THE GUESTBOOK

MADRONA ISLAND
BED & BREAKFAST

ANDREA HURST

A NOVEL

ISBN 13: 9781478163145
ISBN 10: 1478163143

Cover Design: Lidia Vilamajo
Copy Editors/Proof Readers: Audrey Mackaman & Marie DeHaan
Interior Design: Brian C. Short
Marketing: 2MarketBooks

Cover page photo courtesy of Auberge in the Vineyard B&B
http://www.sonomabedbreakfastinnwinecountry.com/

Madrona Island, Washington

Patterns of light danced across Margaret's eyelids as the afternoon sun filtered through the lace curtains of her bedroom, causing her to wake. She had been dreaming of her granddaughter again. A young Lily had pranced around on the old front porch like a little pony, her golden hair soaring behind her as it caught the breeze. But all she had left now were her memories and her good friends.

Margaret propped some pillows behind her and inched her way upright in the old mahogany, four-poster bed. She glanced at the ceramic clock on the nightstand: 3:00 PM. Napping in the afternoon; when had that started? Mary, her housekeeper turned nurse, had been by fussing around her earlier in the day, trying to get Margaret to eat something. But even Mary's buttery shortbread did not tempt her now. Food was a necessity in order to take the medication the doctor had prescribed for, what he called, comfort and quality of life.

Even into her late seventies, she'd felt energetic and kept the inn thriving. Her last decision, closing the doors to her beloved bed and breakfast, was one of the most difficult things she'd ever done. With a low moan of pain, she turned, reached into the antique nightstand, and removed the leather-bound volume: The Guestbook. She stroked the embossed cover and gold leaf lettering: Madrona Island Bed & Breakfast.

Each entry was special to her, each life that crossed her path a gift. A smile broke across the wrinkled surface of her face as she flipped open the book and randomly chose an entry from a young couple who'd lodged in the Rose Suite a few years ago.

> *Maggie,*
> *We can't tell you how much our stay has meant to our marriage. Feeling the love here in this dazzling place helped us find the love for each other again. Thank you for all the little details, from the scrumptious cookies to the fresh baby roses and herbal bouquets. We'll be back.*
> *~Lorna & James*

Margaret shivered and tears threatened to surface. It was so hard to say goodbye. Her life had been rich, finding love again late in life and owning this piece of heaven. Was it just this morning John had stopped by to read to her? She flipped through the well-worn Guestbook, savoring the sweet smell of dried lavender lingering between the pages. In the back, where she kept her special keepsakes, was an old photo of Lily.

"What a sweet girl," whispered Margaret as she gazed at the picture of her only grandchild. Lily had been about nine years old in this one. Her lanky child's body was draped over the old porch swing, her broad smile facing the camera... Lily's last visit. Even now it broke Margaret's heart and anger warmed her cheeks at the wasted time apart.

Silly old woman, she thought, surely by now you have learned to accept the past.

Margaret's mind drifted back to her son Jerold. She'd been

so pleased when he'd married Katherine, and when Lily was born a year later, her heart overflowed. How she'd hoped and prayed he would change when he became a father. In the end, he'd left them all.

She could not go down that "if only" road again. She sighed, long and hard, as her shoulders fell back onto the down pillows. So long ago, so pointless a loss, she mused. Now, more than ever, she knew the only thing that really mattered was being with the ones you love.

Her lawyer and friend, Mike, had delivered the legal papers for her estate today. "Are you certain this is what you want now, Maggie?" he'd asked. She'd only nodded. With all her heart, she hoped that willing the Madrona Island Bed and Breakfast Inn to Lily would bring the same joy to her beloved granddaughter that it had brought her. The ballpoint pen had quivered in her hand as she signed the final document.

The legal papers were stacked neatly on the nightstand, the Guestbook tucked back into the drawer. Margaret pulled the down comforter up to her chin, and the old bed creaked softly as she turned onto her side. As she drifted back to sleep, she was comforted by the thought that John would be by in the morning to check on her.

Chapter One

Brentwood, California

Perched on silk cushions, nestled in the dormer window, Lily watched the rain from her favorite spot in the massive bedroom, a reclusive tower overlooking the winter gardens. In her mind's eye, she saw raindrops seeping deep into the soil, bringing nutrients and working their magic on her dormant plants.

The bedroom door snapped open, interrupting her reverie.

"Lily, it's almost seven and you're not even dressed." Brad, immaculate in a charcoal suit, flung open her closet doors and pulled out a sleek black Dolce & Gabbana dress and Dior evening sandals. "Here, wear these," he said tossing them on the bed. His gold cufflinks shone in the overhead lighting. "And hurry."

"Yes, Brad, I will," she answered for the thousandth time.

He turned to leave. "And wear the diamond necklace I gave you for your birthday."

Lily lifted the delicate dress over her head and slipped her feet into the flimsy shoes before making a last check in the full-length mirror. She prodded the glass surface with her fingers, reassuring herself that it was solid. How could such a complete—and unwanted—transformation take place without her even realizing it was happening? The flawlessly coiffed woman staring back at her was not someone she recognized. The precise arc of her eyebrows conformed to the downturn of her frown, and her wide-set eyes lined in midnight blue were empty of light. Expertly cut blonde hair touched her shoulders and completed her carefully constructed appearance.

Scanning the room, Lily assessed the sterile beige-on-beige master suite with the massive marble fireplace. Everything was in its perfectly designated place, from the signed artwork on the walls to the European crystal vases filled with pale orchids. No detail was left to chance. Brad had made sure of that. The years had flown by like a whirlwind, sucking her in slowly then building momentum as the eye of the storm claimed her.

"Enough of the drama, Lily," she said shaking her head. She pushed her feelings aside and walked downstairs to finish the preparations for the meal ahead. There would only be one VIP guest tonight. She could handle that herself.

The ringing phone barely stirred her as she glided down the staircase. She was not expected to answer it.

At the bottom of the stairs, in the marble entry, Brad stood holding the phone in his hand.

"Your mother is on the phone again. This is the third time she's called." He covered the mouthpiece. "Make it fast."

Lily took the handset and walked over to the window, turning her back to Brad. "Hi, Mom."

"Are you all right, Lily? I've left two messages already."

"Sorry, Brad didn't tell me. You caught us just before a dinner party we're hosting."

Brad paced and pointed emphatically to his watch.

"I'm sorry, Mom; our guests will be arriving soon. I'll have to call you back later." Lily hung up the phone and glared at Brad. "Why didn't you tell me my mother has been calling?"

He shrugged. "So what was it that couldn't wait?"

Lily stepped back and laid the phone on the table. "You didn't give me time to find out, not that it would interest you anyway."

"Suit yourself," he said, moving down the hall. "I'll be in my office if you need me."

+ + + +

Lily was in her element. Her sparkling stainless steel kitchen boasted simmering pots releasing an herby aroma complemented by the yeasty smell of fresh bread. She kicked off her shoes and let her stocking-covered feet take a break. The pungent smell of garlic flooded the room, soothing her frayed nerves.

She glanced at the clock; Brad's new client would arrive in about an hour, and there was still plenty to do. Steadying herself with a deep breath, she prepared the second appetizer tray of crab-stuffed portabella mushrooms smothered with buttery fontina cheese.

A knock at the kitchen door startled her. Her neighbor, Roma, popped her head in. "May I have permission to enter your revered domain?"

Lily wiped her hands on a dishtowel and drew Roma into a hug. "Couldn't be happier to see you."

"Need a taster?" Roma leaned over a simmering pot, inhaling deeply.

Lily held up a spoon. "Sure, try this Bolognese and let me know if it needs anything."

Roma moaned. "Divine, as always."

Roma took a seat at the breakfast bar. She pointed to Lily's bare feet and patted the stool next to her. "Come, sit down.

You're the hostess, not the maid here."

"Tell Brad that, would you? He has me on a tight schedule tonight." Lily drizzled the endive and calamari salad with black truffle oil. She arranged heavily crusted Italian bread and placed the olive paté next to the basket.

"That man," Roma continued. "I suppose he picked out the too-tight dress under your apron as well."

"I don't think my jeans and sweatshirt would have gone over too well tonight," Lily answered.

Roma giggled. "I would love to have seen that." She helped herself to a stuffed mushroom. In a lowered voice she asked, "So, how're the dog rescue capers coming along?"

"Wonderful," Lily whispered, glancing over at the door. "Our group rescued a dog right off the freeway. It was so cute I just wanted to bring it home."

Roma moved over to the stove and watched Lily stir fresh garlic into a pan of sizzling olive oil followed by succulent cubes of lobster. "I know Brad's afraid of dogs, but why didn't you just bring this one home and let him get over it?"

Before she could answer, Brad leaned his head through the kitchen door. "Lots of talking going on in here with you girls, any cooking?" He placed his briefcase down on the table and walked over to the stove.

Lily turned her back to him and continued cooking.

He hovered over her shoulder then proceeded to move through the aromatic kitchen like a general inspecting the appetizer trays, considering wine choices.

"Do your best," he whispered in her ear.

She looked up into his chestnut eyes. How they used to melt her down. "Of course, Brad."

He kissed her cheek. "Did you remember the Dom Pérignon I asked you to pick up?"

Lily caught her breath. She rarely forgot anything he requested, but lately it was difficult just to remember what she was doing next. The Christmas holiday had been a blur. One more party and the season was over.

"No, Brad, I forgot, but we have plenty of excellent champagne in the cellar."

His voice rose. "I told you specifically this client only drinks that label."

"So what do you want me to do, leave the dinner on the stove and go pick some up?"

"Never mind, I'll go," he said, grabbing his keys off the hook by the back door and stamping out.

"Looks like you're in trouble," Roma said with a nervous wink. "Think I'll head home and order take-out." Roma waved as she closed the door behind her.

Lily leaned over the sink, feeling sick; she could not play this part one more time. In the beginning, Brad had been so charming and self-assured. The promises and compliments never seemed to end. She could still hear his words: "Lily, I will take care of you and give you everything you could ever want." Love and security were dangled in front of her, a twenty-two-year-old girl starved for affection.

Thirty years old at her last birthday, and what did she really have to show for it? No children, not even a dog. Brad would not allow the interference in their lifestyle or the mess. So much for being rescued by Prince Charming, she thought. I should have left that fantasy in the fairytale books where it belongs.

The sound of rapid bubbling from the stove pulled her out of her daydream. Adeptly, she lowered the flame and stirred the simmering cream sauce. She rubbed her temples, hoping to stave away the pounding headache that had been threatening throughout the evening.

A chiming sound resonated from the direction of the table. Lily went over to investigate and found Brad's iPhone lit up next to his briefcase. "Text Message from Ashley" flashed across the screen. "Missed Call from Ashley" was indicated below it. Lily started to walk away, but the phone chimed again, prompting her to take a closer look. Ashley again, this time with a picture.

Lily tapped the screen and the message lit up: "Brad, what time do you think you will be able to get away tonight? xoxo Ashley."

She laid the phone back on the table. That was strange. Brad had a dinner party here tonight and it would probably last pretty late, yet he still had plans for after. Lily thought about all the late night calls and trips back to the office. No one named Ashley worked at the office, not that she knew of. And what about the xoxo? Her stomach tightened as she dropped the phone back on the table and returned to the meal. Lily warmed her hands over a simmering pot of lobster bisque. It was a particularly cold December for southern California, and the thick soup would take care of that. She stirred the soup, trying not to turn back to the phone.

Perhaps she should take a peek at the second message? She wandered back to the table and turned the iPhone over in her hand. The phone never left Brad's side unless he was asleep, and even then it was at his bedside. It was not her style to go through his things, but... She pressed the power button and the IMs popped up. She expanded the screen to get a closer look at the photo. A statuesque woman smiled out at her. She looked like she just stepped out of the pages of Vogue: white-blonde hair accented high cheekbones and kohl-lined sapphire eyes. Not a day over twenty-five, Lily thought, studying the black suede boots and body-hugging sweater. Two fingers were raised to her lips, as if to send a kiss.

"See you tonight," was all it said.

Lily scrolled back, amazed by the long list of previous messages from the same woman. Each was inviting; some thanked him for a great night, others promised favors to come.

Her mind swirled as her heart picked up its beats. Mindlessly, she started to count the messages, twenty, thirty, fifty. When she reached over a hundred in less than a month, she stopped counting. She had seen enough. All these weeks with him never around, too busy to deal with her, judging every move she made. He must have been out with this woman.

She placed the phone back on the table. The marriage had been ending for a long time, she just hadn't wanted to face it. But this still hurt, like being sliced open with one of her razor-sharp kitchen knives. One by one, she turned off the burners then washed her knives and placed them back in their cases.

The sound of Brad's Porsche speeding up the front drive caused her to flinch. Lily slid into her shoes and threw off the apron.

Footsteps resounded in the hall before Brad rushed into the kitchen holding the champagne. "I only managed to find two bottles. If you had done what I asked—"

Lily held up his iPhone. "You have some messages."

He snatched it from her hands and checked the screen.

"Too late, Brad, I've already read them," she said.

"How dare you, Lily."

"How dare *you*," she said, holding her ground. She pointed to the half-cooked items on the stove and counter. "You better call your important client and arrange to take him out to dinner, because I won't be catering your meals anymore."

She watched his face morph from anger to bargaining. All she wanted was to get away from him before he saw her burst into tears. A hundred plus text messages. Why had she counted them all?

"Let me explain, Lily, you're over-reacting, it's nothing..."

"Save it, Brad," she said, pushing past him, heading toward the front door.

"Wait," he said, following behind. "Ashley is our new corporate attorney; we're planning a merger."

"I bet you are," Lily said, beginning to laugh. "The xoxo merger, right? Either get out of my way or *you* leave."

He put his arms out to her, his eyes pleading forgiveness. "It's you I love, Lily, from the first day I saw you."

"Right, the first day you saw me and realized what a moldable pawn I would make!"

"Alright," he said, pulling out his keys. "Just know, this is *your* choice."

Lily stood in the foyer and leaned against the wall to catch her breath. Hands freezing, body rigid, an unreal quality took over as she watched her husband walk out the front door and slam it behind him. The sound of Brad's Porsche screeching out the driveway sent a quiver up her spine. Her legs gave way as she crumpled onto the cold marble floor. Immobile, she glared at the oversized carved wooden door. Another ostentatious, unattractive, overbearing piece of décor Brad had chosen. It had been alternately her fortress and her prison, keeping her in this false palace, barring both entrance and exit.

She ripped off her Dior heels and threw them at the door. "I hate these shoes, this house, this marriage…" The long-held tears shook her body. Every accusation Brad had dismissed as her "overreacting" was finally answered with the truth. Why hadn't she trusted herself and left long ago? She let the tears flow.

A cool calmness filled her being. She was done here; the certainty of it swept through her body. She rose from the floor and hastened up the spiral staircase to her bedroom. Her red puffy face stared back at her from the mirror. It was streaked with mascara-colored tears from eye to chin. At least she recognized this person.

She yanked off the clingy dress and laid it neatly on the king-size bed. Beside it she draped the Cartier necklace. The imposing diamond wedding ring would be next to go. She stopped abruptly...this she would keep. It was the only thing of real value that Brad might consider ever truly belonging to her.

Bending over the marble sink in the master bath, she rinsed off the tears and ran a comb through her hair. She pulled out her travel case and tossed in a few toiletries. The walk-in closet presented overwhelming options: silk blouses, cashmere sweaters, designer jeans. Lily tossed her favorite comfortable jeans, warm sweaters, a pale pink cotton sweatshirt, and a comfy pair of tennis shoes into a suitcase. She added a jacket, some warm boots, a couple of shirts and left just enough room to fit some of her prize knives on top.

She leaned over her desk and unlocked the side drawer. It was right where she left it a few weeks ago. Grandma Maggie's will. To my grandaughter, Lily Parkins, it read. Grandma hadn't even known Lily's married name, it had been that long. It continued: is the sole heir to the property known as Madrona Island Bed and Breakfast Inn.

There was a note from her Seattle attorney explaining that Maggie had converted the farm into a successful inn, but that it had been closed for the last year due to Maggie's poor health.

Lily thought about her grandma all alone on the island, sick, lonely. Why hadn't she visited her, or at least called? She'd let fear keep her from what she wanted too long. Flashbacks of a sparkly woman with a wide smile flooded her mind. She could see herself as a young girl, racing her grandma down the grassy path to splash in the cool waters of the Puget Sound. And the batches and batches of chocolate fudge brownies they'd baked together. Often over the years, Lily wished to be back with her grandmother, sharing the old porch swing, picking warm ripe tomatoes right off the vine, not a care in the world. She had no idea if her grandmother would have been receptive after their estrangement, and if her mother would have felt betrayed.

She placed the will in her purse and took one last look around the room she had slept in with her husband for ten years. Reassured that there was nothing left that mattered, she proceeded down the staircase.

In the kitchen, the aroma of garlic and rosemary lingered, the only pleasant memory of a gourmet dinner interrupted. Trays of food littered the counters, dirty pans and food-caked dishes filled the stainless steel sinks. There would be leftovers for tomorrow, but she would not be here to serve them. That would probably be the only reason she would be missed. She took her Global knives and slid them into a side pocket of the suitcase, then surveyed her collection of pots and pans. "No, too much to carry...they can be replaced later."

On the brass hooks by the back door hung the various sets of car keys. Brad had taken the Porsche. Remaining on the rack were the keys for the Mercedes sedan and the Honda SUV, used mostly by the housekeeper for running errands. The black sedan was certainly not her style. The Honda would do just fine.

A disparaging laugh erupted as she realized that Brad would have to clean the kitchen on his own. Surely his new eye-candy had no idea how.

She retrieved her wool coat to ward off the cold, locked the door behind her, and ran quickly through the rain toward the garage. Inside, she threw her bags in the back of the SUV, slid into the driver's seat, and backed out slowly. Lily took one last look at the big house, all lit up against the dark night. She programmed the GPS for Washington State, clutched the steering wheel, and drove off through the misty rain.

Chapter Two

The Washington State ferry cut through the ocean currents much the way Lily was cutting through her life: swiftly, mercilessly, and with a clear destination–Madrona Island. Lily lifted her head to the wind, enjoying the view from the upper deck. A faint silhouette of land emerged through the low-floating fog. She gripped the icy hand railing as the butterflies in her stomach turned to knots.

Doubt crept in like the morning fog. Have I made the right decision to come here? A ray of sun pierced the clouds and lit the water with a thousand glittering flashbulbs. The lush green of the island shore beckoned in the distance, and the sound of lapping waves called to her. The wet winters in the Pacific Northwest were a whole different experience than sunny Southern California.

With a sigh of release, Lily lifted her head. She would face this and she would do it, for the first time in her life, alone. A light gust of wind rolled over the deck, bringing with it the familiar scent of sea air. She tightened her wool scarf and dug her icy hands into her pockets. The ferry's horn blasted, announcing its approach to shore. She turned quickly, almost bumping into a tall, dark-haired man. Their eyes met for a brief second—his intense blue eyes seeming to look right through her. The spark between them was unmistakable. Momentarily stunned, she stared, mesmerized at the striking face before her. "Excuse me," she managed to get out as her eyes searched the deck for the correct staircase.

"No problem," he said, a wide smile crossing his face.

Lily felt a flush creep up her neck into her cheeks as she fled for the stairs. She located her car keys and escaped the icy wind. "I think I just had a hallucination," she laughed to herself. "No *real* man has ever affected me that way before. I'm sure my heart stopped beating." As she climbed into her SUV, she looked up to see the same man taking the last step down from the deck and turning toward her car. For a moment she thought he was following her, but then he continued past and entered a Volvo station wagon two cars behind her.

When she looked up, a ferry worker was waving her to exit and she hadn't even started her car. Fumbling with the keys, she managed to start the engine and exit the ferry onto the two-lane highway. The GPS showed the main highway, which divided the east and west sides of the island. Her gaze drifted out the window to open fields and tree-lined hills. Billowing steel-gray clouds hung low in the sky, and a fine mist dusted her windshield. Hands still frozen, she turned up the heat. This was definitely not the weather she was used to in Los Angeles; it would take some acclimation to be comfortable in this damp, bone-chilling climate.

Up ahead the stoplight turned yellow and she slowed to stop. The street sign offered two alternatives: Grandview, four miles; Forest Glen, ten. Her stomach growled. She couldn't remember the last time she'd eaten. Grandview was the closest, and if her memory was accurate, it would offer a cozy town and a place for a hot lunch. To the right it was then. The road narrowed as towering pines and cedars sprang against the backdrop of the dazzling red bark of Madrona trees.

Lily slipped another CD into the player; smooth jazz fit the mood of the setting. As she entered the city limits, charming older houses trimmed in gingerbread shared the landscape with modern wood homes with massive windows to take advantage of the view. Businesses sprouted up, a realty office in an A-frame cottage, antiques in an old barn. The quaint little town on the west shore proved easy to find. The first view, as she turned on to Front Street, revealed a scene right out of a movie set, turn-of-the-century style. It had been a long time since she'd been here with Grandma Maggie. Her memory wandered to the tall chocolate sodas they used to get at the corner ice cream place. She hoped it was still there. It was somewhere on a back street, if she remembered correctly. Lily passed a hand-carved wood sign with bright letters, *Island Thyme Café & Bakery*. A large picture window revealed a gift shop adjacent to the café. Perfect for lunch, she thought as she looked for a place to park. She could scout for the ice cream parlor later.

Front Street appeared to be the main drag, sporting Grandview Bank and the old ivy-covered brick building that housed the Island County Library. The multitude of shops promised local artisan wares and every kind of food from cookies to sushi. She pulled the car over and headed to the café. Along the way, she paused to admire the expansive view of water and horizon clouds in all shades of gray that hung heavily over the peaks of the Cascade Mountains to the east. The drizzle was rapidly turning into rain as the wind picked up and tugged at her jacket. Raindrops dotted her eyelashes. The smell of wood smoke lingered in the air with the promise of a warm fire, so she zipped her raincoat, flipped up the hood, and hurried towards the café. A new umbrella would be top of her list for her first shopping trip.

The smell of saltwater carried on the wind, but the aroma that spoke the loudest was the whiff of fresh-baked chocolate chip cookies as she opened the door to the café and hurried inside. A well-polished antique wood bar covered the entire left wall.

From behind the counter, a cheerful auburn-haired woman waved to Lily. "Come in and dry out, it's getting nasty out there." She snatched a menu. "Can I get you a seat?"

"Thanks, I would love one."

Lily's eyes washed over the welcoming interior. Just past the old-fashioned bar and down two steps was a cozy dining room with what looked like the original turn-of-the-century oak floor. Tables of every size and shape crowded together in the center with mismatched chairs and tablecloths.

"Would you like a booth or table?"

"A booth is fine," Lily said.

The leather booth where she now sat hugged the back wall, where a picture window overlooked the bay. The rear of the building hung over the water's edge. It must have been on stilts, as it gave the café an appearance of floating over a large inlet. Ominous clouds cast shadows over the pale silver water and seagulls dove for fish, their screams filling the air.

The woman placed a menu in front of her. "I'm Jude and I'll be your waitress. Can I get you something hot to drink first? A latté? Hot cocoa?"

"Cocoa sounds wonderful, thank you." Lily leaned back into the cushioned seat, savoring this place of refuge. There were only a few other patrons in the dining room: a man reading the local paper and nursing a mug of coffee, and a couple quietly talking over a bottle of wine. Plants, old photos, and bold oil paintings lined the oak walls. Jude approached with a cup of cocoa topped with a decadent mound of whipped cream and chocolate shavings. The fragrant steam curled up from the cup in a tantalizing fashion.

"Here you go, should take the chill right out. Are you ready to order?"

Lily scanned the menu. "What would you suggest?"

She beamed at Lily. "Well, being the owner and all, I think everything's spectacular. But let me suggest our special today, homemade potato cheese soup, and a Dungeness crab melt."

Lily's mouth watered. This was a far cry from the chic LA cafés with the small-portioned, no carbs, no fat specials. "That will work!"

"Good choice," Jude said. "I'll have your lunch for you in a jiff."

Old 80s soft rock played in the background, and a fire sparked and smoked behind the glass door of the wood stove. The heavy weight sitting on her shoulders began to dissolve. She leaned back and enjoyed the next few songs as she savored her hot chocolate. She'd made it here, and not even Brad had gotten in her way. She should just stay in this café forever.

Jude bustled over to her table with a gracious smile and placed the tasty lunch before her. "Just let me know if I can get you anything else. Okay?"

Lily shook her head no. Already stuffing the fragrant sandwich into her mouth, all she managed to get out was a muffled "thanks." Pure comfort food, just what she needed right now. And the owner seemed friendly. The house was only ten minutes away, at most; she could make this a regular spot in her new routine. Although, with all these carbs, she couldn't come too often or her new life would also require a new wardrobe.

She was just laying down the fork when Jude approached the table with a dessert menu. Lily looked up and felt instantly comfortable in the warm rays of Jude's smile.

"Save room for dessert today? Our fresh-baked, square-shaped chocolate chip cookies?" Jude asked.

"I don't think I could take one more bite, but I will take one of those cookies to go."

"Only one?"

Lily considered the ice cream store again but decided it could wait for a warmer day. "I'll take two. Do you have them every day?"

Jude pulled out her business card. "Our hours are on the back. Hope to have the cookies every day, but I'm afraid I'm not the best baker and our chef is due to have a baby in a few months."

Lily extended her hand and shook Jude's hand. "My name is Lily, and I guess you could say I'll be living here for a while. Your place is my first stop before I head over to Madrona Island Bed and Breakfast."

"Madrona Island?" Jude said. "Why, they've been closed for a few months now."

"I know, I heard. My grandmother, Margaret Parkins used to own it, and now I suppose, it's mine. I haven't seen the place since I was about nine years old."

Jude's eyes lit up. "You're Maggie's granddaughter? Why, she talked so much about you. I know she would be real pleased to know you're going to be taking over."

"Oh no, I'm not taking it over, I've just come to stay for a while. Actually, I'm really not sure how long I'll be anywhere right now, and I just..." Lily could feel her throat tightening and tears threatening. Why was she telling this perfect stranger so much about her life?

Jude gave her a hug and reassuring pat on the back. "Well, you're home now, and a lot of people will be looking forward to meeting you."

"Home," Lily murmured. "Thank you."

"You just let me know if you need anything...promise?"

Jude said heading over to the counter to bag up a few cookies.

"I may just take you up on that offer," Lily said.

Jude returned with a bag of cookies and placed them on the table. "A small housewarming treat for you, on me."

"You don't have to…"

"I want to," Jude said.

Lily took out her debit card and paid the bill at the bar.

"Don't be afraid to drop in on your neighbors, Betty and Shirley. Those ladies would be more than happy to come by and help you with whatever you need."

"Ok. Great place, great food, I'll be back."

Jude walked with Lily to the door. "I sure miss selling your Grandma's baked goods in the cafe, especially those addictive brownies. They had quite a following."

"I remember them from when I was a little girl. I hope I can find the recipe."

"Well, let me know. Be seeing you soon."

Lily's heart felt as full as her stomach.

✦✦✦✦

The sky showed signs of clearing as Lily wove her way out of town to the main island road. She followed her highlighted map and made the left turn on Sunshine Lane. Interesting name. There sure isn't much of that right now. The road narrowed and veered right toward the water, passing a dormant apple orchard. Fields of wild grasses in hues of browns and reds lined the sloping hill on the other side. As she made the final turn, the muddy road swept down, offering a picturesque view of the yellow and white Victorian farmhouse nestled among the gently inclining acres that finally touched into the blue-green waters of the Puget Sound.

The wheels of the car splashed through the puddles in the

driveway and slowed to rest at the log barrier. She was here. It felt more like being in a dream, some surreal experience. Once out of the car, she watched as the sun broke through the dense clouds in long, thin rays, spraying a silver and gold reflection over the water. The house picked up the beautiful yet eerie glow emanating off the Sound, and the pale yellow paint took on a quality of spun gold. The cedar trees surrounding the pond whistled in the wind, and a flock of birds took noisily to the sky.

She could only stare and wrap her arms about the bulky rain jacket her mother had given her. This magical place had always been her refuge as a child, a place she now hoped would help her find what her heart desired. The sun was dipping below the barely visible peaks of the Olympic Mountains, tinting the sky with vivid shades of orange. It would be dark soon, and yet the idea of going into that house alone almost had her turning back to town. Opening her purse, she pulled out the envelope Grandma's lawyer had sent with the will, and removed the key. The letter spoke of a caretaker, Mary, who had been keeping the house clean and watching over everything these past few months.

She opened the hatchback of the Honda and grabbed some of her things. The rest could wait until the morning. The wraparound porch was exactly the same. The wind rustled the old porch swing, and its familiar creak brought memories of sipping cold lemonade on a warm summer afternoon and watching breathtaking sunsets at dusk. As Lily walked up the wooden steps, memories whirled—laughter mingled with shouting arguments, being ripped away by her mother from this favorite place.

She leaned over the railing, remembering to breathe deep and relax. Ghosts and bad memories. Maybe she'd made a mistake coming here. The ocean's salty scent moved on the breeze, accompanied by squawking seagulls. For just a flash of a moment, she could see herself in the yard with her grandmother, holding the crusts of bread up for the birds to swoop down and pluck from her fingers.

She turned toward the door. Panic caught in her chest, and the tears she thought were cried out threatened another appearance. "Lily, get it together. You can do this. Now go inside."

The soothing smell of old wood and lilac greeted Lily as she pushed open the thick oak door. Her eyes lingered fondly over her favorite room, the parlor. Her grandmother's loving presence was everywhere. With a rush of enthusiasm, she laid down her belongings and started to inspect the rooms of her new home. *Her new home.* Everything was still the same as she remembered: antique sofa and loveseat, oval mahogany table and matching china cabinet. Balancing on a lower shelf, the old white ceramic horse still stood proudly, peeking through the glass doors. The oil painting over the fireplace, with its bright rose and yellow hues, warmed the room. She gingerly touched each picture, vase and figurine. She could almost hear Grandmother Maggie calling. "Lily, my little pony, come inside. I've baked cookies and they're getting cold." She could smell that sweet, warm chocolate even now.

The kitchen was grander than she remembered. The last flicker of sunlight streamed through the large west windows, encouraging the dormant herbs in the clay pots on the sill to blossom. The counters had been retiled in white with a kelly-green trim. There were copper faucets, and pots and pans hanging on an oval rack over the huge six-burner stove made of chrome and pale yellow ceramic. On the shelves were glass mason jars filled with beans, grains, teas, and even miniature rosebuds. Bouquets of dried rosemary, garlic, and lavender hung like trophies of the past spring's garden harvest. Along the tops of the white cabinets was an assorted collection of rose-patterned China teapots.

This kitchen was a place she could cook and bake in a way she had always dreamed of. It was ready for a loving touch and a master's hand. She remembered Jude's words about missing Grandma Maggie's baked goods. She could bring Jude some samples of her own muffins and cookies to sell at the café. A smile spread across her face. She was a master chef, at least she was confident of that. That was one thing she could thank Brad for. Her cooking had to be the best to impress his business contacts, so he had sent her to the finest schools and been a merciless taskmaster. Her smile vanished at the thought of his name. Not here, not now, I will not let thoughts of him ruin this moment.

She retrieved her suitcase and contemplated the steep staircase leading up to the bedrooms, and was half tempted to just curl up on the sofa for the night. But a warm bed sounded well worth the climb. At the top, she dropped the suitcases on the landing and wandered down the hall to choose a bedroom.

The room that had once been her grandmother's was at the corner of the house, and that was where she would sleep tonight. Its dormer window had always been a favorite place to play. Her old room was just past it, but she'd always felt so safe and happy in her grandma's room. She entered and noticed immediately that the room had been redone in a rose décor. Many of the old items were still in place, as if her grandmother would suddenly walk out from the bathroom and say, "Why, Lily, how good to see you after so long." To her dismay, the old poster bed was gone.

The room was now furnished with an ornate, queen-size brass bed and a lovely antique, marble-topped dresser. Lace curtains framed the magnificent picture window with a breathtaking water view. The wood floors glistened, covered here and there by pale rose-patterned antique rugs. Lily sat down in the rocking chair situated in a corner and rocked back and forth in a lulling fashion. Although it looked a bit different now, it still held her loving presence. She remembered snuggling in bed with her grandmother and listening to the wonderful stories Maggie would make up just for her.

All those years they'd been apart, and now here she was… alone. No one was here for her, but Brad sure as heck wasn't alone tonight. She kicked off her shoes and fell face down onto the bed, burying her head in the pillows. The tears came hard. She cried for the lost years and dreams, her fading youth, and ending marriage. Then she climbed under the warm quilt in the brass bed and blessedly fell into a deep sleep.

Chapter Three

Ian unpacked the Volvo station wagon and got his son, Jason, settled in the den with Grandpa John. The cold island wind whipped through the single-pane windows; he reminded himself to replace them next summer. He stared out the kitchen window. He was sure he'd seen lights go on next door at Maggie's place. It could have been Mary getting things cleaned up. It was still hard to believe sweet old Maggie wasn't right next door and going to tap on their door any minute with a plate of steaming hot cookies. He stepped out on the back porch and noticed there was a car in the driveway next door. But it was too dark to see whose it might be.

No more distractions; it was time to paint. The wood stove had heated up his studio, and he was on a tight deadline to complete the pieces for his art opening next month. He scrutinized the unfinished piece on the easel, a bald eagle swooping down across a snow-covered mountain range. Lifting a brush, he began to paint a Buddhist temple in the foreground. The deep crimson walls were a striking contrast to the stark white of the jagged mountain peaks.

His mind wandered back to the ferry and the woman

who'd walked right into him; the crimson flush that had filled her face and framed an amazing pair of hazel eyes. It had been hard to break his own stare, but she'd hurried down the stairs and out of the door so fast, for a moment he thought he'd seen a phantom. It had been a while since a woman had made any real impression. He had his young son, Jason, and Gramps; that was enough... His grief took the rest of the space in his heart.

He dipped a small brush into gold and touched up the roof of the temple and the light in the eagle's eye. With a step back, he observed the painting carefully, waiting for a title to surface in his mind. "Golden Flight" would work. Just two more and he could start planning their placement and assist the gallery with the guest list. Another hot cup of coffee would keep him going all night, but it was getting late and it was time to put Jason to bed.

When his wife, Denise, was alive, there were days when he didn't even say goodnight to his son. He wished he could go back and make up for the time he missed. Being a single parent for four years really turned his life around. For the better, in some ways. The longing for Denise gripped his heart. In the early days after the accident, he was sure he was having a heart attack. Grief takes many forms, the doctor had said.

Gramps and Jason were playing Scrabble, and his precocious son was winning.

"Give your old gramps a break, kid," Ian said placing his hands on Jason's shoulders.

"Dad, don't look over my shoulder, I'm concentrating."

Ian joined them at the dining room table and watched with amusement. His grandfather was obviously doing whatever he could to make sure Jason won, not that Jason needed much help.

"Hey, you two, is this game going to last all night? How

about some sleep?"

Neither looked up as they concentrated on the letters before them. Three generations gathered around a table. It did not escape his attention that they were all males.

Chapter Four

Dawn's light eased through the lace curtains, chasing away the dark shadows of the previous night. Lily took in the rose-themed décor of the bedroom. Morning made everything more real. Grief clung to her like a heavy coat, invaded every cell, and permeated every thought. She realized it was not Brad she was grieving for; it was the dream of a happy marriage, her lost identity... Who was she if not Brad's wife? The sadness weighed on her heart. For a split second she questioned her decision to leave him.

Lily wrapped herself in a terrycloth robe that was in the closet, probably for guests to use. Her warm socks from the night before served as slippers. She smiled to herself, not an outfit Brad would approve of. Certainly he'd made it home by now, and the thought of him having to make his own breakfast gave her great satisfaction. That, and her being gone, would certainly add to his foul mood. Not her problem...not anymore.

She wandered into the bathroom. Her eyes felt puffy, and her hair badly needed washing. A familiar icy fear crept up her spine... What was she going to do now? She turned, ready to retreat back to the bed, but her eyes caught on a small, hand-painted wooden plaque. A single figure sat in a rowboat, oars in hand, navigating the crashing waves. Carved across the bottom were the words, "Pray to God, but row to shore." It was so like her grandmother to have something like this. "I should do a bit of rowing myself, and some prayers wouldn't hurt either," Lily said out loud as she ran her fingers over the carving.

She turned on the shower, dropped her clothes on the tile floor, and stepped in. The steaming water relaxed her tired muscles and washed her dark thoughts down the drain. The herbal scent of the shampoo reminded her of running through her grandmother's garden as a child, carefree...happy. Lily took the large rose-colored towel and dried off quickly to stay warm. She put on her old jeans and her favorite gray sweatshirt with the soft inner lining, then slipped her feet into woolly slippers and headed for the stairs.

The faint scent of coffee drifted up. Am I dreaming? Is that cinnamon rolls I smell? She headed down the stairs, following the blissful aroma. At the kitchen door stood a plump, middle-aged woman with curly black hair, cooking and cleaning up in her kitchen. "Hello?" Lily said.

The woman turned to face her with gentle eyes and an affectionate smile. Taking both of Lily's hands in hers she exclaimed, "Hi there. I'm Mary Gibson, Betty's niece. You must be Lily. I saw your car in the driveway last night and couldn't wait to see you. You're just as lovely as your grandmother described you."

"Betty...?"

"My aunt who lives next door."

Lily pinched herself to be sure she was awake. There was coffee brewing, cinnamon rolls in the oven, and a cheery, rosy-cheeked face happy to see her. She couldn't have dreamt it better.

"How nice to meet you, Mary. You look a bit familiar."

"Ah, that's right, it's been a while since we've seen you around here. We used to play together as kids when I was visiting my aunts." She puttered around the kitchen, taking out the rolls to cool, laying out fresh cream and juice on the kitchen table.

"Why don't you have a seat before your coffee gets cold?"

"I think I will. Everything smells divine."

Mary continued, "You probably don't remember the nice old ladies living next door, my great-aunts Betty and Shirley. I'm *sure* you'll be hearing from them real soon. They know everything going on in this island, and they'll be more than happy to catch you up."

Mary brought over thick ceramic mugs with steaming coffee and hot rolls oozing sweetness. "How about *I* catch you up a bit?"

Lily sipped her coffee, admiring the view from the large picture window. A low fog rested gently against the Olympic range. Shades of pink and crimson reflected off the fog from the rising sun and were mirrored by the waters of the Puget Sound.

"Delicious," Lily managed to get out between bites of the oozing cinnamon roll.

"I've been the official caretaker here since Maggie died. I just come in, tidy up, keep an eye on things."

"I can't thank you enough," Lily said, licking a gooey piece of dough off her finger.

Mary sipped her coffee. "You know, a lot of people will want to meet you. They just loved Maggie."

Lily reached over and gave Mary a hug. "I couldn't have asked for a better welcome."

"Well thanks," Mary said. "I see you slept upstairs last

night? Not sure if you've seen the innkeeper's quarters down-stairs yet. Your grandmother had it built when she opened the inn."

"Did you work for my grandma?"

"Sure did," Mary said, taking another sip of coffee. "Cleaned the rooms, washed the dishes, even helped with the baking sometimes."

"I wish I could have seen it when it was open."

Lily closed her eyes. Why hadn't she called? Life with Brad had taken over everything. "I *am* your family now," he told her, implying that her own family was to be left behind. Which wasn't that difficult at the time, being distant from her mother anyway. She'd never even heard from her dad. But her grandma, if only she had taken the time.

"It was a grand place, always booked up with guests and weddings. Your grandma could really bake. And those brownies!"

"Any idea where the recipe for the brownies is?" Lily asked.

Mary rose and took some of the dishes to the sink. "I know she kept a recipe box around here somewhere. If you want, I could help you look."

Lily took her plate and cup to the sink. "No need, I'll get to it later today. But I need to know where my grandmother lived."

"No problem." Mary dried her hands and turned to Lily. "Follow me, I'll show you the innkeeper's quarters."

Mary led them through the living room and down a short hall to a locked door. The answer to where her grand-mother had slept was: downstairs. Mary pulled a key off her keychain. "Here's the key. I've been keeping it locked because she still has some personal items in there. I packed up most of her clothes and items you might want to go through. They're up in the attic." She pushed open the door. "I'll just leave you alone here to get comfortable while I finish cleaning up the house."

Walking into the room felt like stepping back in time. Her grandmother's old four-poster bed dominated the room with its rich apricot duvet cover and lace pillows. She had wondered why that bed hadn't been upstairs, now she knew. The mahogany nightstand with the fluted legs supported a cream-colored porcelain lamp. There was a large dormer window with a cozy built-in seat that was sprinkled with overstuffed satin cushions. Lily curled up by the window and gazed out at the herb garden. Most of the plants were dried and wilted now, but the rosemary still retained its deep green color. A lone sparrow splashed in the rain-filled birdbath. The rocky paths moved through the dormant vegetable garden and out to the orchard of apple and pear trees. Tall cedars circled the property, creating quiet seclusion and a dramatic backdrop. She hugged her knees and leaned back against the wall. It seemed unbelievable that this was all hers now.

Lily inspected the musty-smelling closet; a few coats and sweaters remained behind. The private bathroom had a large old-fashioned claw-foot tub. Spending time here, in this house, would allow her to learn more about her grandmother. Missed years, missed love. Her mother had kept her estranged from Maggie for almost twelve years, and then when she'd married, it seemed too late to contact her.

Mary popped her head into the room. "Anything I can get you or show you how to use?"

"As a matter of fact, Mary, could you show me where the thermostat is? It's pretty cool in here. And point me in the direction of a good market."

"Sure thing, right this way." Mary pointed to the temperature controls for the up- and downstairs. "Right now, the upstairs guest rooms are closed and only heated a few days a week to keep the mold from setting in. There's chopped wood and kindling behind the shed."

Mary buttoned up her coat and headed for the front door. "Oh yes, there's a brochure in the office alcove off the kitchen if you want more information on the inn. And as far as markets go, I put a few things you might need in the fridge, but the Cascade Market is back out on the main road. Just turn left and go up-island a few miles, you can't miss it."

Lily walked her to the door. Mary threw her arms around Lily in what her grandma used to call a bear hug. "You just call me now if you need anything. I'll be back to check on you in a few days."

Lily watched Mary seem to disappear down the driveway. Perhaps she'd been an apparition after all. She turned and faced the house. "What should I do first? Unpack? Shop?" Her options were unlimited as long as it didn't cost a lot of money, and the sense of freedom made her momentarily giddy. Then the fear returned, this time taking residence in her stomach. "And after I do that...then what?"

✦ ✦ ✦ ✦

Water had drenched Lily's tennis shoes and was seeping into her socks by the time she made it through the muddy yard to her car and back a few times. "Waterproof boots are a must!" She unloaded the Honda through the back door that led to the kitchen, carefully wiping off her muddy shoes on the bristly welcome mat before she brought everything into the innkeeper's quarters. This would be her new residence, and that suited her just fine. After her clothes were hung, she headed into the kitchen and carefully tucked her knives into a drawer.

She better let her mother, Katherine, know where she was.

The thought of calling her and hearing, "I told you so," did not encourage her to pick up the phone. After three rings Lily was ready to get this over with in a voicemail, but her mother picked up.

"Lily, is that you?"

"I'm sorry it took so long to call back. I'm on Madrona Island."

"Are you alright?" her mother asked. "I see your grandma's attorney reached you after all."

Lily contemplated how much to tell her. She really needed an ally right now. "I suppose you want to know what happened with Brad?"

"If you want to tell me."

"This isn't like you, Mom, treading carefully."

"Lily, I assume you've had about enough of someone pressuring you and I—"

"Are you implying Brad pressures me? Are you?" Lily held her finger over the end call button.

"I really don't want to argue with you."

"Oh, Mother, I've been so stupid…"

"It's all right. I'm here, we'll work this out together," Katherine said.

Her mother seemed a different person than she'd carried in her memory all these years. During their last visit Lily had noticed telltale lines around her mother's eyes and the gray hairs at her temples spoke of aging. But her eyes had always been kind.

"Thank you, Mom. I didn't mean to turn on you."

"I know, Lily, you've been through a lot. Do you want to tell me what happened?"

"It's Brad." She took a deep breath, pushing back another flood of tears. "I've left him."

"I see," her mother said.

"I know you've always disliked him."

"It's not about me, Lily. Are you happy with him?"

"No, I'm not, not for a long time. I wanted to leave, but I just had no idea what I'd do or where I'd go."

"Lily, you're so smart and talented. You can do anything you want."

"If I only knew what I wanted." Lily remembered how hard her mother had worked to support them after her father walked out. She could start a catering business, but she was so tired of the whole LA scene.

"So, why don't you take your alimony and run?"

"You know Brad. He'll make my life hell if I try to get a cent from that marriage."

"Here in California, there are community property laws."

"I just can't deal with divorce attorneys yet." Lily closed her eyes, willing all these decisions to disappear. "But I guess I better find one soon."

"I'll put out some feelers for you. You will need one in California. But right now you just need to take care of yourself for a while."

Lily laughed. "If I can remember how."

Chapter Five

Two days to herself had given her a chance to catch up on some sleep, but now it was time to see exactly what she had inherited. The plumbing was leaking on the kitchen sink and the house badly needed a painting, on the outside at least. Lily located the office area tucked under the stairs. A computer was on the desk but nothing more. She turned it on and searched for Internet. No connection. For now her cell phone would have to do for checking email. Lily sifted through the items in the desk, searching until she found the brochure. She adjourned to the rocking chair in the parlor to peruse its contents. Madrona Island Bed & Breakfast–Maggie Parkins, Innkeeper. The glossy cover featured a beautiful photo of the inn framed in a gold leaf oval. The front yard was alive with vibrant color: lilac plants bloomed wild along the path to the entry; scarlet, apricot and yellow Hollyhocks towered against the garden fence, complemented by white daisies. The wraparound porch was adorned with ceramic hanging pots overflowing with cascades of fuchsias in pinks and white. A climbing rose wound its way up a lattice arbor and a tulip tree was in full bloom. The cornflower blue water glistened in the

distance and the snowy peaked Olympic Mountains dominated the sky. Underneath this dreamlike picture, in a perfect
script, was written:

*Let your worries drift out to sea from our majestic
perch on picturesque and romantic Madrona Island.
Turn of the century country hospitality.*

Inside the brochure was a small snapshot of each room
with a brief description. She popped out of the chair and headed upstairs to investigate the rooms firsthand. The first door
on the right was labeled the English Lavender Room. She read
its description aloud. "This comfy and cozy suite, in lavender
and green floral décor, features quaint English teapots, cups,
saucers, and lilac bouquets. A white picket fence headboard
complements the queen bed and ultra-plush down quilt." Lily
lay back on the bed and sank into its luxurious comfort. She
took in the beautiful room, the purple velvet loveseat in front
of the fireplace, the dormer window with a sweeping view
of mountains through the rose garden. "What a lovely room
Grandma created."

She rose and continued down the hall to the Peaches n'
Cream Suite. "This fresh and cheerful room offers pale peach
walls with butter cream trim," she read aloud. "Sounds good
enough to eat," she giggled.

The canopy bed was draped in apricot-tinted satin and
accented by hand-embroidered pillows. The sitting area featured a turn-of-the-century fainting couch and an old-fashioned Victrola. She walked over to the window and admired
the view of the gardens. "A perfect setting for romance," the
brochure said.

She reviewed the brochure; the Rose Suite was where she
had spent the night on the other side of the staircase. Lily stood

in the doorway, breathing in the light scent of the petal-filled flower cushions and bouquets of dried roses. It was lovely.

One more room awaited her discovery, the Honeymoon Suite. This secluded suite, with a sitting area nestled in the round windowed turret, had an impressive hand-carved four-poster bed and a wood-burning fireplace to stay snug and warm. Lily looked out at the outstanding mountain, water, and sunset views from the tower peak. She could see a man and young boy chasing a dog along the ocean shore. The sun peeking through the clouds made it tempting to go outside for a walk and look around.

She stuck her head into the bathroom. A heart-shaped Jacuzzi tub for two was built under a window facing out to the Sound. A painted sink sat on a ceramic pedestal.

Lily was transfixed; she actually lived in this enchanting place. She read on about the amenities and then turned to the back of the brochure. Mouthwatering, homemade breakfasts: "Enjoy our specialties–Lavender Orange Stuffed French Toast, Dungeness Crab Quiche, Loganberry Honey Scones, and our unique Washington Apple-Stuffed Croissants drizzled with molten caramel."

Yum… Where in the world were these recipes? She hurried down the stairs to scour the kitchen for the recipe box Mary thought was stored there. In a top drawer, she found the old wooden box that she remembered from when she was a little girl.

"Here it is!"

She lifted the lid and pulled out a card filled with a handwritten recipe.

"There are hundreds in here. What a find!" She scanned through the recipes, pulling out several cards to create a grocery list with. "Off to the store, stock up, and have a baking day tomorrow."

Lily bundled up in her coat and wool scarf and headed for the car. The air was clean and crisp after the rain, and there were patches of blue in the sky. She navigated her way to the main road and headed up-island to the market. Just as Mary had said, it was easy to find. A quaint hand-painted sign with a cornucopia of fruits and vegetables surrounded by a rainbow heralded the Cascade Country Market. The small exterior was deceiving, Lily soon discovered. Bountiful bins of colorful vegetables and fruits lured her into the produce section. She loaded up the cart with Jonigold apples and juicy-looking pears. The freshly washed arugula would make a splendid salad and omelet filler. The purple potatoes, sweet onions, carrots, and celery would add flavor to a chill-thawing chicken soup. Much of the produce was labeled with the name of a local farm.

Lily wandered over to the bread section and lightly squeezed Matt's Killer Sprouted Wheat bread...soft and still slightly warm. Her cart was filling quickly with local raspberry-infused honey, hand-pressed cider, free-range brown speckled eggs, creamy goat cheese mixed with herbs, and a bottle of Island White wine. The rich smell of fresh-ground coffee demanded an about face and a trip down the aisle tantalizing her senses. She picked up the slick, bright-red package with a towering lighthouse on it—Madrona Brew, Fresh Roasted Island Coffee. "A must," she said as she placed it in the already overflowing basket and headed for the checkout.

A middle-aged man in a flannel shirt and overalls was humming as he bagged up the groceries for the lady in front of the line. Then he waved Lily in and started unloading her cart.

"Morning," he said with a smile. "Did you find everything you need?"

"Looks like I bought up the whole store!"

The man continued ringing up the groceries. "Are you visiting?"

"Well, not quite. Actually, I'm living over at the Madrona Island B&B and plan to do some cooking."

"Margaret's old B&B? You must be her granddaughter, been hearing about you. I'm Dana Hansen, your local grocer, ma'am." His hearty handshake certainly felt safe and welcoming.

"Lily." She couldn't remember the last time she felt that comfortable, especially around a man.

"Looks like you're planning on doing some baking too. We sure miss those home-baked brownies that your grandma used to make for us to sell in the bakery. Think you might have some extra?"

Lily smiled. "Maybe. First I'm just going to do some experimenting, but I'll bring samples soon."

When Dana totaled her bill, she had a moment of pause. For ten years now, she never thought about how much her groceries rang up to. She needed these ingredients to make some products to show Jude. But she better start budgeting after this. Surely, Mary could help her figure something out. She paid in cash and left the store, arms piled with groceries and recipe ideas spinning in her head as she drove the few miles home. Was this a Stepford island, or was everyone really this nice?

Lily pulled into her driveway, gravel rolling under her tires, and parked in front. As she opened the trunk, she realized she should have driven around to the back door. Heck with it, she thought as she tried to juggle several bags between her arms and shoulders.

"Can I help you with those, little lady?"

Lily jumped and almost dropped the groceries. An elderly man reached over and caught a few bags. "I hope I don't have that effect on all the women," he said with a broad smile. "Time for introductions, I think. I'm your neighbor next door to the north. McPherson, John McPherson, and this here is my faithful canine companion, Gretel."

"I'm Lily," she said, regaining her composure. She placed the bags on the ground and bent down to pet the large black dog that had come up behind her.

"Yes, I know. You look a lot like your grandma, and she told me so much about you." He picked up some of the grocery bags and followed her to the house. "I kinda miss helping around here, and I think Gretel does too. Shall I carry these into the kitchen for you?"

Lily looked up at his gray hair neatly tucked under a baseball hat and the warm brown eyes encircled by deep smile lines. She thought he was probably close to eighty. This was a good man. Two in one day? She must have left the planet, not just LA.

"Come on in, Mr. McPherson. I could use the help and some company, to be honest. I've just been here a couple of days, wandering around in this big old house, having this great conversation with myself."

He chuckled. "I have plenty of those myself with the kids gone and Margaret..." He stopped there and stared at Lily as if he had said something wrong.

"You knew my grandmother?"

His gaze dropped to the old floral carpet then up at her again. Sadness crossed his face, making him look old and dimming the light of his smile. "I knew her well, to tell you the truth...I sure loved her."

For a moment they just stared at each other. A deep understanding passed between them. "You know, Mr. McPherson, I just went crazy and bought all this food in town, and you would do me a great favor if you would join me for dinner tonight."

The smile was back. He stood and tipped his hat. "Would love to, but my grandson and his boy are visiting. They'll be leaving on Sunday to catch the ferry and head on home."

"How about Sunday dinner then, say around five?"

His smile was contagious. "Sounds like something to look forward to."

"Okay, but I must warn you, I'll be doing some experimenting with recipes and you'll be the guinea pig."

John headed for the door. "Five it is then. See you on Sunday."

Lily entered the house and turned up the thermostat in the hall then laid down her purse. She slid her cell phone out to check for messages. One new message. She checked the call record but it said private caller. She put the phone in her pocket and hurried back to the kitchen to put everything away. Flushed with excitement, she tore through the bags, sorting ingredients and putting away a month of supplies. She enjoyed knowing that her biggest decision was what to make for dinner, but not as a mandatory, graded performance like it had been for Brad. Brad...almost a whole day without thinking of him.

The heater had kept the house warm and welcoming, but a cup of hot tea would be perfect now. She turned on the copper kettle to boil and pulled out her phone to check the voicemail.

"This is Brad, Lily. I miss you. Are you planning to come home soon? I'd be happy to come up to Washington and bring you back."

His voice was sweet, almost purring, but the edge was there. How did he know where she was?

The message continued, "We can make a little vacation out of it, take the coast route. Call me, you know the number.

Today would be good. Love you."

Her stomach lurched and her world crumbled. He'd found her in only a few days. How thoughtless she'd been, using her debit card on the way up and in the café. He knew her maiden name, and it was the same as her grandmother's. It must have been easy to figure she was heading to her grandmother's house. The one she'd always talked about.

Was there nowhere to go that was safe? Hers alone? She pounded on the kitchen counter with both fists. She was no longer his property. This was her home, and she had no intention of going back.

"He can take his veiled threats and yell them down the toilet for all I care. For once in my life, I'm going to face him head on."

Heart beating, pulse racing, Lily dialed Brad's number. "Answer, darn it, pick up the phone."

"This is Brad."

"Brad, it's Lily. I know you already know that. Just listen for once, will you?" She heard his low chuckle and heat raced to her face. "I want you to leave me alone. Neither your threats nor your promises are going to change my mind."

It didn't take much for him to show his true motives. Brad's voice was cold and steady. "I really don't care whether you change your mind or not. I don't want a divorce and if you push me much further, you'll get nothing, Lily."

The kettle boiled furiously and she pulled it off the burner.

"There are laws to protect me, Brad, and community property. That house is half mine. I lived there for almost ten years." She thought of every meal she had cooked, every room she had cleaned, painted, decorated, and loved. The rose garden and the koi pond were hers...hers.

"As usual, you don't know what you're talking about, sweetheart. Not only did you abandon your house and home when you left, but that same law you're talking about…it says this is not community property. Remember a little thing called a quit claim deed you signed?"

"You told me it was my home and that we didn't need to put my name on the deed. You lied, Brad."

"It's your word against mine, and who do you think they'll believe, Lily? You, who barely worked a day of our marriage? You, who just walked out without giving me a chance to work things out? Or me?"

If he'd been in front of her, she would have strangled him. "You always did have a way with the truth, a way to twist it so it always suited what you wanted."

"Of course, Lily, if you can't see it my way, my attorney is just waiting for my call. And by the way, I closed our joint checking account," he said casually, "so your debit card will be declined in any further purchases."

The room started to spin and she grabbed the nearest chair for balance. Calm down, she told herself, get a grip. "You can't do that Brad, my name is on it too."

"Yes, dear, but I am the primary account holder in this family, and I can do anything I want. Now how about we put this behind us and you just come home."

"Don't call again. I will notify you when I get an attorney and if you have something to say, say it to him!"

She slammed the phone down with every ounce of strength she had left and tried to slow her breath. Thank goodness her mother had helped her put some cash aside. No credit cards, money running out, all assets in Brad's name, no spousal support yet…it was almost insurmountable. She took a deep breath and closed her eyes, taking stock. She had enough food for quite a while. She had herself, this place, everything would be all right. "He has underestimated his so-called trophy wife this time," she said aloud.

She paced the kitchen floor, thinking about all of the gourmet cooking and pastry classes she'd taken; surely they could be her ticket to some kind of income. "I will do what I do best...cook, that's what I love to do anyway," she murmured to herself. Jude had asked her about selling baked goods to her café, and the brownies seem to be in high demand.

First thing I need to do is to find that secret recipe for the incredible brownies Grandma Maggie used to make. Then, I need to get Internet installed. She looked first through the many recipes in the wood box in the kitchen, but none were for brownies. Next she rummaged through the kitchen drawers and cabinets. Having no luck there either, she searched the office desk. Methodically she moved through the inn, opening drawers and closets until she reached her new quarters. In the small office of her bedroom, she rifled through the file drawers by the desk. There were records for a mail order business for the brownies and the Mt. Rainer cookies, and it looked very lucrative.

If only she knew her grandmother better, she might know where to find the darned thing. Hand-me-down family recipes could be scarce when you had no contact with your family. Standing by the bed, she scanned the room.

"Of course!" The mahogany and marble nightstand had an old-fashioned keyhole in the top drawer. Lily gave the drawer a yank, and to her surprise, it slid right open. No recipe, but tucked away in the back of the drawer was a periwinkle-colored, leather-bound book with gold embossed letters on the cover: Guestbook—Madrona Island Bed & Breakfast.

Lily flopped on the bed and placed the book in her lap. She ran her fingers along the leather surface then opened it, savoring the faint scent of dried lavender. She flipped gingerly through the pages, noting the dated journal entries from the previous years. She could imagine the B&B filled with people, mouthwatering aromas wafting up from the kitchen, guests on the porch sipping tea and watching the sunset. A beautifully scripted entry caught her attention.

June 30, 2007
We woke up to the most spectacular view of the Sound and the mountains. It made all the exhaustion from our wedding day just fade away. The sunrays filled the wonderfully romantic room, and the gourmet breakfast delivered to our door made our first morning as husband and wife a serene and exceptional experience. Thank you for your kindness.
Billee & Rex Winston

With eyes closed, Lily imagined the bride in her white lace negligee stretched out on the canopy bed, her hair mussed and spilling over the apricot satin pillowcase, a flush of happiness on her face. She saw the bursting colors of the sunrise peering over the snow-peaked mountains, reflecting vividly in the misty waters of the Sound. And there was her grandmother, carrying a silver tray graced by a bud vase filled with a single long-stemmed red rose. China plates garnished with fresh mint and orange nasturtiums held a succulent quiche, ripe strawberries, and steaming coffee. The soft knock on the door by Margaret would send the bride scurrying to fetch the tray to share with her husband.

The scene faded, and with it Lily's spirits. She recalled her own wedding night with Brad at the upscale five-star hotel in Palm Springs. Two nights only. Brad had work to do, after all. No roses, no romance, only, "Lily, I think that little black swimsuit would be more appropriate, and watch the desserts, it's starting to look a little tight on you." For God's sake, she'd worn a size three when they married.

He always knew just what to do. Back then it had seemed endearing; he was teaching her, taking care of her. Broad-shouldered, dazzling smile, and heart-stopping golden brown eyes, he'd been hard to resist. Now she could see he was just trying to mold her into the image of the perfect wife he wanted, right down to her suit size and the color of her hair.

Tears welling up, she turned the pages filled with happy memories and love shared, hoping somehow she'd find in this book the secret to the life she was missing. These people knew how to be happy.

Saturday
> *This place is so peaceful even the birds nest on it.*
> *Geneva, age 8*

The little girl had drawn a picture of a bird's nest in the peak of the roof. So sweet. How she wanted a little girl of her own. Each entry ended with almost the same sentiment:

> *A beautiful, memory-making weekend. Thank you.*
> *~Paula*

The familiar emptiness pressed down on her heart. She'd always longed for someone to share special moments like these with. A book filled with happy memories from other people. At least it was possible for some. But for now, and she must remember, by choice, she was alone, and it was time to find an attorney. She had her grandmother's memories to keep her company; maybe they would work their magic on her life too.

Chapter Six

To create a muted, fog-like effect, Ian added a watercolor wash in a pale gray over his newest painting. The raven, large and perched off center, stared back at him with his cocked head and piercing yellow eye. The black creature guarded the entrance to a distant land, where fields rolled gently toward a great sea. Only the raven knew the depths to which a person must delve within his own soul to find the coveted password—the key to this hallowed place where one's deepest dreams and desires manifested themselves upon the misty air, fulfilling the longings of the heart.

Ian scrawled his signature in the bottom corner and stepped back to assess the finished painting. Ravens were revered in certain cultures, considered messengers from the gods. He stared into the yellow eye, searched for the wisdom that would lead him through the gates and down to the sea. For a moment, he reflected on the metaphor. His own heart was so guarded, the happiness he sought was locked away, and a mysterious scavenger held the key but was unwilling to reveal the secret password. For Ian, ravens had always repre-sented death and decay, but this raven held some ancient wisdom, some knowledge yet to unfold that would restore him.

Outside his studio in the old refurbished barn, romping through his Grandfather John's yard, Jason was playing with the dog. It was a wonder how well that young boy had healed after losing his mother. He should follow his son's example. Jason was as bright and playful as any seven-year-old; perhaps it was a blessing that his memory had faded over the last four years, and as youth can do, he moved on, finding simple pleasure in the skipping of rocks along the water's surface or chasing his grandpa's big black dog, Gretel.

The door of his studio slammed shut and Jason skidded in. He was tall for his age. Sandy blond hair fell across his forehead, framing his dark eyes.

"Dad, Dad, you gotta come out here. Gretel is chasing a baby bunny." The boy reached for his dad's coat, "C'mon, hurry."

"Okay, Jason, calm down. We'll go get that silly dog and bring her home." Ian tossed on his blue down parka and followed his boy outside.

Jason started running across the yard. "She ran across the field toward Aunt Maggie's old house. Follow me."

The field was damp and muddy from the constant pounding of winter rain, and their boots made a sloshing sound as they crossed.

"Gretel," Jason yelled at the top of his voice. "Come home."

Ian chuckled to himself. In the distance, he could see the dog had abandoned her pursuit of the rabbit and was making her way up the steps to her once favorite place–the porch at Maggie's farmhouse. The dog remembered the luscious treats and warm reception from her old friend and still wandered back occasionally, waiting for Maggie to return. Unlike a child, you could not tell a dog that her loved one had gone to heaven. It was hard to imagine the kind old woman, with her twinkling eyes and generous spirit, was not there anymore. Those fresh-made dog biscuits she had concocted were not only Gretel's favorites, but were in high demand by pet owners throughout the island.

Ian walked across the stone path. "Come, Gretel, she's not there anymore, girl." He reached over and scratched behind the dog's ears. "Yeah, we know, we miss her too."

All heads went up and were taken aback when the front door opened and a young woman peeked out to see what was going on.

Ian stammered, "Excuse us, Miss…"

"Lily."

Jason took the lead. "Grandpa's dog, Gretel, was chasing a bunny and I didn't want her to hurt it so I got my dad to help me catch her but she ran over here. This is my Auntie Maggie's house, what are you doing here?"

Ian laughed. "Whoa, Jason, take a breath."

"I quite understand, Jason," Lily said warmly. "I wouldn't want to let a baby bunny get hurt either." She made eye contract with Ian, then reached out to shake Jason's hand. "I'm Lily Parkins, and who are you?"

"Jason McPherson, and this is my dad, his name's Ian."

"Well nice to meet you both, Jason and Ian. I guess we're going to be neighbors for a while."

Ian stared at the tall, attractive woman. Something was so familiar about her. Those sad blue-green eyes, he'd seen them somewhere. Then it hit him, it was her, the woman on the ferry, the one who had almost knocked him down. He could not forget that face. A raven's caw cut the air; an omen.

Jason cocked his head and stared at Lily. "We're not really neighbors. My Gramps lives here and we visit on the weekends. Except in the summer, we live here almost all summer.

The rest of the time we live in Lahomish, on the other side of the water, and my dad is an artist and I know how to paint too."

"Jason, buddy, let's not tell Lily our whole life story. I think it's time we head home and let Lily get on with her day."

Lily bent down and met the boy's eyes. "Jason, sometime you could come over and tell me more about your painting. And I could make some of my killer chocolate chip cookies for you and your grandpa too."

Ian looked into Lily's eyes—she meant every word. Something inside him shifted, melted ever so slightly; a light, long out, flickered.

"Jason, say goodbye to Lily, we got to get going."

"Nice to meet you, Miss Lily. I'll be back and bring some of my drawings too," Jason said.

Lily, smiling broadly, looked up at Ian. "I'll look forward to it, Jason."

Ian longed to look back at the farmhouse as they walked, but he willed himself to look straight ahead. Lily never did say what she was doing there. It was possible his grandfather knew her story, not that he was really interested. The last thing he needed right now was another distraction with the art show deadline looming over him. Her eyes told a story he was not sure he wanted to know.

Chapter Seven

Lily watched Ian's tall, slim body move easily across the moist field back toward his house. Dark, tussled hair curled over the back collar of his flannel shirt. He looked so…earthy was the word that came to mind, solid. Not at all like Brad. This was not a way to be thinking right now; another man in her life was not what she needed. The damp chill was starting to set in as the sun took refuge behind some slate-gray clouds. She sighed; a warm body beside her, a soft touch would be so nice. "Ahh," she whispered in the air.

The boy was running ahead, chasing the black dog as they neared the back door porch. Wood smoke curled up from the chimney and reminded her to try again to start a fire. Both boys—well Ian was definitely a man—had a sadness that hung over them like the murky fog starting to roll in over the water. She rubbed her arms to warm up as she turned and hurried up her steps. The wood, paper, and matches awaited her not-so-deft hands; she wished she had asked Ian to show her how to start a fire…in the wood burner, that is.

Despite the chilly day, Lily watched an elderly woman wearing a baseball hat and a down vest traipsing across the muddy front yard, heading right for her front porch.

"Yoo-hoo, anybody home?" called the old woman as she rapped on the front door.

Lily opened the door to find a spry-looking woman with electric blue eyes holding a bundle of kindling wood.

"Can I come in? You must be the granddaughter we all heard so much about. I'm your neighbor, Betty. My sister, Shirley, and I live right next door, so if you need anything, you just wander over and ask. We wanted to give you a little time to settle in before we came calling. Well, at least I did. Shirley wanted to stomp right over the day you arrived."

Shaking the rough and calloused hand Betty had extended, Lily replied, "Good morning. I'm Lily. It's nice to meet you."

Betty walked in as if she lived there and laid the kindling by the fireplace. "Thought you might be needin' some of this kindling with the weather still being so cold. Your wood's been settin' out there a long time and might be a bit wet."

Lily looked with dismay at the kindling and the fireplace. She was embarrassed to let this obviously very competent, self-assured woman, who had to be more than twice Lily's age, know that she had never lit a fire before in her life. The only heat source she knew was the thermostat. And thank goodness this old house had one. "I'm so happy you came by, Betty, and thanks for the sticks, I mean..."

"Kindling," Betty piped in. Her bright blue eyes noticed Lily's longing glance toward the thermostat. Quickly assessing the situation, Betty said, with a gentle diplomacy, "Just roll your sleeves up and I'll give you a lesson in fire starting. Be sure you start by opening the flue up inside here."

Betty pulled up the metal latch. "Real important, Lily, you gotta open up that flue first so the smoke goes outside." Betty wadded up some old newspapers sitting next to the hearth and set the balls of paper into the stove. "Then you take the kindling and make a grid out of it like this." She began to arrange the wood. "Leave plenty of room for air to circulate, but make sure it's a tight enough grid to catch fire. You'll get the hang of it with a little practice. Here, you try it. Can't rely on that propane tank all winter and spring, or you'll be broke before you know it."

Lily stacked some thin slivers of wood in place, and as Betty coached her, she set a few small logs on top. Betty handed her the long matches. "Light the side edges and get the fire going." She leaned over and blew a bit of air onto the flames to get them to rise.

The pungent smell of wood smoke started to fill the room. Lily stood back and admired their work. She loved the crackling sounds as the flames leapt up over the logs. Already the room was feeling toasty from the roaring fire. "Thanks, Betty, for the Fire Building 101 lesson. Now, how about a cup of coffee and a snack?"

"Coffee's great, but no food for me. Got lots to do today, no time to eat. Plumbing's leaking again and that darn front step is rotting out."

Lily poured some coffee and sat down at the table with Betty. "Did you have to call a plumber and a carpenter?" Lily asked.

"Heck no," Betty answered, "I do all that myself. Got my tools in the basement and two good hands. That's all I need."

How different her new neighbor was from any woman Lily had ever met in Los Angeles. She tried to guess Betty's age—probably late 70s—and she still had more energy than Lily had ever had in her entire life. "I am so glad you came by, Betty. I don't know many people on the island yet."

Betty gulped a mouthful of coffee. "Well, Lily, your grandmother knew just about everyone in these parts—and was loved by them, too. You'll be meeting folks soon. They've all heard so much about you from Maggie, they'll be wanting to meet you themselves. My busy-body sister will probably be over here talking your ear off as soon as she manages to wake up and get all her make-up on. And then there's John next door over yonder. He's a good egg."

Lily fried up some bacon to make a breakfast sandwich. "Betty, are you sure I can't interest you in a small breakfast?"

"Alright, I think I will. That smells too good. It's not often I eat anything so fancy, I'm too lazy to cook for myself. Shirley's the one who usually makes a big fuss over cooking."

Lily served the breakfast and sat down at the kitchen table. She watched Betty bite into her bacon sandwich with gusto. The older woman's face was weathered but radiant, lit by sparkling eyes and a kind smile.

Swallowing, Betty continued, "I used to see you on your visits over here. I remember you running outside with your grandma, chasing those seagulls, laughing and having a good old time. Shirley wasn't living here back then, she came back to the island after her husband died, let's see…about twelve or thirteen years ago. We both adored your grandma."

"Sounds like you knew my grandmother pretty well."

"You betcha." Betty smiled while she gobbled down more of the bacon and egg sandwich. "Pretty feisty lady that one. Almost single-handedly she turned this place into a B&B after having to sell the café when your dad left. No easy job either, after all those darn taxes just kept going up. It's those tourists running around up here, buying summer places, kicking the property values up. But Maggie had the right attitude; she took what looked like a problem and turned it into a constructive solution."

Lily sighed. "I wish I could have helped. I regret not taking the time to get to know Grandma better. I thought about her often enough, but my marriage was so demanding and I kind of lost myself in it somewhere."

Betty patted Lily's hand. "Well, you're here now and that's all that matters."

"Yeah, I guess so. Now, if I can at least learn to build a fire, there's hope for me yet. That's of course if Brad, my soon to be ex-husband, doesn't show up and try to drag me back to LA."

"Give yourself time girl, and don't go borrowing trouble," Betty said. "I'm sure you've got a good head on your shoulders, just like your grandma. It'll all work out."

Betty took her plate to the sink and washed it off. "Well, I best be going now. Just holler if you need anything," she said heading for the back door. "And thanks for the breakfast. You needn't have bothered, though. I'm just fine with crackers in the morning."

Lily sipped her coffee. With an example like Betty to follow, she could not fail. Lily quickly did the dishes and sat down to make a list of things to accomplish today. Top of the list was to try chopping some more kindling with the axe she'd found in the shed.

She zipped up her jacket and grabbed the heavy gloves she'd found in the hall closet. "I'll do some chopping and carry in a load to start a fire. Lily Mitchell...no, Lily Parkins... country girl! I like the sound of that." She pushed her hair up under a warm cap and headed outside.

Roosters crowed in the distance. Lily remembered her grandma saying roosters did not have the sense to know the time of day. She inhaled the sweet scent of saltwater. The morning dampness penetrated her heavy jeans, permeating to the bone. Kneeling, she balanced the small chopped hardwood on its side and began to slice off small pieces with the ax. It felt good to be focused on a simple task. Tomorrow, she might call her mother and get some names of attorneys.

Chapter Eight

Out of her bedroom window, Lily saw the mail truck pull up and deposit something in her box. Nine a.m., right on time. She tied her shoes, grabbed a sweater, and headed outside. A priority mail packet from an attorney in Los Angeles was waiting for her. *Just what I need this morning, something to spoil my breakfast.* There was a plain white envelope with no return address on it addressed to her. She brought the mail inside and opened the anonymous one first.

Don't get too comfortable in the house, it doesn't belong to you.

No signature, just a veiled threat. It was not Brad's style to do something like this. Was it a prank? It was obvious someone did not want her in this house. Should she tell someone about the note or just ignore it? There were more important things to deal with for now like the big envelope. She ripped it open. With shaky hands, she pulled out the contents, a list of debts and assets for her to review from Brad's attorney. "How dare he! How *dare* he!" Her heart pounded so loud she didn't know which frightened her more, its racing sound or her gasping breath. She crumpled the pages and then shredded them into tiny pieces. Fists clenched, she paced the floor.

"The bastard! Didn't he already take enough?" Lily said to the ceiling. I need to sit down. She pulled out her cell phone and dialed her mother as she walked toward the parlor.

"I received paperwork from Brad today, he wants everything. Wait until he hears I inherited property from Grandma, he'll probably want half of that too."

"Lily, he doesn't have a chance of taking your inherited property. He is just bluffing to force you to come back."

"I don't know why he would want me back. Probably he doesn't want to part with any of his possessions, including me."

"I'm sorry I haven't been there more for you these last years."

"It's alright Mom, I was pretty distant myself."

"When you married Brad, the irony of all my choices and where they led us hit me hard. I didn't want you to make the same mistakes I did."

Lily laughed. "The joke, I think, was on both of us. Here, all this time I thought you were proud of me marrying a man like Brad. I was afraid to tell you what my life with him was really like. I thought you would blame me."

"Never, Lily. It takes a lot of guts to walk out on a marriage that provides financial security and looks so perfect from the outside."

"I wish I could take credit for walking out on my own volition before all the ugly lies were rubbed in my face." The text messages, the pictures, how could she tell her mother? "He cheated on me. I found out and he didn't even care."

The only sound was the hum of the furnace.

"Don't look back, Lily. You did your best to hold a marriage together, certainly. I understand that."

Her mother's words hit deep. As a child, Lily had resented

Katherine ripping her away from her home and her grand-mother, but now she understood what it was like to be in an abusive marriage. Her mother took them away to start a new life. "I love you, Mom. Thanks for being here. I know it hasn't always been easy for you, either."

"It's going to be all right," Katherine said. "He can threaten all he wants. I found a good divorce attorney who will see us right away. When can you come down?"

"Go ahead and make an appointment. The sooner the better."

"Can you be ready to fly out Monday morning Lily?"

"Absolutely."

"Good," Katherine said. "I will take care of the flight arrangements and email you a confirmation. I'll see you at LAX."

The kindness of her mother's act reminded her she was not alone. "Thanks, Mom. It's not just about the money anymore. For once, I'm fighting for me."

♦ ♦ ♦ ♦

After the morning mail, weeding was proving to be very therapeutic. Lily pulled out a tall weed, roots soaked in mud, and tossed it in a bucket. From behind the hedge that led up from the sisters' cottage, she heard a low whistle. A woman appeared, dressed for a magazine shoot with a perfectly matched teal-blue pantsuit and shoe combination, white camel coat, silk scarf, and a double strand of pearls peeking over the collar of her blouse. The golden haired, perfectly coiffed, and made up woman looked to be around 80. She was startlingly out of place in this rustic setting. Shirley, Lily surmised with a smile. Lily waved and watched the woman precariously balancing a basket as she stepped over the mud puddles and onto the steppingstones leading up through the dormant garden to Lily's house. She reminded Lily of a regal mother lion.

Lily wiped her hands on her jeans. "Hello," she called out as she walked down the hill to greet the woman. "You must be Shirley. I've already heard so much about you."

"Nothing good, would be my bet!" Shirley said with a hearty laugh. "Here, take this darn basket I brought you before I drop it all out on the ground."

Lily took the wicker basket and peered in. It looked like enough food for a family of ten. "Why, thank you, Shirley. People sure are nice around here."

"Well, some of us are anyway," she said glancing back at her cottage.

Lily led the way back to the house, opening the door for Shirley to enter the warm kitchen.

"I presume you're Lily."

"Yes, of course."

With a dazzling smile and a strong booming voice, Shirley proceeded, "Good to meet you in person. You *are* a pretty one." Her crystal blue eyes seemed not to miss anything. "Looks like there's still some city left in you. I'd have been over here sooner, but my hip's been giving me some trouble. Getting old is no fun at all."

Lily took Shirley's arm and guided her into the parlor, then placed the basket on the coffee table. These sisters couldn't be more different.

"Here, have a seat by the fire, I'll put some more wood on," Lily said, helping Shirley into the club chair nearest the warm flames.

Shirley observed the pile of fresh kindling in the corner. "Looks like my sister's already been here this morning. Leave it to her to be out early getting dirty doing something."

Lily laughed. "Can I get you something warm to drink?"

"Well, actually, the thermos in the basket is filled with super-rich hot chocolate, and the Tupperware has fresh cinnamon whipped cream."

"Yumm," Lily said opening the lid and taking a sniff. "A woman after my own heart. And what's this? Looks like banana bread. I'll go get us some cups from the kitchen and slice some of the bread."

Shirley yelled in after her, "The butter pickle potato salad probably needs to be refrigerated, but the chicken can stay out."

As Lily emptied the basket, she knew one thing for sure—she'd never go hungry around here. She carried in the cups of hot cocoa and a plate of the bread and sat down beside Shirley. "Thank you for your wonderful welcome. What more could a woman ask for?"

Shirley's smile lit the room. "I would have brought flowers too, but none are blooming yet. It's too early in the season, and there's been too much damn rain."

The parlor filled with the sweet aroma of warm chocolate and the faint scent of cinnamon. Shirley glared at Lily. "Are you single?"

Lily was taken aback by this direct inquiry about her personal life, and she paused for a moment before answering. "I'm filing for a divorce, actually."

Shirley didn't miss a beat. "Have you seen that cute grandson of John McPherson's next door? He's a real looker if you ask me. That Ian McPherson doesn't need a purse or a nurse like some of these single old men here on the island."

Lily had to think for a minute—a purse...a nurse? Oh she got it—men looking for money or someone to take care of them. Pretty clever, she thought. "I'm not looking for any man right now. I think I've had just about enough of them in my life, thank you."

Shirley eyed her again. "You're young, you'll get over that quick enough. Don't let a good one get away, especially when he's right next door!"

The thought of that handsome young man right next door was a bit close for comfort.

"So, Lily, what do you plan to do with your time? It can get pretty dull around here, especially in winter."

Dull sounded fine to her right now. "I haven't got that far in my plans yet. I'm mostly just getting through each day."

"We'll have to fix that," Shirley said finishing off her last sip of cocoa. "You young people should be having some fun too, unlike my sister, who just can't stop working. Darn stubborn Betty, still climbing up ladders at her age. Her idea of shopping is a nice trip to the hardware store!"

They heard a knock at the door and Betty poked her head in. "Did I hear someone say my name? I bet that's you, Shirley, in there talking so loud."

Lily stood. "Come on in, Betty."

"She's already let herself in, uninvited, I might add," Shirley said.

Betty shook her head dismissively. "What are you girls having, a tea party?"

"It's cocoa, can't you smell it?" chirped Shirley.

"Now, now, girls," Lily said with a laugh. "Would you like some cocoa and banana bread, Betty?"

"Oh no, I'm not staying. No time. I'm off to town to pick up supplies and thought I'd check in one more time to see if you needed anything."

"You think this nice girl needs a wrench or a screwdriver?" Shirley griped. "You just about live at that hardware store, and buy your wardrobe from it too."

Betty flipped her hand at Shirley. "Don't mind her,

someone's got to keep us from floating away or trippin' down those front steps. Speakin' of which, I better check that leak under your kitchen sink again too."

Leaky sinks, fading paint, Lily hoped the house was not going to turn out to be a burden. "Thanks Betty, whenever you have time."

Lily held up the picnic basket still filled with goodies. "Shirley brought me enough food to cater a wedding."

Shirley let out a loud laugh. "No weddings around here with us old maids and you, young one, not even divorced yet. The hapless dog that always hangs around here will help you with the leftovers."

Betty zipped up her parka and pulled her hat down over her ears. "I'll be off then." She stared at her sister, "We can't all be fashion plates. I happen to like my parka and work boots, thank you."

"I don't know why you can't just sit down and take a rest for a while," Shirley complained. "Just call a plumber. Dad left us enough money to buy that old hardware store if we wanted to."

"Rest, what's that?" Betty asked coyly. "Plenty of time for that when I die." With a wave, she left the house.

Shirley started to rise from her chair, and Lily offered her a hand. "Well, don't be a stranger, Lily. We're right next door if you need anything."

"So good to meet you, and thanks so much for the goodies." Lily gave Shirley a warm hug.

Shirley beamed. "Now make sure you do something fun today," she said as she headed down the front steps hugging the banister.

"You know," Lily said, "I think I will bake up some cupcakes and cookies and then take them into town next week and see if Jude is interested in selling them in her café."

"Great idea, I bet she'll be very happy to do just that."

Uplifted and motivated, Lily headed to the kitchen to experiment with some baked goods that might appeal to Jude for the café. But first she would check her email on her cell phone and see if her mother had secured an appointment yet with a lawyer.

Chapter Nine

*L*ily was glad John was coming to Sunday dinner tonight. Cooking gave her something to focus on, and keep her mind off her meeting with the lawyer on Tuesday. For this dinner party, there would be no Brad leering over her shoulder, making demands, and commanding perfection. This would be a friendly dinner with the neighbor.

A knock at the door had her wondering who might be coming for a visit now. She opened the door to find John McPherson with Gretel at his side.

"I wasn't expecting you so early. Come in," Lily said. "You too, Gretel."

The dog wagged its tail and sat at Lily's feet, tilting her head up with an expectant gaze.

"Gretel's trained to do that for a treat, I'm afraid. Maggie always had a jar of biscuits waiting."

Lily moved toward the kitchen. "Well, let me see what I can find, then." She took out a slice of cheddar cheese and rolled it into a ball. "Here you go, girl."

Lily motioned for John to sit down at the table with her. "Can I make you a cup of coffee?"

"No, had my fill this morning, but thanks. We're just stopping in for a minute with a question for you."

"How can I help you?" she said.

John hesitated for a moment. "I didn't realize Ian and the boy were staying an extra day this weekend because of winter break, so I thought we might do our dinner on Monday instead?"

All the food was prepped and there was so much. She hated the thought of eating alone again tonight. "No problem, I told you I have enough food for the whole neighborhood. Just bring them along for dinner as well."

"You sure?" John asked. "Don't want to impose."

Lily laid her hand on his. "I'm happy to have you all over."

"Much thanks. See you at five o'clock sharp then." He stood and whistled for Gretel to follow him out the back door.

◆ ◆ ◆

The doorbell rang precisely at five. Right on time, Lily thought as she finished brushing her hair and adding a quick dash of lipstick. She opened the door to find John McPherson looking dapper, holding a bottle of sparkling cider, and wearing a warm smile. Beside him was Ian, wearing a dark blue sweater that set off his eyes, and Jason, holding a bouquet of carnations.

"Well, come on in," she said.

"For you, Lily," Jason said, handing her the flowers.

"Thank you, Jason. How thoughtful of you."

They wiped their boots on the welcome mat and stepped inside.

Lily took their coats. "Hope you're all hungry."

"Sure am, and if it tastes as good as it smells in here, we are in for a real treat," John said.

Lily led them into the dining room. "Go ahead and take a seat, and I'll bring out something warming to drink."

As Ian brushed past her, she caught the scent of cedar. He was taller than she remembered and so far had not said a word.

John ran a finger along the china dishes, embroidered napkins, and sparkling silverware. "I hope you didn't go to all this trouble just for us boys."

Lily laughed. "It's nothing fancy, just some old-fashioned comfort food with a gourmet touch. Believe me, it's a pleasure to have such wonderful dinner companions."

"We don't eat like this at home...ever," Jason said.

"How about hot chocolate for you, Jason?" Lily asked. "John, Ian, I have planned a Pinot Noir with dinner, but I can get you a cocktail first if you like."

Both men just stared at her. This was not Brentwood, California. She should probably have offered a beer.

Ian's gaze was tinged with humor. "I'll have the Pinot."

"Me too," John followed quickly.

After serving the drinks, Lily retreated into the kitchen. She leaned on the counter; just keep it simple, she reminded herself, no pressure. The pungent smell of garlic filled the toasty kitchen. She admired the layered meatloaf; seasoned ground turkey sandwiched a center of goat cheese and spinach. She placed a generous slice on each plate and then added a large mound of garlic mashed potatoes smothered in homemade gravy and a few sprigs of sautéed broccoli. She carried a plate in each hand, serving her guests first and then herself. The only empty seat at the table was next to Ian.

"My goodness, what a feast you made here," John said as he covered his lap with his napkin.

Ian held up his wine glass for a toast. Gazing directly at her he said, "To friends and family," then clicked her glass.

His lips circled the glass as he sipped the deep red wine. For a moment there was no one else in the room. She could not take her eyes off him.

Ian dug into the meatloaf, and the ecstatic look on his face filled Lily with pleasure. She forced herself to look away.

"So, John," she began between bites. "How long have you lived on the island?"

"My family has been here a long time. You know all the land you can see from your place to the bluff, and past Betty and Shirley's place to the bay? All of that was once McPherson land. My grandfather bought about 125 acres for a whopping $1,500 in the early 1900s."

"You couldn't even buy a garden patch for that much now!" Lily said.

Lily watched Ian joke around with his son over trying the goat cheese filling. The two of them seemed so easy with each other.

John shook his head, remembering. "My, how times have changed."

"How did you end up in Washington?" Lily asked between bites, fully aware of but trying to ignore the sparks she felt passing between her and Ian.

"Well, Granddad and his brother decided to bring their wives here to live near the ocean teeming with fish. Their first home was a one-room log house."

Lily tried to imagine what Madrona Island had looked like back then, pretty remote. Not a place she would necessarily want to settle in. The struggle to survive must have kept the family pretty busy; it could have been what held them together so long.

"Your family has a very rich history alright. Ian, do you live off island?" She said hoping to bring him into the conversation.

"Some of the time," Jason popped in. "We have a house in Lahomish."

Ian nodded. "I teach art at the community college there. But the gallery I primarily show in and my studio are located around the corner from Jude's café here on the island."

An artist, she should have known. He had that deep, otherworldly look. She wondered what simmered just below the surface.

Ian laid his fork down and pointed to his plate. "You are quite the artist yourself. You might enjoy attending my art opening in town in a few weeks?"

Lily could feel herself blush. "Sure. I can see if Jude would like to come along too."

"Of course," Ian said staring back at his plate.

The room was quiet while everyone worked on cleaning their plates.

"Best meal I've had in a very long time," John said swirling his last bite of meatloaf around the plate to sweep up every last drop of gravy.

"How about seconds?" she asked.

"I think I'm just fine."

"Ok, as long as you save room for dessert."

Ian lifted the wine bottle and offered to refill their glasses, "Shall we polish off the wine first?"

John placed his fork down and with a wistful look pointed toward the Sound. "See that bay out there? My grandfather used to talk about ships that smuggled rum close in to shore and dropped the bottles in the water. Well, they'd float right in on the tide and land on the beach."

"Thank goodness the laws and times have changed some since then," Lily said with a laugh. "I would hate to find bottles of rum floating up on my beach."

"I'd like that," Jason said, scraping his plate clean with his fork and licking off every drop.

Ian laughed. "I bet you would, son."

"Great meal, great chef," Ian said with a dazzling smile.

She placed her hand on his. "And good company makes it so much nicer." It was unlike her to touch a stranger's hand. And for that matter, to hug a neighbor either. She laughed to herself. In Los Angeles, they might sue you for doing something like that.

"If you ever want a tour of the island farms that sell direct, let me know and I'll be your guide," Ian said.

"That would be great, just let me know when you're available." She wished she had not used the word "available." It sounded so impersonal. It was such a relaxed dinner, unlike anything she'd experienced in the last few years, and she just didn't know how to act.

"I'll be back in a few weeks for the art opening," he said.

"Sure, just let me know, I'll be here," Lily said. She'd almost said, "It's a date."

"There's wild berries in the summer, too, great for pies," Jason said licking his lips.

John tousled Jason's hair. "When your gramps was a kid, we used to pick wild strawberries then take the boat out into the bay to fish. It was a great place to spend a childhood. It still is."

Lily remembered vividly the time she'd spent here as a child. It had been a haven, hanging out with her grandmother in the kitchen baking cookies, making strawberry jam, running along the shore chasing seagulls and collecting shells.

"We've taken up the whole evening with our stories, how about you? I'm sure your story is so much more interesting than mine," John said.

"I doubt that. Moved to Los Angeles, got married, getting divorced, and I'm back now." Lily regarded the man in front of her. He had history, ancestors, and hardships to overcome, yet his attitude was so filled with humor and grace.

She turned to Jason. "So how does hot-out-of-the-oven blueberry apple crisp, topped with vanilla bean gelato sound?"

Jason scrunched his face in deep thought. "What's gelato?"

"A really soft, creamy ice cream," Ian answered. "It's yummy, trust me!"

John patted his stomach. "Somehow I'll find room! I can't remember the last time I had a meal this delicious. I am sure, though, it must have been prepared in that very same kitchen by your grandmother."

Lily gave him a grateful smile and rose to clear the table. Dessert and coffee followed, milk for Jason.

When it was time to leave, first Grandpa John then Jason gave her a big hug. Ian lurked behind them. Lily hoped he wouldn't give her a big hug, too; she was afraid of her reaction. He took her hand. "Thank you for a wonderful evening."

A jolt shot up her arm as his warm fingers pressed into hers.

"You...you're welcome," she stammered closing the door behind them.

Lily hummed while she cleaned up the kitchen. She turned off all of the lights and headed for bed. Tomorrow she would get focused, make some decisions. Tonight, she felt content as she pulled the down comforter up over her shoulders. Her thoughts floated to Ian's warm touch. She wouldn't see him for a few weeks; it would give her time to cool down.

Chapter Ten

An unending veil of brown smog floated above the city as Lily's plane landed. One long shuttle ride, one short ferry ride, one fast flight, and Lily rolled her carry-on through LAX airport and headed for baggage claim where her mother would pick her up. The airport was a zoo, as usual. Thousands of people, all talking on their cell phones, all pushing and rushing somewhere, reminded her why she left this city.

Her mother's Toyota was waiting at the curb for her. Lily waved, threw her bag in the back and hopped in the passenger seat. For a moment they just stared at each other.

"Thanks for being here," Lily said.

Her mother's arms surrounded her and it felt wonderful to return the hug. Car horns blasted and Lily snapped her seat belt while Katherine pulled out into traffic.

"How about we stop for a quick dinner and then head home, have some tea, and talk?"

Lily nodded. "Perfect."

After eating, the traffic was almost clear when they entered the freeway. When they reached the valley, they exited at Laurel Canyon Boulevard and drove a few short blocks into the foothills of Studio City. Katherine pulled up in the driveway of their ranch-style home. The familiar porch light glowed as if to welcome her.

What am I doing back here with my mother at thirty years old? The dim glow in the windows of her old front bedroom reminded her how long it had been since she lived in this house. When they'd moved in, she'd been in high school and was thrilled to have a nice room and a pool of their own. She closed her eyes. "One night," she reassured herself. "Just one night and then I can return to the island."

"Lily, why don't you come inside?"

Lily fumbled with the door locks and stepped out of the car. "Sorry, it's been a long day."

Katherine picked up a suitcase and led her into the house. "I've fixed up your old room for you."

"Thanks, Mom. I just want to sleep."

Silently, they walked to her bedroom. Katherine placed the suitcase on the bed.

Lily turned to her mother. "I didn't tell you everything. I found over one hundred text messages between Brad and his gorgeous new corporate attorney, including barely clad pictures and endearments. Such a cliché these days in LA: wife turns thirty, husband goes for younger model." Tears welled in her eyes and she brushed them away. "I'm done crying, and if he thinks I am going to just quietly leave, he is very mistaken!"

"I'm sorry," Katherine said reaching over and getting Lily a tissue. "That must have really hurt."

"It did."

"Don't worry, honey. Tomorrow we will have a top attorney working for you."

"Thanks, Mom."

"I'll shut the door for you then. Sleep well, Lily."

She wilted into the overstuffed chair and dropped her purse on the floor. Her eyes drifted over the familiar objects: the prize-winning seascape she painted in college still hung above the brass bed, set off by the azure walls she had insisted on in her teens. The oak dresser with the carved mirror displayed her colorful shell and rock collection on an antique glass tray. But the cream-colored curtains were new; the royal blue velvet drapes that had hung over the sliding glass doors were long gone.

It held a comfortable familiarity, but still it didn't feel like home. The oversized house she lived in with Brad never had, either. Only one place had ever held that feeling: Grandma Maggie's farm. She rummaged through her bag for a nightshirt, pulled it over her head, and snuggled in under the down comforter. Sleep was the only thing on her mind.

◆ ◆ ◆

The Century City high-rise cast an ominous shadow that matched Lily's dark mood. Thank God her mother was by her side to face this business with a divorce attorney. Karl Goldberg, a.k.a. the bulldog of the courtroom, had come very highly recommended by a good friend of her mother's.

Lily hesitated at the elevator. "I really wish we could just settle this out of court."

Katherine pressed the button for the penthouse. "Lily, this is one divorce where your wishes will only be granted if you have a fairy godfather, and right now he is located on the top floor!"

The elevator doors opened to a lush reception area filled with soft leather sofas, potted orchids, and carved glass tables holding neatly stacked glossy magazines. The entire office was framed by floor-to-ceiling windows, revealing a view that reached all the way to the Pacific Ocean. All Lily could think about was how his bill would probably match this high-rent office.

As Katherine checked in at reception, Lily wandered over to stare out the windows. She located the Brentwood neighborhood where she'd spent so many years with Brad. He was probably busy changing the locks and hiding valuables right this moment. The nerve of him trying to keep everything and then demanding she pay half of all the debts. She turned her back on the view with resignation, crossed the room, laid her briefcase at her feet, and sank into the mauve Giovanni couch beside her mother.

A perfectly dressed and coifed woman hurried into reception, her high heels clicking smartly on the wood floor. Her icy gaze would have caused the most courageous heart to quiver. "You must be Lily Mitchell. Do you have all of your papers ready?"

Lily nodded.

"Mr. Goldberg is still in court, but we expect him shortly. Can I get you an espresso or a Pellegrino?"

Lily looked at her mother, who shook her head no. "Just a Pellegrino would be great."

"I didn't sign anything," Lily confided in her mother. "The signatures can wait until I see if I want to retain him or not."

"Your choice, Lily. Just remember, this one is paid to be on your side."

The atmosphere shifted, as if a storm were rolling in, when a tall, powerfully built man in a well-tailored Armani suit burst into the reception area. He directed a dazzling smile at them. "So sorry to be late, ladies, but the case ran a little over." He reached out a perfectly manicured hand. "I'm Karl Goldberg. Please call me Karl."

"Lily Mitchell," she said with a firm handshake, noticing the Rolex watch on his wrist—the exact model Brad wore.

"Come on in, make yourself comfortable."

Karl pointed them to two high-back leather chairs. He seated himself behind a vast oak desk in a throne-like chair. The power emanating from his stature, the cool penetrating eyes, and his steel handshake spoke volumes. Lily felt small and insignificant, a familiar feeling, but not one she wanted to have again. She took a deep breath, put her shoulders back, and met his stare directly. She'd seen this type before during the many dinner parties in which she played perfect hostess. He lived for the power of winning, and money was his aphrodisiac. She reminded herself that the decision to employ this man—or not—was entirely hers alone.

Karl leaned forward over the desk and clasped his hands on top. "This husband of yours is attempting to squeeze you into a very small corner and is fighting hard not to give up even *that* bit of real estate in the divorce."

Lily took a moment to gather her thoughts. She sipped her water, hoping it would help wash away the bitter taste in her mouth.

"Well, Karl, that is exactly why we're here!"

His booming laugh resonated off the expensively decorated walls. "Touché," he said, giving Lily a thumbs up. "I see I do not have to worry about you being ready for the fight ahead. But don't worry, I've literally wiped the courtroom floor with these types before."

The image of Brad spread across the courtroom floor in his designer suit provided the comic relief she needed to relax. She sized up Goldberg…clever and confident.

"Why don't we go over the particulars and see where we stand?" asked Katherine.

"Quite wise to know our enemy in detail," Karl replied.

"I lived in that home with him as his wife for ten years. That must count for something."

"Of course it does, and I am sure the judge will see it that way too when we're finished. We will ask for him to buy you out of the house at current market value or sell it and give you fifty percent. However," he said shuffling papers, "I see there is a pretty steep second mortgage on the home as well. Did you know about that?"

Lily closed her eyes and clasped her hands over them, willing this all to go away. She felt the urge to run out the door, but where could she go to outrace this opponent? It was now or never.

"No, I didn't know that. I just inherited a farmhouse on an island in Washington State from my Grandmother. I'm living there now. Does he have any claim over it?"

Carl leaned forward. "Technically, it is part of your separate estate. He cannot make a claim on it. However, its net worth may affect your level of spousal support."

Katherine went on to explain to the attorney how the home was turned into a bed and breakfast, but was no longer operating.

"Well, that's another matter altogether, ladies. If the property can be shown to be viable, Lily will probably be given a certain amount of time to earn a projected income. It's a good place for you to be for now while I handle this messy business here."

Karl rambled on about temporary spousal support, tax returns, hidden money. Lily could see where all this would lead, and the lawyer fees would be never ending.

"We can fill out some papers today, arrange to have him served. In California, judgment takes six months and a day. If you like, we can file this week, so if all goes well, the divorce will be final just after July fourth...Independence Day."

Both women laughed. "A fitting arrangement if I ever heard one," Katherine replied.

Katherine pulled out her checkbook and looked at her daughter. "Lily, I would like to pay half of the retainer for you, at least for now."

Lily tried to speak, but no words would form from her closed throat. She managed to get out, "Thanks Mom. I'll pay you back as soon as I can."

Karl escorted them to the door. "Don't worry, ladies. I am in your court now. If he bothers you, just tell him to talk to your lawyer."

When they reached their car, Katherine pulled out her keys, "I have one word to say...chocolate!"

Lily laughed. "Ditto."

"And while we're at it, we can stop at Macy's and pick you up a some clothes as a late Christmas present from me."

Lily looked out the window at the city streets jammed with buildings and traffic. She longed to return to the big trees, sweeping water views, and snow-peaked mountains. She didn't belong here. The opportunity for a fresh start felt like sunshine after this foul weather time of her life. First chocolate, then shopping, the airport, and home.

Chapter Eleven

One minute she was trapped in a nightmare running from Brad as he chased her down a dark alley, and the next she was wide-awake in her grandmother's four-poster bed, staring at the alarm clock. 3:00 AM. A sense of panic made it hard to catch her breath. Her heart raced. She forced herself out of bed, pulled aside the curtains, and looked out at the total blackness. The island certainly wasn't the manicured McMansions of Brentwood she was used to seeing, with their overuse of electric lights blazing down every street and screaming, "Look at me!" These unlit, pitch-black country roads, dark by four in the afternoon in this dead of winter, made her leery to venture out by car at night. For a moment, she wondered if she had traded in one prison for another.

After her trip to Los Angeles, the days had flown by, blending together one gray morning after another. She hadn't seen anyone except Mary in what seemed like forever, and was too lazy and cold to venture into town. She had avoided the neighbors and hid out in the house.

"Boy it's cold." She dove back under the down quilt and mentally measured how many steps it was to the thermostat.

Jude from the café had called a few times. She was really a nice woman and kept insisting Lily come visit and bring some of her baked goods in to sell.

Lily made an effort to steady her breath and let the heavy fog sitting on her brain lift a bit. What was she supposed to do next? She was not even sure who she was anymore. Her stomach growled loudly. When was the last time she had eaten a meal? John's friendly company had helped briefly, but her lawyer had called and said there had been no progress on getting temporary alimony. It hadn't helped to overdose on caffeine every day. It just jolted her out of time and space and obviously was not allowing her to sleep peacefully.

She wanted her grandmother. The Guestbook would have to be the next best thing. She pulled it from the drawer and glided through the pages. So many people had stayed here.

> *Thank you for letting us hide out in your peaceful little sanctuary.*
> *It feels so good to be away from all the dramas of life - the bunnies put on a spectacular show. And I can't wait to try my new recipes.*
> *~Marsha & Chad*

A recipe card fell from the back of the book and drifted to the floor. Lily turned the well-worn card over–Mt. Rainier cookies. She read over the ingredients, punctuating them with an occasional blissful sigh, then closed her eyes and imagined–chocolate ganache, peanut butter, powdered sugar. Heavenly!

She flipped to the back of the Guestbook and saw an envelope overflowing with more precious recipes. She sensed aromas floating up from the kitchen and could hear her grandma's soft hum as she baked. She thought again of Jude's offer to sell her baked goods and specialties to the Island Café as her grandma had once done. Could she do it?

"I'm going to have to get up sometime, might as well do it now." She pulled the afghan off the bed and wrapped it around her like a huge cocoon, slid on her slippers, then proceeded through the office to the parlor. She about attacked the thermostat putting it up to the highest temperature, then headed to the kitchen, determined to get something accomplished today. Avoiding the cold wood floor, she stood on the braided rug by the sink, filled the copper kettle, and put it on the stove. She opened the glass cupboard doors and searched for some tea. The shelves were well-stocked, and everything was in its place, as if her grandmother would be returning home anytime now. Lily chose a thick ceramic mug and some loose leaf green tea. She poured the steamy water into the cup and warmed her hands around it while she waited for it to steep.

Bundled and cozy, she plopped into a chair in the parlor and began to sip her tea. Another whole day lay ahead and she had no idea how to fill it. It was as if she'd been transported to some other world and now her life had come to a complete halt. Outside the window, a moist fog rose off the trees, and the dampness seeped through the windows. Maybe she would just sit here all day. She had walked out of her old life, but the future was another matter. It terrified her.

Tears threatened. Uninvited, Brad's voice crept into her head, taunting her: "And just how are you going to support yourself? You've never worked a day since you were married. Who's going to take care of you now?"

"No more," she said, standing abruptly. "I'm tired of tears and I don't have to listen to this anymore."

She reorganized the kitchen in earnest. After moving, sorting and labeling the entire kitchen, she finally collapsed into a chair. The sun was coming up, and a rose hue colored the sky and tinted the moist grass in the yard. A magical scene of color and light danced over the fields as far as she could see. She half expected fairies to come out and play. A sense of rightness filled her. She could almost hear her grandmother's voice. "All is well, my Lily."

The sky was alternating colors from deep slate to blinding silver. A lone hawk caught the currents and glided on the breeze. She should count her blessings: her mother was becoming her friend, her neighbors were like family, and Brad lived two states away.

A soft knock at the back door and a "Yoo-hoo" announced Mary's arrival. She entered the kitchen in her sweats and no jacket. She was obviously acclimated.

"I brought you some hot quiche and biscuits." She popped the lid on the Tupperware. The herby egg mixture, mingled with the yeasty bread, lured Lily to the table. Mary placed everything on the table next to a pot of soft butter.

"Thanks, Mary, I'm not used to someone cooking for me."

Mary broke open a biscuit and smothered it in butter. "A good home-cooked meal will fix up anything that ails you. Go on, dig in."

The fragrant meal was definitely comfort food. She was not alone, not really, Lily reminded herself. Mary was here, Betty and Shirley were right next-door, and that kind Mr. McPherson and his cute dog seemed to keep an eye out for her. And there were sweet Jason and Ian…

"Glad to see you eat. Now, I'll just get about my business of cleaning up around here. Ok, Lil?"

No one had called her Lil since her grandma, and that young boy with his father. She kind of liked it. John had told her Ian should be arriving today, she had no problem remembering that.

Mary rose and began cleaning up the dishes, singing as

she worked. "Don't mind me, I'll take care of things around here. Why don't you bundle up and head into town, cause some trouble!"

"Mary, I can't remember the last time I caused that kind of trouble."

"Well, it's about time then, I'd say."

"Good idea. While I'm out, I can pick up some groceries too." A trip to town would allow Lily to talk to Jude about baking for her café. A good long walk might be therapeutic too.

She took a shower and bundled up in a sweater and jeans. She pulled on a coat, lopped her purse over her shoulder, and headed for town to pick up a few more ingredients. Raindrops glistened on pine boughs, and the air was clear as a diamond. All this rain certainly had its purpose, to replenish the dormant growth. It might work on her soul as well.

✦ ✦ ✦

By the time she returned home, the sun was just a memory and Mary was gone. The dampness penetrated the locked doors and windows and took up residence inside Lily's bones. She definitely had not acclimated to the island weather yet. When the heck was spring around here? The fire was dimming in the wood burner and needed refreshing. Carefully, she added a few logs from the pile she had carried in and prodded them into place with the steel poker. Who would ever have thought, even six months ago, that she would be dressed in old jeans and flannel, building her own fires to stay warm? The propane heat was so expensive, she was glad she had an alternative. A sense of contentment crept up unexpectedly.

She called Jude and set up a meeting with her for four o'clock today, after the lunch rush. All she had to do now was get everything baked to perfection. The scent of her home-baked scones wafted into the parlor and drew her back to the kitchen. The complementary aroma of fresh-ground coffee mingled in the air, causing her to lick her lips in anticipation. On the counter, the softening cream cheese, tangy zest, and nutmeg were ready for her to mix into the icing for the orange scones. She emptied them into a bowl and worked all the ingredients together with a spatula, then slid her finger along the edge of the bowl and popped a glob of icing into her mouth.

"Yumm!"

Using the crocheted potholders, she slid the scones out of the oven and onto the cooling rack. After generously frosting each of them, she poured a large mug of Seattle coffee and sat down in the kitchen nook. This would hopefully be the first batch to sell and begin her prosperous business venture.

◆ ◆ ◆

Lily entered the Island Café just after lunch, arms filled with plastic containers. She was greeted by Jude's perpetual smile. "Lily, come in. What have you got for me here?" Jude lifted a plastic lid and took a whiff. "Amazing, can't wait to try them."

Lily laid the trays on the counter and carefully removed all of the lids. "Three varieties for you to choose from, and they'll still be fresh for tomorrow's breakfast."

Jude pulled out a plate and fork to taste them. "Can I get you something to drink? A mocha or cappuccino?

"Thanks, make it a mocha. It's that kind of day."

Jude pressed the brew button and started steaming the milk, then handed Lily a foamy delight. "Extra chocolate, extra hot, just the way you like it. And it's on the house, no arguments from you, my friend."

The woman's kindness touched her deeply. Except for

Roma in LA, it had been a long time since she'd had a friend or anyone who really seemed to care about her. "Thanks, Jude," she managed to get out between sips, her lips covered in mocha-colored foam. "I have some other recipe ideas for the café bakery, too. I also wanted to run by you an idea I have to do a mail order business at home. Are you sure this is a good time?"

Jude put her arm around Lily's shoulders and gave her a squishy hug. "It's always a good time for you to come by. Let's go over to the table by the window and have a look."

Lily pulled out a sample of each of the warm scones and put them on a plate. Using the knife she'd brought, she cut a bite-sized piece out of each and made a sample plate for Jude.

Jude popped the frosted orange scone into her mouth. "A bite of heaven! More please."

Lily lifted the plate up for Jude to choose between the cinnamon and the lemon thyme.

"The lemon thyme is divine." Jude took a sip of water and popped the fragrant cinnamon scone into her mouth. This time she only moaned. "How many did you bring? I want them all."

"A dozen of each, but I can always bring more. Just let me know."

Jude carried the Tupperware filled with scones to the kitchen and came back with her checkbook. "I can sell these for $3.00 a piece, with a great markup. How does that work for you?"

"Perfect," Lily said. She watched Jude write a check for her first sale for the soon-to-be Grandma Maggie's Baking Company. She looked at the check. "There's a bit extra here?"

Jude smiled. "For delivery costs."

"You're always so kind to me Jude, so—"

"Lily, it's easy to be kind to you. Now tell me what it is

you really want to talk about. You look like you're holding back a storm."

Lily began to sob, tears rolling down her cheeks. "I just don't know what to do. First I get anonymous threats in the mail, then there's Brad's constant pressure."

Jude frowned. "What do you mean threats?"

Lily shook her head. "It's probably nothing, some prank."

"What did it say?"

"Well," Lily said, "something about the house not belonging to me and not to get comfortable."

Jude's face turned pale. "No name?"

"Nothing," Lily said. "I hardly thought about it until now because I was too preoccupied with Brad cancelling the credit cards and freezing our joint checking account. I had to fly down to L.A. and meet with an attorney."

Jude reached across the table and took Lily's hands. "You should have told me sooner. As for that no-good, soon-to-be-ex-husband of yours, just let me get my hands on him."

Lily laughed out loud. "I'd like to see that!"

"Believe me, I'll be right there at your side helping you. He will *not* win. Now, let's see those other recipe ideas you were talking about and get to work making you a bakeress extraordinaire!"

♦ ♦ ♦ ♦

The afternoon meeting at the café was coming along very nicely. Jude had ordered enough baked goods to keep Lily in the kitchen for many hours, not to mention help her pay some bills.

Lily sipped the last of her very tasty mocha. "I had the McPhersons over for dinner a few weeks ago."

Jude's eyes twinkled. "How did that go?"

"They're a wonderful family." Lily thought about the warm meal and even warmer company.

Jude winked at her. "That Ian's pretty nice himself."

"I'm not interested in dating right now."

"Wow, Lily, who said anything about dating? Not me."

The front door chimed and Lily looked up. For a moment, she thought the tall redheaded woman had a glow around her. She blinked and looked again. It was gone now. Must have been the sunlight hitting that radiant hair, only there was no sunlight today.

The lithe woman wandered over to the bar. Jude rose to greet her. Was there anyone Jude did not know?

The woman's presence was startling. The model-thin body sculpted into old jeans and wrapped with a colorful coat looked like she belonged in a magazine. A deep purple scarf was wrapped around her elegant neck and glowed as if it were specked with moonlight.

Caught staring, Lily lowered her eyes and studied her coffee cup. The two women were heading in her direction.

"Lily," Jude said, "I'd like you to meet a fellow entrepreneur here in town, Kyla."

Kyla took Lily's outreached hand and stared into her eyes. "You're Lily."

Lily wasn't sure if it was a question or a statement.

Jude went on, "Kyla owns *Tea & Comfort* in the cottage shop down the block. You must get over there and try some of her homemade brews and scented candles."

Tea and herbal products sounded intriguing, but Lily wondered where the comfort part of the name came in. No sooner had that thought crossed her mind than Kyla spoke the answer to her unvoiced question.

"My homegrown remedies, teas, and scents bring well-being to many of my customers."

"Not to mention the ambiance and those delicious licorice tea cakes," Jude piped in.

"I would love to come by sometime," Lily said.

Kyla's emerald eyes twinkled, "Do come. I can brew up some transition tea for you." With that, Kyla turned and headed for a table alone in the corner.

For a moment, Lily felt disoriented, and her appetite seemed to have vanished. Maybe she would pay this woman a visit sometime soon…or maybe not.

Jude rose to clear off the dishes and headed toward the kitchen. "I gotta get back to work before the dinner crowd comes in. Have a good day."

And with that, Lily's first successful sale was concluded.

Chapter Twelve

*J*ude watched Lily walk out the café door. She was a bit worried about that girl and had a pretty good idea who'd sent the note. Lily's father. Rumor had it the last ten years her dear old dad had been in and out of rehab and in jail for a bungled check fraud scam. The last thing Lily needed right now was for Jerold Parkins to waltz back into her life and demand his rights to the house. That girl had been through enough.

Jude went behind the bar and looked up Mike's number, the attorney in town. The phone rang once before the gruff voice answered. He was all bark and no bite. That is, unless you crossed him.

"Hi, hope I'm not bothering you. It's Jude. Can I interest you in coming down for a free bacon burger and a beer?" She knew he could never turn down that offer. "No, nothing is wrong," she answered. "I just have some questions."

Jude ordered the burger and pulled out a bottle of Pale Ale and a chilled glass. True to his word, Mike popped in the door a minute later wearing his favorite Mariners baseball hat.

"Right on time," Jude said, motioning for him to follow her to a quiet booth in the corner. She set the bottle down on the table and slid into the seat opposite him.

"So what's up that requires my immediate presence?" he asked.

His eyes looked concerned. He was the real deal when it came to a friend. "It's not about me."

"Okay," he said. "So who?"

Jude sighed. "I think Jerold Perkins is back in town and looking to cause trouble."

Mike scrunched his face, narrowing his eyes. "I'd heard he was calling lawyers around the island looking for representation for something. He knew better than to call me. After what he did to Maggie, I would have kicked his butt."

"And he deserves it, if anyone does."

Karen brought over the oversized bacon burger, oozing out the sides with cheese, and placed it before Mike. "Enjoy."

He took a giant bite and rinsed it down with a gulp of ale. Between bites he asked, "So what makes you think he's back?"

"Lily, Maggie's granddaughter, stopped by this morning and told me she received an anonymous note telling her not to get too comfortable in her house because it didn't belong to her. Who else would do something like that?"

"You're probably right," Mike said. "Jerold was most likely shopping for a lawyer to help break the will."

"Damn him, can he get away with that?"

"Probably not, but that won't stop him from trying. I'll put some feelers out and see what I can do."

Jude got up and hugged Mike. "I can't thank you enough. Free lunches for a week."

Mike waved her way. "Not necessary. I'm happy to do it."

"Well at least have another Pale Ale and dessert, on me."

Mike smiled and took another large bite from the burger.

Jude walked back to check what the customers at the bar

wanted for lunch. As she worked, her mind drifted back to Lily. Mike would do all he could, she was sure of that. Just how far would Jerold go? She better call John McPherson, Lily's neighbor, and tell him to keep an out for anyone suspicious hanging around. She liked Lily and wanted to see her succeed. Maggie would have been so proud to see her granddaughter here, baking in her kitchen. Jude secretly hoped Lily would stay and reopen the inn. She fit right in here on Madrona Island.

Chapter Thirteen

*L*ily leaned out the parlor window and watched Jason running in the field between their houses with Gretel. A flicker of joy caught her off guard. She had promised Jason a special snack and something for the dog, too. He'd probably like some of those chocolate chip cookies she'd baked this morning, and so would John. The pumpkin dog treats she'd experimented with could be tried out on Gretel. She could fix up a basket…why not? The memory of Ian's sapphire eyes almost had her abandoning her plans. She should not encourage that attraction. But they were neighbors; she should be friendly. She selected a straw basket and lined it with a checkered linen napkin. The cookies were still warm, and the chocolate chunks still glistened under the light.

Parka on, she started across the slushy field toward John's house. Jason must have gone inside, but she could see Gretel stop, lift her head and sniff the air, then race like the wind to greet her. Lily bent and stroked the shiny black fur, fending off the wet kisses and trying to keep her balance.

"Down, girl," Ian said with a clap of his hands, "let the poor lady stand up."

Lily looked up to see Ian's tall, lanky frame shadowing her. Grasping the basket, she stood. "It's okay, she's a real sweetheart."

"That she is," he said, patting the dog's head affectionately. "Can I give you a hand with that basket?"

She hesitated. "Sure. These are for Jason and your Grandpa John. A little snack for Gretel, too."

Ian lifted the napkin and inhaled. "And for me too, I hope."

His lopsided grin unnerved her. "Of course, sure, for you too."

"Jason's inside, would you like to come in?"

"That would be nice."

Ian held the door open for her and she hurried through, followed by Gretel. "We have a visitor," he announced. "And she's bearing gifts."

Jason was at his father's side in a flash, his hand in the basket, snatching a cookie. "Cookies," he mumbled, mouth full, "and they're still hot!"

Ian grabbed some napkins, placing them on the table. "Should I get the milk? Make coffee?"

Everyone looked at Lily. "Well, I guess I could stay awhile."

John rose from his easy chair. "It's settled then," he said, offering Lily a chair at the dining room table. "We can use some good company around here, especially such a lovely lady."

John laid out some napkins and poured everyone a large glass of milk.

"These are great," Jason said, wiping the oozing chocolate off his chin with his shirt sleeve.

"Use a napkin," Ian said.

"Thanks, next time I'll bring some of my scones for you

all to try."

John took a big drink of milk and picked up another cookie. "So, Lily, how are you getting along over there in that big house?"

Lily wiped the sides of her lips, hoping to remove any of the melted chocolate in a dignified way. "I'm finding my way around, doing some baking for the Island Café."

"Starting a little business, it sounds like," Ian said.

"I'm considering calling it Grandma Maggie's Baking Company. And if I ever find my grandmother's famous brownie recipe, I can go mail order as well."

"Ambitious. Let me know if I can help you with designing a label or something." Ian leaned over the basket and lifted up the last cookie. "Who wants it?" he said, looking right at Jason. He dropped it in his son's outstretched hand. "See how much I love you?"

It was obvious to Lily just how much love there was; the way any kid would want to be loved...or any adult, for that matter.

Lily picked up the basket. "Pretty fast work, boys. Next time I'll bring more."

John stood to walk her to the door. "Happy to have you over any time. Where you off to?"

"I think I'll take a little walk along the water before the sun is gone. See you all later."

Ian followed her outside. "Mind if I join you?"

She didn't want to lead him on. After all, she wasn't even divorced yet. But his look was so sincere, and some company would be nice. "Sure, I'll go drop off the basket and meet you down by the beach in a few."

✦✦✦✦

She walked into her bedroom and threw on a warmer turtleneck. At the hall closet, she added a scarf, gloves, and her down coat, then threw open the front door and headed briskly toward the beach. The air was crisp, and it froze the end of her nose. She tucked her hands into her jacket pockets and moved carefully over the large pieces of driftwood.

She found Ian waiting for her at the water's edge, staring out over the vast Sound. He waved for her to join him.

She hurried her step to reach him. This company would be very nice.

"Tide's out," he said, "plenty of room to explore."

They walked together, bracing against the wind. Although rocky in places, it was worth the effort to negotiate the jumble of stones to view this incredible scenery. Crescent Bay's popular sandy area was just around the bend, where the bluffs reached the sand.

"Tide pools," Ian said stepping up on some low exposed rocks.

Lily slipped off her gloves and put them in her pocket before picking up a smooth orange rock. She ran her finger back and forth over its surface.

"Looks like agate," Ian said. "You can tell from the soapy feel.

He ran his finger over the rock and sliding it against the soft inner side of her hand. "See how it's semi-transparent. It's probably an Agate."

Lily placed the stone in her jacket pocket and kept her hand there as she headed down the beach. Hidden in the minute puddles were some tiny shells still completely intact brought in on the ebbing tide.

Ian had a camera around his neck and he commented on the gentle winter light and the colors it evoked.

They continued down the beach, lost in the song of gulls,

Lily gathering little treasures, Ian stopping occasionally to get a shot of a bird in flight, or an angle of light reflecting off the trees. Even without conversing, she felt comfortable walking with him, content to let this beautiful day wash over them. When they rounded the next bend, the beach area narrowed as cascading cliffs came right down to the sand, infringing on the walking space. Patches of various grasses grew along the steep bank, and an occasional Madrona tree clung to the flimsy earth at cockeyed angles. Lily remembered her grandmother showing her the smooth, red bark of the Madronas. How their branches grew out like arms and legs in the middle of a dance, always seeking the sun.

She watched Ian taking pictures of the marvelous trees. His body moved with grace as he positioned himself to get just the right shot. "You know," he said, "the Madrona tree is a Native American sacred tree. Some even call it the tree of knowledge."

"It is a special tree, for sure. No wonder this island was named after it."

As far as she could see, they were alone on the beach. There were hiking trails leading up the bluffs, but no one was in sight. A few clouds had blown in, bringing with them a light drizzle. Silver white sunrays burst through the clouds, pooling light on the ocean's surface. A full rainbow perched across the sky, sparkling with color. Lily reached skyward and then twirled in the sand, relishing her freedom as the wind danced in her hair.

Ian moved around her, snapping pictures as she moved. Lowering the camera, he joined her dance.

Laughing, she finally collapsed on to the sand. Ian dropped beside her.

"Look," he said, pointing out to sea.

A small brown head was bobbing up and down, seeming to look right at her. "It's a seal," she said, standing and brushing the sand off her pant legs before running down to the water to get a better look. The seal continued to dive and resurface, always coming back up and looking back at her on the shore. "Well, hello, my new friend," she said.

Ian snapped shots as the seal played hide and seek in the water.

"This is such a magical place," Lily said.

Ian took her hand. "That it is."

His hand felt warm and steady and she did not want to let go.

Lily glanced back over her footprints. The house looked a long way away, and the tide seemed to be creeping up quite a lot closer now. "We'd better head back. The tide's coming in, and I sure don't want to have to hike out of here over those cliffs."

"You're right. I don't even have my cell with me to call for our rescue."

Hand in hand, they sprinted down the beach, trying to beat the incoming tide. When they reached Ian's property, they clamored over the driftwood wall and back up on dry land until they reached his deck.

"I'm drenched," Lily said. "But it was worth it."

Ian wiped the raindrops off her forehead. "Do you want to come in and warm up?"

The thought of warming up by a fire with him at her side was alluring and unsettling at the same time. "Thanks," she said, "but I think I better get home and get changed into something dry."

"Are you still interested in going out to the local farms?" Ian asked.

Lily thought about delicious fresh produce, eggs, and cheeses, but remembered her dwindling funds. "I'll let you know."

Ian shrugged. "Okay."

Lily turned to go before the chilling night penetrated her damp clothes any more.

"Thanks for the walk," Ian yelled after her.

"Any time," she called back.

Chapter Fourteen

The unpaved road threw up a muddy film that clung like glue to the ruby red paint of Brad's Porsche. "So much for having the car detailed," Brad muttered. "This damn dirt road sure isn't doing it any good." He down shifted into second gear as he rounded the last sharp curve and followed the wooden sign that read "Inn." As if some invisible person hovered above the car, he yelled to the sky, "She *would* have to decide to come to the end of the world."

From the vantage point atop the bluff, he could see the country inn. His face registered loathing. "Looks just a little too much like home. Leave it to Lily to find some place to dredge up my fondest memories." His laugh had a sardonic ring. "I spend every waking moment trying to escape my past and she moves into the perfect replica."

He parked the car and moved slowly up the wooden steps of the veranda. He could almost see his father rocking ever so slowly in the corner and smell his stinking, alcohol breath. His body jerked involuntarily at the memory. He surveyed the house and property with the keen eye of a businessman. Looks pretty run down. I don't know if the house is worth much, but the property surely must be. I'll check with a realtor in town before I leave, he thought.

Brad held the two dozen long-stemmed roses behind his back and knocked on the screen door, waited a second, then impatiently rang the bell. He hated to admit that he missed her, and he sure as hell didn't want to deal with splitting community property in a divorce proceeding. For a moment, the prospect of failure curdled in his gut.

"Just a minute, I'll be right there," Lily called out. Anxiety moved like a current through his body. His shiny, black shoe rapped on the porch. What was taking so long? He slowed his breath, and a well-polished smile slid into place.

✦ ✦ ✦

She was under no pressure to do anything today, and it felt surprisingly good. No long lists of errands, no clients to charm and entertain, no gardeners or housekeepers to supervise, just baking in her new kitchen. Lily felt her shoulders relax.

She switched off the blender and listened. Was that the doorbell? Sure enough, there it is, she thought as she quickly rinsed the oil off her hands. She disliked being interrupted in the middle of creating a new culinary masterpiece. With the back of her hand, she brushed a wisp of stray hair from her face and hurried for the door. The image behind the screen door caused her to gasp. "Brad, what are you doing here?"

He stood on the porch holding a huge bouquet of blood-red roses, sporting a wide grin. Time stopped. Her hand went abruptly to her stomach.

"Aren't you going to invite me in, sweetheart?" His words were candy-coated, and all she could think of were M&M's. Slick and shiny on the outside, but dark on the inside. "After all, I came all this way to see your new place." Warning bells went off in her head. Her lawyer had told her to have no communication with him, but Brad didn't like to hear no, and she was alone in the house. She could handle this.

"We can talk on the porch," she said never taking her eyes off him.

His face dropped. "Lily, I came all the way out here. If you will take a few minutes to listen to what I have to say, I'll leave quietly after that."

She showed him into the parlor but did not offer him a seat. She reluctantly accepted the bouquet and placed them on the table for now. "What brings you here to Madrona?"

"I just followed my heart and this is where it led me." He stood there, a pleading look on his face.

Lily remained standing and stared at the ridiculous imitation of a benevolent smile smeared across his face. He reached out and took her hand. There was an awkward silence as she released his hand and retreated backward.

His eyes registered pain, and for a moment she felt pity. It yanked at her heart, beckoning her to console him, but she would not go there.

"Don't you have anything to say to me, Lily?"

Moments of silence passed and when she did not answer, a red flush of anger washed across his face and then disappeared. She could guess the reason; it probably wasn't going as he'd planned, and as she knew, he always had a plan.

"If you have nothing else to say, I have to get back to my baking."

She watched him regain his composure and survey the room. "You've made this place real cozy now, Lily, just right for a summer house."

Her eyes narrowed. "Thanks, Brad, is that why you're here? To scout the property?"

With a deep breath, she pushed back her shoulders and

ANDREA HURST

stood to her full height of 5'7". Brad smiled indulgently, as he would to a child.

A hot flash of discomfort crept up her neck and face. To hide her dismay, she grabbed the flowers off the table. "I think I'll put these in some water. I'll just go get a vase."

Brad sprang to the kitchen doorway and placed his body in front of her, pulling her into an awkward embrace. She smelled his expensive aftershave, the one he had started wearing just before she found the text messages. The smell nauseated her. He'd never worn the fragrance she'd given him. She squirmed out of his arms and set the flowers in the sink.

He moved closer. "You're looking good, Lily, real good." He tilted her chin up to meet his gaze. "I've really missed you. I realize now what a mistake I made letting you leave. Can you ever forgive me?"

Lily glared at him. She couldn't believe her ears. Brad apologizing? This was a first. The other woman must have left. Or else his divorce attorney told him he would have to share half of everything with her.

"Have you nothing to say, Lily? I'm asking you to come back with me."

He looked so sincere. She scanned the kitchen, a room that had become such a comfort to her. She inched backwards, moving toward the door. Brad's eyes never left her.

"There is no sense both of us wasting money on lawyers. We can keep this place. It can be our vacation house. Or we can sell it and buy ourselves a real dream house at the ocean like you always wanted."

All Lily heard was "we" and "ours." This place was *hers*, and she realized in that instant that she had no intention of leaving it. She looked at the man she had been married to and all she felt was disgust. It must have shown in her eyes, because Brad's face contorted and he lunged toward her.

104

"Don't come any closer, Brad," she cried, moving around him, out of the kitchen and into the front hall.

"Ah, come on now, Lily," he said cajolingly. But the grimace on his face conveyed his patience was at an end.

"I mean it, Brad, just stay back." Lily inched toward the front door. Goosebumps crept up her skin, her heart pounded in her ears.

Brad sprang forward and grabbed her arm.

"You inherited this godforsaken place while we were still married. And in case you have forgotten, the divorce is not final. Legally, whether you like it or not, darling, you're still my wife and this house is still half mine."

To Lily's utter humiliation and horror, she began to cry.

Brad's grip loosened, and mistaking her tears for victory, he pulled her in for a hug. "It will be okay, Lily. Come home, let me take care of you."

Brad withdrew a handkerchief from his pocket and handed it to her. She snatched it and wiped her eyes then willed herself to remember the hundred plus text messages she'd seen on Brad's phone. She steadied her nerves, and her resolve returned.

"My lawyer says this place is not community property."

He reached out his hand to her. "Why don't you just come home, let things go back to normal? We can put this all away and forget about it."

"It may be hard for you to believe, Brad, but I really don't care about that house. You can have it and everything you picked out in it." She took a deep breath and straightened her shoulders. "Now, I want you out of this house."

"You know, if you don't cooperate, I can make things very difficult for you." He touched her cheek. "I'd rather not, Lily. We did have our good times."

She looked him square in the eyes. "Brad, that threat

works both ways."

A quick look of surprise crossed his face. Then his eyes narrowed and he laughed.

Lily's gaze darted to the window, where she could see Gretel, John's large black dog, trotting up the porch for a visit. She almost laughed out loud and faked a cough to cover it. The one thing Brad was afraid of was dogs, and the hundred-pound Gretel would terrify him. With a quick turn, she pushed open the screen door and dropped down on one knee. "Why, hello, girl, come here and give me a kiss." Gretel leaped inside and licked Lily's face. Her arms went around the dog's neck.

Brad backed up toward the door. "Very cute, Lily. Now get that dog out of here."

"I think not, Brad. She's welcome here and you're not. In fact, all I have to do is let her know that and she'll be all over you." Lily had no idea if this was true, but she liked how it sounded. As if to affirm the truth of it, Gretel looked over at Brad, bared her rather large canines, and made a low, menacing growl.

"You've made your point, Lily, but so have I. If you aren't packed up and home within one week, I *will* see you in court. The law is on my side, so you better kiss this place goodbye." Brad yanked his car keys out of his pocket. "Hold on to that stupid dog so I can get back to civilization."

Lily kept her hand firmly on the dog's collar. The front door slammed as Brad stormed out. She watched him pound down the path to his car. The engine gunned and the Porsche sped out of the driveway, spewing a cloud of dirt behind it. Lily dropped to both knees and hugged Gretel fiercely. Finally free to let the tears come, they spilled down her face. The dog nuzzled in close and moaned softly. Lily wept into the soft black fur while Gretel stood firm for both of them.

"Quite a chorus going on in here. Hope I'm not intruding," Ian said, sticking his head in the screen door.

Lily couldn't help but laugh at the picture she and Gretel must make. She wiped her eyes, and taking the hand Ian offered her, she rose from her knees. His hand felt so warm and steadying, she almost wished he wouldn't let go.

"I heard some race car driver tearing up the dirt out there. Are you ok?"

The gentleness of his voice, and the pure sense of relief, brought fresh tears to Lily's eyes.

"Hey now," he said squeezing her hand. "I didn't mean to make you cry again."

It was all just too much. Lily gave in, buried her head in Ian's shoulder and sobbed. "It's ok, it's all ok," he whispered. And for just a moment, everything was.

"You must think all I do is cry," she sniveled. "I do think after today I will be all cried out."

"Listen, I know all about tears. You feel free to let them out anytime."

He knew how to make her smile. Acutely aware of his tender arms around her, she pulled back a little and tried to regain her composure. "Well, the least I can do to thank you for your kindness is to invite you to dinner. I was working on some new recipes before my soon-to-be-ex-husband arrived."

"Well, I wouldn't want to intrude if you're having company."

"Believe me, that was not company. And he is *not* coming back."

"I have an idea. Do you like Northern Italian food?" he asked. "My treat."

"How could I resist such an offer? Are you cooking?"

Ian laughed. "You better hope not. The Deano's Bistro in Forest Glen has some pretty tasty food. How about I pick you up at seven o'clock, get you out and away from your troubles for a while?"

"Formal or casual?" she asked with a grin.

"I think the establishment requires black tie, but if you don't have one with you, I have an extra you can borrow."

They laughed together. Like everywhere else in town, jeans were probably the attire of choice. Ian walked toward the door. "I'll just let myself out now. See you at seven."

"Thank you so much again, Ian." She leaned down and scratched Gretel behind her ears. "And you too, girl. Fresh-baked dog biscuits are in order."

Lily watched him cross over the field separating their properties, Gretel running to catch up with him. The sun broke through the clouds, casting gold and pink hues across the sky. The country air and sweet smell of saltwater mixed with the permeating scent of damp soil and forest. His closeness lingered on her skin. His penetrating blue eyes seemed to look right through her; she hoped he liked what they saw. "Ah, Lily," she sighed, "you better get your mind back in the kitchen and leave enough time to get cleaned up by seven."

Chapter Fifteen

$\mathcal{L}$ ily punched in Jude's number on her cell phone.

"Island Thyme Café, Jude speaking."

"Hi, it's Lily, do you have a sec?"

"Sure thing, Lil, what's up?"

"Brad paid me a visit and I told him to get out."

"Good for you, way to go Lil."

Lily sat down in the velvet rocker, reconsidering her impulsively extended invitation from Ian. "And…"

Jude laughed, "What did you do now, Lil?"

Lily exhaled sharply. "Ian invited me to dinner."

"And you accepted, I hope."

"Yes, Jude, I did. Now stop laughing, I'm serious."

"So why are you calling me? Certainly not for seduction ideas."

"Ok, Jude, I'm sorry I called. I just thought you…"

"Would talk you out of it, Lily?"

The clock said 6:15. Was it too late to cancel? "Yes, I mean, no. I don't know."

"Just be happy, smile, and wear a killer outfit, ok?"

What would she wear? Phone in hand, she headed for her

closet and started laying sweaters out on the bed. "I get it, have fun, stop worrying."

"Right!"

"Red or pink?"

"Underwear?"

"Of course not, Jude, sweaters!"

"Depends on your mood, and your hopes for the evening."

Lily chose the pink sweater. "Pink then. I have no plans for the evening, just dinner."

"Doesn't sound like much fun, I'm afraid," Jude said.

"I'm jumping in the shower now. I'll call you tomorrow."

✦ ✦ ✦ ✦

Lily glanced at the clock. Five minutes to seven. Yikes!

She thought of Jude's suggestions. Her most flattering jeans were set off by a rose pink chenille sweater. Her now almost-shoulder-length blonde hair was freshly washed, and the pink lip gloss added color to a Washington white complexion. She was ready...well sort of. Her pulse raced and she felt a bit light-headed. She was probably coming down with something and should cancel, she thought.

She reminded herself aloud, "It's only a nice neighbor taking me out for a casual dinner, now calm down." So what if he was a tall, very handsome man with a wide dimpled smile... and those eyes... Enough!

The sound of the doorbell did nothing to calm her demeanor. Lily opened the door to see a rather "spiffed up" Ian with hair neatly combed back, a rugged but dapper Eddie Bauer jacket, and nice-fitting jeans.

"Come on in, Ian."

He handed her a purple, beautifully designed, blown-glass vase. "For you."

110

"How beautiful. You really didn't need to bring anything."

Ian shook off his jacket. "Just something I made in one of the classes I teach at the college. I kind of like that one, and you'll need all the vases you can get when your garden out front hits full bloom."

She placed the vase on the coffee table and then hung up his jacket. "Would you like a glass of wine or something?"

"Sure, why not."

His closeness unnerved her in a completely different way than Brad's had only a few hours ago. But her impulse was the same...to run, at least into the kitchen. "Go ahead and make yourself comfortable in the parlor. I'll be right back."

She returned holding two glasses.

"What time is the reservation?" she asked, handing him a glass of prosecco.

Ian sipped the sparkling wine. "We have a few minutes. It's at 7:30. Hope you're hungry."

"Getting there. You?"

"Always."

His smile threw her off balance. Lily took a moment to get her bearings. What the heck's happening to me? The first good-looking man I meet and I'm turning into a puddle? Forget it! No more drowning in shallow water, no matter how blue his eyes are.

✦✦✦✦

The pungent smell of spicy tomato sauce wafted out the door as they entered the candle-lit restaurant. Tables covered in blue-checkered cloths, a vase with a single red rose, and a white candle, were all filled with patrons and baskets of crusty bread.

"Right this way, Ian" the waiter invited. "Shall I bring a bottle of your favorite Pinot Noir?" he asked. It was obvious Ian had been here many times before.

Lily nodded her ascent. "Works for me."

The waiter handed them the menus. "The soup today is minestrone garnished with mascarpone."

"Say no more," Ian said. He looked at Lily. "Shall we start with two?"

"And a bruschetta to share, please."

"Good choice," Ian said as they continued to review the menu.

The Willamette Valley Pinot was opened and their glasses filled. She raised her glass to his. "A toast, to new friends." They clinked glasses. The subtle flavors of strawberry and peach tantalized her taste buds.

The crisp, fragrant bread arrived on a hand-painted plate. Lily took a nibble and let the flavors melt in her mouth. Ian seemed to be watching her every bite.

She raised an eyebrow in mock dismay, then broke a smile. "Here have a taste." She held the cheesy slice to his mouth. A spark of electricity shot up her arm as his lips wrapped over the bite. As he slowly savored the flavor, he uttered a low moan of pleasure.

She ate quietly, wondering what to talk about.

"So far away. Want to share your thoughts?" he said.

Lily blushed. "Sorry."

He touched her hands with his fingertips. "Forgiven."

"Actually, I was thinking how well things are starting to work out. I've learned to light a fire, and I'll be baking for Island Thyme Café."

"Great idea," he said between bites. "The town has sure missed Maggie's treats...for humans *and* for dogs."

"My grandmother...I wish I could have known her better."

"She spoke of you often, and I know wherever she is, she's happy you're here now."

"Thanks, Ian. That means a lot to me."

The waiter returned to the table and took their order.

Lily wondered what she was doing here with this man she barely knew. Did he bring a new woman here every week? It was just a friendly dinner, she reminded herself.

Neither one of them spoke for a while. Lily squirmed in her chair trying to think of what to say next.

"I'm a bit awkward at this, I'm afraid," Ian said. "It's been a long time since I've been on a date."

So he considered this a date. Why would such an attractive man not have been on a date in a long time? Not for her to ask. "You sure have a cute little boy," she said. "Does he live with you fulltime?"

In Los Angeles, this was the perfectly normal thing to say, but the minute it came out of her mouth, she wasn't sure it was here.

Ian laid his fork down. She watched emotions cross his face. "Jason's mother died three years ago."

"Oh, I'm so sorry. I didn't know." Of all things to talk about, could she have picked a worse subject?

"You would have found out soon enough anyway," he said. "It was a car accident…a drunk driver." He pushed the food around on his plate. "It if wasn't for my grandfather, I don't know how we would have made it through."

She thought about the sadness that shadowed Ian and Jason. This was it. Her heart went out to him. "If you ever just want to talk, I'm here."

"Thanks. That means a lot," he said.

The only noise at their table now was the scraping of forks on the plates. Trays of delicious-looking food passed by as waiters scurried to serve their customers. Lily savored the herby flavored pasta. It was a really good meal, she decided.

"So, how long do you plan to stay on the island?" Ian asked. "Must be a lot different than Southern California."

"It was never my choice to live there," she said. "My mom brought me to California when I was a young girl. I never really felt at home there." She noticed she had not answered the question about how long she planned to stay. Truthfully, she had no idea. But when she looked into his eyes, the thought of leaving was not on her mind.

"I've had a few shows in Los Angeles. It's not my kind of town either," Ian said. "But New York, that's another place altogether. When I show my work in the galleries there, I try to spend an extra week or two."

"I'd love to see New York sometime," she said, taking the last bite of her dinner.

Ian finished up the last of the pasta on his plate and washed it down with wine. With a very serious expression, he leaned over to her. "So, tell me what I've been waiting all night to find out…"

Lily eyes widened, her breath came quickly. Thoughts whirled in her brain, some quite pleasant, as she waited for him to finish his sentence. He seemed to be purposely drawing this out, and she hoped he could not see her squirming.

One elbow on the table, fist resting under his chin, he met her eyes with a probing look. "What would you like for dessert?"

She released her breath, laughing. "No rest time after such a big dinner?"

"Absolutely not," he replied in earnest.

"In that case," Lily said, "I did notice Tiramisu on the menu."

Ian called the waiter over and ordered two with espressos.

"Great, it's their specialty."

Lily stole a glance at Ian's profile. He was handsome, and his full lips looked kissable. He turned back and caught her gaze. Say something, Lily, something neutral. "What medium do you generally work in as an artist?"

Warm tones of candle flame danced across his face. "I paint, mostly in oils, and occasionally I work with glass. When I'm not playing hooky over here on the island, teaching pays the bills."

"Where else do you show your work?" Lily said sounding a little too Los Angeles for her taste.

He inched his chair closer to her, and the room seemed suddenly much too warm. "As a matter of fact," he continued, "the gallery in town here carries my work almost exclusively."

Lily sipped her coffee. "I'll have to go by and have a look."

Ian finished the last bite of whipped cream and laid his fork down, leaning back with a contented sigh.

"If you're interested, we're installing the new show I told you about this week, and the opening reception is next Friday. Why don't you venture out and have a look?"

"Sounds perfect, I'll put it on my busy social calendar," she said.

"On second thought," he said, "is it too short notice to commission some of your dessert items for the opening?"

Lily shook her head. "I don't think so. I can come up with a short menu for you to choose from tomorrow." Her first catering commission on the island, and she had no idea what to charge him. She would ask Jude tomorrow.

"Nothing gooey or with icing please," he said with a smile. "And here's my card with email and cell number in case you need to reach me."

"Right, of course." She could see it now, icing all over his artwork!

"You choose whatever you think is appropriate for about fifty guests and would be complementary with the local Madrona Vineyard's wine selection. I leave the menu in your very competent hands."

She was well aware he was now holding those "competent" hands. His fingers caressed the back of her hands. She could barely breathe and pulled her hands back into her lap. Was this his price for offering her a job?

"It's getting late," she said.

"Of course, I don't want to wear you out. Would you like anything else before we go?"

"Not another bite. It was a wonderful meal. Thank you."

After Ian took care of the check, they walked outside. The wind had picked up, and Lily wrapped her arms around herself and ran for the car.

"You're cold," Ian said, turning up the heat in the car.

One minute he seemed kind, the next she just wasn't sure what to think. Trusting another man was not high on her priority list.

The night-light lit up the porch as he walked her to her door then turned to leave. Regret that he was leaving was met equally with doubts about seeing him again. "Oh, I almost forgot. Hold on a sec, I have a bag of fresh baked dog biscuits for Gretel."

She went inside then returned to the porch and handed Ian the package.

Doggy bag in hand, Ian hopped down the stairs. He took a few steps and stopped to look up. "The stars are amazing tonight. Come on out and have a quick look, Lily."

She walked over and tilted her head up to view the starlit heavens. "So beautiful," she sighed. "There are so many of them."

Ian placed his coat around her shoulders, leaving his arm

to linger there as well. "Yes," he whispered, "so beautiful." But as Lily turned to acknowledge his words, his eyes were on her, not the heavens.

His lips brushed hers with a gentle whisper of a kiss. "Thank you again for the wonderful evening," he said.

Ian turned and walked to his car. It took her a few seconds to realize she was still wearing his jacket.

"Your coat," she called after him. She peeled it off and tossed it into his outstretched arms. Lily returned to the porch and watched Ian disappear into the cloudless night.

Chapter Sixteen

The test baking to decide on the final items for Ian's art opening had gone well this week, and she was pretty sure what the final menu would be. As she put the finishing touches on her latest recipe, the phone rang. Lily checked the caller ID, it was her lawyer. She picked up phone and just listened; every sentence he said pounded into her gut. "I understand," she told him. "I'll get back to you."

She hung up and staggered over to a chair to support her wobbly legs. Brad had been gone just a little more than a week, and now this phone call from Karl. It was unbelievable the lows that Brad would stoop to in order to get his way and get her back. The lawyer had been a little encouraging, but his words about what might happen still rang in her ears.

He was claiming to be broke, saying she owed half the debts, and was probably hiding money every place he knew. Even their cars were leased, except for the Honda she had driven away in, and that made it community property. Nothing was a solid asset she could count on. It was too much to bear. Their whole life together had been based in smoke and mirrors.

She rifled through her divorce folder looking for the name of the forensic accountant her mother had located for her. She wondered how she was going to pay for that too. But without professional help to uncover assets and income, she was lost and would come away with nothing. It might be best to walk away. No one won with Brad, and there was nothing to win but more debt. She would certainly consider that.

But now she had to make a list of all the jewelry and clothes that had been gifts from Brad to prove that they were not part of her debt. She thought of the Cartier watches and diamond necklaces, the imported French dresses and shoes; he had bought them all to make her shine for the outside world. She didn't want or need them now, and she would be damned if she would pay for half of them. Besides, she had left them all behind, and he could sell them or burn them for all she cared. At least she was not liable for any debt he incurred after she moved out.

Exhaustion set in, and all she wanted to do was go lie down in her bed and hide under the covers. All this debt, no income, cancelled credit cards. She tried to remember what the good news was. She dropped into her bed and burst into tears. There was no one to comfort her or come to her rescue. For a moment she thought of Ian, so tender and kind. She was pretty sure he would be there if she reached out to him. It would feel so good to have a sympathetic friend. But she did not want to turn to another man to save her. It was time she did that for herself.

She had a friend in Jude, she had her mother, and she had her grandmother, whose presence filled every room with her love. She could feel Grandma Maggie as if she were here, sitting on the bed, encouraging her and making her smile. Lily wiped her tears and sat up in bed. She opened the nightstand drawer, pulled out the Guestbook, and propped it open on her lap.

A few pictures fell out that had been pressed between the pages. One was of her as a little girl playing in the flower garden. Another was of her father giving her a piggyback ride. Her father...she had not thought of him in years. He was a vague memory of someone fun, but someone dark. He'd been around then and sober, most of the time. All of her happy memories were at her grandmother's, except for the last one before they left the island. Her father driving off in a huff with that woman in the car, her mother in tears yelling for Lily to get in the car, Grandma Maggie saying over and over, "I'm so sorry this happened, Katherine, so sorry." After he had abandoned them, Lily had never heard from him again. She thought about how bitter her mother had been, how confused she herself was. She knew he'd gone off with another woman, but as a child, she hadn't understood really what that meant. Didn't he love them anymore?

Over the years, she'd never thought much about how it might have affected Grandma Maggie, who'd just recently become a widow herself, to have her son take off. How alone her grandmother must have felt after Katherine swooped them off to California to make sure Lily's father never found them, and then cut off contact with her grandmother just to be sure. Maggie lost her only grandchild at the same time as her only son. The last picture showed her grandmother wearing her classic and radiant smile. No matter how much pain she had been through, her grandmother had put on a smile and managed to start a successful bed and breakfast, and help others too.

She sifted through some of the pages, and her eye caught on a particular entry written before the B&B closed.

Dear Innkeeper,

You will never know how much my stay here has meant to me, and how it has changed my life. I arrived so very depressed, having just been told of my diagnosis. Yes, I know I did not tell you. But, Margaret, you seemed to sense my need, and I did not want to burden you. The cool breezes, the gentle serenity of this island, and this cozy Inn soothed my aching heart. Your special brand of kindness, generosity of spirit, and contagious smile helped open my heart. You gave so much. I felt encouraged by your words. You helped me to find the courage to trust my instincts and have the strength to pursue my course of treatments. A healing does not come close to describing the magic I experienced here in this enchanted place. Many blessings to you, my Innkeeper Angel,
Marie

Lily closed the book abruptly. She felt like she was trespassing in someone else's world. Always, there was someone with problems greater than her own to remind her to be grateful. The woman's courage shone brightly and sent a surge of strength to Lily's own spirit. Surely this place would work its magic on her too—actually, if she were honest, it already had.

Her mind drifted again to Ian, as it did so often these days. He seemed too good to be true, and the timing could not be more wrong. She needed all her energy and focus just to deal with Brad and their divorce, not to mention figuring out her financial situation. Perhaps someday she would feel safe enough to think about love again, but not now. She had no idea what she really wanted, but she was determined to figure it out. Cooking and baking had always been a passion, so it was a natural place to start. And get a dog...or two. A trip to the local animal shelter was definitely in her future.

She skimmed through the Guestbook pages and caught a neatly folded letter as it fell out from the back of the book. It was addressed to her grandmother. She was about to slip it back into the book when her eyes caught on the first line.

Dear Margaret,

I'm kind of rusty in the love letter department, but I know I have to tell you how I feel. After my wife Carol died, I never thought that I would find love again in this life. But I have been blessed twice. You've always been there, waving across the field with that big smile, bringing me dinner so I wouldn't starve after Carol's stroke, taking care of me. Your heart was big enough to weather my stormy moods and despair after her death.

Sometimes I feel like a silly old man falling in love this way. My heart skips a beat whenever I see you, and at my age that might be dangerous! I don't know quite why you love me, but I thank God you do.

When the Heavens see fit to send love your way, only a darn fool would turn down a gift like that. Margaret, you are my light, my reason each day for waking, and my last thought when I turn off the light to sleep. I give you all my heart, all my soul, for as long as I'm here on this Earth.

I love you,
John

John? John McPherson next door? It had to be. Lily laughed with delight. Her grandmother had not been all alone after all. Relief lightened her heart. She liked the idea that love was a gift. Could be she was more like her grandmother than she knew. They sure had the same taste in men. John was a bit old for her, but Ian...

Lily jumped out of bed, ran a brush through her hair, and bundled up to head into town. The nasty weather accounted for all the empty parking spaces on Front Street, so she was able to park right in front of the café.

A few tables were filled with people finishing what looked to be a late lunch, and a couple of men were drinking beers at the bar. Jude looked up from some paperwork and waved Lily over to a table by the picture window.

"Beautiful view today of gray and more gray!" Jude said.

"Nothing one of your Grande Mochas won't fix."

Jude raised an eyebrow. "One of those sorts of days?"

Lily nodded. "When you have time to talk…"

"Be right back," Jude said.

Lily sat and looked out the window. It was about zero visibility today. No rain, but dense grayness and light fog put her in the mood for a nap, one that lasted all day. She checked her watch: two o'clock. She'd better not stay too long and have to drive home in this weather once it got dark. Which, in February, was still around five-ish in the afternoon.

Jude placed the steaming mocha in front of her and joined Lily at the table. "So give, what's up?"

Lily took a few sips and savored the warm foamy drink before answering. "Same old thing. My lawyer called today, and it's just more bad news."

"I'm sorry to hear that," Jude said with genuine sympathy. "Drink up, let the marvelous mixture of chocolate and sugar do its work."

The mocha and the good company were definitely soothing Lily's frayed nerves. She would find a way to work things out. Brad was not going to intimidate her anymore.

"So, tell me about your dinner with Ian," Jude whispered, making sure no one else heard.

"Oh right, I forgot."

"You forgot! That bad?"

Lily broke a smile, "No, it was good, fun and..."

"And what?"

"I don't know what I think about Ian. He offered me some work catering his art opening."

"That's great news," Jude said.

"Is it?"

"Lily, Ian's a great guy. If he offers you work, trust me, he is not looking for something in return."

Lily lowered her eyes. In Los Angeles, anyone that gave anything expected to get something in return. She was not used to someone just being kind with no hidden agenda. "I just don't want to get involved with another man right now."

She could feel Jude's eyes boring into her and looked up.

"What?" Lily asked.

"Just take your time. You'll know what to do," Jude said.

It had been a long time since someone trusted her to know what to do. She hoped Jude was right.

Jude stood and started clearing off the table. "So, shall we dress up and go to Ian's art opening together? I'll invite Kyla to join us too."

"Sounds great." Lily laid some cash on the table for the coffee and waved goodbye, feeling a lot better than when she had arrived.

Outside, the sun was doing its best to break through the thick, dark clouds, and Lily wasn't ready to go home and be alone just yet. Why not wander over to the art gallery and peek through the window at Ian's work? After all, she did have to know what kind of event she was catering for. She walked around the corner and located the Raven Gallery.

Resting her forehead and hands on the glass, she could make out the large paintings being mounted on the walls by gallery staff. The front door was locked when she tried to go in.

"Lily, is that you?"

She turned quickly, almost stumbling into the handsome man standing before her. "Ian…"

He laughed. Was he laughing at her? Did she look foolish?

"Couldn't wait for the show, I see," Ian said. "Did you want your own private viewing?"

She felt her face flush and heat rise to her already restricted throat. "Well, I, yes, no, I mean, yes, I was curious. And I was trying to get a sense of your work before I finalize the menu for your opening."

"I see." He just stood there with what she hoped was a friendly grin on his face. "Ok, well, come on in."

Her breath released. "Thanks, just for a minute, I have lots of planning and shopping to do this afternoon for your event." She was glad she could think of something to say. It wasn't like she had nothing better to do than seek him out.

He pulled the key from his pocket and opened the door. Motioning for Lily to step inside, he said, "I'm not usually on the island on Thursdays, but I came early this week to set up the show. Hope you'll stay after you drop off the desserts."

Lily nodded. "Of course."

"Only a few of the paintings are unwrapped and some are still being mounted, but I'll show you one of my favorites." He walked over to a brick wall and he pointed to a painting under a spotlight of a Kingfisher suspended in outer space overlooking the Earth.

"The detail is amazing on this one, the eye looks right through me," Lily said.

"I named this one 'Eye on the World.' In ancient China, the Kingfisher was thought to be a symbol of beauty and it is generally seen as an omen for peace and good fortune."

He showed her a few more paintings and then escorted

her to the door. "Don't want to spoil the show for you."

"Right," she said. "I look forward to seeing more of your work."

She felt his eyes on her as she walked down the sidewalk back to her car. She hoped she could keep steady footing with her head so giddy. If she could run, she would, but what would he think then? What in the world did he think now?

Chapter Seventeen

Lily finished blowing her hair dry and studied her face in the bathroom mirror, then applied a little more color to her eyes and a touch more blush. "That's as good as it gets," she said, heading to the bedroom. She rifled through her closet, trying to decide what to wear. "Saved by the bell," she said, picking up the ringing phone.

Jude's voice came through loud and clear. "It's going to be a girls' night out, so dress up, for God's sake. Put on some of those fancy city clothes left from your old life."

"Actually, Jude, I dumped most of the clothes in the same place I dumped my soon-to-be-ex-husband!"

Jude's robust laughter filled the room through the phone. "Good call, Lily. I'll be right over with some of my skinny clothes I have stuffed in the back of my closet. Get out your shoes and jewelry, and we'll get you all fixed up. Be there in a jiff."

When she'd dropped off the perfectly constructed desserts earlier today, wardrobe had been no problem...she wore sweats. Ian had written her a check, all business. But now, she wanted to look good. And not just for Ian, she told herself.

Lily hung up the phone and wandered over to her dresser to review her meager jewelry collection. All she had brought with her when she fled Brentwood were some freshwater black pearl earrings, a hand-crafted hummingbird necklace she had bought at an art fair in Santa Barbara, and the new watch her mother had given her for Christmas. The hummingbird was delicately crafted in silver, and the wings were filled with iridescent moonstones and purple tanzanite. All of the Stella McCartney and Armani dress shoes were definitely left behind. She did have the sense to keep her black Stuart Weitzman knee-high boots, and they looked great with everything.

The rumble of Jude's little MGB sports car in the driveway prompted Lily to head for the door. Jude's arms were overflowing with clothes as she made a dramatic entrance, dressed from head to toe in varying shades of red silk with a black satin, full-length opera coat. "Here, let me help you," Lily said as she hopped down the steps and relieved Jude of some of the load. "Just drop everything on the bed for now."

Jude picked out a long black silk skirt with a handkerchief hem and a periwinkle-colored chenille sweater and handed them to Lily. "Okay, let the fashion show begin. Hurry up, girl, we haven't got all night."

Lily pulled the sweater on then discarded her jeans and slid on the skirt. It landed perfectly mid-shin and had a nice swing to it. She added her boots and twirled around to face Jude. "What d'ya think?"

"Absolutely gorgeous. Your eyes really jump out with that periwinkle blue. I think the first outfit is the charm."

Lily smiled at her reflection in the mirror. She added the black pearl earrings and held up the silver necklace against the sweater. Perfect. "I love it, Jude. Hardly a trace of California Barbie left."

"Out with the old and hello Pacific Northwest, artfully independent woman!"

"Thank you, Jude. It's so nice to have a friend like you." Lily spontaneously gave Jude a ferocious hug.

"Enough stalling. It's time to head into town and hook up with Kyla. She's meeting us at the gallery. And looking like that, you had better watch out for the artsy, single island men that hang out at these things."

Lily grabbed her purse and wool coat. "Thanks for the words of encouragement. Do you want me to drive?"

Jude finished buttoning up her dazzling, floor-length velvet coat and wrapped a colorful scarf around her neck. "Why don't you follow me? I want you to have a good time there, drink some wine, have some fun. I'll be the designated driver home if you need me to. If I weaken and have a cocktail or two, we can have a slumber party at my house."

✦ ✦ ✦

When they entered the art studio, Jude, waving to everyone she passed, headed straight to the wine bar. Lily scanned the room for Ian and located him across the room talking to an attractive woman. He had a glass of wine in one hand and was making animated gestures with the other. Her heart skipped a beat, and the blast of heat on her face was not from the warmth of the room. She was jealous. She could not believe it. One dinner, one very small kiss, and she was jealous! He looked up and met her eyes gazing at him. Embarrassment caused her to turn away and head for the wine bar near the window.

Kyla was just leaving the bar and had two glasses of Chardonnay in hand. "There you are," she said. "Jude told me you were here somewhere. I thought I'd save you the wait and bring you a glass as well."

Lily took a large sip and then another. "Thank you. Shall we look at the paintings?" She could hear Jude's distinctive laugh over in a corner, and they followed the sound.

"Lily, come here, I want you to meet someone," said Jude waving her hand. "Lily this is Cherise. She owns the Raven Gallery."

The woman was dazzling, dressed in hand-painted silk and strands of saltwater pearls. Lily shook Cherise's hand. "Nice to meet you."

"Love the desserts you made, Lily. I must get your number. Do you have a card?"

"Not yet," Lily stumbled for a moment. "I'll give you a call next week."

Cherise was off as fast as she had appeared. Another attractive woman, no wonder Ian has a show here, Lily thought. She watched the well-coiffed woman as she worked the room. Eclectic, was the first word that came to mind. Cherise was so elegant and seemed comfortable in her own skin.

Lily saw Ian walking toward her, but just steps away, he was intercepted by Cherise leading a well-dressed couple. Lily leaned over discreetly to listen to the conversation.

"Ian, darling," drawled Cherise, "I want you to meet Bob and Helen Cosby. They came over all the way here from Mercer Island." Lily couldn't believe she was actually eavesdropping. She downed her wine and sought out Jude, determined to forget about Ian and have a good time with her woman friends.

Lily joined Jude and Kyla as they moved from painting to painting. "Some of his best work I've seen," commented Kyla.

"Really?" said Lily, moving into their conversation. "I haven't seen his work before. It's very distinctive, blending a bit of Native American and Asian influence together in a unique style."

"Somewhere on his mother's side is quite a bit of Native American heritage. He definitely taps into that with his work," Jude added.

Kyla continued, "And you know he traveled with his mother through Japan for several years as a teen."

"No, I didn't know," answered Lily. "I really don't know much about him." But Kyla sure did, she noticed. Her eyes drifted involuntarily around the room again, looking for Ian just as he turned a corner and headed right for them.

"Ladies," he said, approaching with a big smile and a hug for each of them. "Welcome and thank you for coming. Grandpa John just left, he'll be sorry he missed you." He put his arm around Lily's shoulder. "So, which is your favorite?"

Lily was still recovering from her reaction to his touch and did not realize he was looking right at her. Flustered, she turned to see Kyla and Jude eying her as well. "The one with the misty sunset really moved me."

"Hmm," he said, shaking his head up and down slowly. "That is a recent one inspired after a walk along Crescent Bay."

To her dismay, she felt the top of her lip break out in a sweat. Did he mean *their* walk on the beach? She could hardly breathe and fanned her face with her hand. "The crowd," she gestured. "It's a bit hot in here. I think I'll step outside for some cool air."

Jude followed her to the door. "Are you nuts? It's thirty degrees out there tonight."

Lily opened the door, stepped outside, and then jumped back in. "You're not kidding." She stood by the door, calming herself. "I think I need another glass of wine. What about you, Jude?"

Jude contemplated the question for about three seconds. "Twist my arm, I'd love one too. And some more of the crab puffs and cheesy things they're walking around with on those trays."

At the bar, both women ordered another drink. A large boisterous man swept over and wrapped Jude in his arms. "My lady, how nice to see you," he said in a mock old English accent.

Jude looked delighted. "Lily, this is Stanton, he does Shakespeare in the Park here in the summer."

Lily shook his rather sweaty hand and forced a smile. Stanton gave her a quick once-over, then turned and continued his conversation with Jude.

Wine in hand, Lily wandered off and found an empty, overstuffed chair in a quiet alcove by a window. From this comfortable position she could people watch and still be part of the party. No sooner had she sat down than a man with a long silver ponytail and wearing a faded leather jacket sat in the empty seat beside her. "Hi, pretty lady, I'm Tom. Are you new here?"

Inwardly she groaned. "Yes, I am."

"Do you know the artist?" he asked.

Lily looked over the crowd to Ian, who was now talking to Kyla. "A little bit. Actually, we only met recently."

Tom continued. "He's quite well-known, done shows in New York and Europe, too. In fact, we've shown at a few of the same galleries."

"Really," she answered without interest. "What type of artist are you?"

"A potter," he said. He pointed toward the entrance. "You see that large planter over there with the bonsai tree in it? The one with the spikes and opalescent glaze. That's one of mine."

Lily eyed the pot, definitely not her style. She smiled politely. "I've never seen anything quite like it before."

"I know, my style is very distinct. If you would like to see more, I have my own studio up-island, and I would be glad to give you a private showing anytime."

"Well, thank you, Tom" she said as she reluctantly gave up her place of refuge. "I'll keep that in mind."

Tom rose to follow her. "Here, let me give you my card."

Lily pocketed the card and headed toward the ladies' room. He hadn't even asked her name; at least that was a break. Before she reached the door, she caught a glimpse of Ian walking into the back room of the studio with his arm around Kyla. The door shut and the two of them disappeared. What was that about? she wondered. Just how many women is he interested in? The word "womanizer" crossed her mind, and she dismissed it, along with her interest in him, as she moved to the sanctity of the women's restroom.

"Lily?" Her name was being called from outside the stall.

"Jude? How did you know it was me?"

"No one has boots like that on this island," Jude yelled out over the sound of the toilet flushing. "I saw our resident Don Juan Tom talking to you earlier. I almost came to your rescue."

Lily groaned. "Thanks for the thought. I made a quick exit into here. I think I'm about ready to go home."

"How about one more glass of wine, Lily? The night is still young."

"Ok, but just one, and then let's find Kyla and call it a night. This art scene reminds me too much of Los Angeles, and Ian seems to be quite busy and involved."

Jude laughed. "You could say that."

Kyla reappeared from her private meeting with Ian looking a bit flushed in the face. As Kyla joined them for another glass of wine at the bar, Lily felt her hackles rise. "Looks like people are starting to head home, it's almost eleven. What do you think, ladies?"

"I'm ready," volunteered Lily.

"Okay, let's get our coats," Jude said, standing a bit unsteadily.

Ian met them at the door. "Thanks again for coming. I'm sorry I didn't have more time to chat with you all."

"Was the show successful?" asked Jude.

"We did pretty well. A few pieces sold and I made some good contacts for future commissions."

Lily placed her hand on the door, pulled, and started outside. "Someone's in a hurry to leave," whispered Jude as she followed close behind.

"Drive carefully, ladies," Ian called after them.

"Hold up, Lily," Jude said, catching up to her with Kyla in tow. She threw an arm around Lily. "So, my coconspirators in crime and wine, how about we take this party down the street to my house for the night, have a girls' all-nighter at my place?"

Lily considered the offer. She wouldn't have to drive, and she wouldn't have to ask Jude, who'd had several glasses of wine, to drive her home down a dark island road. Plus, she'd have good company for the night in Jude. Kyla, she wasn't sure about. Still, a no-brainer decision for sure. "Sounds good to me. Are you in, Kyla?"

Kyla hesitated. "C'mon, Kyla," urged Jude. "Let your hair down, have a little fun and girl bonding time."

"Okay, but only if you'll make your Mexican coffee drink for us."

"Deal," Jude agreed.

The threesome strolled arm-in-arm down Front Street. At Cedar Street they walked the few blocks back to the café. "Look at the stunning scarf in Cousin's Boutique," Lily said as she leaned in close to peer through the storefront window. "I love hand-woven chenille. I'll bet it costs a fortune."

"Come on, Lily," Jude said, scooting her along. "It's too cold out here for window shopping. We can come back tomorrow and check it out then." They approached the wooden steps alongside the back of the building that led up to Jude's apartment above the café. "Careful on the stairs. They get slippery with the frost."

Jude fumbled with her keys, her unsteady hand making it difficult to get the key into the lock of her front door. "Almost!" she giggled drunkenly as she bent to pick up the keys that had slid out of her hand.

Lily bent over to help retrieve them, banging her head into Jude's. "Ouch!" she cried, rubbing her forehead. "I guess sometimes two heads are *not* better than one."

Kyla groaned. "All right, ladies. Let me handle this. After all, I only had two glasses of wine and you two had…I don't know how many." Kyla confiscated the keys from Jude, unlocked the door, turned on a few Tiffany lamps, and led the way into the expansive living room. She immediately claimed Jude's burgundy velvet antique fainting couch and made herself comfortable.

Lily slipped off her boots and left them at the front door. The polished wooden floors and the lush oriental rugs felt luxurious against her bare feet. She walked across the parquet wood floor to gaze out the oversized picture window that seemed to be floating on air above the water. "What an amazing view you have, Jude. There are so many stars out. If I lived here, I would never leave this window."

"It is hard sometimes. It's an even better view up here than from the café. You can see the Cascade peaks on a clear day. I was sold on this place the minute I walked into this room."

Lily followed Jude into the kitchen and watched as she began the process of making Mexican coffee. Jude added cocoa powder, a pinch of cinnamon and nutmeg, then retrieved the

Kahlua bottle from the wet bar. "The coffee will be ready in a few," Jude said.

Lily inhaled the aromatic smell of fresh brewing coffee. "May I see the rest of your place, Jude?"

"Sure, I'll give you the grand tour."

Jude led Lily down the hall and into one of bedrooms. "Here's the master suite," Jude said as she flipped on an overhead chandelier.

"Looks like a true boudoir where secret trysts are enjoyed."

"Right," Jude sighed. "The procession of gentlemen coming to my door is never ending."

Lily ran her hand over the satin duvet cover and fingered the delicate lace pillows on the bed. "These are gorgeous. When I think of my flannel sheets and bulky down comforter in its woolen duvet, I feel like a tom-boy next to you."

Jude draped an arm over Lily's shoulder. "If Prince Charming shows up at your door, or for that matter a hot one night stand-in prince, my boudoir is at your disposal."

Kyla called from the living room, "Are you two coming back out here to keep me company before I fall asleep? I thought we were having a party."

"Hold your horses, Kyla," Jude said as she returned and pulled some tall mugs down from the kitchen shelf. She poured generous amounts of Kahlua in each cup, topped it off with spiced coffee, then plopped a mound of whipped cream and a dusting of Dutch chocolate before handing them to her guests.

Lily curled up in a well-cushioned wicker rocker next to the couch and sipped her Mexican coffee. "Ian is quite a talented artist. I was very impressed by his work tonight," she said.

"Are you sure you mean his work and not his bod!"

"Jude, I didn't say that, I didn't mean, I mean…"

Jude laughed. "Girl, it's all right, you didn't have to *say it*, your eyes never left him."

"Was I that obvious?"

Kyla sat up and leaned in closer to Lily. "To us women who don't miss much, yes, it was obvious. But to Ian, I doubt it."

Lily squirmed in her seat. "I'm not really looking for love right now; I mean, I'm not even divorced yet."

"So what?" Jude said taking a big gulp of her drink. "When did that ever stop true love?"

Lily turned to Kyla. "You seem to know him pretty well. He appears to like you."

"We're just friends, nothing more," Kyla said.

Jude stood up and changed the subject. "So, does anyone have any juicy town gossip? Or shall we start the party with some true confessions."

"I vote for true confessions, but only if you go first, Jude," Kyla answered.

"Okay, okay, I *do* have a secret to share. You know how my cook, Karen, is pregnant and about to go on permanent leave? Well, I've been thinking about bringing on a more 'gourmet' chef. Someone to jazz things up a bit. And I think I may have found someone."

"And…" Kyla prodded.

"Well, he's smokin' hot, a little mysterious, and *single*."

"But can he cook?" asked Lily, grinning.

Kyla laughed, "Possibly that doesn't matter!"

Lily blushed, "Oh right, right."

"Not so fast, you two. It happens he's Cordon Bleu trained and apprenticed at a three-star Michelin restaurant in Spain. And he's currently the executive chef at the Grand Hotel in Seattle."

"So why would he want to come here to such an isolated place like Madrona Island?" Kyla asked. "Your café, as wonderful as it is, is not exactly an upwardly mobile career move for a guy like him."

Jude sighed. "That's the question I'm trying to get answered before I make up my mind to hire him and tell Karen. He says he just wants a change. Maybe you could do a tea leaf reading for me, Kyla, help me figure this out?"

"You do tea leaf readings?" Lily asked with surprise.

"For some people I do. I would do it for you if you wanted one."

Jude clapped her hands. "Yes, Lily, you have to try one."

Lily paused. "I'll think about it. You know, possibly the chef just wants a change of scenery, a fresh start somewhere new...like me."

Both women stared intently at Lily, waiting for her to reveal more. Lily warmed her hands on the porcelain mug. "As you know, Jude, I left my marriage to Brad. I guess you could call him an arrogant, overbearing, self-centered jerk."

"That's letting it all out, Lily," Jude said, nodding her head in approval.

Lily paused and smiled. It was nice to have girlfriends she could talk to and not have to always be the "nice girl," overwhelmed by Brad telling her day and night what to do, what to wear, what to say, how to act. She continued, "Unfortunately, Brad doesn't like to lose his possessions, and I was his prized possession–he's making it extremely difficult for me to negotiate a divorce and a fair settlement."

Kyla leveled her green-eyed gaze on Lily, then spoke softly. "Is he threatening you?"

"Not exactly, not yet, anyway. Just lying, withholding money, manipulating everything to try to force me to come back."

"That's more than enough threat." Jude shook her head sadly.

"Stay true to yourself, Lily," Kyla said. "True freedom always has a price, but it is so worth it."

Lily looked into Kyla's piercing green eyes. Shadows of grief played along the dark-rimmed edges, and it occurred to her that the cost of Kyla's own freedom, whatever that was, still weighed heavily upon her. Lily's heart went out to her. She wished this woman would open up to her, just a little more.

Jude went to get the coffee pot. "Okay, let's lighten up, ladies. Ex-husbands and their wonderful attributes and charades can be quite amusing viewed from a distance."

She refilled their cups with coffee and Kahlua, then relaxed into the plush sofa. "Take my ex. He marries me, promises eternal love, then, when our daughter is just three years old, he freaks out and starts whining about wanting his freedom. And you know how I found out he meant what he said...in the headlines of our local newspaper!"

"What, you're kidding!" chimed Lily and Kyla.

"No, 'Mr. I–want-out' was cheating on me with the young and gorgeous wife of our neighbor. The two lovebirds were out on a date, driving drunk, got in an accident, and almost killed someone."

"That's how you found out? How humiliating!" said Lily. "At least I found out in the privacy of my own home when I found over a hundred racy text messages on my husband's phone to a gorgeous blonde. Pictures too!"

Jude raised an eyebrow. "Not too discreet, that soon-to-be-ex of yours." She continued, "Well, I divorced mine, and he took off with the neighbor's wife to who knows where and tried not to pay a dime of child support. But I got him good."

A sly grin crossed Kyla's face. "Tell us more."

"I went to court and the judge sided with me big time. I got a tidy sum, enough to buy this cafe and eventually send my daughter, Lindsay, to college."

"Wow," Lily said. "Where's your daughter now?"

"She's finishing up her business degree at Duke. I'm very proud of her."

Jude and Lily turned their attention to Kyla. "Your turn," they said in unison.

Kyla's eyes darted around the room nervously, resting on the front door then back again to the floor beneath her. "I guess it's not too hard to guess from my looks, but my mother and grandmother were both Irish. They were gypsies, of sorts, and healers. The authentic kind from a long family line."

"Really!" they both said.

"When I was growing up, we had medicinal herbs growing in our backyard, from lavender to garlic. The windowsills were filled with mint and sage in rainbow colors. People would line up at our door to wait for an appointment to get help with their various ills–arthritis, indigestion, impotence, insomnia–there wasn't much my family didn't have a natural remedy for."

"And now you own *Tea & Comfort*. It's perfect," said Lily. "Turning your heritage into a successful business."

Kyla looked at Lily. "I do love my work *now*, but in high school I was so embarrassed by my family that I never brought anyone home. I was always alone and wanted to escape to a different world, one where I would fit in."

Jude prodded, "So, what did you do before you came to the island?"

Kyla took a deep breath; her eyes distant, obviously filled with a memory somewhere far away. "Suffice to say, it was the complete opposite of my life now, but that's a long story I'll save for another night."

"Oh, c'mon," said Jude. "I always tell you everything."

"That's just your way, Jude, not mine."

Kyla folded her arms across her chest and leaned back. She was finished talking.

Jude broke the silence. "Are you ladies ready for sleep, or would you prefer a quick batch of fudge brownies?"

"Brownies!" Lily said, rising from her chair. "I'll even help make them. Where's the flour and …?"

"Whoa," said Jude. "I have a box of brownie mix that I throw a few eggs and water into and we'll have some chewy treats in no time."

"I can see this is going to be an all-nighter." Lily followed Jude into the kitchen; she didn't feel much like sleeping anyway.

Chapter Eighteen

Ian looked out the back door window and craned his head to see if Lily's car was coming down her drive yet. Where the heck was she? It was almost eleven o'clock in the morning. Obviously, she had not come home last night. Flashes of a car accident set his heart racing. Not another Denise. His breath came faster, and he needed to sit down. A warm hand took his arm and guided him to the couch.

"I know what you're thinking son, and I'm sure she's fine." His grandfather guided him to a chair and took a seat across from him at the kitchen table. "She probably stayed in town with Jude. Good idea, too, with all the wine drinking going on at those openings."

Ian looked into his grandfather's eyes and felt a calmness settling in. "You're right, we would have heard if anything went wrong. I just don't like her not coming home or calling…" He stopped himself abruptly, amazed by what he had just said. She didn't owe him a call. She really didn't owe him anything at all. And yet he already felt so attached. Ian pushed himself from the chair and started for the door. "You're right, Gramps, thanks for the reminder. I think I'll go out to the studio and get some painting done."

"Hold on, Ian. How about we talk a bit, have some coffee?"

"You always could see right through me. Am I that obvious?"

Ian held fast at the door. He wanted to run out to the old barn that held his studio, bury himself in his work, drown out the feelings that fought to resurface from the depths where he had banished them after his wife's death. John laughed. "I'm afraid when it comes to women, the men in this family fall pretty hard, once they finally fall. And Lily is the kind of woman who comes along very rarely."

Ian started a fresh pot of coffee, then joined his grandfather in the den. "The timing is just so bad. She's not even divorced yet. I don't want to scare her off." Ian remembered the look in Lily's eyes when he'd moved in for a kiss. It looked a lot like terror. That soon-to-be-ex-husband of hers must have really caused some damage.

John nodded his head in agreement. "Sometimes you just have to stand firm with your feelings, be patient, and let the tide turn toward you. Fear can be contagious, you know."

Ian knew about fear of getting involved. For the last few years the minute any woman started to get close, he'd taken off running. His head perked up at the distant sound of a car rolling down the gravel drive next door. His eyes met his grandfather's, and they both burst out laughing and headed for the window. John put his arm around Ian with a tight squeeze. "See, I told you she was fine. Why don't you head over there just to be sure?"

Ian's eyes glimmered. "Wouldn't it seem like overkill, like I was pouncing on her the minute she got home?"

John gave him a nudge. "Stop thinking so much and get going."

✦✦✦✦

I'm getting too old to pull all-nighters, Lily thought. Exhaustion was setting in after staying up half the night. She walked down the driveway to check the mail, hoping it would be filled with something besides bills and divorce papers. She was surprised to see Ian walking across the field, waving at her. Memories of him flirting with the women at the gallery reminded her to remain cool and distant.

"Good morning, Lily."

He looked awful cute this morning, she had to admit. "Morning, Ian."

"I thought I'd thank you in person for the desserts," he said. "They were a big hit at the opening."

"Thanks, that's good to hear." She reached in, pulled out the mail, and started back toward the house.

He followed close on her heels. "Did you enjoy the show?"

"Actually, Ian, I'm pretty tired. Jude, Kyla, and I had quite an evening after we left the gallery." She saw his face drop and knew she was not being kind. A chilling wind blew off the Sound and a piece of mail flew from her hands.

Ian caught it in mid-air and handed it to her. "Alright, sure. Would you like to take a walk later, when you're rested, if the wind dies down?"

"Possibly. I am out of kindling and need to cut some."

"My specialty," Ian said. "Point the way, I'm at your service."

"Thanks, Ian, the wood is out by the back porch. I'm going to change, then I'll meet you out there."

Here he was being so nice again. Did she read him wrong last night? She didn't trust her judgment when it came to men, particularly now. She brought the mail in and went out the back door to see how Ian was doing with the wood.

Lily watched Ian chop kindling for a while and thought about all the things she should be doing instead, like looking for the brownie recipe or taking a nap. How can one man make me feel so darn uncomfortable? she wondered. It's those eyes. It should be illegal for them to be so blue. He was obviously trying hard to be helpful. Not interested, walk away, Lily, the voice in her head said. Don't you see the red warning light over his head?

Just as he finished chopping the stack, the sun broke through the clouds.

"Feel any better? Up for a walk now, Lily?"

She felt that sinking feeling again in her stomach. Before she could stop them, words came out of her mouth. "Sure, just a short one. I have to get back soon."

The tide was out and the wet beach stretched for miles. Her fatigue dissolved as she watched each foamy wave retreat. Wisps of pink crossed a pale sky and set off the Olympic Mountains in the distance.

Ian picked up a small iridescent shell and rinsed it in the waves. "A shell for your thoughts," he said as he handed it over to Lily.

She held it in her hand. "A pretty one, too, delicate, unique...good taste."

"So, does that mean I pass inspection?" he said, standing straight at mock attention.

Arms folded across her chest, Lily stared up at the man standing at attention before her. Despite herself, she had to admit the shaggy dark hair blowing across the olive-skinned face framed a handsome and seemingly thoughtful man.

"I suppose, but only time will tell." Jaded, crossed her mind. That is how she sounded. After Brad, any man was suspicious until proven otherwise, no matter how hard her heart pounded when she stood beside him.

As they meandered along the shore, it crossed her mind how they made a striking pair. He tall and dark, long, lean arms; and her, slim but strong frame and straw-colored hair reflecting sunlight and playing with the breeze.

A gnarly piece of driftwood suggested the perfect seat to watch the sun drifting in and out of the clouds. The tide rolled ashore, edging away grains of sand, turning it into foaming mud.

"Let's sit here awhile. Couldn't find a better view," he said.

Lily sat, curled her legs up to her chest, and hugged them close. The quiet passed between them, but with a marked comfortableness, like a married couple after years of being together.

"I love this spot. Thank you for showing it to me, Ian."

"I know it well. I've taken many photos here and brought my easel on a few occasions."

"I'd like to see the new pieces you're working on." There it was again, words coming out of her mouth that she didn't mean to say. Lily, get a grip, she thought. Yes, he is very good-looking, and yes, it is hard to breathe or think straight around him, but he is, remember, a man.

She looked away, afraid to hear his next comment, hoping it would not be some awful line about coming over to his place sometime.

"Whenever you would like, Lily, stop by my studio. Or I could drop by your place sometime and bring a few."

Hmmm, a safe, polite answer. Possibly more points for him.

The water was just beginning to reach their toes when they realized the tide was definitely coming in.

Ian jumped up. "How stupid of me not to notice the tide. Come on, Lily, before we have to climb out over the cliffs. Let's head back." He took her hand and brought her to her feet.

Lily looked back at the steep, sandy, unstable cliff behind them. Hiking out was not an option.

Running hand-in-hand, they took for the higher beach area, jumping old logs and heading for the path leading back to the steps bordering John's property. The bottom step had just started to fill with water. Ian hopped up a few steps and reached a hand out to guide her up to the dry plateau. He pulled her in close for a moment and pressed his face into her hair. Almost visible sparks flew between them. He gently touched her cheek, leaning in for a kiss, but the terror she knew was showing through her eyes must have stopped him. Releasing her, he stepped back, eyes resting softly on her face.

"When you're ready, Lily, I'll be here."

Before she could answer, Ian started for his house.

She watched him walk across the field. Melancholy filled her heart. He seemed so perfect. Why couldn't she at least give him a chance?

Chapter Nineteen

February continued to be a long, wet month. Lily turned the calendar page; tomorrow was March first. Jude had promised her that the days would begin to get longer and the sun would appear more often.

Lily paced her bedroom floor. She was sick of worrying and dealing with divorce issues, and there was really nothing more she could do in the house. Mary kept it spotless, and she had tested every recipe that she thought Jude and the grocer might buy from her. Cash was flowing in steadily, just enough to cover the utilities and food, but the promised temporary alimony had never materialized.

She sat down on the edge of the bed and pulled out the Guestbook. With closed eyes, she opened to a random page and read the entry:

> *Three friends came to stay looking for rest and relaxation. We found a priceless treasure of views, sunrises, stargazing, and magical walks along the sand. We giggled all night, and it replenished our souls. Thank you for sharing your beauty with the rest of the world. We leave here wiser and happier women.*

Lily glanced out the window. She could use some R&R herself. The rain had finally stopped, and there were patches of blue in the sky. If she left now, she could run into town, find something very chocolaty to lift her spirits, and possibly hit the thrift shop as well. The decision propelled her out of the house and into the car. She headed up Sunshine Lane toward the main road, humming "Happy Days are Here Again." Her grandmother had loved to sing that song and make up new lyrics for it. Lily's favorite verse had been something like: It's time for a chocolate soda again.

Perfect. That's what she'd do. A bit of shopping and then a tall soda at the old- fashioned ice cream place. She turned on the radio and sang along to some of the pop songs. The day was hers to do whatever she wanted with it.

Weekday parking was pretty easy to get in town, so she pulled the car right in front of Island Creamery. The "open" sign was a welcome sight. Many of the shops closed during winter months or were open only on the weekend. Memories of coming here with her grandmother flooded her mind. How she wished Maggie were here. The booth where they used to sit in the window was filled with a little girl and an elderly woman, probably her grandmother. If only she could go back in time. But she had the present. Her grandmother left her the inn and wanted her to thrive and be happy there. She would do everything in her power to make that happen. But she could not walk into the ice cream place until her heart settled.

Hands that Help Thrift was right across the street. Lily wandered over and peeked through the window. Crowded. This was a popular destination shop for the locals.

She pushed open the door and began scouting. The front shelves were full of dishes, vases, knickknacks, and other memorabilia. She picked up an antique rose teacup and saucer set. The smooth surface and markings on the bottom of the cup revealed it was English bone china. It would be lovely for serving morning tea and coffee to guests in the Rose Suite at Madrona Island Bed and Breakfast. If it was still open. Lily imagined putting a tray together: steaming coffee, warm almond croissants, a small dish of fresh fruit garnished with herbs from her garden, a bud vase with fresh-picked flowers. How would she get the money to reopen it? Reluctantly, she placed the teacup back on the shelf and wandered toward the back, where the clothing was.

"Lily, is that you, dear?"

Lily turned to see her neighbor, Shirley, trying on a fancy hat in the mirror.

"Shirley, so good to see you."

"What do you think of this hat? Too much for me?"

Lily suppressed a smile. Was anything too much for Shirley? "I think it's very flattering. The red velvet brim sets off your blonde hair quite nicely."

Shirley leaned toward the mirror. "You think so?"

"Absolutely," Lily replied.

Shirley pulled the hat off and put it in her plastic basket with the rest of her finds. "Let's find something for you now, Lily."

They perused the racks of clothing, pulling out a sweater here, a jacket there.

"What do you think of this?" Shirley asked, holding up a teal green sweater with a cowl neck.

Lily checked the label. It was a good brand and just her size. "Love it." The price was $3.99. "Can't beat the price, even I can afford that."

"And," Shirley said, "I have the perfect scarf to go with that at home. I'll bring it over and see what you think."

Lily could only imagine what the scarf might look like,

but the offer was kind.

"Ready to check out?" Shirley asked.

"Ready when you are."

After they paid for their purchases, Lily helped Shirley put her new items in her car. "Where you headed now?" Shirley asked.

"I thought I might head across the street and have a tall chocolate soda. Want to join me?" Lily asked.

Shirley looped her large gold handbag over her shoulder. "Let's go. Two sodas, my treat."

The ice cream parlor looked exactly the way it had almost twenty years ago when Lily had last been here. They were seated in a red leather booth that glistened in the overhead lights. The gray Formica table still had a coin-operated jukebox on it. Lily pulled out a few quarters and dropped them in the slot. "What would you like to hear, Shirley?"

Lily turned each page slowly, reading the song titles out loud. "How about the Everly Brothers or 'Put Your Head on my Shoulder' by Paul Anka? Or, if you like, 'Don't Be Cruel,' by the King?"

"Love them all, you pick," Shirley said.

A famous crooner's voice echoed through the parlor on the brassy speakers as they both read over the laminated menu.

"Can I take your order?" the waitress asked, holding a pencil and order pad in her hands.

"I'll have the cheeseburger with fries and a vanilla Coke," Shirley said.

"I'll have the grilled chicken sandwich and a chocolate soda with vanilla ice cream," Lily said.

Shirley laid her menu down and looked intently at Lily. "So, tell me the truth, how are you doing?"

Lily was taken aback for a moment. Shirley did not mince words. But she knew this woman would listen and give her honest feedback. "To tell you the truth, I've been going over my finances and trying to figure out if I could make a go of reopening the B&B."

"I'm sure you can do anything you set your mind to," Shirley said.

Lily thought about the court battle still going on and how up in the air her financial stability was. Could she even consider such an ambitious plan as starting a new business?

"Do you really think so, Shirley?"

"Of course. You know, your grandmother, after all her losses, managed to get that place together, open the inn and have a thriving business. You're a lot like her, you know."

"I am?" Lily asked.

"You just need a bit more confidence in yourself. Don't let that cheating husband of yours bring you down. In fact, show him just what you're made of."

The waitress brought their food over and placed it on the table. Lily sipped on her creamy soda while she watched Shirley pour ketchup over her fries and cut her burger in half before diving into her lunch. Her grandmother had lost her husband. Only a year later her only son, Lily's father, had borrowed money and left town after deserting his wife and daughter. If that wasn't enough, Katherine had skipped the state with Lily in hand, and they had never spoken again. If her grandmother could get through all that and still run a business with such love and grace, so could Lily.

"Your grandmother just did what she loved, and everything worked out just fine. It will for you too," Shirley said, stuffing another fry in her mouth.

Lily took a bite of her sandwich and washed it down with another sip from the long straw in her soda. "I'm so glad you were her friend."

Shirley's eyes looked warm and sympathetic. "Don't

waste time on the past. Your grandmother would only want you to be happy. That dad of yours caused lots of heartache. It was *not* your fault."

Happy...Lily let that word resonate in her head. Other than as a child here on the island and for a few brief moments with Brad, she had not known much happiness. Perhaps it was time she did. "I'm so glad my grandmother had you and Betty as neighbors and friends."

Shirley winked at Lily. "We had some good times together. It wasn't all hard work, there was plenty of play."

"I bet there was," Lily said with a smile.

When the check came, Shirley insisted on paying. "Well at least let me leave the tip," Lily said.

"Not today," Shirley said, taking cash out of her large pocketbook. "My treat."

"Where are you off to?" Lily asked.

"Grocery store, then home for a nap," Shirley replied. "See you soon."

Lily headed back to her car and settled into the driver's seat. Before fastening her seatbelt, she let their conversation wash through her mind. Three generations of women with challenges all centered around the men in their lives. Her grandmother had overcome her grief, had success and happiness in her life. Her mother had done much the same. It was Lily's turn.

Chapter Twenty

Ian stood at the doorway, kicked some mud off his boots, and wiped the soles on the coarse welcome mat. The kitchen wood stove kept the pine-paneled room toasty and was a welcome refuge from the constant rain, the howling wind, the sting of rejection. He'd been gone a few weeks and was really looking forward to seeing Lily again. But when he stopped by to ask her out for dinner, she'd made some excuse about being too tired.

"Sit down, Ian, I'll make us some coffee," John offered. Ian moved toward the stove to help, but John waved him away. "Hey, your old gramps can do it himself. Sit down, take a load off."

Ian removed his coat, plopped into the carved oak dining chair, and stared out the window toward Lily's farmhouse. John brought two mugs of coffee over and joined Ian at the old Formica kitchen table. Ian had loved the bright shiny red surface as a boy, but it was pretty faded now.

"How's your work coming along for the show in New York?"

"Going well, Gramps. One show behind me where I sold

several paintings, and another show coming up in April."

"Good thing so many people turned out for your show with this lousy weather." John took a sip of his coffee. "Oh, by the way, Jason went over to Wilcox's house to play with Tim. He wants to know if he can spend the night."

Ian rose and walked over to the phone. "Sure, I'll give them a call." As he dialed, Ian stared out the window, watching the light of day fading and the ominous gray clouds turning slowly black.

"Hi, it's Ian, hear my kid's there again and wants to spend the night." Ian could hear the boys shouting in the background while Ida Wilcox assured him it was fine. "Sure, I'll pick up Jason in the morning."

Ian sat back down and stirred his coffee. With Jason gone, he could work all the rest of the day and night.

John brought the coffee pot over to refill their cups. "Looks like you've got someone on your mind, son."

Ian looked up and stared into the kind eyes of his grandfather. "Yep."

"When you look confused like that, it reminds me when you were a little boy and I used to take you on my lap to talk out your problems."

"I'm a bit too old for that now," Ian said wryly.

"And too big!" John laughed. "Last thing I want to do is see you hurting again, boy. After Denise died, you were so depressed I was afraid I was going to lose you too."

"If it wasn't for little Jason, that might have happened. But no way I would ever leave my son."

The fire in the wood stove was waning. John added some fresh wood and kindling, and the flames licked the edges then burst into flame.

"So, Gramps, you seem to be the expert on women in this family. I sure could use some advice."

John fell into his chair laughing. "Me? An expert?"

"Don't laugh so hard, you know what I mean. You lost Grandma Carol and you still were able to love again."

Ian watched how mentioning Carol's name still brought a twinge of pain to John's face.

"You really never get over losing someone you love, Ian. I won't kid you, it hurts. I don't want to use trite phrases like 'life goes on,' but the fact is, it does. And I believe the human heart can love again. When Maggie and I got together after we both had lost our spouses, I had all those feelings you have, too. Guilt about caring for another woman, confusion, and fear of ever having to lose someone I love again."

The room filled with silence. Ian knew that each of them was remembering the common thread of loss that bound them together—losing a wife, watching her die. For John, watching Carol suffer a stroke right after their 50th wedding anniversary was devastating. She'd been paralyzed and unable to speak. With deep love and gentle care, he'd nursed her at home for months until she finally slipped away in her sleep. John had found her one morning, resting peacefully in their bed, the one they had shared for more than 50 years. Ian wondered how John had ever gotten out of bed after that.

"It is a hard, long road back, son. I never thought I'd wake up happy to see another morning after that. You gotta remember, I was almost 71 years old when it happened. You, Ian, are a young man, and you have a responsibility to your son to make a happy family life for him. Denise would want you both to be happy, you know that."

Ian clenched his teeth, trying to hold back the sorrow and tears that blurred his vision. He wiped them away briskly with his flannel shirt sleeve. "See what an idiot I am? I still can't even think of her without welling up in the faucet department."

"Doesn't mean you can't have feelings for another woman. I notice you've been over visiting that nice Lily next door."

Ian jumped from the chair and began to pace the room. Then he stopped abruptly and met his grandfather's eyes. "I asked her to dinner tonight. Yes...when I'm around her, I feel emotions that I thought were long gone. I don't know what to think. She's not even divorced yet, and it's plain she is not ready for some guy hitting on her now. But I just keep thinking about her and then find myself over there offering to help out."

"Just let yourself do what comes natural. She's a real nice young woman and she could use some help about now."

"Yeah, I guess you're right," Ian said as he grabbed his coat. "I think I'll go out to the studio and do some painting."

"You do that, Ian. I'll heat up some supper in a little while and come get you."

Chapter Twenty-One

*L*ily looked at her watch. It was after four, and the nap had revived her. She wondered if Jude would like to meet for a glass of wine before dinner. She *needed* someone to talk to. Why did she turn Ian down for dinner? She really did want to go. And such a lame excuse, telling him she was too tired. And now, when he saw her drive away, he was going to know she was not too tired to do something else. When she got to town, she parked the car and headed to Island Thyme Café. Lily pushed open the door and almost bumped right into Jude.

"My, my, Lily, you look a little flushed. Hangover? In love?" She motioned to the bar. "Have a glass of wine, we'll sit and talk."

Lily plopped onto the barstool. "Why did I have to meet him? I sure don't need another man in my life right now."

"By 'him,' I assume you mean Ian. Spill the beans, let's have it," Jude said, pouring some wine.

Lily gulped down the flowery Chardonnay. "I'm finally free, building my own life. Ian is…just an interruption."

Jude burst out laughing. "I told you he was a hottie."

Lily glared at Jude. "Why does he have to seem so perfect?

He's kind, understanding, and those blue eyes..."

"Here, have a little more wine. So, what would be so bad about dating him?"

"When I'm around him, I feel like I'm melting, losing myself again, and I don't want another man to control me, ever." Jude shifted on her stool. "Take it slow and see what happens. Ian's a good guy, and you'll know when and if it's right."

"I don't know what I want. The only thing I do know is what I *don't* want, and that could fill a book. I read some entries in my grandma's Guestbook, and the couples all seem so happy. Sometimes I think I want that for myself. Then I remember Brad."

"All men are not Brad. Or like your father. It's an unfair comparison." Jude raised her glass. "Let's toast. To happy endings."

Reluctantly, Lily lifted her glass and echoed the sentiment. "To happy endings." She sighed. "You know, I even love his grandfather and his kid. Can't you see us as one big, happy family? Do things like that ever come *true?*"

"Ask Kyla," Jude said holding up her glass for a toast. "She's the tea leaf reader."

✦ ✦ ✦ ✦

Lily had just come into town to look at another view of gray, and now here she was letting Jude drag her over to Kyla's for a reading.

Jude gave Lily's arm a little tug. "Come on, Lily. Kyla's not going to bite, she's just gonna read a few tea leaves for you."

Lily was not so sure about that. There was something different about Kyla, something that spoke of secret knowings and mysterious powers. She had opened up at their slumber party a little, but still. "I've never done this before. How does she do these things? What's her background?"

Jude stopped on the entry step to the quaint shop and turned to face Lily. "It's not like you're going to a witch's den or some TV psychic. Kyla's the real thing."

"How is that supposed to make me feel better? Just what exactly *is* the real thing?"

Jude chuckled and leaned in close to whisper in Lily's ear. "A Green Witch, not to be mistaken for a sandwich!"

Lily pulled away with alarm and started back toward the car. "I suppose you think that's really funny. I've heard of people who work with plants and herbs being referred to in that way. I just never heard of them doing tea leaf readings. I think I'll pass."

Jude caught up to Lily and put her arms around her. Patting her fondly on the back, she said, "Lily, I'm sorry. You just looked so scared, I couldn't resist teasing you. Really, Kyla is the most amazing reader. Her insight and healing methods will blow you away...gently, that is. Just try it, for me?"

Lily looked warily at the sign above the inviting wood door: *Tea & Comfort.* Both sounded pretty good to her right now. And she *was* curious. It couldn't hurt to give this a try. With all the other new things she was doing, she just might find this quite intriguing. "Oh, all right," she exhaled sharply. "Let's go."

They heard the tinkling of chimes as they walked through the doorway. A portly Siamese cat sat perched on the windowsill, obviously hoping for a few weak rays of sun to pour through. The shop smelled woody and spicy. Shelves filled with glass jars packed with herbs and dried flowers lined the walls. Other antique wood shelves were lined with teapots and cups in every shape, size, color, and pattern. Near the cash register, a low table was covered with baskets filled with homemade soaps in scents from jasmine to lemon verbena.

Tall pillar candles lined the windowsill, each wrapped with a ribbon holding a fresh herb knotted into it. Jude was right, this place was amazing. Lily wandered around sniffing each item, admiring the herb and flower arrangements resting on ledges atop the windows and doors and the hand-painted floral designs on the walls and shelves. Enchanting was the only way to describe it.

Kyla emerged from behind some deep-violet curtains. "Good morning, ladies, welcome. I just brewed a fresh pot of chamomile tea with rose petals. How about joining me? Just sit anywhere and I'll bring it out."

Jude and Lily walked over to the other side of the store, where there was a small tearoom filled with round tables covered in lace or floral-print tablecloths. Each table was set with fresh flowers in a bud vase.

An affirmative chorus of "ahhh" filled the tearoom. Lily picked a table by the front window where she could pet the Siamese cat that sat on the sill and they could look out between the lace curtains to the flowerpots outside. Even in early March, with all this rain and cold, Kyla had flowers and herbs growing out there. She really did have a green thumb. Lily sank into the comfortable chair. Just the girls having tea; she liked the feel of that simple act.

"I baked some of those anise-lemon cream scones you like, Jude, so help yourself." Kyla placed a white china plate edged with a rose pattern onto the middle of the table. The scones were warm and smelled of a fresh garden. The teapot looked like a rose garden trimmed with spun gold, and when the tea was poured into the cups, it glowed with a golden hue.

Lily tasted the scone. "It's like biting into spring. I feel like I'm sitting in a garden basking in the early morning sun."

Kyla laughed. "You're an easy one to transport! Now let me see that dainty hand of yours." Kyla took Lily's right hand

and turned it over to look at her palm. "Hmm, strong-willed and very creative."

"My hand says that about me?"

"And much more," Kyla answered. "But you're not here for this. I have some imported black tea brewing in the back, and we'll see what those leaves have to say."

After sipping the fragrant tea together for a while, Jude rose from the table. "Well, girls, I think I'll go do some window shopping and pretend I'm on vacation for an hour before I have to go back to the café. Have fun. Lunch tomorrow, my place. Okay, Lil?"

"See you then," Lily said.

Kyla led Lily through the velvet curtains and into a small back parlor with a kitchenette. An overstuffed couch was laden with colorful pillows and a small table flanked by two wingback chairs stood by the wood stove, catching its warmth. The table, covered with a multi-colored, embroidered silk scarf, held a scented pillar candle flaming in the center.

"Take a seat," Kyla said, pointing to one of the chairs. She handed Lily a wide-rimmed, petite cup of hot liquid. Loose tea leaves floated on the surface and others sank slowly to the bottom. "I like to use white cups because they make a clean canvas for the reading."

"We drink it first?" Lily asked.

Kyla laughed. "That's usually what you do with tea. Just enjoy it. Think about those parts of your life where you'd like some clarity as you sip it down."

Lily finished most of her tea and waited for what would happen next.

"Now," Kyla said, "put the cup in your left hand and swirl the tea leaves around three times in a clockwise direction."

Lily watched the leaves float around in a circular motion

and thought of her life, swirling all around her in much the same way. She laid the cup down. "Okay, what's next?"

Kyla took the handle of the cup and tipped it sideways, slowly draining the last bit of tea into the saucer. Then she set the cup on the table in front of her guest with the handle pointing toward Lily.

Lily watched as Kyla leaned over the cup, how her gaze softened and her eyes clouded over after she took a slow deep breath.

"Much to see, much to tell," Kyla said. "Coming from darkness, but moving to light. Detours, the leaves show two paths, one is lit and ends in heart-pink roses; the other is dry desert and ends in tears."

Lily let out her breath, unaware that she had been holding it. "Do you see that in the leaves? How do you know what it means?"

Kyla's eyes focused back into the room. "I was taught the skill from my Irish grandmother, and my mother. This tea ritual has been in our family for generations. You can Google Tasseography if you want a definition."

"I will."

"It's not what you may think of as magic," Kyla continued. "The patterns and symbols are an excellent tool for tapping into the unconscious. Of course, my grandmother believed it was a lot more than that."

"How does it work for you, Kyla?"

"I use the ancient interpretations, but I also listen and see what I am shown in my head and heart as well. Look yourself at the leaves and tell me what you see."

Lily stared into the cup, waiting for impressions to form. She could feel Kyla's eyes on her and felt a bit exposed. She pointed to a cluster of tea leaves near the top of the cup. "This image looks like a picket fence."

Kyla turned her focus to the spot Lily was pointing to. "Yes, it does, and near the rim, too. Generally symbols near the top of the cup mean something will happen soon, or are happening now. A fence represents a block, a temporary setback that prevents you from moving in the direction you need to go."

Kyla's eyes scanned the inside of the cup then closed. "The leaves show a split mind and a wavering heart that wants to be set free. The wings of your soul seek flight, to rise and reach the freedom of the stars. But, there is still a small amount of murky water around your mind. It is not clear yet, time and choices. It is your path to claim." With that, Kyla opened her eyes and looked directly at Lily.

Lily stared back, feeling a sudden, inexplicable, deep connection with the woman across the table. Kyla's words rang true. They touched her, yet frightened her as well. Lily pointed to an image that looked like a large, thick branch. "And this image?"

"Hmmm, an injustice is weighing heavily on your mind and heart. But there is a perfect circle further down, do you see it?" Lily nodded her head. "And next to it, what appears to be a star. These are very positive indicators of triumph and happiness, but they are in the distance, not quite in sight yet."

Lily waited for Kyla to focus back to her again. "Can I ask a specific question?"

"Of course."

"There is someone I worry about, don't trust. Can you see anything on him?"

Kyla pointed to a wavy trail of tea leaves. "This looks like a snake, perhaps apropos of this man?"

Lily laughed uneasily. "I'd say so."

"The snake can mean an enemy, someone quiet and deceptive ready to strike. But remember, Lily, if you rise above its lowly crawl, snake medicine is one of great wisdom. By its placement in the cup, I see it forcing you to gather strength and encouraging you to find greater self-knowledge."

Lily paused, taking it all in. Strangely, it made sense and reminded her just how important her choices were now and not to underestimate Brad or the strange letters.

"All in all, Lily, this is a very positive reading. Tears line the bottom of the cup, but the strong image of the sun is in your future. It is up to you to choose to follow its bright rays." Kyla stood, stretched, and inhaled deeply. Then she picked up the teacup, brought it to the sink, and rinsed it out.

Kyla's words resonated deep within Lily. Disturbing emotions played at the surface of Lily's heart, but she also felt a well of strength building up inside. Jude was right. She *did* feel amazing—lighter and more clear-headed.

"Thank you so much, Kyla. That was very special and meant a lot to me." She felt the urge to embrace the slim woman standing before her, but something kept her from reaching out.

"Come on in the front, Lily. I'll make you a special tea blend to take home, and I'll give you an herbal candle to help with focus and calmness." Kyla pulled some jars off the shelf and began preparing the special formula.

Lily picked a brochure off the counter and read over the afternoon tea menu. She could almost taste each item; finger sandwiches with Devonshire cream and fresh fruit preserves, fresh greens and herb salads, and an amazing array of teas graced the page. She wandered around again, enjoying the soaps and candles. "I love your shop, Kyla. I feel so comfortable here. The name *Tea & Comfort* is perfect. Do you make the candles too?"

Kyla measured then poured herbs into a clear plastic bag and labeled it. Without looking up, she answered, "I grow many of the herbs in my garden and have a large barn where I make the candles, soaps, and lotions. I do have a young helper, so I can't take all the credit." Kyla handed her a glass jar labeled *Calm & Serenity*. "This is an aromatic jar. Leave it on a kitchen counter or your coffee table, and whenever you walk by it, lift the lid and take a whiff. The herbs will uplift your spirit and calm any anxiety."

Lily lifted the lid and inhaled slowly. The smell was divine, probably in more ways than one, she thought, chuckling quietly to herself. "What's in this heavenly concoction?"

"Fresh, dried herbs mostly, some thyme, oatstraw, rosemary, rose petals, and a touch of cardamom. And here is your tea, made to order."

Lily read the label, *Courage & Triumph Blend.*

"For you, I combined sage for concentration, chamomile and linden flower for calmness and confidence, and fennel seed for balance and joy. Be sure to add fresh island honey to the brew. And, as a housewarming gift—and to brew your tea in, of course—choose any teapot on the shelf that calls to your heart."

"Kyla, you've been so generous already, please let me pay you for the teapot, at least."

Kyla looked directly at Lily. "Receiving gifts is an art in itself. Now choose the one that speaks to you."

Lily wandered over to the shelf of teapots. The English garden ones were beautiful, and so were the small Japanese pots. She ran her hand over a delicate midnight blue clay pot. Images of dragonflies were carved along the base and handle. This one was hers.

Kyla wrapped the pot in tissue and inserted it into a gift box. "Good choice. Dragonflies signify new beginnings and new unions...sometimes marriage."

"No way," Lily said. "New beginnings, yes, marriage...I

don't think so."

Very briefly, Kyla's eyes clouded over as they had during the tea leaf reading. "You never know what gifts await you, Lily. Keep your mind and your heart open."

Arms filled with her new presents all wrapped with bows and cellophane, Lily nudged open the front door. The chimes rang softly, signaling an end to the magical experience.

Chapter Twenty-Two

The snake struck fast and hard through the morning mail.

There would be a court-ordered hearing to have her vocationally evaluated before spousal support could be determined. When her new Madrona Island house had been a successfully run B&B, her grandmother's tax form showed a profit of close to $50,000 a year. So now, if she was going to stay here, that would be calculated as potential income for her against any alimony payments. It felt so unfair. She had no idea how to run a bed and breakfast, nor did she have the money to get it going again. But that didn't matter to Brad. It was either that or get a job, or no alimony.

She didn't need his damn money. The walls felt like they were closing in on her. Fists clenched, she paced the room. There was only one way out of his grasp, to let him keep everything and walk away. Now! She'd been fine before she met him and she would be again. She would find a way to earn the money to reopen the Inn even if it meant baking day and night. Lily grabbed her keys and slammed the door on the way out.

✦ ✦ ✦ ✦

Jude checked the clock. It was almost 1:00, where was Lily? A few minutes later Lily blew in the door like a whirlwind.

"Sorry I'm late. Why is it when you're in a hurry there is always someone driving 15 miles an hour in front of you?"

"Come on and sit down at the booth over here. I want to hear all about Kyla's reading over lunch."

Lily followed her to a booth and threw her keys down on the table.

"Do I dare ask what is wrong?" Jude said.

"Nothing. Everything."

Jude stayed quiet waiting for Lily to open up to her. The poor woman had enough on her plate. What now? Jude ventured into what she hoped was calmer water. "How was the reading with Kyla?"

"She was right on target."

"And?"

"It made me think a lot about what I'm going to do with my life," Lily answered.

"Sounds intense," Jude said, waving the waitress over to take their order. "Two lunch specials," she ordered, "and two glasses of Madrona White." She turned back to Lily. "So, did you come up with anything?"

"Lots to think about. Mostly money."

Jude stared at her. "And can I help?"

Lily stared at the table. "We could brainstorm sometime soon about how to build my baking business up."

"Happy to share my business expertise. Making money cures a lot of ills."

Lily laughed. "And while you're at it, if I don't see the sun soon, I may just stop getting out of bed."

Karen personally brought over their food and wine and placed them on the table in front of them.

"Thanks," Jude said. "The long, drab winter has made me stir-crazy. Business is down and so are everyone's spirits."

Outside the window, sheets of rain splashed into the gray water of the Sound. "Enough," Jude proclaimed. She laid down her fork and walked briskly to grab a pen, paper, and manila folder from a shelf underneath the bar.

It was time to put some long-range plans into motion and to do what always worked in times like these…have a party! She yelled into the kitchen, "Karen, come on out here, and leave your apron behind." A very pregnant Karen waddled into the dining room and joined them at the table by the window.

"What's up, boss?"

Jude held up the page and pointed to the bold letters at the top—Island Café Spring Fling, March 20th. "Time to get these rain-soaked locals out of their houses before the whole town turns moldy. We need to spread some spring cheer around." She waved her hands around the café. "Flowers, I want color everywhere, roses, tulips, daffodils, and carnations in every color. And fabulous food. That will be your department, Karen. Are you up to it?"

Karen patted her protruding belly. "Sure, as long as this little guy stays put and doesn't cause any trouble."

Jude sighed. "Lily, I hate to lose this girl. Soon Karen will only be available very part time, if that."

"What about the chef who contacted you?" Lily said, sipping her wine.

"I had to think about it a bit more," Jude said.

"No time like the present," Karen said.

"Well, I received an email a few days ago from the candidate, and he's still interested. His name's Ryan—quite an impressive résumé, and his references checked out well. I did a phone interview to see what his story is. Karen, you will always be my top chef, but I think you will have your hands full soon with two little ones."

"That's fantastic, Jude. When can he start?"

"As soon as I call him and tell him he has the job. I wanted to run it by you first, Karen." Jude turned to Lily. "And I hope you, Lily, will look over his résumé and see what you think."

Jude placed the manila folder with the résumé inside beside Lily's plate. "He's worked in some pretty high-class places in Seattle, but he wants out of the city and the limelight. Look where he's worked: a very chi-chi restaurant in Los Angeles, some of the finest hotels in San Francisco, and then the award-winning Grand Hotel in Seattle. I threw in free rent in the apartment above the café as an enticement."

Karen pulled her cell phone out of her pocket. "No time like the present! Give him a call. He can help with the Spring Fling."

Lily perused Ryan's résumé. "Seems top notch. It does seem odd he'd want to leave all that glamour for a country restaurant. But it will certainly be our gain."

Jude dialed the number on the résumé. The phone rang and a resonant voice answered. "Hello. Ryan? It's Jude over at the Island Thyme Café. After our phone interview and discussing everything with my current chef, I have decided that if you're still available, I would like to offer you the job."

There were a few seconds of silence before Ryan answered. "Sounds good to me, just about right, actually. I can be there tomorrow if the apartment is ready."

"It's ready...when you are...which appears to be now," Jude told him.

"We're having a meeting to plan a Spring Fling tomorrow afternoon if you can make it. That will be a good event to introduce you to everyone and announce the new menu changes I expect you'll be suggesting."

"I'll just take down the driving directions and see you by noon tomorrow," he answered.

Jude hung up the phone. She took a few bites of her now cold lunch. "He'll be here tomorrow. He seemed anxious to start."

Lily smiled. "Not running from the law I hope."

"He's running from something, is my guess."

"The sooner the better is fine with me," Karen said. "Don't worry, I'll be here to show him the ropes and to check him out for you. Now, let's get down to business."

Karen took the pen and started writing down ideas. "How about we push all the tables back against the walls and windows and create a small dance floor? We could do a buffet over near the bar and get my brother and his band to get everyone up and dancing."

"Great ideas," Lily said.

"We could charge one admission price for food and music, and the bar drinks could be extra," Jude added. "Might as well make a profit. Soon I'll probably have a higher food overhead. I still can't believe Ryan was happy with the apartment above the café, all he can eat, and island wages."

Karen jotted down some food ideas. "Hot appetizers, finger food, maybe some chili, what do you think?"

"How about I bring some cornbread and apple pies?" Lily volunteered.

"Perfect," Karen said.

Jude looked at Karen. She was loyal and a hard worker, but not overly inventive when it came to the menu. Maybe Ryan would add some spice to the café. "How about we wait for our new gourmet chef tomorrow and see what he has in mind?"

"Perfect. Shall we meet after the lunch rush, say three o'clock?" Lily asked.

"Works for me, boss," Karen said.

"Me too, although it has not been much of a rush lately. Thanks for all your help, both of you." Jude stood to clear off the lunch dishes. Karen and Lily followed close behind with dishes in hand.

"Prep's done for dinner," Karen said. "See ya tomorrow, Jude."

"Sure thing. Get off your feet now." Jude turned to Lily. "You'll be one of the first to meet my mysterious new chef."

"Hmmmm....wonder what he looks like?"

Jude laughed. She had grown quickly to love Lily. She applauded her innocence and determination, and she could relate to her struggle for survival. "I Googled him. Just show up. You won't be disappointed mañana."

"I'll be here at three," Lily said, leaving and shutting the door behind her.

Jude started setting the tables for dinner; it was not too hard handling everything almost alone during the quiet winter months, but it sure would be nice to have Ryan coming on board. Maybe in more ways than one.

✦ ✦ ✦ ✦

Ryan arrived promptly at noon the next day. He drove up in his dark blue Saab and unloaded a couple of boxes and a suitcase. Jude noticed that he was traveling very light, and again wondered what he was leaving behind. Why was he coming here and so eager to start? Don't think about it, she told herself, just be happy he's yours. In the kitchen, anyway!

Jude took him around the side of the building to the narrow front stairs that led to the loft apartment above the front of the café. "Watch the steps, they get slippery in the rain, and we sure get plenty of that." Jude kept talking to fill the silence and to dispel her slight discomfort. "You'll have a great westward view. When the clouds clear, you can see the sunset over the Olympic Mountains. Lots of eagles out there too. The binoculars are on the windowsill."

"Thanks," he murmured as he unloaded his things and started putting away some obviously pricey cookware. "This will do just fine." A slim smile crossed his face. An attempt to be polite, Jude thought. He was definitely the quiet type.

"Just let me know if you need anything. I'll see you at three for the meeting."

Jude went downstairs to start greeting the lunch crowd and was amazed to see Ryan enter the kitchen just a few minutes later. He put on a chef's coat and started cooking with Karen. Jude set things up for lunch and waited for customers to arrive.

Some local city workers entered, their parkas slick with rain. "Here, let me help you guys out of those wet coats," Jude said as she took the dripping garments and hung them on the oak coat rack. "How about a warm table by the fire for you two?" The men nodded gratefully. Jude placed their menus down and pointed to the board with the specials. "We have some great chili today, and"—she strained her eyes to see the addition put there by unfamiliar writing—"it looks like we have some cream of broccoli soup as well. Just give a wave when you're ready."

Lunch hour was slow, but several regulars came in for a hot lunch and a warm place to get out of the rain. The bell rang over the front door, announcing a customer. "Menus, boys?"

"Not today, Jude, just the usual."

She seated the men and walked to the kitchen door. "Ryan,

two gourmet double-cheeseburgers. Hold the fat."

Ryan gave her a perplexed look.

"It's a joke, Ryan." Note to self, lighten that man up a bit.

Around 2:30, Jude cleaned off the last of the tables and brought paper and pen over to a large booth, where they all could meet and go over the Spring Fling ideas. She thought about Lily and Kyla; we all could use a little fun about now. It had been a long winter. And what better time to surprise everyone with her new chef and to taste the exquisite cuisine he had promised to deliver?

Ryan strolled out from the kitchen. He looked pretty good in his black chef's coat. Jude's heart leapt at the sight of him. Not too tall, buff around the arms and chest, mid-forties probably. A strand of sandy blond hair toppled over his brow, and the rest was pulled back into a short ponytail at the back of his neck. A day-old beard covered his well-carved jaw. His deep-set black eyes wore a guarded expression. Fire danced in those eyes, but so did beware.

Jude had seen Ryan's photo with his résumé, but in person he was a very different story. What was she thinking? He wasn't here a day yet and her mind was wandering where it definitely should not go. He was an employee, here only to help her expand the business.

"Are we ready to meet?" Karen yelled, popping her head out the kitchen door.

"Ready soon as Lily gets here," Jude called back. Just as she uttered those words, Lily strolled through the door looking like she was dressed for the Arctic Circle.

Jude waved Lily over. "Lily, meet Ryan, our new chef."

Lily shook the chef's hand. "Nice to meet you."

Everyone slid into the booth and put their notes on the table. Ryan began passing out copies of a sample menu for the event. "I put these ideas together quickly on my break."

Jude glanced over the menu. Happy hour appetizers: Crab canapés, shitake mushrooms stuffed with baked brie, tuna tartare.

Jude tilted her head. "Ryan, I like the idea of a Happy Hour to get them in the door early and drinking, but the menu may need a little adjusting for now. We want to begin to introduce high concept menu items, but blend them with familiar items as well. This party will be mostly locals. Think country, not city. Size matters, and quantity, and of course, quality. A few tree huggers, a few tree cutters, your basic city escapees, artists, writers...you got it?" Why did everything she said sound so damn sexual to her today? This man was really throwing her off. She usually could keep her cool around her personnel.

Ryan looked over and grinned. "I got it. How about blue corn nachos smothered in cheese and lime mango salsa, some chicken wings drenched in cayenne and barbeque sauce, stuffed potatoes with bacon and gruyere..."

Karen patted him on the shoulder. "You learn fast! My mouth is watering. Loads of fat, wonderful smells, hot, spicy and plenty of it. The whole town will come running when they hear about this menu."

"I'm still happy to bring cornbread and apple pie," Lily said.

"Lily does all our baking for the café right now. Scones, cinnamon rolls, a few pies."

"Do you bake?" Lily asked Ryan.

"Savory is more my thing," he replied. "I usually leave desserts to the pastry chef."

Lily smiled. "Well, in this case, that's me."

Jude inconspicuously scooted over a few inches so that her leg would stop brushing Ryan's. That, and she was sure he could hear her heart as it pounded loudly in her chest. Ryan looked over and Jude offered her warmest smile. Cool as a cucumber, no response, just the professional demeanor talking on about the rest of the menu. Maybe this Spring Fling would light a little fire under him. In fact, Ryan was not the only man she hoped to cheer up a bit... Ian needed a little confidence-building with Lily.

Shifting her attention back to the meeting she said, "So, as a professional chef, have you ever planned a Spring Fling before?"

"You got me there, Jude. I can't say that I have, but I'm sure my experience and skills won't disappoint you."

I bet not, thought Jude, I bet not. "Ryan, we want to get the word of mouth started at this party. We want people talking about the new menu and the new imported big city chef. We want them to have fun and start coming out from their winter hibernation."

"Sounds good to me," Lily said.

Jude stood up and surveyed the room. "So, after the Happy Hour in the bar, we want them to stay, have a buffet dinner in the dining room, drink from the cash bar, dance and party with a capital P."

Ryan stood too. "We can make that happen."

"Good," Karen said, struggling to get to her feet. "'Cause I'm ready to go home and take a nap."

"Go home and get off your feet for a while, if that husband of yours will let you. See you tomorrow," Jude said, waving after her.

Lily rose to follow. "Let me know what else you need from me."

"I want you both to dress up for this party. No aprons. I'm going to wear my silky red dress and put a flower in my hair. And Ryan, you'd look good in a cowboy hat." Jude could see Ryan tightening up and his expression freezing. "Totally optional," she said with a chuckle.

"Country life is a bit different, Ryan, I've been finding that out myself," Lily said. "I came here from Los Angeles."

Jude held Ryan's gaze. "It's certainly a long way from your last kitchen at the elegant Land and Sea in the heart of Seattle." Jude watched his expression, hoping he would relax and feel comfortable staying on the island.

Moments of silence ticked by.

"Are you sure this is what you want to do?" she asked Ryan.

She watched Ryan scan the café, glance out at the water and back again. "Yes," he said in a warmer tone. "I left the city behind. I want to cook great food in a more relaxed atmosphere, draw more clientele for you. Not sure about the cowboy hat, though, hope that's not a deal breaker," he said with a wry smile, the first one of the day.

Jude laughed out loud. "Okay, no cowboy hat."

"For me either," Lily said.

Jude watched Ryan snap back into professional mode. "I'll work up the rest of the menu for your approval. Will tomorrow be soon enough?"

"Of course," Jude answered. "Lily and I will work on the decorations, flyers, and invitations. Remember, think spring." She watched Ryan retreat back into the kitchen and couldn't help thinking he reminded her of a feral cat retreating into a cave.

Lily leaned over and whispered, "Not a real friendly one, is he?" With that, they both burst out laughing and then covered their mouths so as not to be heard. "Jude, he sure better cook as well as that résumé says, 'cause I have a feeling his personality is not going to win a lot of friends right off the bat."

"You can say that again! Thanks for coming out for the

meeting."

Lily put her Arctic gear back on and headed for the door. "No problem, this is going to be fun."

Jude watched her leave. Things were changing around here, shifting. She wondered what Lily really thought of her bringing on a new chef. And Karen. Ryan had studied abroad at a three-star Michelin restaurant. What brought him here in answer to her ad was still a mystery.

The peaceful beaches and breathtaking scenery of Madrona Island attracted a wide variety of people. Some came here to heal, some to search for other things. The island drew many tourists during the warmer season. Each person had his or her own story. She certainly had hers. Jude stared out the window, watching the early night start to fall over the water. Misty, gray fog was settling in among the hills. Ryan's story would come out when he was ready to tell it. For now, she needed to keep her mind on business.

Chapter Twenty-Three

After running into town in the afternoon to drop the sheets of flaky cornbread and still-warm apple pies by the café, Lily hurried home to shower and get ready for the evening. She couldn't remember ever going to a Spring Fling before, so she was not sure whether to wear the new teal sweater, or something more subdued. She tried on the sweater and admired the way it draped off her shoulders. It would look good with her dress jeans. She could wear her low heels to dance in and the silver dangly earrings her mother gave her at Christmas. The party would be an excellent place to network and let people know about her baking services.

John McPherson had agreed to act as the designated driver, especially since Lily's car was starting to overheat on a regular basis. She'd try to remember to ask Mary tomorrow the name of her mechanic friend who worked cheap. Lily would be one of the passengers in John's Chevrolet's large back seat, along with Betty and Shirley, while Ian would ride in front. They would be here any moment. All she needed was her wool coat and the hand-knit cashmere scarf Shirley had made for her to keep warm. She wrapped the luscious scarf around her neck, admiring the beautiful shades of pink and purple that ran through it.

A car drove down the driveway, crunching gravel and sending its headlights over her lawn. She ran out the front door just as Ian stepped out of the car and opened the back door for her.

"Thanks," she said, jumping in and fastening her seatbelt. Betty was in jeans, a blue button-up shirt, and matching cardigan sweater. Shirley was decked out in a bright green wool coat with big black buttons. Shiny black pants caught the overhead light as Lily sat down beside her.

"You look so nice, Lily," Shirley said. "And I see you're wearing the scarf I gave you."

Shirley beamed as Lily fingered the scarf. "I do love it."

"Who's got time to sit around knitting when there's so much to do?" Betty folded her arms across her chest. "Spent this first day of spring on that darn back porch making sure you don't fall through it next time you head out there."

Ian turned his head. "Can you use some help, Betty? I'm here for a few days."

"Yeah, I could." Betty looked pleased.

"I'll put it on my calendar for tomorrow," he said. "Anything else you three lovely ladies need right now?" Ian's gaze settled on Lily. "I hope you all will have a dance with me tonight."

Shirley groaned. "Not with my bad hip, and Betty has two left feet. Best stick with Lily if you want to dance."

"Speak for yourself," Betty snapped back at her sister.

"Save one for me too, Lily," John perked up from the front seat.

Shirley clapped her hands. "You'll be the belle of the ball, Lily."

Lily was glad it was somewhat dark in the car. She could

feel the flush of embarrassment creep up her neck and face. "You two sisters look pretty gorgeous yourself tonight," she said.

A light rain coated the windows, but the temperature was definitely getting warmer. Not California warm, but at least Lily wasn't freezing every minute.

"Here we are, everyone," John said as they pulled into a parking space across the street from the café. John hopped out of the car and opened the back door for his passengers. He looked pretty dapper in his blue plaid Pendleton shirt and what Lily assumed were his dress jeans.

Ian helped everyone out of the car and escorted them through the front door of the café. It was barely past five, but the party was already underway. The long, polished oak bar was two-deep in people holding glass mugs of foaming beer or stemmed glasses filled with wine.

Some men at the bar called out to them. "Hey, John, Ian, good to see you."

Jude was off down in the dining room, dashing around in her red dress, as promised. Even from a distance, Lily felt the warmth of that amazing woman's smile.

Each table held vases of daffodils, and the oak beams in the ceiling shimmered with tiny sparkling lights. Over the sound of people's laughter and conversation, Lily heard the Island Blues band. They were accompanied by a wiry fiddle player as they played the old Eagles song "Take it Easy."

The five musicians and their amps barely fit on the small stage set up in the corner of the dining room, but they really added to the party atmosphere.

"Let's grab a table and get settled." John led the way to an empty booth near the corner of the room. "Ladies first," he said, waving his hand toward the cushioned seats.

"Except Lily," Ian said. "She can sit here at the end next

to me."

"Here you are!" Jude glided over to their table and leaned over to kiss John's cheek. "Thanks for bringing the whole gang."

"It looks like a good turnout so far," Lily said. She recognized some of the people from town, people she'd come to know over the last three months. There was Dana the grocer, out of his apron and looking dapper, who waved at her when they walked by, and Lisa, the nice woman from the bank whose husband was a potter. A rowdy group ranging in age from a girl who didn't look old enough to be drinking, to a very white-haired man, was doing a lot of laughing at the big round table near the bar. "Looks like everyone's having fun at that table," Lily said.

Jude craned her neck to see whom Lily was referring to. "Oh, that's the local writer's group that comes in every Wednesday night to discuss their books and to consume many large bottles of wine."

"They look like a lively group."

Jude fanned herself with her hand. "One's a well-published Brit. He's a regular here now. Even the sheriff's a writer on this island."

"The flowers make it look just like spring," Shirley said. "You've done a good job, Jude."

Audrey, the librarian, stopped at the table to greet everyone. "It's so good to see everyone out. It has been a long winter." She hugged Jude and was off to the next table.

"Can you believe Ryan has not even been able to leave the kitchen yet?" Jude said. "Seems everyone here is loving the new food."

"Who's Ryan?" Shirley asked. "New chef? What kinda food are you talking about?"

Jude's smile reminded Lily of the Cheshire cat. "Yes, new

chef. Just head over to the buffet and you'll see."

Then Jude was off as fast as she'd arrived, greeting more customers at the door and scurrying around inspecting the buffet and bar. Lily wasn't hungry yet, but a glass of wine would be wonderful. As if reading her mind, Ian rose and took drink orders from everyone at the table. She watched him walk over to the bar. His dark jeans hugged his lean legs, showing off his long stride, and the black button-down shirt he wore emphasized his broad shoulders. Her mind was on him more than she would like.

"How about we get us some food, ladies?" John stood to help Shirley out of the booth.

Betty popped up and led the way. "What about you, Lily?" she asked.

"I think I'll wait to eat. You all go ahead."

Lily saw a flash of red hair over toward the bar. Kyla had arrived. She looked like a sea goddess dressed in a fluid turquoise silk kimono, her long red curls glowing around her face and shoulders. Lily saw Ian hand Kyla a glass of wine and watched them toast. A shiver went down her spine. Jealousy rearing its head. Were they really just friends? She shook it away then turned her head back to the band. The female vocalist, dressed in a vintage purple velvet dress and bright-colored shawl, was belting out an old Stevie Nicks song about landslides bringing you down. She could feel the shaky ground beneath her own feet about now.

Ian reappeared and placed two glasses of wine down, then scooted in next to Lily. "I ran into Kyla at the bar. Glad to see her out and about."

Lily sipped her wine. "Why is that?"

Ian looked confused. "Why is what?"

"Why are you glad to see Kyla out?"

He laughed. Sometimes his laugh was maddening, like

he saw right through her and was assuring her nothing was wrong. "Kyla's a bit of a recluse is all. She tends to isolate. How do you like the wine? It's from a local vineyard."

Lily let the wine reveal its flavors in her mouth. A bit of cherry and peach. "Light, delicious. Very nice."

John and the ladies returned to the table with plates piled with food.

"Looks good," Ian said.

"Lots of fancy stuff, too, but that's not for me." Betty buttered her cornbread. "Just got some of Jude's famous chili and this girl's cornbread," she said nodding at Lily. "Caesar salad too."

"Where's the coffee?" Shirley asked while trying to take a dainty bite out of a BBQ wing sloppy with sauce.

"I ordered some for you," Ian said. "They'll bring it out when a fresh pot finishes brewing."

John pointed to his plate. "They're calling these Thai mussels. There's some ginger and coconut in them. Want to try one?"

Lily opened her mouth for a bite as John delivered a forkful. She closed her eyes and savored the subtle taste of curry spice combined with cilantro and the other flavors. "Excellent."

The lights dimmed, and the band, now kicked into high gear, started playing some old rock 'n' roll. A few couples dominated the dance floor.

"You two better get out there and dance before it gets too crowded." Shirley nudged Ian. "Go ahead, ask her."

He stood and offered his hand to Lily. "May I have this dance?"

It had been a long time since she'd danced like this. It took a minute to relax, let go, and just move with the music. Ian said something inaudible to her.

She leaned in closer. "Too loud, can't hear you."

He put his lips to her ear. "I'm not sure I can make it through a whole song of this stuff."

When she looked up at him, he was smiling. His body swayed and seemed to move with hers. Even with this free-style dancing, they were in sync. In the soft light, she admired the angles of Ian's face, the chiseled cheekbones and strong jaw. She'd forgotten just how enjoyable dancing could be. Kyla waved as she danced by with a partner old enough to be her grandfather.

The song ended and everyone applauded. Just as they started back to the table, the band switched to a slow tune. Ian drew her into his arms. She rested her cheek on his shoulder as they swayed to the dreamy melody of "Wonderful Tonight." The room and all the people melted away. She could dance like this all night. He pulled her closer and even the music disappeared. The abrupt sound of clapping brought her back. The electric guitar plunged into "Here Comes the Sun."

"Shall we sit this one out?" Ian asked.

"Definitely."

He took her hand and led her into the back hallway out of sight.

"Where are you taking me?" she asked.

"Over here," he whispered. Out of sight now, he whisked her into his arms for a kiss. Her body was electric, sparks flew between them, and her knees went weak as his lips crushed hers.

Loudly, someone cleared his throat. Ian and Lily turned, startled to see the new chef, Ryan, staring at them and pointing to a storage closet behind them. "Ah, excuse me," he said, "but I need to get some supplies."

Lily giggled. "So sorry," she said, dragging Ian back toward the dining room and smack into Shirley and John.

"You two look flushed. Did you have fun on the dance floor?" Shirley said.

John caught Lily's eye. "Save a dance for me too. But nothing too wild."

"Of course," she answered with a warm smile, almost bumping into Kyla at the buffet.

Lily hurried back to the booth, trying not to make eye contact with Ian. She did not want to burst out laughing. Perhaps she'd had one glass of wine too many.

As soon as they were seated again, Jude approached their table, Ryan in his black chef's coat in tow. "So, everyone, this is my new star chef, Ryan Carr."

Ian put his hand out, suppressing a smile. "Welcome to the island."

Ryan put out his hand, but looked a bit uncomfortable. Lily figured he must spend most of his time in the kitchen, not with the guests. Jude would fix that soon enough.

"Have you tried Ryan's smoked salmon pâté yet?" Jude asked.

"Not yet," Lily said, "but Ian and I were just going to head over to get some food."

"Don't let us stop you," Jude said, taking Ryan's arm and moving him on to the next table.

Shirley gave Lily a wink. "Hey, that Ryan is a hottie."

Betty nudged her sister. "Don't go getting any ideas, he's young enough to be your grandson."

The food line was long. Lily could see the very pregnant Karen at the front handing out plates and directing people to both sides of the table.

Everywhere she looked, people were laughing and having fun. "I think the Fling has turned out to be a great success," Lily said.

Ian nodded. "About this time of year, everyone on the island is getting cabin fever. How are you holding out your first winter here after living in California?"

"Pretty good, got making a fire down and staying busy with my baking business. I've been thinking about volunteering at the local animal shelter, but there's always so much to do lately."

Ian laughed. "Wait until spring and summer. The tourists take over then, and you'll have trouble finding a parking place near town."

Lily wasn't so sure she'd like all those people flooding onto the island, but they would be good for business. If she opened the B&B again, those tourists would probably fill it. It was something to think about.

"Hey, guys, you made it," Karen said, handing them a still warm white plate.

"Shouldn't you be off your feet?" Lily asked.

"It doesn't get much easier than handing out plates. And when I get tired, my husband," she pointed at the nice-looking young man at the table behind her, "well, Mark takes over."

Even with all the people running through the line, the buffet looked appetizing and well-stocked. One point or possibly two for Ryan, Lily thought.

Back at the table was quiet as everyone cleaned their plates. Between the great band, people-watching, the food, and, of course, the wonderful company, Lily couldn't remember having had a better time. It sure beat those stuffy, highly elegant dinner parties she and Brad used to put on. And that kiss...

"This is my kind of song," John said, humming along to "Singing in the Rain." "Shall we have our dance now, Lily?"

With a wide smile, Lily took John's arm and he led her to the dance floor. Playfully, he glided her across the floor. "Sorry, I'm a bit rusty," he said.

Several people in the room started singing along with the familiar, beloved melody. John and Lily joined the chorus as they danced. "What a glorious feeling, I'm happy again."

John twirled her into a spin and back again. "You're a masterful dancer," Lily said, catching her breath.

When the song ended, John kissed her hand and thanked her before leading her back to the table.

"Anyone else for a dance with me?" John asked when they reached the table.

Ian raised his hand. John just shook his head and took a seat.

"So how's everyone doing?" John asked.

Shirley sighed, "I hate to be a party pooper, but I am getting a bit tired."

"You're always a bit tired," Betty said. "Why don't you let the young ones enjoy themselves a little more?"

"That's okay," Lily said. "I'm ready to go when everyone else is."

"In that case, I'd say it's time to say our goodbyes." John rose and offered his hand to Shirley as she slid out of the booth and steadied herself on her feet. They stopped at the bar to say goodbye to Kyla and thank Jude for a great evening. Once outside, coats on, they hurried to the car. John turned on the engine and blasted the defroster to clear the windows. "First stop, I'll drop off the sisters, then a quick stop for Lily."

After what felt like a long drive on the dark, foggy, forested roads, they dropped off Betty and Shirley. Lily could see her porch light from the driveway and was glad she'd turned the heat on before she'd left the house.

Ian stepped out of the car and opened the back door for her. "Mind if I come in for a minute?"

It really wasn't late, and a nightcap with Ian sounded pretty good. "Sure, I'll make us some hot chocolate with Baileys."

"Gramps, I'm staying here. I'll just walk home later. You go on home now."

John waved. "Have fun, you two."

Lily unlocked the door and stepped inside. "I left the thermostat on, but it's still cold in here."

Ian moved toward the wood burner. "Why don't I build us a warm fire?"

"Sounds great, and I'll go mix up our drinks." Truthfully, it felt good to have a man helping around the house. Coming in alone most nights to this big place, with all the empty bedrooms, didn't do much to boost one's spirits. Lily poured some Valrhona chocolate powder into a pan of warming milk then whisked in some sugar. In two glass mugs, she poured a little Baileys and filled the rest of the glass with the hot chocolate. She carried them out into the parlor. Ian was sitting on the loveseat facing the fire, the flames reflecting a rosy glow off his face. She handed him his glass and sat down beside him.

"To spring," she said, raising her glass.

He smiled and clicked her glass. "To spring," he agreed. "It takes a while to get used to the cold, but you will. By next winter you'll barely need a coat." Ian put his arm around her shoulder.

Lily cuddled into his shoulder, savoring the warmth of his body. She wondered where she would be next winter. Hopefully the divorce would be long over and her life would have some direction. She sipped her cocoa and watched the flames through the glass door of the stove. There was nothing more she could want in this moment.

Ian brushed the top of her head with a kiss. "I have an idea you just might like."

She looked up into the dark pools of his eyes. "Yes?" she whispered.

He lifted her chin and pressed his soft lips to hers. The kiss was light, sweet like the first sip of a good wine. "I know a place," he said, "where even *you* will be warm."

Her mind wandered to the large bed upstairs in the Rose Suite, its satin duvet over the feathery down comforter. She imagined his long, lean body next to hers.

"There is a natural hot springs just a ferry ride away over on the Olympic Peninsula. I could whisk you over there tomorrow for a long, hot soak."

It was not what she was expecting, but it was very tempting. A small part of her was disappointed that her fantasy of the suite did not manifest. But the thought of a day of soaking beside Ian in warm, temperate waters in a beautiful natural setting was very appealing. "Sounds glorious."

Ian walked over to the stove and put more logs in the fire. The ashes were molten red and sparks flew as he placed in the new logs.

"What time shall we leave tomorrow?" Lily asked.

He settled back beside her on the couch. "We should probably get an early start, say eight a.m.?"

Lily checked the antique clock on the mantle. It was almost eleven now, and the drink and warmth had worked its magic. She was ready for sleep. "That'll work if we call it a night now."

He took her hand as they walked to the door. The moment right before a man left was always awkward, before she knew if he would kiss her goodbye. He pulled her close, his eyes caressing her face. Slowly, his lips found hers. Drowning in sensation, Lily deepened his kiss. His lips tasted of chocolate and cream, and his intoxicating smell of woods and musk had her melting in his arms. His fingers stroked her neck, lingered through her hair, as his tongue danced in her mouth. Encircled in his arms, she could hardly breathe. The bliss of losing herself so completely was new and enticing.

"You are so beautiful, Lily," he whispered, pulling back and taking her hands in his. "I best go and let you get some sleep." His eyes were filled with longing.

Reluctantly she let her fingers drift from his. "I'll see you in the morning."

"Sleep well," he said, "and don't forget a bathing suit."

When the door shut behind her, Lily leaned back against it for support, then let out a long sigh. She wasn't sure she would sleep at all now. And if she did, she knew where her dreams would take her.

Chapter Twenty-Four

Ian maneuvered his dark blue Volvo wagon onto the small Kitsap state ferry. A dockworker wearing a bright orange vest raised his weathered palm, indicating that Ian should halt his car. Ian turned off the ignition and zipped up his jacket. "Would you like to go up on deck? The ride's about thirty minutes, and the view's better up there, too."

Lily tightened the knot on her wool scarf and exited the car, leaving her canvas bag in the backseat. "I love ferry rides," she said, skipping up the metal staircase. She yanked ineffectively on the heavy door to the deck.

Ian reached over her and opened the door, waving her to enter first. "Be my guest."

The ferry's horn boomed as it began its lumbering voyage across the Puget Sound to the Olympic Peninsula. Lily pressed her nose up to the icy window at the bow of the ship. She hugged her coat closer to her body. "The Olympics are blanketed in snow," she said, giving Ian a questioning look. "Won't it be cold up there?"

He walked up behind her, put his hands around her shoulders, and rested his chin on top of her head. "The elevation of the hot springs is pretty low. We might see a little snow on the ground, but the waters are a steady 103 degrees."

"It's getting into and out of the water I'm worried about," she said with a shiver.

"I'll make sure you're warm," he said, kissing the top of her head.

"I'm sure you will, but how about a cup of hot cocoa for now?"

"Not a problem. One cup of hot cocoa coming right up, the best the snack bar has to offer."

She watched him walk down the ferry aisle. What was she doing here alone, with this incredibly striking man whose kindness was warming her heart? Just standing next to him left her feeling disoriented. The proximity of his lips left her longing for more sweet kisses. But the timing was wrong, not now, not yet. She really should get right back on the ferry in Port Olympia and go home...alone. She turned back to the window and watched the ferry glide through the twirling currents. The sun flashed through the fast-moving clouds, painting patches of color across the gray waters. It was not that long ago a similar ferry brought her to Madrona Island. She could not have made a better decision. Things were still uncertain, but for now, the waters were calm and she was building a new life. Enjoy the moment, she urged herself silently.

A splash of orange sunlight tinged the water before muting to a coppery gray. It reminded her of herself. Water had no color of its own, it could only reflect. She was discovering who she was now without being a reflection of Brad. She had no wish to become a new reflection of yet another man.

Ian returned with two paper cups, steam rising and filling the air with the aroma of milk chocolate. The impact of his smile erased all the thoughts of caution that had just paraded across her brain.

"It's a bit watery, but tasty," he said handing her a cup.

She inhaled the warm Hershey's aroma and took a sip. "Thank you, Ian, this is just perfect."

The landing dock emerged as they rounded the last bend of the journey. "All passengers, please return to your cars," boomed over the loud speaker. They proceeded down the steps, fighting the cold winds coming off the currents, and hurried into the warm protection of the Volvo wagon. Ian started the motor, turned up the heater, and waited for the all clear to exit. Lily gripped the armrest, anticipation building in her stomach.

Tall evergreens lined the narrow two-lane road that hugged the coast. Charming little towns sandwiched between wide-open meadows lush with winter vegetation dotted the landscape. She could imagine how beautiful it would be in the spring when everything was blooming. Following the sign indicating the turn off for Cedar Hot Springs, Ian guided the car up the narrow hillside road. "Ready for a little adventure, Lily? We're almost there."

She hesitated. Was she? "Sure, yes, ready."

"Good," he said, stealing his eyes off the road to glance at her.

As the road climbed in elevation, Lily stared out the window at the half-frozen waterfalls trickling down the hillsides. They proceeded across an ancient-looking wooden bridge flanked on both sides by overgrown ferns and gnarly bare branches. "What an enchanted place."

He grinned. "Just wait."

The road curved sharply to the left before entering a narrow driveway leading to the Cedar Hot Springs Lodge. After parking the car, Ian walked around to open Lily's door. He tossed the backpack with their swimsuits and sundries over his shoulder and took her hand.

Glass doors at the entrance of the massive lodge opened to a lobby with floor-to-ceiling windows sporting a view of the cedar and pine forest. A high wood-beamed ceiling added to the openness of the space. In one corner, a river rock fireplace was ablaze with a roaring fire. After registering for day passes, they retreated to the dressing rooms to change into their swimsuits. Wrapped up tight in the plush terrycloth robe provided by the lodge, Lily walked outside toward the warm springs. Ian was sitting on the edge of a stone-lined pool, his legs dangling in the water. A few people were soaking on the other side of the pool. He waved her over.

She was so nervous about revealing herself in a bathing suit that she almost slipped on the steps as she made her grand entrance. Hair piled high in a clip, she dropped her robe to the deck and descended quickly into the bubbling water. The sting of circulation from the heat melted rapidly into comforting warmth. She peeked discreetly at Ian's body. His olive-skinned shoulders were sculpted with sinewy muscles, and his skin was slick from the steaming spring. Water beads glistened across his smooth, firm chest.

She could feel Ian's eyes on her pale skin as she had waded over to join him in the bubbling water. His smooth skin was a stark contrast next to her porcelain complexion.

"Shall we?" He dropped his body into the water and reached his hand out to her.

"Ahhhh, it's so warm and wonderful," she said. They sat on the submerged benches lining the pool. Every muscle in her body melted; she leaned back and closed her eyes. A lone raven cawed in the distance as the steam and mist danced across her face and hair.

She opened her eyes and let the smell of the cedar forest and cold, fresh air fill her. White patches of snow lined the hillside rich with evergreens and ferns. "Thank you for bringing me here, it's wonderful."

"I'm glad we came on a Sunday. It's not very crowded because everyone is going home today." Ian put his arm around her and lightly massaged her shoulders. "These waters have healing properties. The Native Americans believed they could heal ailments of body and soul."

"I can see why, I don't remember the last time I felt this relaxed." The other couple in the pool climbed out, leaving Ian and Lily the only ones there. Lily wasn't sure mixing these luscious waters and Ian's steaming body was such a good idea. But her defenses were melting right along with the tension in her muscles.

Ian's moist male scent in such close proximity, and his scantily clad body, shot up the temperature of the pool a bit too high. She rose up to allow the winter air to cool down the flush across her face and neck. She could feel Ian's penetrating gaze caress her body. She shyly stole a look at him. For a moment, the impulse to run overwhelmed her. Everything felt too perfect and her gun-shy heart rebelled.

"Is the pool too warm for you?" Ian inquired.

She shook her head, "No, no, it's wonderful really." She slid back under the water, closed her eyes, and let the springs blissfully saturate every cell of her body.

Ian brushed a wisp of damp hair from her forehead. The gesture jolted her back to the moment, back into his mesmerizing eyes that were focused directly on her lips. His fingers caressed the skin of her cheek, lingered on the surface of her mouth. Resistance melting, her lips parted in longing and anticipation. The gentle kiss was disarming, her ardent response coming from a place she'd never known before.

With a rapid intake of breath, she pulled back. Time was suspended, everything around her blurred as she fought to regain control. "I think I need to get out," she said, scrambling up the steps. "The heat is making me a bit light headed." She wrapped herself in the terrycloth robe and pulled it tight.

Ian was right behind her, helping to secure the sash. He braced her shoulder to steady her. "Let's try some food and drink. It might help."

Relieved to move away from the pools, she readily agreed. It was after two in the afternoon, and she'd not eaten since breakfast, early that morning.

After exiting the dressing room, back in her warm clothes, Lily entered the dining room. Her composure was now restored. Ian, dressed in a teal-blue sweater, was waiting at a table by the window. Her breath caught at his good looks.

"How are you feeling?" he asked.

"I'm feeling much better now, thank you." She sat down and picked up a menu.

"Glad to hear it."

She watched him scan his menu. His hair was still moist and curling a little at the base of his neck. He looked up, and the sight of his crooked smile made her bury her face back in the menu. One minute she couldn't take her eyes off him and the next she felt like a shy schoolgirl.

A waiter appeared and announced the specials. "I can recommend our winter warm up: cream of potato leek soup, salmon in puffed pastry and mixed winter vegetable frittata."

"Sounds perfect," Lily said.

"Make it two," Ian followed. "Would you like a glass of wine, Lily?"

She nodded and the waiter pointed to an exquisite bottle of Oregon Pinot Gris on the wine list.

"A perfect complement," Ian said, ordering a bottle.

The daylight was dimming outside, and remnants of the deep scarlet and gold sunset reflected through the trees and across the small patches of snow along the ground. Busboys lit the candles on the table while the waiter poured their wine. Lily took a sip of her wine. It was floral, but not too sweet. Time seemed to slow as each course came out and they polished off the bottle of wine. Classical music played in the background as night fell. She did not want this to end. The waiter approached their table with a large tray of tempting-looking desserts. Lily shook her head no. "Not another bite for me."

Ian laughed. "As incredible as they look, I have to pass too."

"Shall I get your check then, sir?" the waiter asked.

"That would be fine," Ian answered.

Ian and Lily held hands across the table.

"It's getting dark and it's a long drive back down the mountain," Ian said.

Lily looked out the window at the black night. The roads would be slippery, and they had been drinking. Not a good match at all.

"We could see if they have a cabin available and leave first thing in the morning," he continued. "All I have to do is call home and let Grandpa John and Jason know I'll be home tomorrow."

Her heart leapt. She closed her eyes, imagining drifting off to sleep in Ian's arms. She opened her eyes and searched his.

"No pressure, Lily. I'll sleep on the couch if you want."

The kindness in his expression confirmed what her heart told her; she could trust this man. "Yes, let's stay."

✦✦✦

Ian made sure Lily was comfortable in a wicker rocker in the lobby, then proceeded to the reception desk to request a cabin for the night. The clerk handed him the key to the River Suite. Ian noticed the Cedar Hot Springs t-shirts for sale behind the counter and bought two extra-large shirts to act as pajamas for the night.

"A souvenir?" Lily asked when Ian returned and held up his purchase.

"A nightshirt," he said, grinning. "Only the best for you." He tossed it and she caught it mid-air.

"How thoughtful," she laughed.

Hand in hand, they walked along the well-lit path and located the cedar and stone cabin with a wooden deck hanging out over the river rock bed.

Ian unlocked the door, turned on the light, and laid his backpack on the small desk. The wood-paneled cabin consisted of a sitting area with a stone fireplace, a separate bedroom, and a large bath. French doors opened onto the deck facing out to the river.

"How cozy." Lily approached the fireplace. "There's even a bundle of firewood."

"Is that a hint?" Ian asked.

"I am fully capable of building one myself now," Lily said.

"Of course you are. Still, I'm happy to do it." Ian knelt then laid some kindling down and struck a large match from a tin next to the fireplace. It caught quickly, and he placed some of the cut wood in angles on top of the licking flames. "This should warm things up a bit." As if he needed that. Just one look at Lily and that was all the heat he needed.

"Look at this," Lily said, holding up two hand-carved walking sticks. "These are for us to use if we go for a hike in the forest. And a trail guide too."

Ian ran his hand up the smooth dark wood of the walking stick, noting the precision carving and curved handle. "Excellent craftsmanship."

He watched Lily wander about the cabin. "There's a coffee maker and fluffy towels in the bathroom," she said, returning to the main room, curling into the cushy sofa and tossing off her shoes.

"Would you like a foot massage?" Ian asked, sliding over next to her.

She lifted her leg and placed her foot in his lap. "Sounds nice."

He watched her close her eyes and lean her head back into the sofa. Gently, he removed her socks then massaged each toe. His fingers slipped between the toes and worked their way down her foot. Faint sighs of contentment were the only sound as he stroked the soles of her feet.

"Are you getting sleepy?" he asked.

She opened her eyes, and he knew the answer to the question.

"A bit," she said, obviously trying to force herself awake.

"Bedroom's all yours," he said.

Ian watched as she entered the bedroom and closed the door behind her. The aging couch opened to a bed, the desk clerk had told him. He checked the small closet for extra blankets and a pillow and started to make up the bed.

"You awake?" Lily stood in the door in nothing but the extra-large t-shirt.

Ian nodded, His eyes feasting on the silhouette of her body beneath the thin shirt.

"I can't bear to think of you on that uncomfortable old sofa-bed. There's a warm down comforter on the bed and plenty of space for you."

"I think I'll take you up on that offer!" Ian tossed the scratchy wool blanket on the sofa and followed her into the bedroom.

"To sleep only," Lily said.

He looked at her long, creamy legs and doubted he could just sleep beside her. But the last thing he wanted to say was no to her. He followed her into the bedroom and watched her hop into the bed and pull the covers up to her chin.

Ian slipped off his jeans and t-shirt and lay down far to the other side of the mattress over by the window.

"Thanks," he said, "this is so much better."

"You're welcome." Lily switched off the light and they both lay there in the total darkness of a moonless night.

Ian closed his eyes and tried not to think about her warm, soft body only a few inches away. He flipped on one side then the other. This was impossible; there was no way he would be able to sleep. He considered going back out to the couch but did not want to wake her with his movements. Then she turned over and he knew she was awake, too. Every part of his being longed to take her in his arms, to bury his face in her silky hair and... Stop, he told himself, think of something else.

"Ian?"

He considered not answering, but that was ridiculous. "Yes, Lily?"

"I can't sleep. Would you hold me?"

She did not have to ask twice. He rolled toward her and wrapped her in his arms. Lily laid her head into his shoulder. He kissed her hair and let his lips linger across her forehead and cheek. When she lifted her face to his, their lips met in a soft kiss that quickly deepened into a passionate embrace. Lily raked her fingers through his hair, her hands caressing his neck and running down his back. He tightened his embrace as she pressed her body into his.

"Lily," he gasped. "I want you. You don't know how much."

She moaned as he lifted her t-shirt over her head and

tossed it to the floor. He traced her perfect breasts with his fingertips then bent to gently kiss them. "So beautiful," he whispered.

Lily pulled him into her silky, moist body, whispering his name, running her tongue down his neck while her fingers gripped his back.

He rolled her beneath him as he placed his slick body, burning with passion, over hers. He drifted, lost in an ecstasy he never thought he'd find again.

✦✦✦

Ian smiled in his sleep. He was dreaming of Lily, dreaming he could smell the sweet herbal scent of her hair, that her warm body with its silk skin was cuddled beside him. He reached out and felt the warmth of her leg under his hand, and it startled him. He was fully awake now, and the memory of the night rushed back to him. He smiled. Perched on one elbow, he marveled at the remarkable woman sleeping beside him. She looked like a sleeping angel, golden hair swirled across the pillow like a halo around her lovely face.

She stirred and his heartbeat picked up speed. He did not want to wake her. Fear gripped his heart. What if she woke up and was upset at finding herself in bed with him? He had pushed gently, but not against her will. She was like a newborn colt, stumbling around on fragile legs trying to walk by herself. He wanted to protect her and give her that chance. He did not mean to rush her, but his passion for her had overtaken him. Despite their obvious attraction for one another, until now her fear had kept her from letting go. He hoped something had changed for them last night and that now he could open his heart to her. The realization that he had grown so fond of her hit him with a gale force.

Agitated, he carefully lifted off the blanket and slid out of bed. He retrieved his jeans and t-shirt from the floor and slipped them on. He paced the oak floor, intermittently glancing over at Lily to be sure his silent vigil did not wake her. What was he doing? She was not even divorced, and he was in a very vulnerable position himself, opening his heart to someone who could just as easily return to her husband, leave the island. Just the thought of it terrified him; he could not bear to lose another woman he loved.

He remembered his sketchpad and pencils in his backpack. With supplies in hand, he quietly positioned himself in the wicker chair opposite the bed and studied his subject with an artist's eye and distance. Yes…this feels better, he thought, just draw and don't think. He sketched her face with broad strokes, highlighting the angular cheekbones and wide curvaceous lips. Her long neck and shapely shoulders peeked above the fluffy down comforter. He drew the bed floating on abstract images of bubbling, misty water. Enormous heron wings crossed the sky, casting shadows on the cedar trees below. Ian surveyed his sketch and smiled. It would make a good painting someday.

"You look very pleased with yourself," a female voice said with a giggle.

Taken aback, Ian looked up to see Lily sitting up in bed, sporting a teasing grin. "Absorbed in your work?" she joked. "Let me see what you've drawn."

He laid his drawing down. "Later, when it's ready."

"Brr, it's cold in here," she said, pulling the covers up to her chin.

Ian moved to the bed and bent over to give her a soft kiss on the lips. "Good morning, beautiful. Do you want me to come under the covers and warm you up?" He saw hesitation in her eyes and the way they darted to the clock. He straightened up. "How about I turn on the heat, put on some shoes, and get us some lattés from the lobby?"

"Great idea. Any food would be appreciated too," Lily said.

He put on his tennis shoes and pulled a charcoal-gray sweatshirt over his head. "I think I remember something about a continental breakfast. Be back in a sec."

Ian hummed as he sauntered down the hall. "Good sign she wants to stay for breakfast," he mumbled to himself. The lobby was toasty and filled with the smell of fresh pastries and coffee. At the start of the buffet were trays with extendable legs that could be pulled down if you wanted breakfast in bed. Great idea, he thought. He filled the tray with flaky croissants, thick loganberry jam, and a glass custard cup filled with fruit salad.

A young attendant walked by with refills for the buffet tables, and Ian stopped him with a question. "Where's the coffee?"

He pointed to the automatic espresso machine on the other side of the lobby. "It's self-serve, sir. Real easy, though, just push a button for the kind you want. Mochas, lattés, you pick."

Ian perched two large round cups on the tray and headed for the machine. He pushed the various buttons, and within minutes the cups were filled with steaming lattés. Balancing the tray carefully, he walked back to the cabin and used his foot to knock on the door.

Lily answered wrapped in a terrycloth robe provided by the lodge. She looked at the trays full of food. "Yum. Great job, Ian."

"You haven't seen the best part yet. Hop back in bed."

Lily frowned.

"Trust me."

She jumped on the bed and stuffed a few pillows behind

her back. Ian lifted a tray and released the wooden legs. "Voila!" he said, grinning. "Breakfast in bed."

He placed the tray legs over Lily's lap first, and then joined her in bed. He loved watching her eat. She savored every flaky bite of jam-covered croissant with a childlike pleasure. The comfortable silence between them as they ate felt natural and right. The clock registered 10:30 a.m. Ian hated the thought that they would have to check out today. Maybe it was best they left soon, that he backed off a little and gave her some space.

"Check out is at noon," Ian said between bites.

Lily looked up at him, but he couldn't distinguish the look in her eyes.

She took a last sip of her coffee. "Would you like to shower first?" she asked.

After last night, he was kind of hoping they would shower together, but it was obvious she was starting to pull away again. "You go," he said. She looked uncomfortable about getting out of bed. Ian turned his back to her. "Not looking, all clear."

He felt her slip out of the bed and heard the bathroom door close behind her. A sharp pain crossed his chest. He did not want this to be just a one-night stand. He got out of bed and rolled up the drawing he'd made while Lily slept, then retreated to the sitting area so she could have her privacy when she came out of the shower. We'll leave as soon as she's ready, he told himself. And then? He just wouldn't think about it right now.

◆ ◆ ◆ ◆

Lily stared out the passenger window, admiring the view on the drive down the mountain road. Neither one of them had spoken since they got in the car. The awkwardness of the situation caught in her throat. Last night seemed like a dream. She had melted into his arms until she no longer knew where her body stopped and his began. His smooth, strong body... she could barely think of it without sighing. But now, in the light of day, without the wine and soothing hot waters of the spring, she felt shy, uncertain. He seemed anxious to get back in bed with her this morning, but she'd panicked. She could see the pain in his eyes when she asked to shower alone, but she needed some space to figure this all out.

She glanced over at him and longed to run her fingers along his carved cheekbones and down to his unbelievably soft lips. Just thinking of his kisses left her knees weak. Ian did not look back at her. She wouldn't blame him for being upset. Last night she'd thrown herself into his wondrous arms without a protest. Then this morning she was embarrassed for him to see her naked. Any woman would want him, and it was clear many women did. What was she doing? She was not even divorced and had no idea where her life was going. It would be so easy to turn to him, to let his kisses wash all her cares away. But at what price?

The waters of the Sound were a solid gray as the ferry made its silent crossing in the dense fog. Was it only yesterday that Ian brought her hot chocolate from the snack bar?

"We're lucky the ferry is still running in this weather," Ian said.

She searched her mind for something to say, something to smooth the tension. "Thank you for sharing that wonderful place with me," she finally said.

He turned to face her. Hope flickered in his eyes. "I'm glad you enjoyed it. I sure did."

"Who wouldn't?" she said.

The ferry horn blasted, alerting passengers to return to

their cars. They hurried down the stairs and back into the Volvo. "I'll turn the heat on as soon as they let us start the cars," Ian said.

She wanted to rest her head on his shoulder, feel his warmth pour into her. But she hesitated. She did not want to lead him on when she just wasn't sure what she felt or what she wanted. He had been through enough pain, too.

When he pulled into her driveway, Ian carried her bag and walked her to the door.

"I'll see you next week when I return to the Island," he said.

Impulsively, Lily threw her arms around his neck and hugged him. He returned her hug, but eventually he dropped his arms, releasing her, and walked back to the car.

Back inside the house, Lily tossed her bag of clothes on the floor of her room in the innkeeper's quarters. She lay down on top of the neatly made bed. It was hard to say goodbye when he'd dropped her at her door. Hard to watch him leave the island for the week. But some time apart was exactly what she thought would be best, and that is what she would tell him. Her nerve was failing as she thought about calling and telling him she needed a break. Then she remembered he had given her his business card. She could email him. It was cowardly, but she knew if she heard his voice or looked into those soulful eyes, she might back down.

She got up and rummaged through her desk until she found the card. Ian McPherson—Artist, it said. The computer took a minute to boot up. Lily composed the words carefully. She just needed some time apart to think. She cared about him, but timing and circumstances made it too hard right now. She signed it, "with affection, Lily." She hesitated before hitting send. Her heart screamed no, but it was the right thing to do... for now. She pressed send, closed the computer, and wondered how she would face this day.

Chapter Twenty-Five

The tendrils of fog crept down the jagged cliff nesting in the crags, dispersing into thin fingers as they reached for the sky. The effect reminded Lily of the ancient isle of Avalon, floating in the mist, only visible to those with the sight…the privileged few. If you answered its call, the island lured you in; first to its darkest places, testing your strength, revealing your weaknesses. But for those who survived the initiation, unparalleled beauty was revealed. And she had survived not only the winter turning mercifully toward spring, but the dark places that divorce had driven her to.

The fog spilled into the cove, looking like steam rising above a boiling pot. Layers of silver and blue filled the bay. She had a lot of work to do today, business was picking up. Lily had her day planned filling orders for Jude and for the local grocery's deli. She checked her calendar for the exact numbers. It was Saturday, and she'd seen Ian's car arrive last night. He had not been back to the island in almost two weeks. Not since she sent the email. His reply had been sweet, that he would wait until she was ready. Lily missed him but was much more focused on her work without him there.

Out the office window she noticed someone walking toward her drive. It was Ian crossing the field with a bouquet of tulips. "Ugh, I told him I needed some space," she muttered to herself. She watched him walk to the old mailbox and put the bouquet inside, then turn and walk away. Disappointment gripped her. He could have come inside, she thought. No…good. He's keeping his distance. Oh, I don't know what I want! She resisted the urge to go to the mailbox, take the flowers, and run after him. Instead she waited a few minutes before heading out there.

The dusty path going up the driveway to the mailbox was bordered by blooming irises, wild pink lupines, and fragrant herbs. Since winter had turned to spring and summer's promise was in the air, the meadow was starting to turn to shades of emerald, and the towering pines flanking it provided shade for the wild ferns. The sun was climbing overhead and just starting to penetrate the misty fog.

She retrieved the pink tulips and today's mail, brought them into the kitchen, and laid them on the counter. The note said: *Lily, miss seeing you. Come by or call when you have time. ~Ian*

Short, simple, to the point. She weighed the note in her hand. Communication was not one of his strongest points, but then she had told him to give her some space. He seemed too good to be true, just like Brad had at first. There was no way she was going to rush into anything; she had a business to build, a future to figure out.

They were a stark contrast to the blood-red roses Brad had brought her. Lily tried to decide whether to place them in a vase or into the garbage. The vase won out. Pretty tricky. He brings me flowers so when I look at them I think of him. Possibly the garbage can was the better choice after all.

She ruffled through the mail and found another plain envelope with no return address. Her heart dropped into her stomach as she ripped it open.

You might as well start packing because the house will be mine soon.

Who was sending these and why? It was not Brad. Some crazy person probably. It made Lily uneasy, but she crushed the note in her hand and threw it in the wastebasket.

On to something more pleasurable, like trying out her new finds from the overflowing recipe box her grandmother had left in the kitchen. She opened the box and turned a well-worn card over. Yum, lavender orange syrup over stuffed French toast, sounds like a breakfast from a dream. She read over the ingredients, punctuating them with the occasional blissful sigh, then closed her eyes and imagined–fresh-squeezed orange juice, just-picked lavender sprigs from the garden, cinnamon, vanilla, and thick maple syrup drizzled over puffy French toast browned in butter, stuffed with cream cheese and orange zest. Heavenly!

She flipped through the box overflowing with more precious recipes. She sensed aromas floating up from the kitchen and could hear her grandma's soft hum as she cooked.

Her taste buds were alert as she read over what must have been her grandmother's favorites: Lemon coconut bread pudding, potato sour cream pie, asparagus feta frittata, bittersweet chocolate cherry muffins. Her hands itched to cook them all. But who would eat them? She spread cards from every category across the table: breakfast treats, salads, baked goods, gourmet casseroles, and specials of the house. There were certainly enough of them to make a go of it as a decent business and run a full bed and breakfast at some point. Some of the other restaurants in town would carry a few products too.

She held up the two index cards written in her grandmother's distinct hand. Quickly assessing the ingredients, Lily knew these would be scrumptious and would work for Jude and the deli at Cascade Market. She could produce these in individual sizes or in a large batch. Customers would love this Fennel Sausage Frittata with artichoke hearts and provolone cheese.

Her mouth watered as she read each ingredient. Ideas for a packaging logo flooded her mind. A cute label with the name, Grandma Maggie's Baking Company. The second card held a recipe with multiple uses–Inn Style Cookies.

Perfect! Cookies, batches and batches, would adorn her kitchen counters starting today. Besides selling them to the stores, they might work for a mail order item as well. Of course, when she reopened the B&B, they could be her afternoon cookie jar filler.

She would show Brad…she would show herself.

She could hear Mary arriving through the front door and went to greet her.

"Afternoon, Lily. I brought some fresh eggs and just-pressed apple juice from Wasson's Farm." Mary smelled the flowers. "Oh, how lovely. Secret admirer?"

"I'm glad you like them. They're yours. Please take them home with you."

Mary replied, "But they're beautiful and they're yours."

Lily insisted.

"Consider them gone," Mary said. "Now, what's on the menu today?"

Lily started taking out ingredients. "We're baking cranberry scones and chocolate cherry cookies."

"Let's roll up our sleeves and get to work." Mary's melodic humming blended with sounds from the mixer and helped brighten the cold spring morning.

Lily measured out the dark chocolate, sour cream, butter

and sugar, and blended in the cherries while Mary greased the pans. "We're doing three dozen of each today. I made the quiches earlier. One is pesto and feta and the other is mushroom and spinach."

Mary mixed and cooled and packed several batches, then washed all of the pots and pans. Lily wondered how she could ever do all this without her. Lily hoped her grandmother's trust was paying Mary well for the upkeep.

Mary dried her hands and approached Lily.

"Hate to remind you, but there's still a dang leak under the kitchen sink. Looks like it might be getting worse."

"I'll deal with it, tomorrow, promise," Lily said.

Mary zipped up her coat. "Don't wait too long. I'm sure my Aunt Betty would be happy to come over and fix it right up for you."

"Great idea, thanks." Lily waved goodbye and Mary walked out the back path past the pond to her home up the hill.

✦✦✦✦

"You've been looking out that window all morning, son. If it hasn't appeared by now, it's probably not going to."

Ian turned away from the window and took a seat at the kitchen table. "You're probably right, Gramps. Any coffee left?"

John poured them both a cup and joined Ian at the table.

"I just can't lose her, not now that I finally found her."

John patted Ian on the back. "The course of true love is not always smooth."

"Right," he said, breaking a smile. "And I suppose you know just what I should do now that she's pulled away?"

John sipped his coffee. "You know what to do. It may not

be your strongest quality, but patience is what's called for."

"I know, I know. But what if she's never ready, what if she decides not to stay here, what if…?"

John held a palm out to stop. "Whoa, boy, all those what ifs are going to get you nowhere. If Lily is anything like her grandmother, and I think she is, she'll find her way."

There was nothing more he could do. His gramps was right. Worrying was driving him crazy anyway. He needed to work, to start another painting, and he knew just which one it would be.

Ian rose and rinsed his cup out in the sink. "Thanks for the coffee and advice, Gramps. I'm off to the studio."

"Any time. Try trusting a little. It just might work."

Ian walked out the back door and looked over to Lily's place. Smoke rose from her chimney and he could smell the baking aromas from Lily's house drifting across the field as he walked to his studio in the old barn. His mouth watered. He'd really like to drop in for samples and tried to think of an excuse to do so. But no, he decided, he didn't want to rush her or push her away. She had not called after he dropped off the flowers this morning, and that was probably a sign she had not changed her mind about taking a break in their relationship.

One thing he did know now, his feelings for Lily were real. Her kindness to his son, his grandfather, her neighbors, and even to Gretel showed her generous heart. He admired her creativity and the inner strength it took for her to leave a bad marriage and be willing to start again. She was an amazing woman, and he could wait as long as it took. The week away in New York for his art opening only confirmed that. He could not stop thinking of her. All the beautiful women in New York, and all he wanted to do was come home to Madrona Island and be with Lily.

Sometimes his impatience got the best of him, but his heart could not take another loss. Gramps's wisdom prevailed, as always, in his mind. Do whatever it takes to help her feel safe. After that piece of work she had as a husband, Brad, no wonder she was gun shy to get involved with another man. He would never hurt her. For now he would do whatever he could to support her choices and watch her bloom. And keep his hands off, as hard as it was.

Ian took out the sketch and placed it beside his easel with the new canvas on it. He closed his eyes and could see the images, mist, steam, a river, and golden hair across a pillow of clouds.

✦✦✦✦

It was a day well spent baking with Mary, and Lily felt the satisfaction of creating great food that would bring in money and pay a few of the many bills. Speaking of bills, she better go pick up the mail from the table where she'd left it.

There was a notification from the county, a large envelope from her attorney, and a colored paper full of ads for this week's special at the Cascade Market. Butter was on sale; she'd needed to run in and pick some up. She closed her eyes and took a deep breath. She could wait until tomorrow to open the remaining mail. But if she did, she probably would not sleep all night worrying. Sitting down at the dining room table, she ripped open the notice from the county. In large red letters, a statement for property taxes was marked past due. The note said something about a reassessment of the property value. Heart pounding, her eyes raced to the bottom of the page to see the amount: $3,500. It might as well have been three million, it was more than she could afford right now.

She rubbed the back of her neck, fighting off the tight

shoulders and building headache. "Do I dare open the one from the attorney?" Tears threatened at the thought of what was waiting inside the envelope. "Might as well get it all over with, tear the bandage off fast."

She ripped it open and spilled the contents onto the table. On embossed stationery, Karl had typed her a note. A large packet of forms filled with numbers was attached. Her breath stopped as she read the note.

Lily,

This is to notify you that we have finished the evaluation of all property and assets in regard to your divorce proceedings with Brad Mitchell. I am afraid it is not good news. There is nothing of any real value that would warrant going to court over. In regards to the Brentwood home, the house has a higher mortgage than it is valued at and is facing foreclosure. Most all of the assets, including the automobiles are leased. Due to exorbitant credit card bills, Brad is filing for bankruptcy. If you still would like to retain my services, I will need another $10,000 retainer to continue with these proceedings and quite a bit more if this case goes to court. My suggestion is you consider using a mediator to finish off the final divorce agreement.

Good luck,

Karl Goldberg, Attorney at Law

Ominous blue-black clouds hung in the dark sky out her window. Rain pounded down on her roof and flew into her windows sideways. Fatigue and a chill that penetrated through her bones seemed impossible to shake. She'd lost her appetite for dinner. Every muscle in her body was tight and longed for a luxurious soak and the comfort it would bring.

The thought of a hot bath in the deep, claw-foot bathtub in the Honeymoon Suite sounded inviting. The rain had stopped as fast as it started, and from the small bathroom window, she could see the last rays of the sunset turning the sky shades of rose and violet. The night sky crept in from the east, and the dark clouds headed south toward Seattle. Under the sink she found all types of bath powders and potions. She chose the deep green "Total Relaxation" salts, turned on the hot water, and dropped two handfuls of the eucalyptus-scented powder into the water. As a final touch, she squeezed pale orange liquid bubble bath under the old brass faucet.

On the shelf over the tub was a collection of candles, some shaped like shells, some like flowers, and others like pillars. Ceremoniously, she lit each one, lowered the light, and watched the room fill with a rosy glow. Iridescent suds foamed in the tub, lit only by candlelight. The night sky claimed the scene outside. She caught a glimpse out the window of the silver moon rising above the Olympics as she eased her aching body into the hot water. She melted back, eyes closed. *Magic, pure magic,* she thought.

She remembered when she and Ian had sat in the hot springs together, entangled in each other's arms. Her heart raced with the memory. A vision of his full lips, parted and warm, increased her longing. Sinking down into the caressing suds, she released her breath and let the herbal water pull the tension from her muscles. She pushed Ian from her mind and let the moment be enough.

Chapter Twenty-Six

It was 7:00 a.m. Who the heck was calling this early in the morning? Lily wondered. She hadn't even finished making coffee yet. The caller ID on the kitchen phone showed Brad's number. She hesitated. Under their lawyer's instructions, they were not supposed to speak directly to each other. What did it matter now? After that letter, there was no way she could continue to retain a lawyer. She might as well start dealing with Brad directly.

"Hello," she answered.

"Lily, this is Brad, please don't hang up."

She sighed. "I wasn't planning to. I received a letter from my lawyer we need to discuss." She added water and turned on the coffee pot.

"I received the same letter," he said.

The line got quiet, and Lily wondered if they had lost the connection. Very softly, she heard Brad speak.

"I'm sorry."

She couldn't believe what she was hearing. She couldn't remember him ever apologizing, at least not for many years. Feelings surfaced, but she couldn't distinguish whether they were of pity or just familiarity.

"It's all my fault, Lily. I ruined everything. I just wanted you to be happy, for us to have a good life. Then everything started falling apart. I thought if I could just mortgage the house, buy more time…"

The aroma of fresh-made coffee filled the room. Lily paced, trying to catch her breath. "You should have told me, Brad."

"I know, I know," he said.

"You should have told me a lot of things. Like about the affair…"

Brad's voice escalated. "That's over now, done. I was just crazy and made a mistake. You're the only one I love, Lily, always have been."

It was all too much, and she couldn't get any words out for fear she would break down crying. She should probably hang up.

"Lily, let's drop all this divorce stuff, stop feeding money to the bloodthirsty lawyers."

"What about mediation?" she said.

"We have over ten years invested in this marriage. We could start again, have a family."

She shook her head from side to side. Now he brings up a child, the one thing I really wanted and he wouldn't even consider.

"I have to think about all this. I'll get back to you."

"I'll be waiting, Lily. I love you."

She almost said love you, too, but caught herself and said goodbye. She felt dizzy and made her way to the rocker in the parlor to sit down. It was early May, and on days like this, she still needed to light a fire. She pulled the knitted throw around her, rocked and stared out the window toward the Sound. If she stopped the divorce, it would be one less thing weighing on her shoulders, one less responsibility. This house, the taxes, the leaking plumbing, no money coming from the divorce, and she still owed the attorney.

If only everything could go back the way it was before, simple, uncomplicated. Was it really? Brad took care of everything, but then she could never make a choice on her own. Could he really change? And Ian, was he just a fantasy, too good to be true? An artist who buried himself in his work and was still in love with the wife he lost? Was she kidding herself that she could make a business work on this small island? The dark, damp thoughts matched the clouds closing in on the house and grounds.

Maybe she would just go back to bed. There were no clients who needed a delivery today. Then she remembered, Betty had offered to come over this morning around eight and take a look at the leak in the kitchen. That was late for Betty; sometimes Lily saw their lights on before six in the morning. She walked back in the kitchen and poured herself a cup of coffee. If the plumbing needed expensive parts, it would have to just go on leaking. She better get dressed before Betty arrived bursting with energy.

At 8:00 AM sharp, Betty knocked on the kitchen door then poked her head in. "Yoo-hoo, you up, girl?"

Lily wandered into the kitchen. "Sure am, thanks for coming by."

Betty had arrived with a large toolbox and a flashlight. She got down on her knees by the kitchen sink. "Let me get a look under here and see what's happening."

Lily held her breath; she did not need any more bad news.

"Looks like you need some new piping, probably a snake down the drain to clean it all out, too. I can get an estimate on the parts and do the labor myself."

"Thanks, Betty, what a kind offer. But I'm afraid I'm short

of cash right now."

Betty stood and washed her hands in the sink. "No problem, we can loan you the money and get this fixed up. And Mary's willing to keep working until you can pay her."

"What are you talking about paying Mary? Doesn't my grandmother's estate pay her directly?"

Betty shook her head. "Not for a while now, I'm afraid. She doesn't mind. None of us do."

Someone being that nice was the last straw, and Lily started to cry.

Betty looked confused. "Did I say something wrong?"

"No, no, of course not. That is so kind of you. I'm just overwhelmed right now. Not been a great few days."

"It'll work out, always does," Betty said, picking up her tools. "Loan's available if you want it, just let us know."

Lily took a plastic container of cookies down from the shelf and handed them to her neighbor. "Thanks again."

Right now, she needed time to think. She could call her mother and go over the pros and cons of Brad's offer. Maybe she wouldn't. Her mother would go ballistic at the thought of Brad, no matter how many apologies he made. And she'd offer her more money. She'd already done enough to help. A list might help instead, weigh out her options. She was still married to him, was it worth another try?

The Guestbook. She would open it to wherever it led her. Her grandmother would help guide her. She retrieved it from the nightstand and propped up on her bed. The book was beautiful; she could imagine Grandma Maggie holding it in her hands. Lily closed her eyes and opened the book to an entry near the end.

Maggie,
    We were so glad to be some of your last guests at the

Inn. We were just devastated when were heard you were closing this place. There will never be another quite like it. Here for you if you need us.
   Rowena and Mare–Coupeville, WA

Lily closed the book. She had let so many people down. Her grandmother, her mother, her husband, herself. If only she had been here for her grandma, maybe she could have helped her keep Madrona Island Inn open. She could be there for her husband now, help him rebuild, open a business in LA, where the economy was a little better. She turned to the last entry of the Guestbook.

Dear Lily the Innkeeper,
   I hope you enjoy this place as much as I have, and that love finds you here as it did me.
   Love,
   Your Grandma Maggie

She dropped the book on the bed. Her grandmother's last message to her. An Innkeeper. How could she pull it off with all the issues facing her? How could she not? She did not want to disappoint her grandmother once again. It all came down to what she herself wanted at this moment and what she was willing to do to get it.

She thought about Betty walking the path back home in hiking boots, jeans, a parka, and knit hat. What a sight to see. Eighty years old and she's offering to fix my kitchen plumbing. The women here on the island were something else. She could learn from them. So were some of the men, come to think of it. Like the nice mechanic who offered to fix her car for the cost of the parts and cookies for the next month.

She should bring some cookies over to Grandpa John and

a few extra for Ian and Jason. She'd been kind of a recluse lately, and they could be a peace offering of sorts.

After retrieving a batch from the kitchen, Lily threw on a coat and started across the field. Spring grasses were coming up, and it was getting harder to walk across. John said he'd get his driving mower out soon and take care of it. Jason was sitting on a bench outside, playing a game with a friend. What a sweet kid, she hadn't seen him in a while either.

"Cookies!" he said, jumping to his feet.

Lily waved. "Plenty for all of you."

She looked over to the door and saw Ian's sinewy body leaning against the frame. This was going to be harder than she thought. One look at him and she wanted…she didn't want to think about what she wanted.

She held up the container. "Brought some cookies for you all."

Grandpa John joined Ian at the door. "Lily, so good to see you." He walked down the porch steps and gave her a big hug. "Come on in. Ian, get the milk out."

John stopped for a moment leaning against the door frame.

"Are you alright?" Lily asked.

"Fine, fine," he said, "Just a bit dizzy there for a moment."

The young boys followed behind and gathered at the kitchen table. "What kind are they?" Jason asked.

"I tried some new kinds, I hope you like them. One is chocolate chunk with salted caramel, and the other is my grandma's Inn Style cookies. You might have had those before."

"I remember those," Ian said, his eyes searching hers. "They're great."

She held his gaze; there was no anger there, only longing. Could it really be for her?

John and the boys scarfed down the cookies, but Ian hadn't

moved from his place by the stove. Lily picked up a couple Inn Style cookies, placed them on a napkin, and brought them over to Ian.

"Thanks," he said, taking a bite. "Taste pretty good, you have the touch." He reached over and took her hand. "I've missed you."

Shoving the last of a cookie in his mouth, Jason rose. "Dad, are we still going fishing today? We've been waiting all day."

"Wanna go?" he asked Lily.

"I can't. I've got to deal with the new property assessment and some other paperwork."

"You too?" John said, rinsing her now empty plastic container out in his sink. "Shirley was over here screamin' this morning, and I plan to go into the tax assessors office tomorrow and fight these tax raises. In this economy, who are they kidding?"

"Can I come?" Lily asked. "They have me as overdue too."

"Sure thing. With the inn being closed and all, I'm sure we can work something out with them." John leaned over and whispered in her ear, "If you need a little loan, you just let me know." He winked. "And no interest."

All these people offering to loan her money was very touching. But how would she ever pay them back if she accepted?

She turned to Ian. "You all have fun fishing today. I better get back to work."

"Bye, Lily, thanks for the cookies. C'mon Dad." Jason raced out the door with his friend toward the Volvo.

"I guess I'm being paged." Ian kissed her forehead. "Let me know if there is anything I can do to help with that tax situation."

She watched him walk toward the car. Gretel started barking and raced after him.

"Come on, girl," Ian said, opening up the passenger door for the dog.

He waved as he started down the drive...the perfect dad.

Lily crossed the field and headed behind the house to one of her favorite spots on the property, the old pond. The rotting wood made her doubt whether the short dock leading out over the water would hold her weight, but the lure of the evening mist diffusing hues of violet and turquoise over the still water drew her down the rickety structure. Ghostly shadows of trees cast in the fading light undulated over the surface of the water. She felt as if she could just keep on walking, floating over the water, toward the sloping meadow and well-lit windows on the far side of the large pond. Ripples pushed the water up the shore like a small tide, and reeds ruffled in a slight breeze.

Looking up, she searched for the source of a tap-tap-tapping and saw two rowboats tied up together, knocking against each other as if to say hello in Morse code. She inhaled deeply. The air was redolent of green things and damp earth, and it filled her with pleasure. All thoughts of her former city life fell away. Careful to keep her balance, she bent forward and let her hand skim the water's surface. "Like silk," she whispered. Cool enough to raise goose bumps up her arms, yet tantalizing enough to encourage her to sit at the dock's edge, pull off her shoes, and dangle her feet in.

Her toes wriggled below the water's surface as she contemplated the scene. In the reeds, an almost imperceptible motion caught her eye. She was not alone after all. He was large, very gray in the dimming light, but his magnificent profile was unmistakable. Balanced with precision on one leg, he blended well into the foliage. Without a speck of warning, his long beak moved toward the water like an arrow shot from an archer's bow. Dinner...silver scales shimmered in the faltering light of dusk, and the fish briskly disappeared down the throat of the Great Blue Heron. To her amazement, the splendid bird suddenly took to the sky, gliding away on wings spread wide. She imagined he was late getting home tonight, or perhaps, like herself, no one was waiting anxiously for his return.

Chapter Twenty-Seven

Why had she answered it? The mechanic was coming over today, and she was sure it was the driver calling for directions. Lily closed her cell phone and let it drop to the floor. How did he get her number? Only Brad, her attorney and her mother had it. She stumbled back and fell onto the couch. Memories assaulted her, yelling and fighting, all her clothes and dolls being thrown into suitcases, driving away without saying goodbye, even to her Grandma Maggie. How could he do it? How could her father, who hadn't even spoken to her in almost twenty years, pull the rug out from under her again?

The notes, it had to be him. She tried to breathe, but she choked on her tears. She curled into a ball on the sofa and tried to block out the world. Her daddy wanted her house, this house, and he was suing her to get it. The room spun and filled with a ringing. The sound was familiar, her cell phone. She watched it light up on the floor; it was Brad. At least he took care of her, gave her a home, never abandoned her, and still wanted her back.

In a daze, she opened the lid and whispered, "Hello."

"Lily, is that you? Are you all right?"

She whimpered into the phone. "He wants the house…"

"Who is he? Who wants the house?"

"My father."

"Lily, try to calm down. What do you mean? Your father called you?"

Lily dried her tears with her sleeve. "He's suing me for this house. Says my grandmother wasn't in her right mind when she left the family home to me and not him, her only child."

"The SOB. He doesn't even bother to see if you're alive for twenty years, and now he wants to take the house out from under you? What a guy."

Phone in hand, Lily walked into the kitchen for a glass of water. Brad's voice was calming; he was on her side. The taxes, the mounting costs to maintain the place much less start a business, and now this horrible lawsuit with her father were just too much to face alone.

His voice was smooth and settling. "Honey, it will be okay. I'll call my lawyer and get this handled, today. Don't be afraid. Your father will never bother you again."

She sipped her water then took a deep breath. "Thank you, Brad, that is very kind."

"I love you, Lily. I will make this go away. Now, make some tea and forget about it."

"I'll try."

"I don't like you being alone. Do you want me to fly up there? We can talk, work some things out."

She hesitated. "Yes, Brad, please come."

"I'll catch a plane."

✦✦✦✦

Lily checked her hair in the mirror one more time. Why was she nervous? It was only Brad coming by…yet he'd sounded so nice the last time they talked–like the old days, when they were dating and she didn't have to cautiously measure his every word. He'd called her from the airport. She couldn't believe how fast he had taken care of the lawsuit with her father. It had magically disappeared, and he'd said he'd find a way to pay the back taxes and handle everything.

She went back into the kitchen to check the oven. Dark coffee, half and half, his favorite cinnamon scones turning a golden brown. A nice afternoon treat. What am I thinking? This isn't a date. Why am I going through all this trouble? Do I still care about him? A flicker of hope kindled in her heart. She fantasized about keeping the family together. A baby. A golden dog playing fetch in the emerald yard. The phone broke her reverie. I hope he's not going to be late or not show up at all.

"Lil, it's Jude. Is he there yet?"

Lily released her held breath. "Not yet, but any time now." Telling Jude had been hard, but she wanted any support she could get.

Jude continued, "Well, remember, keep your guard up."

"He's being great so far."

Jude interrupted. "I know, I know. Just call me when he leaves, okay?"

Jude sounded concerned. She might be right. This was a foolish move. Her mind was so fuzzy she could barely think. Lily stared at the old grandfather clock that dominated the parlor and listened to its low, steady tick tock, tick tock, like her heartbeat...like a bomb.

Tires hit the gravel in the driveway, and through the picture window she watched dust fly into the air. Brad parked the BMW convertible in front of the entrance, like a limousine arriving for a pick up. The sound of his steps mounting the porch sent a spasm shooting through her solar plexus, noticeably not reaching the few inches higher to her heart.

She opened the door. "'Morning, Brad." She smiled and reached for the exquisite bouquet of lavender roses he held out to her.

Brad kissed her cheek and whispered, "See, Lily, I still remember your favorite flower."

He followed her into the kitchen and sat at the old oak table, now covered with lace, silver, and china. "You always could set an elegant table. Just one of your many talents."

Lily busied herself serving coffee and warm cinnamon rolls with homemade pumpkin butter. She placed a tangy Waldorf salad and a thick slice of Walla Walla onion quiche on the fine bone china plates that were so prized by her grandmother on the table, then sat down facing Brad. She tossed her food around the plate nervously, hardly able to eat, while Brad was obviously savoring each bite, stopping only to stare into her eyes.

"I can't tell you how good it feels to sit beside you and share a homemade meal," he said. He took her hands in his. "Lily, I've missed you. I've been so lonely without you." His grip tightened. "I want you to come home. With me. As soon as possible."

Her words caught in her throat. The chair, the room, and even her breath were closing in on her now. Ian's face flashed before her, his smile, the longing in his eyes.

Brad continued. "Lily, you *know* I love you." His pitch rose. "Please, I'll do *anything* you want. A baby, even a dog, if you'll just come home."

Home, Lily thought. She wanted to go home. She always had, since she was a little girl. Their house in Brentwood flashed across her mind–safe, perfect, grand, but *home?* Brad had managed to keep it from foreclosure...for now. Lily turned her fingers in her hair and looked at the man across the table. She saw a little boy, the pain in his eyes, like a sad puppy. She knew the depth of his anguish from growing up so lost, almost homeless, hungry. How could she say no to him? He'd suffered so much loss, as had she. Perhaps together…?

Brad touched her cheek. "Lily, my Lily. I need you." She stood up and went to him, nestled in his lap. He kissed her forehead, her eyes, her lips. And just held her.

Momentary safety filled her being. At what price? a voice in her head whispered.

After breakfast, Lily showed him around the house and gardens. Brad kept his arm around her as they surveyed the property.

"This was my grandmother's parlor," she said. "When I was a little girl, we'd cut out paper dolls here and have tea parties."

Brad wandered over to the mahogany china cabinet. "This looks like an old piece. Could be worth some money. Have you had it appraised?"

"Brad! I can't sell these things. They're all I have left of my grandmother's memory. See this white china horse here? It's almost a hundred years old. Grandma Maggie played with it, my mother played with it, and I used to take it out on the porch and pretend I rode it away to a magical place."

She walked over to the Italian hand-painted Ginori ruby and pink carnation plates. "See these antique plates on the wall? Grandma Maggie served me her scrumptious French toast on these and….."

Brad interrupted. "I get it, Lily. But really, you'll have to start thinking about what you'll do with all this *stuff* when you move back."

Lily got very quiet. This *stuff*, this place, and everything in it, was a part of her, the self she was just getting to know… and like. She straightened her spine and took a step toward him. "I don't remember giving you a definite answer, Brad."

His face paled and he moved quickly to hold her. "Sorry, Lily. I mean it. Whatever you want."

Her body stiffened in his arms. His hands felt cold on her skin. He crushed his lips against her mouth, moaning her name. Everything in her fought for release, for air, for freedom. She pushed him away. "So, Brad, just what were your plans for *my* bed and breakfast here on Madrona Island?"

"Well, I thought we could sell it and take the money and buy a great beach house in Malibu, just like you always wanted."

"No, Brad. That was what *you* always wanted. Do you even have any idea what *I* want?"

He took a deep breath and tried to mask his strain with a smile. "I'm trying, Lily. Certainly you don't plan to stay cooped up here, isolated, with nothing but old memories forever? I thought we could move on to a new life together."

It all became clear to her then… If they sold the bed and breakfast, the proceeds from the sale would co-mingle as community property, and he would have his hands on her money and, with it, her future. She looked closely behind the little boy veneer. He was still the same self-centered, controlling man he'd always been. He had just put on a new mask. His needs, his wants, the child and dog were an empty promise to lure her back. He'd taken advantage of her in a weakened moment, and she had allowed it.

"I need to take some time and think about your offer. I'm not ready to make any decisions," Lily said.

"You want me to wait *how long*? Come on, come back with me now. I have the car, we could pack a few things."

"No." The strength in her voice astonished her.

Brad paused. "No *now*? Or no *forever*?" he asked.

She saw his jaw tighten. The veins in his forehead began to

throb. "You belong with me, Lily." She stared past him out the window, noticed the sun playing on the water of the Sound, the light breeze moving through the pines. She loved those old lace curtains on that window, the polished oak floor still smelling as it did when she was a little girl. *This* was home. What had she been thinking? It was time to stop letting men stand in her way.

"My life is here now. This is what I want."

He stared at her, his face morphing from shock, to grief, to anger. "After I fixed everything for you, now you're telling me to leave?"

"Consider what you did for me a parting gift. I won't ask for anything else."

He stared at her. She could only imagine what was going on in his mind. "Fine, you just stay here. But don't call me if you can't pay the bills or expect to see me except inside a courtroom."

He stamped toward the door and yanked it open. The pain in his eyes was blazing. "I hope your knickknacks and old chintz keep you good company."

He slammed the door on the way out, and for a split second, she longed to run and comfort him. But it would be like trying to comfort a rabid dog. It would only end up biting her and infecting her in the end. She watched him race away, and relief flooded her limbs and left her exhausted.

Lily, delicate flower, fragile...no more! She imagined a tiger lily, bright with color, exotic and mysterious. She cleaned up the coffee cups and banged around the kitchen.

"How dare he!" she said, pacing the floor, "trying to get my own inheritance from my grandmother. My chance at an independent life, my own success. He thinks he can just pull that out from under me? He has underestimated his sweet Lily.

"No more," she said with a grin. "Here, Lily, let me balance the checkbook, it's too much for you. You just write the checks and look pretty." He took care of everything, alright, like I was some prize possession he kept for display.

Her inner boiling point erupted, and the feeling of release left her charged with energy. It was all crystal clear now. No matter what obstacle presented itself, she would find a way to make it work here, with the bed and breakfast. She would tear the place apart if she had to and find that brownie recipe.

+ + + +

Brad gunned the engine and raced down the curving dirt road, forcefully changing gears, grinding them the way he was grinding his teeth. He wiped the sweat from his forehead with the back of his hand. He entered the highway, accelerating briskly, topping seventy-five miles an hour on the country road. "Damn her! Dammit Lily! What are you thinking?" He was panting. His stomach churned. Every muscle in his body was knotted and ready to spring. "I can't even breathe on this accursed island."

He rolled the roof down, trying to get some fresh, cool air to bring down the heat of his body. Over and over he replayed the scene with Lily in his mind...he had lost...he had lost her. Furiously, he blinked his eyes, trying desperately to stop the oncoming tears. He downshifted, slammed on the brakes, and made a hard turn down a small forested lane. The car slid to the side of the road, and he threw open the door and ran to a tree, bracing himself with one hand as the contents of his stomach rebelled and forced their way out and onto the fern-covered soil. There seemed no end to the heaves, which ultimately became dry and empty. Finally, he sank to his knees and covered his eyes with his moist palms. Guttural

moans turned to tears. He choked, rambled, "Lily, my Lily…
alone, always alone…there's no one." Tears washed down the
well-groomed face, and like a little boy, he used his sleeves to
wipe his eyes and nose. "She's mine. If I can't have her…." He
leaned back against the cedar tree; the bark felt comforting,
and the cool moist earth crept up through his slacks.

Eventually, he stood and brushed himself off, regaining
his composure. "There are other women, I don't need her."

With renewed resolve, Brad headed back to the car. The
driver's door was still open, as if some madman had left hur-
riedly while being chased by a demon. He pulled out a comb
and fixed his hair, using the rearview mirror. He pulled back
onto the country highway, his brain now back in full gear. He
kept glaring at the cell phone on the dash, waiting for the bars
to indicate a signal. When he reached the ferry dock, the bars
came up and he dialed his attorney. "Rick, it's Brad. I'm leaving Washington, first plane I can catch. I'll be in to see you
tomorrow to sign papers."

He knew now she would not come back. As much as it
tore at his gut to lose, it was time to move on. He would start
again with someone who appreciated him. Let Lily rot in the
country. She'd never see a dime from him, he'd make sure of
that.

Chapter Twenty-Eight

Lily wrapped herself in a wool shawl and retreated to the porch swing, which swayed with the light wind. Brad's visit was unnerving. She rocked back and forth like the tides, letting the steady rhythm calm her jangled nerves. The sunset expanded across the horizon, casting a pale shade of violet across the snowy peaks of the Olympic Mountains. Deep shades of pink and gold reflected then dispersed across the watery inlet. On the grassy rise by the McPherson barn, deer munched in the grass, foraging for supper.

A trusty blue heron, always the last bird she saw in the sky, made his way home, racing the darkening sky. She clutched the shawl tighter as the icy breeze brushed through her hair, leaving behind it the scent of the sea. Her shoulders dropped, releasing what felt like a great weight of worry. Decisions needed to be made, it was time. She couldn't procrastinate, pretend, or avoid any longer.

As the sun cast a bronze ray across the crystal water, an idea surfaced, resonating clearly in her mind and heart. She would re-open the bed and breakfast, and do it soon. She could see the newly decorated rooms, smell the fabulous delicacies she would create in the farmhouse kitchen. The book-keeper had kept accurate records until about a year ago when the B&B closed. The inn had shown a good profit, especially in the summer months. If her grandmother could do it...she could too!

She walked inside and retrieved the Guestbook from her nightstand. She held it snugly to her chest, as if to infuse the love it held into her spirit. It was almost like having her grand-mother at her side. It might look a bit silly doing this, she thought, but at least she felt less alone now. "Okay, work your magic," she said as she closed her eyes and opened the book to reveal its contents. Written, in a flawless script, the entries read:

There is no place I would rather be than here at Ma-drona Island B&B on this beautiful island. No matter how big my problems, they melt away when I am here.
~Cate P.   Seattle, WA

This inn was a Godsend. Staying here during the time our home was being repaired from the flood really helped us recover from the shock. Thank you, Margaret, for all your kindness.
Tesia and Jan–just down the road

Your hospitality touched my heart. I so enjoyed the opportunity to center and reflect with the wind and the tides. The time here reminded me how all things are pos-sible.
Barb–Santa Rosa, CA

Lily wondered how her grandmother must have felt knowing she had been instrumental in delivering such loving and peaceful experiences to so many people from all kinds of families and backgrounds. She walked into the parlor and looked at the bright, wide-open kitchen waiting to be used, the long oak table and chairs with no one to sit on them. Upstairs, the fluffy beds remained empty. There were hundreds of people who might want to stay here again, people who still called to ask for reservations. She too could bring that kind of joy to others.

In fact, she would love to do it. It would demand everything she enjoyed and was good at: making rooms beautiful, growing flowers and herbs, creating and serving gourmet meals that would tantalize the palate and warm the soul. And when she found that darn brownie recipe, the mail order potential was unlimited; she could sell them all over the world. The image of herself as the Brownie Queen draped in robes and a crown, and Brad groveling at her feet, was very satisfying. She could expand the brownie flavors, use herbs like lavender in them, or create a spicy cayenne brownie bite.

No time like the present to create the Madrona Island Bed and Breakfast website. And blog. She had plenty of experience blogging anonymously for the Angel Paws Shelter in Los Angeles. She went to the computer in the office, opened her web browser and typed in "buy a domain name." "Let's try www. MadronaIslandBandB.com. Yes, it's available!"

The ideas flowed, and she had to share them with someone. She would call Jude and Kyla, meet for drinks and celebrate. A certainty swept over her like a cool wave on a hot day. Anything was possible here…even finding a new dream of her own. And her grandmother would have been so pleased. She took one last glimpse out the window at the sun dropping below the horizon, reflecting off the blazing red bark of the Madrona trees. Somewhere, it was rising for a new day. For her, Madrona Island B&B would be her own personal sunrise.

Chapter Twenty-Nine

The smells radiating through the house made Lily's mouth water. The peach cobbler with a mascarpone cheese center was baking at a low temperature and spicing up the air with smells of summer. She checked the tomato, mushroom, and garlic sauce simmering on the stove and filled the pasta pot with water to pre-boil. The table was set for eight. Her seven dearest friends were in the parlor, awaiting the official announcement that she was reopening the inn.

"Table set, check. Pinot Noir breathing, check. Caesar salad on the table. What am I forgetting? Ah, the apple cider for Jason."

She removed the French bread from under the broiler and placed the cookie sheet on the counter. Humming softly, she brushed fine olive oil over the warm slices and then rubbed each one with a fresh garlic clove. Each piece was lightly sprinkled with grated Parmesan cheese, a splash of kosher salt, and fresh ground pepper, then set on a serving dish. She popped a spoon in the mushroom sauce for a taste.

Ian poked his head in the kitchen. "The smells are killing me, hope you don't mind if I take a peek?"

"Help yourself, there's a spoon on the counter. No fingers!" The timer went off on the buzzer, and she hurried to the stove to drain the al dente pasta, smother it with sauce, and bring the steaming plates to the table.

"Ian, can you start carrying these to the table?"

"Sure thing."

She entered the parlor, the wine in one hand and the cider in another. "Everyone to the table."

After each guest took their seat, she filled their glasses while Ian served the pasta.

"Have a seat, Lily," Jude said. "We can handle it from here."

Lily joined them at the table and held up her glass for a toast. All eyes were on her. Kyla raised an eyebrow in expectation.

"Out with it," Shirley demanded.

With a broad smile, Lily made the toast. "To the reopening of Madrona Island Bed and Breakfast, and to the new innkeeper...me!"

Everyone clicked their glasses, offering congratulations.

"About time," Shirley said. "I knew you'd figure it out."

"And with no help from you, I might add," Betty said, glaring at her sister.

Jude held up her glass next. "To friends."

"To new beginnings," Kyla said.

"And to lots of cookies!" Jason said, holding up his glass of cider.

Lily looked from face to face. This was her new family. She wished her mom could be here. Katherine had promised to come up and help with the painting soon. And she had insisted on sending a check. Everyone she loved would be in one place soon, right here on Madrona Island.

Ian caught her gaze. "I'd be happy to help in any way.

Along with my painting, my carpentry skills are pretty good too."

"Not as good as mine," John said with a smile. "I'll be over tomorrow to work on that picket fence up front. Think I have some white paint for it too."

She smiled. "That'll help. I'm going to be on a very tight budget."

"I'll take care of the plumbing problems," Betty said.

Not to be outdone, Shirley offered to help with the decorating.

"I forgot to tell you," John said. "Went to the county a few days ago. You weren't available, so I asked about your property, too. Turns out they had no idea the inn was closed. Changed everything. And nothing was overdue, it was an oversight with all the legal papers and such."

Lily breathed a sigh of relief. "Thank you so much, John."

He tipped his hat to her. "Any time."

"I can hammer nails," Jason said.

"And I'll feed all the workers from my kitchen," Jude said. "I know a few guys who will be happy to help. I'll send them over."

"Thanks, all of you." Lily twirled the spaghetti with her fork and took her first bite. She noticed Ian's plate was almost empty already, and only one piece of bruschetta remained. "When was the last time you had a home-cooked meal, Ian?"

"Caught me," he said with a grin. He winked at John. "Grandpa's chili is good, but it really has been a while." He looked over at her sheepishly. "Pretty obvious, is it? Should I slow down to a more dignified pace?"

"Forget it," Lily said. "Just enjoy. I don't think we need to worry about being dignified here tonight."

It was a pleasure to see people truly relish her cooking. It reminded her just how wonderful it felt to bring joy to people through her culinary creations. Tomorrow she would start preparing the menu for the new B&B.

Lily ate a few more bites then rose to clear off the plates. "Why don't you all go sit by the fire in the parlor, and I'll brew some coffee and finish up the dessert."

"I'll help," Jude said.

"I'm making my way to the parlor now as instructed," Ian said with a smile.

In the kitchen, she plated the cobblers, put them on a tray, and dressed them with a dollop of fresh whipped cream. She handed Jude the tray of cobbler. "Be right there. Thanks, Jude."

Carefully, she poured the coffee into china cups—a hot chocolate for Jason—and placed them on a wooden cart that she wheeled into the parlor. As she entered the room, Ian gestured for her to take a seat beside him. She served the coffee then joined him on the loveseat, but not too close. For now, they were just friends. The only sound in the room was the tapping of the forks on the china plates and the crackling of the fire.

Without a doubt, Lily knew she had made the right decision. Just like her grandma used to say: Things always worked out if you just let them.

Chapter Thirty

There was so much to do, and just under two months to do it in. The list just kept getting longer and longer. The grand re-opening was set for July fourth, and thanks to finding Grandma's mailing list, all the invitations were out in the mail and through email. If it weren't for all her friends on the island pitching in, this miraculous event would not be occurring.

Lily and Mary surveyed the timeline. White picket fence: repainted. Wood floors: polished. Guestrooms: in process of being painted, but still not finished. And she still needed to find some inexpensive new decorating items for the house and garden. The farmer's market started this second Saturday in May, and Jude assured her that everything could be found there.

Mary pulled out a pad of paper and pen. "I think it's time we planned out the menu for the big party."

Lily went over to her desk and opened up her computer. "C'mon over and have a look. I have a few ideas."

Mary pulled over a chair and joined her at the desk. "Champagne, pretty fancy."

Lily laughed. "It is a celebration, in more than one way. I'll be just about officially divorced by that day as well."

"Well, champagne it is then!"

Lily scrolled through the list. "How does this sound? We'll bake some honey raisin, rosemary, and olive breads and then a whole table of meat and cheese platters and fresh salads."

"Good, and I can make my goddess fruit salad and ask Shirley to bring her famous potato salad."

"Perfect," Lily said, making notations on the document. "I'll whip up some fresh guacamole, hummus, and an assortment of crackers. And my new island quiche with scallops, bacon, and Swiss."

Lily's fingers picked across the keyboard, creating a long list of groceries and supplies needed. "Wow, lots to buy." She thought about the deposits coming in for the guests that would be renting rooms that weekend. If that kept up, this would surely work out just fine.

Mary patted her shoulder. "Don't worry, Lily, everyone will want to bring stuff. I can organize that. In fact, I'm sure Jude will bring plenty too."

"What about music, know anyone?" Lily asked.

"Do I know anyone?" Mary said. "My cousin, Seth, plays a mean guitar with his band, and I guarantee he'll work for free. So will the amazing flute and harp group at my church."

Lily threw her arms around Mary. "What would I do without you?"

"I better go before you make me cry." Mary took her chair back to the table and reached for her purse. "Wait, we forgot the best part. What about dessert?"

"No problem there," Lily said. "For one, I'm going to find that killer brownie recipe and I can bake up bunches of Inn Style cookies."

"I'll bake pies," Mary said. "Loganberry and apple sound

good?"

Lily rubbed her stomach. "Wish I had a piece right now."

"Back tomorrow," Mary said, closing the door behind her.

It was only 2:00, and Lily still had time to put another Facebook announcement up about the inn's grand opening before Dana from Cascade Market and his brother arrived. His wife had just had twin girls, and he still managed to find the time to help her. She would thank them all with the best grand opening party they had ever seen.

Dana's truck pulled into the driveway, and Lily hurried outside to greet them.

"Hey, Lily, this is my brother, Murray, he's an electrician. I dragged him along to take a look at the old wiring."

Lily shook his hand. "Thanks so much for coming over." She could tell they were brothers with one look. Both were slim, auburn-haired, and had kind smiles. "Can I get you both some homemade lemonade and cookies?"

The brothers looked at each other then nodded in agreement. "Which cookie is on the menu today?" Dana asked.

"I'll surprise you," Lily said, turning back toward the house.

"Sounds good, we'll just get to work and stay out of your hair."

The postal truck pulled up, and Cyndi, the mail carrier, held up a bunch of mail out her window and tucked it in the box before driving off. Dread churned in Lily's stomach at the anticipation of Brad's response to her final divorce terms she'd asked her attorney to deliver. She wanted this divorce to be over. Money was coming in pretty steadily from her baking business, but it just wasn't enough for upkeep on the place and the costs of remodeling. She refused to take any loans. As it was, she was accepting much too much help from Ian with repairs, and from Jude, for a myriad of things. Good people, those two, she thought. I owe them so much.

The newly hand-painted mailbox looked like a fancy birdhouse with little windows and brightly colored shutters. Wild morning glories wove their way up the base, creating a fairytale effect. Lily pulled open the latch and reached in to retrieve the mail. A large manila envelope sat on top. It was from her attorney.

"Guess I can't avoid this much longer," she murmured under her breath.

Lily looked around at the acres of beauty she had come to love. The perfect tranquil spot on the water, the lovely pale yellow farmhouse with its wraparound porch, and the iridescent blue waves of the Sound moving over the sand. This was something she did not want to lose; this was home. She could see John working in his garden next door and hear Gretel barking at the crows. She was comfortable, happy, accepted here. This was her place, it always was and she hoped it always would be. Not even Brad could change that.

Returning to the farmhouse, she kicked off her shoes, dropped the rest of the mail on the entry table, and carried the large envelope to her bedroom. Somehow she felt safer there, fortified by the presence of her grandmother. Her stocking feet wore a path back and forth over the mauve carpet as she worked up enough courage to open the papers. Maybe she should call her mother first? Of course not, her mother would just tell her to open and read it.

"Okay, okay." Lily curled up in the big overstuffed floral chair and threw the rainbow-colored chenille spread, a gift from Kyla, over her legs. Heart pounding, she tore open the envelope and started to read. So much legal nonsense to wade through, but finally she got to the results of what six months of legal battling had brought her. She couldn't believe it. She jumped up and threw the papers in the air. "Yes! Yes," she said dancing around the room. She had to tell someone immediately or she would burst.

Her mom's answering machine picked up. "Mom, are you there? It's important. Mom?"

For a moment she feared her mother would be too busy to talk to her, just like when she'd been growing up. She remembered the calls when she was home alone after school. "Lily, just microwave something from the freezer, I'll be late. Lily, I'm sorry to miss your recital, but I have to work, Lily, Lily..."

"Lily, are you there?"

"Yes, Mom, I'm here. Thanks for taking my call."

"Of course. Is everything all right?"

"I received the response to the final terms I offered Brad." She heard Katherine catch her breath. "And?"

"And," Lily said, "it's over! I got everything I asked for." Lily tossed off the spread and danced around the room. "I keep Grandma's house free and clear, my car, and I am debt free."

"That's all?" Katherine asked. "What about alimony?"

"Mom, there was nothing really to take. I have what I wanted most. I'm free of Brad, and Madrona Island B&B is mine. Brad keeps the mortgaged house, his failing business, and everything else, including all the debt."

Katherine chuckled. "Sounds fair to me. I'm sure, with his resourcefulness, he'll land on his feet again. So, how's everything else going? The baking business doing well?"

"Very well. I'm busy with orders from the Island Thyme Café every day, and from other shops too. You wouldn't believe all the help I am getting from my friends here with the remodel. Reservations are pouring in for the Inn after I found Grandma's address list and sent out a mailer announcing the grand re-opening."

"Good thinking! Your grandmother was very industrious. You obviously inherited that from her. She managed to keep her home and property for all those years, even with the high property taxes and overhead."

"I hope I can do as well as her, Mom."

"You will, Lily; you're a lot like her. Creative, strong-willed, kind, and very likeable!"

"Thanks, Mom. I'll let you go now." Lily hesitated for a moment with the words she really wanted to say. "Love you, Mom."

"Love you too, Lily. See you soon."

♦ ♦ ♦ ♦

Saturday morning dawned bright and sunny. After completing her list of items she wanted to buy, Lily went into the house and called Jude to meet her at the farmer's market. Maybe they would hit a few thrift shops too.

The Island Farmer's and Flea Market sprawled over several acres around a pond on what used to be an old chicken farm nestled in a central valley of the island. Some of the dilapidated chicken coops had been cleaned thoroughly and turned into stalls to show off the fine wares for sale–from local honey and fresh fruit, to used baby furniture and handmade crafts. The dirt parking lot was filled with cars, and crowds of tourists and locals meandered along the straw-covered paths to find bargains and delicacies. Children ran along the edge of the pond chasing ducks. Family dogs wandered along with their people. The sun was out, and after a long winter, it was a welcome relief.

Lily stepped out of the car, happy to finally be wearing sandals and a light cotton blouse. The lively sights and rich smells left her wondering where to go first.

Jude bounced out of the car and, hands on her hips, surveyed the scene. "Pretty nice spread today. Yum, I smell cinnamon rolls. Brett must be here. Let's go."

Lily had heard of Brett's famous cinnamon rolls and was glad she would finally be able to taste one. Brett's booth consisted of boxes of gigantic cinnamon rolls, half iced, half plain.

"What'll you have?" he asked with a smile.

"Two with the icing," Jude said. "And this is Lily, owns Maggie's old place."

Brett shook her hand, "Nice to meet you. I hear you're gonna be opening the B&B again soon?"

"Word travels fast," Lily said. "Hope you'll come to the grand opening July fourth."

"Wouldn't miss it. I'll bring the missus and the kids too."

They wandered on, admiring other booths. The scent of fresh kettle corn permeated the air. A booth overflowing with fresh-picked produce called to Lily, but the lilac-scented soaps and creams won out as her first destination. "Delightful," she declared. Lily turned to a young woman wearing a colorful print blouse and blue jeans. Her dark hair swung down her back in a single long braid. "Do you make these yourself?" Lily asked.

"Sure do, out at the Lavender Farm," she said. "We also do tea-rose-scented soaps. They're in the back. Come on in and have a look." Hearing the word "rose," Lily had a flash of inspiration. She would place local handmade soaps and hand creams in each guestroom, in the color and scent associated with the room. She would use rose, lavender, and for the Honeymoon Suite, jasmine. Lemon verbena for the pale yellow room would be perfect. She liked the idea of supporting her community's businesspeople. Lily turned over the thick, hardy, sweet-smelling soaps, holding each to her nose, and exhaled, "Aaahhhh." She tried the fragrant cream on her own hands and squirted the rose onto Jude's hands.

Jude leaned in close and whispered, "Are you thinking what I'm thinking?"

Lily nodded her head a definite yes.

"Kyla can make up some products for you," Jude continued.

"Right, I'll give her a call." Lily took the Lavender Farm's card, planning on visiting the website that night.

The next booth had fresh goat milk and creamy goat cheese samples smothered over crackers. This is a must have, Lily thought. "Hi, I'm Lily Parkins," she said, stumbling a little on her maiden name, "and this is my friend, Jude. I own Madrona Island Bed and Breakfast, and I wonder if we could talk sometime about stocking your products at my inn?"

"Happy to talk any time. I love that old place. My husband and I were married there a few years back." She reached out her hand. "Gina Marino, nice to meet you, Lily."

Lily took Gina's card and price list and promised to call soon. She and Jude moved along the gift and craft booths, passing candles and pottery, crocheted potholders and wood carvings. The produce and flower area lay straight ahead. One of the larger old chicken coops was strung with every size of hanging basket, each one filled with ferns and flowers, ivy and herbs. Perfect for her front porch. On the ground there were some clay pots full of seedlings ready to plant, marked with little signs telling the name and whether they took shade or sun. She could use those to fill out the garden.

"Jim, so good to see you," exclaimed Jude as she hugged the tall, long-haired gardener in the planter stall. "Lily, come meet Jim, the best gardener on the island." The two exchanged hellos.

Jude questioned him. "Haven't seen you around town for a while, I was wondering if you'd be at the market." Jim stared at Jude for a minute too long, Lily noticed; sort of a shy but interested look. She'd just leave them alone for a little while. "Jude, I'll be right back. I'm going to check out the old dishes and stuff over there."

The table was covered with old, mismatched pieces of china. Lily looked at the price on the soap dishes and teapots covered in baby roses. They would go perfectly in the rose suite. The old restored aprons hanging on a rack reminded her of the aprons worn by women in 1950s television shows. There sure was no shortage of creative people on this island.

After purchasing a few items, she wandered along sampling smoked hazelnuts, golden honey, and fresh-pressed apple cider. It was a pure delight to her senses. On the opposite side of a duck-covered pond was the flea market, which was of special interest to Lily today. She was hoping to find some unusual planters to put in the garden and along the walkways, and some more knickknacks for the guest rooms. Walking in that direction, she noticed Jason and a friend feeding the ducks. "Hi, Lily," he called out as he ran by. She smiled as she turned to wave at them. She stepped back and plowed right into Ian.

"Sorry there, Lily, I was just trying to keep up with the boys. Where are you heading?"

"Across the pond to look for this and that for my place." She could feel the heat of his presence. She had not seen him in a t-shirt before—well, not one that fit him, anyway; it nicely highlighted his smooth, solid muscles. "I best get on with my shopping."

"Can you use an extra pair of hands to carry your purchases? I have Granddad's pickup with me if you need it," he offered.

"Sure," she said.

Ian fell into step beside Lily as they strolled through the flea market. Old wooden tables laid end to end were covered with every imaginable thing, from CDs to toasters. Lily meandered up and down the aisles and spotted a small old-fashioned wooden wheelbarrow with metal handles. It would be perfect with colorful nasturtiums flowing out of it, placed just off the rocky path leading to her pond. "How much?" she asked.

"Six dollars and it's yours, miss."

"Sold!" She was pleased with her first purchase. Ian followed close behind, pushing the wheelbarrow. She noticed the amused look in his eyes but chose to ignore it. "I'll be happy to push it myself," she said.

"No problem, this way your hands will be free to pick up other finds." She wasn't used to a man who was patient while she shopped, and helpful. Brad wouldn't last five minutes shopping here. Jude caught up to them and joined in the search for treasures.

When everyone's arms were full, including the wheelbarrow, Jude suggested they call it a day.

"A profitable excursion, I would say, Lily," Ian commented as he loaded several items into the back of the truck. "I'll follow you home and drop this off."

"I have to drop Jude off first, so I'll meet you there in a while. Thanks, Ian." Lily loaded the crate of fresh brown eggs into the back seat of her car and the still frozen, just-pressed apple cider onto the floor.

"Quite helpful, that Ian," Jude said with a sly smile.

"Look who's talking. You've been smiling like a Cheshire cat ever since you bumped into Jim. So, what's up with that?"

"Oh, he's just a good friend."

Lily smirked. "Does he know that?"

"Besides," Jude said, "I have my eye on someone else."

"Let me guess," Lily said. "Does he wear a black chef's coat?"

Jude just smiled.

Chapter Thirty-One

*L*ily turned off the burner and lifted the bacon out of the pan to drain on a paper towel. The familiar thump, thump on the porch stairs alerted her that Gretel was approaching. The sound of the hundred-pound dog's paws scratching the screen door sent Lily running to let her in. "Okay, Gretel, come on in."

The shiny black dog rubbed against her legs and covered her hands in doggie kisses. "Yes, yes, I love you too," she said, petting her soft fur. "Okay, enough kisses you silly girl. You're just in time for breakfast."

Gretel knew the routine. Wagging her tail, she followed Lily into the kitchen for a treat.

"I have some thick bacon today, will that please you?" Lily made the dog sit before tossing her a small piece. Gretel swallowed the bacon in one bite. To be truthful, Lily knew Gretel would eat *anything*. She'd found that out the day Gretel lifted her giant paws up onto the counter and snatched a whole stick of butter. Lily had tried to grab it out of the dog's mouth, only to feel completely ridiculous when the butter squeezed between her fingers as it was being swallowed whole in Gretel's giant mouth.

Lily patted her leg. "Come on, girl, sounds like someone's at the door." Ian's tall frame was standing behind the screen and she felt her heart start to pound.

"Knock, knock. You there, Lily? I think my dog wandered over again."

Lily looked at the dog with a mock scowl and walked to the door.

"The runaway is here, come on in," Lily said holding the screen door open. "I'm afraid it was the bacon that brought her over this time."

Ian grinned. "The smell would bring me over too."

Gretel bounded happily over to Ian for some petting and sat down hard on his foot. "Look at her. With the whole floor to sit on, she picks my foot." Ian scratched behind Gretel's ears and stroked her coat.

Lily knelt down and ran her fingers over the dog's sleek ebony fur. She could feel the energy flowing from him through the dog to her. Small beads of sweat broke out on the top of her lip. She looked into his eyes and could see passion. She knew he wished he were stroking her, and that Gretel was only a stand in. She wanted to reach over and touch his face, his hair, kiss his lips. Her eyes met his. Was that a smirk?

He was laughing! Ian was laughing at her like he'd read her mind. Feeling foolish, a flush rising up her neck, she quickly stood up. "I, ah, I need to go finish breakfast."

Ian rose quickly and grabbed her lightly from behind. He turned her around to face him. "I am not laughing *at* you, Lily. You fight me so hard, yet your eyes tell me a different story. I just wish you could let go, just for a minute."

The warmth of his hands on her arms set off waves of desire. She could feel his breath on her face. His lips brushed hers. She curved her arms around his neck and deepened the kiss, tasting and probing his mouth. The heat between them built. She was lost in his arms, bliss coloring her world.

She broke the embrace and took a few steps. What she saw completely broke her. His eyes were filled with love and pain; she had hurt him. Her heart reached out. "Ian, oh Ian, I'm sorry." She was holding him now, stroking his head. He had lost a lot too. He was not Brad. "I do care," she whispered, "just give me a little more time. There is so much happening at once, with the divorce and trying to reopen the B&B."

"Of course," he said. "Meanwhile, I'll just hang around and help out. I've been working up a new logo for your product labels."

"But, Ian, you know I can't pay you right now, and I can't just let you work for free."

Ian smiled. "I think I smell something really good in the kitchen, and I haven't had breakfast yet."

"Oh, I see. Paid in food! In that case, can I talk you into staying for breakfast? Your dog has already sampled the bacon and found it to her liking."

Ian started for the kitchen. "Thought you'd never ask. And how about later we take a short walk on the beach?"

He was pushing it, but the sun was out today. A short walk would do her good, help stretch her tight muscles from painting. "Okay, but only if we get a lot accomplished today. Now let's eat."

✦✦✦✦

They stood together gazing out over the Sound like two silhouettes, outlined by the setting sun. Shades of deep rose blended with a full spectrum of golds and purples that seemed to dance on the water's surface, reflecting back the vibrant palette in the sky. The island ferry was making its nightly crossing in the distance, and a lone heron flapped slowly home.

Ian draped his arm around Lily's shoulder and nuzzled closer. "I'm happy, Lily, content. I can wait as long as it takes for you to feel the same."

Lily looked up into his deep blue eyes and felt herself falling into them. Into this man, into his heart. The feeling of happiness and complete rightness overtook her. But could she trust it?

"I...I need to go, Ian, let's head back."

He held her tight. "Whoa, filly, not this time. You look like a spooked horse."

The image of a spooked horse hit home. Images rushed through her head. Pictures of watching her mother run from her father, of herself as a young girl running from her mother, and as a woman running from Brad's words and insults whirled through her mind. Panic rose up, the walls closed in, no way out, no one to help. She burst into tears. Ian pulled her gently into his arms.

She fought him off half-heartedly. "I hate crying, let me go. I'm okay," she managed to get out. Then something inside her just let go, of the pain, of the fight, of the struggle of having to do it alone. Her body surrendered into the warmth and comfort and Ian's arms.

"Ian," she whispered.

The sun made its final descent behind the Olympic Mountains, and night began to set in. He took her hand and they started back. Lily shivered, the breeze off the water had ice in it.

They picked up their pace. "Let's go inside," she said. "We can build a fire. And I'll make fresh chocolate chip cookies."

"Ah, you know the way to my heart. Race you back and I'll even give you a head start. Go!"

Lily's long legs made her a fast sprinter, and the two hit

the wooden porch at the same time. Out of breath and laughing, Ian picked her up and started to carry her into the house. He stopped at the doorway. "Permission, Lily?"

"Permission granted, Ian."

He carried her to the parlor, and they curled up together in front of the fireplace.

"Better?" Ian asked.

"Yes," Lily said, yawning into her hand.

They sat there together, staring into the fire, just holding each other for a long while. To Lily, it felt like they'd always been together. Always.

"It's getting late and we have a big day of work tomorrow." Ian rose and started for the door. "I'll be here first thing and get started on the painting."

"Good night," she said. Lily laid her head on the sofa arm and let herself drift off to sleep.

✦✦✦✦

She was already late getting supplies for the day and chastised herself all the way into town.

She parked and headed first for *Tea & Comfort* to pick up a few items. Kyla's head perked up from a book when the bell announced Lily's entry.

"Good morning, Lily," she said, her eyes narrowing.

"Why do I always feel under inspection when you look at me that way?" Lily grumbled.

Kyla came out from behind the counter and took Lily's hand. "Looks like you could use some tea. Let's go in the back."

Lily sank into the velvet rocker, her mind wandering to last night and Ian's passionate kiss. Business first, she reminded herself.

Kyla set two steaming cups of tea on the pedestal table beside the lavender candle. "Something weighing on your mind, Lily?"

Lily hesitated, blowing on the hot tea and taking a small sip. "It's Ian." She could feel her blush as it warmed her face and neck. Was it safe to share this with Kyla?

"That bad, is it?"

Lily tried to will back her memories, Kyla saw too much. "Good, bad...the timing is wrong."

Kyla was quiet, her gaze in the distance. Lily wished she could read the redhead's thoughts and the secrets she kept so guarded. Silence filled the room, the only sound the clinking of the teacups as they rested back into their saucers.

Kyla's eyes looked like a deep well. "Lily, the problem with running away from love is that you never know if it will find you again."

Her words pierced Lily's heart. The two women stared at each other, a recognition passing between them like a spark. Kyla rose collecting the teacups. "I really must get back to work now. Your packages are on the front counter."

Lily stared after her from the back room. One sentence from Kyla and her whole world went upside down. She had a lot to do and would just go home and face it now.

✦✦✦✦

There were lists upon lists scattered across her office desk. Lily's calendar was scribbled in with appointments. Meet Kyla to discuss soaps, candles, and teas, check with the carpenter, match paint chips, finish final edits for Ian to design the brochure. In the daily reminder block, red letters caught the eye—Remember to Blog and find the Brownie Recipe!

"Yoo-hoo!" Betty's voice resonated as she walked in the

screen door. "Anyone home?"

"Hello, hello," Lily said, throwing her arms around Betty. "I'm so excited, so much to do."

"Wow, girl, I know. I'm here to volunteer my services." Betty hugged her and patted her on the back. "I'm happy to do it. Now, where shall I start? Plumbing done, what else do you need? Got a couple big saws in the basement if you need anything cut."

Lily marveled at how an almost 80-year-old woman could be so spry. "Well, let me think...how are you at painting trim?"

"Just point me toward the brushes. I'll go get my ladder if you think you need one."

"We might. Can you come back this afternoon?"

The phone started ringing again, and Lily waved good-bye to Betty and rushed to answer it. It was an offer from an editor at *Coast Flight Magazine* to do a spread on the grand re-opening. Her mother was arriving tomorrow, thank goodness, and could take over making the reservations and fielding the calls.

She glanced at the clock, where was Mary at? It was already after 3:00. Mary slid in the door a second later and stood at attention. "Reporting for work."

Lily paced the kitchen floor. "Mary, if we're going to re-open by the fourth, we have a lot to do. How many extra hours a week can you give me in the next month or so? I promise I'll pay you soon."

"Don't worry about it. I have some time, and I'm sure there are others who'll help. We could clean out the pond. Aunt Shirley will spiff up your garden, and Aunt Betty has more energy than the two of us together and nothing but time." Mary started for the door. "Let's go outside and see what else needs to be spruced up."

They stepped out and surveyed the grounds. A few yellow tulips were still blooming among the late rhododendrons, and the bright magenta azaleas were in full display. "Start a list, Mary," Lily said. "We'll have to find someone to fix these fences and plant some grass in the brown spots."

"Hey, ladies. What are you talking about so intensely?" Lily looked up to see John, a big smile across his face, as usual.

"Making a list of everything that still needs to be done," Mary said.

John stared at the fence. "Needs some patch-up, that's for sure. I think I can help you, though. Got some extra fencing in the garage, some tools, and plenty of nails." He pointed to the front of the house. "Needs paint, Lily. No way around it. Charm is one thing, but I think it's a year past that."

"I think you're right," Lily said with a frown.

He put a friendly arm around Lily's shoulders. "Don't worry, dear. It'll all get done."

She looked at John. This is what it felt like to have a real father. She sprinted up onto the porch. "I got it. White trim! That'll brighten it right up. We can leave these porch rails blue, add a few more hanging baskets and some new cushions for the swing." For a moment, she was lost in her vision and stood there imagining.

Mary took furious notes, trying to keep up. "Great idea, less expensive too."

John headed back toward his house. "I'll be back tomorrow, ladies, and I'll bring some fencing and white paint."

"That would be great," Lily said. "We're having the big work party and *Coast Flight Magazine* is coming to take some photos of the inn. I insisted they come on a Saturday so everyone can be in the picture."

"I'll be there, and I'll help spread the word."

She waved after him. "I'll cook up a great lunch with lots

of cookies and lemonade too." Lily turned to Mary. "This island certainly works its magic."

Mary smiled. "Only for those it loves."

Chapter Thirty-Two

Someone else was cooking her breakfast for a change. Kyla had suggested that Lily pick the place for their meeting today, and she couldn't wait to see the samples of herbal soaps, scented creams, and specialty teas Kyla had designed exclusively for Madrona Island Bed and Breakfast. Matt's Diner was the perfect not-too-greasy spoon, and it sounded pretty darn good right now.

The bell over the door rang as she entered the diner, and she was greeted by a waitress in a crisp orange apron who looked like she'd stepped out of the 1940s. "Morning, ma'am, table for one?"

Kyla was nowhere in sight, and for once Lily was glad to say, "Table for two, please."

Lily slid into the red vinyl seat of a corner booth and opened her laminated menu. A light breeze from the ceiling fans sent the mouth-watering smell of sizzling bacon her way.

"Coffee for you today?" the waitress asked.

Gratefully, Lily turned the white coffee mug right side up. It was the perfect fit for this place—coffee shop coffee—watered down but warm and pleasing. The clanging of dishes, pots, and pans were the background music, accompanied by the low buzz of people talking. The place was crowded, mostly with locals. Some had on worn t-shirts and baseball caps, faded jeans and nylon parkas, typical island dress.

Lily perused every item on the menu. The hot homemade biscuits with sweet butter, smothered in loganberry jam, were a must. The four-egg Spanish omelet with home-fried potatoes was tempting, and the blueberry sour cream pancakes sounded downright decadent.

"'Morning, Lily," Kyla said as she slid into the booth. She placed a large basket filled with samples right next to her on the seat. "What looks good to eat?"

Lily peeked over, trying to see what was in the basket.

Kyla held up the menu to block her view. "Food first... business second. I'm starved, and the smell in here isn't helping. Okay?"

"Well, I guess I can wait a few minutes longer. And as for the food... everything looks good, too good!"

Kyla scanned the menu. "I think I'll order the cinnamon roll French toast," she announced.

"Not fair," Lily said. "Talk about overkill, how can you eat like that and look like you do?"

"What are you talking about? With all those goodies you're always making, you look pretty good yourself."

Lily decided on fried eggs over easy, hash browns, thick crisp bacon, and of course, a buttermilk biscuit with their specialty, marionberry jam.

After they ordered, Kyla reached into the basket and pulled out a product order form. "Here's a preliminary list of the products I've come up with. I do think they'll suit your business and clientele very well."

She slid the lavender-colored paper across the table for Lily to take a look.

Tea & Comfort Kyla Nolan, Proprietor

"I love your logo," Lily said. "Who designed it for you?"

Kyla waved the waitress over for a refill on her coffee. "Ian did a splendid job on it."

Lily tensed. Kyla and Ian really seemed to know each other pretty well. It was silly to be jealous, she wasn't technically dating Ian.

"He's doing my design too," Lily said, watching for a reaction from Kyla. There was absolutely none. She scanned the products. "Oh, I love this; rainforest mist shampoo and lemon verbena conditioner." She closed her eyes and inhaled the imagined scents of lemon balm and honeysuckle rose candles. She visualized the color-matched votives placed in antique glass holders on every dresser.

Kyla pointed to a section marked teas. "I have included morning and afternoon teas, and some special love blends as well."

"Love teas?" Sure enough, there they were: rosewater, chamomile spice, and chocolate mint. "I think these will be a hit."

Kyla's Cheshire smile crossed her beautiful face. "So do I."

She imagined the smell of a rich cinnamon stick brew being poured from a silver pot for afternoon tea. "Kyla, this list is amazing. It's perfect. Thank you so much!"

"Lily, you deserve to have your dream come true, this one and many more. Don't forget that."

The waitress appeared and placed the steaming hot breakfasts on the table. "Can I get you anything else, more coffee, ladies?" Both women shook their heads.

Lily dove into her meal, savoring every flavorful bite.

Salty bacon mixed with creamy, golden egg yolk, crisp-edged hash browns dusted with salt and pepper, and a moist, flakey biscuit smothered in jam...this was heaven.

Between bites, Lily shared her plan. "I've drawn up breakfast menus for the B&B. I want them to make guests feel satisfied, comforted, and delighted, just like this one." She took a large bite out of her biscuit then continued. "You know, Kyla, I'll need a taste tester sometime soon to sample my recipes. Are you willing to take on the job?"

"Depends on what you're sampling," Kyla replied between bites of French toast dripping with maple syrup.

"Sage omelets, pork rind quiche, spinach biscuits..."

"Ugh!" Kyla replied with raised eyebrows.

"Caught you. Just kidding. How does Lavender Orange French toast, black currant scones, and apple turkey sausage quiche sound for starters?"

Kyla nodded appreciatively while continuing to relish her breakfast.

Lily wiped the jam off her lips with her napkin. "When would be a good time for you to come by? Before opening your shop sometime or on a Sunday? We could have champagne mimosas, sample goodies, and talk."

Kyla's eyes narrowed as she stared at Lily for a few long seconds. "Okay. Let's do it."

Kyla was finally opening up to her a little, Lily was happy to see. She was curious to know why this young woman who was tall, model-thin, and strikingly beautiful with her cascading red hair, had opened up a quaint tea room on this relatively remote island.

"It's a deal, Kyla. How about this Sunday?"

Kyla nodded in agreement as she finished off the last bite of her breakfast. She removed the packaged samples from her basket and stood to go. "Gotta hurry back and open *Tea &*

Comfort." Kyla laid a ten dollar bill on the table. "This should cover my part. Here are a few samples for you to smell and try out. You can let me know your opinions on Sunday. Bye for now."

Lily watched her walk out the door. There was something frail about her demeanor, but she sensed that this woman also held a deep well of strength. She took a last sip of now cold coffee, grabbed the check, and headed for the door. Today she would work on the breakfast menus, and a few recipes for afternoon tea treats. Tomorrow was the interview, and she had to be ready.

++++

Saturday morning was bright and sunny, perfect to get lots of work done. Lily put on some jeans and an old sweatshirt and went into the kitchen to make coffee and heat up cinnamon rolls for the early arrivals. Later she would change into some nice clothes for the shoot. The photographers from the magazine were coming at noon, and she had promised them a lunch buffet.

Cars honked as they made their way into her drive. She stepped out on the porch and waved. Dana, the grocer, was there with his brother, another friend, and lots of tools. Jude was right behind them, her car loaded with food for the buffet table.

"Morning," Lily called. "Coffee and pastries in the kitchen."

"Sounds good." Jude and Kyla carried trays of sandwiches past her and into the kitchen. "This should feed the army that will show up. Everyone wants to help and be in the picture, even Kyla has come in jeans."

The place was a whirl of energy, loose boards being nailed,

trim painted, yards cut, and Betty out there planting shrubs and flowers. Ian was up on a ladder finishing.

"Lily, what would you like me to do with your order?" Kyla asked.

Jude peeked over the rim of a basket. "They smell wonderful. Let's put them out in all the rooms and parlor."

Lily surveyed the baskets of candles, soaps, and other items to put around the inn. "Yes, let's put them out now." They went upstairs and started in the Rose Suite. The tall, freshly made pillar candles in pale rose were placed in a glass holder on the antique oak dresser. The sweet scent immediately brightened the room. Before she could move to the next room, the doorbell rang and Lily froze.

"Go," Jude said, "we'll finish up here and meet up with you."

Lily hurried downstairs and stopped at the entry. Standing at the door, suitcase in hand, was her mother. "Mom!" Lily raced over, opened the door, and hugged her. "You made it."

"Of course," Katherine said. "You think I'd miss anything this important?"

"How long can you stay?"

"I'm here for the work weekend," Katherine said. "But I'll be back for the grand opening for sure."

Lily hugged her mother again. "Kyla, Jude," she yelled up the stairs. "Come meet my mother. Mom, these are my best friends."

"So good to meet you both." Katherine picked up her suitcase from the floor where she'd dropped it. "Point me to a place to sleep and then put me to work."

"We'll start setting out the lunch buffet," Jude said.

"We'll be right there." Lily put her mother temporarily in the Rose Suite, as it was the only one that was completed.

Katherine put a few things away and tied a sweatshirt around her waist. "The place looks amazing. You've done a marvelous job. And all these people helping you."

"I'm pretty lucky."

"It's not just luck, my girl. Now let's go help your friends with the buffet."

✦✦✦✦

The table was set out with mounds of potato salad, sandwiches on dark rye and country white bread, and pink lemonade. Shirley brought over bouquets of fresh-picked lilies in shades of yellows and reds and bright white daisies. Puffy lemon meringue and chocolate cream pies were set out with floral paper plates, and napkins completed the table.

"They're here," Jason yelled as he ran up the front porch steps.

A large van was parked in her drive, partially on the grass, and two men were unloading lights and equipment while one gave orders. He looked the part of typical photographer. Khaki button-up shirt with sleeves rolled back, tight jeans, and a two-day beard.

"Hi, I'm Lily, the innkeeper."

He shook her hand. "CJ, we're here for the shoot."

She pointed to the side yard. "We have lunch laid out on the lawn by the pond if you'd like to start there."

He yelled to his crew. "Set up over there by the pond." He put a camera over his shoulder and walked across the drive toward the buffet. "We'll shoot first, take a lunch break, and then do a few of the front and interiors."

Lily walked ahead to show the way. "Sounds good to me."

She watched them set up lights and agonize over each picture. First close ups, then wide-angle shots.

CJ waved at his crew to take a break. "Lily, let's break for lunch. All these locals here today gathered around the table will make a great shot."

"Sure thing." Lily gathered up her friends and insisted they come have lunch.

Lily entered the kitchen. "You too, Jude and Kyla, come out for lunch and get in the photo."

Kyla's face paled. "What picture?"

"Oh, it's *Coast Flight Magazine.* Isn't it wonderful? They're doing a spread on the grand opening of Madrona Island B&B."

"That's wonderful," Jude said, taking Kyla's arm. "You *are* coming, just turn your face if you don't want your picture taken."

Lily looked back. Kyla was trailing behind. "Come on, let's get there and have lunch."

The scene at the table took Lily's breath away. All the people she loved, laughing, smiling, and obviously enjoying her food. What an amazing picture it would make in the magazine, too.

Chapter Thirty-Three

Dusk was falling as the sun made its last appearance before dropping behind the horizon. Lily wondered if it were too late to go over to John's house. He would love to sample her new cookie recipe, and she wanted to tell him about getting her building permit in the mail today for the final remodel. Ian was back on the mainland for a few more days, so John was alone. She leaned out the window and looked between the trees across to the barn-red farmhouse. The lights in his kitchen were still on. In his deep warm voice he had said, "Lily, you are welcome any time, you hear? Anytime." Carefully, she placed the still-warm cookies on a china plate and wrapped them with cellophane.

The path leading across the field between the two homes was well-worn from years of foot traffic. She couldn't wait to tell him the good news; after all, he was her number one fan and cheerleader. It was easy to see why her grandmother had fallen in love with this kind and thoughtful man. The twinkle in John's eyes and that wide smile would have taken her heart too if he were fifty years younger. His grandson wasn't half bad either.

As she approached the front steps, she heard Gretel barking inside. The screen door was locked, so she rapped on the frame. "John, it's Lily. Are you home?"

Gretel's barks became a low whimper, and Lily's heart suddenly went cold. Something was wrong. She raised her voice and pounded harder on the door. "John, are you there? Let me in."

Her gut instinct told her to move fast. She turned and ran around to the back of the house, trying not to trip on the long hose stretched across the yard. The back door was unlocked, and she rushed in and followed the sound of the dog's cries. Sprawled across the living room floor, unconscious, was John.

Lily gasped and ran over to him. There was a large gash on the side of his head and blood pooling under it. He'd probably hit his head on the corner of the coffee table when he fell. Her mind raced, trying to figure out what to do next. She crouched down and felt for a pulse in his neck. "Damn, I can't find it." She placed her ear closer to his face to see if he was still breathing. He was, barely. She tried to revive him.

"John, wake up. John, it's Lily." She could see his chest rise and fall in a ragged fashion, but there was no response. Help, she needed help. Quickly, she moved to the kitchen and grabbed the phone. With shaky hands, she dialed 911. "Please help, there's a man here, he's unconscious, we need an ambulance. Yes, about 80 years old, unconscious." The operator asked for a location. Lily rattled off the address. "Off Sunrise Lane just outside of Grandview. Please hurry."

Ian, she had to reach Ian. She saw his mainland number posted on the wall over the phone and began to dial. "Jason?"

"Hey, Lily, is that you?" the boy said with a yawn.

"It's me, Jason, this is important. Is your dad there?"

"Yeah, he's in his studio, as usual."

"Jason, listen, please run and get him real fast. Okay?"

Lily heard Jason drop the phone and listened to his footsteps pattering across the floor. Outside the kitchen window, an ambulance siren blared and she breathed a bit easier. They were coming, help was coming.

Out of breath, Ian answered the phone, "Lily, are you all right?"

"Yes, no, Ian, it's John. I found him unconscious on the living room floor."

"Is he breathing?"

"Yes, barely. I already called 911 and I think they're almost here. Please hurry, Ian."

"Lily, I'll be there as fast as I can and meet you at the hospital. And thank you."

"Of course, Ian, I love him too." Lights blinking, siren low, the red truck pulled up to the house. "They're here. I'll call your cell from the hospital. Bye."

Frantically, she unhooked the screen door and ran into the driveway, waving her hands over her head to attract the paramedics. Two men jumped out of the cab. One opened the back of the ambulance and grabbed a stretcher, and the other lifted a medical kit and followed Lily into the house.

She led them through the door. "He's in here on the floor." From the corner of the room, she watched them check his vitals, place an oxygen mask over his face, and slide his limp body onto a stretcher.

"Ma'am, we'll be taking him to Forest Glen Hospital. You can meet us in emergency if you want."

She looked up at this helper in the night and was grateful. "Thank you, please take good care of him, he's very special."

"Sure will. Don't you worry, he'll be all right. You know where the hospital is?"

"Yes," Lily whispered.

"Well, drive careful now, we'll take good care of your

grandfather."

She hoped his words were true.

Lily moved quickly over the darkening path, illuminated just enough by the full moon for her to find her way back to her house. She could barely open the front door, her hand was shaking so badly. John had to be all right, she just couldn't bear losing him. And Ian, how would he ever survive this?

She gathered her purse, keys, and a sweater and headed for her car. Once on the highway, the roads were clear, and she was able to make good time. Apprehension built as she turned the corner and saw the hospital. "Right, go right, okay, the emergency entrance. You can do it, Lily." The small two-story brick building was the only hospital on the island. Lily rushed through the glass doors and headed for the nurse's station.

"Excuse me, an ambulance just brought in a John McPherson. Is he all right? Can I see him?"

The nurse checked her records. "Yes, they just brought him in. Can you provide insurance information?"

"No...I can't, but can you tell me if he's okay?"

"His status has not been reported yet. But the doctors are with him. Are you a relative?"

Exasperated, Lily told the nurse she was his granddaughter. She wished Ian were here.

The nurse continued. "Well, you can't go in right now, but I'll let the doctor know you're here."

Lily could tell she would get nowhere with this nurse who seemed immune to tragedy. She looked at the entrance to the patient area and considered making a run for it. Surely I'd be considered some nut running through the halls yelling, "John, John." They'd probably put me in a room too. It was black dark out now, almost nine o'clock, and her best option was to take a chair. Feet up, knees to her chest, she wrapped herself in her long sweater and began to rock to an imagined beat. With any luck, Ian would be here soon, and he was family and should be able to find out more.

✦✦✦✦

Ian hesitated, wondering whether or not to bring Jason and put him through this ordeal with his great grandpa. At seven years old, Jason had already lost his mother, and he adored his grandfather. Ian considered leaving his son next door at Mrs. Williams's house, but knew Jason would never forgive him. If it hadn't been for this darn workshop he had to teach, he would have been on the island when it happened.

"Jason," he said gently.

Jason yawned. "Dad, what's wrong?"

"Son, you have to get dressed. Grandpa's sick and we need to go over to the island right away."

Eyes wide, Jason asked, "Is he okay, is he gonna be okay?"

Ian continued packing a duffle bag with enough clothes for a few days. "I hope so, Jason. He had to go to the hospital, but Lily is with him and we'll be there real soon."

"Okay, Dad. Should I bring something for Grandpa?"

Ian grabbed his son and hugged him tight. "Just yourself, Jason. That's all Grandpa will want." Ian bundled Jason up, jumped into the Volvo, and headed south to the ferry. If he were lucky, he could catch the 8:30 ferry and be at the hospital in an hour. He wished he could swim across and get there sooner. At least the roads were dry, the sky was clear, there was none of the usual fog to slow the ferry. He felt comforted knowing that Lily was there, a sense of safety and familiarity that he had felt with his wife, only this time, it was not Denise. It was Lily.

The ferry was just loading as they paid the fare, and the

dock worker waved their car onboard. Jason had dozed off in his seat. Ian's mind wandered. He really should call his mother. She was so far away, and he didn't know what time it was in Mexico City. He fumbled with his cell phone scrolling for her number. He hated himself for hesitating. John was her father, after all, and she would want to know.

He pictured his mother in her bright floral dress, barefoot, paintbrush in hand. When she had first moved there, he resented her for leaving him alone with Jason. But she had smiled and said, "You'll do fine, Ian. You have a strong spirit." His Bohemian mother, brave, full of life and a sense of adventure. Before, when he'd been so low, he thought her selfish. But now he could understand her artist's soul and need for adventure.

He'd followed his passion, shown his work in galleries throughout the world and become successful. His son was doing well in school and had good friends, and now even Ian's heart had done the unthinkable: healed and fallen in love again. He dialed her number. "Mom, it's me. Did I wake you?"

Guitar music floated in the background.

"Ian, my love! You sound dreadful. Are you all right?"

"I'm fine, Mom. It's Grandpa." He heard her gasp and then some quick words in Spanish, followed by the guitar music stopping.

"Mom, he's at Forest Glen Hospital. Jason and I are on our way there now. I thought you'd want to know. I have a friend on the island, Lily, she's with him now."

"Of course, Ian. What's wrong? Did he fall?" Then her voice started to break. "I love that old man. You tell him, if he really needs me, I'll be there. But he's a tough one. I expect he'll be up and about in no time."

"I'll tell him, Mom, and call you from the hospital when I know more."

The ferry horn sounded as the boat slid into its dock. Jason opened his eyes and sat up. "We're almost there, right, Dad?" Ian shook his head and turned away. The look in the boy's eyes broke his heart.

◆◆◆◆

Jason pushed through the hospital doors and ran into Lily's open arms. "Hey, Jason, I'm so glad you're here," she said. "Your grandpa's still in with the doctors."

Ian looked down at her and wished he didn't feel so helpless. Their eyes met. He read volumes in her look. One arm around Jason, she stood, walked to Ian, and put her other arm around his shoulder. He embraced them both and exhaled for the first time since Lily's phone call. A doctor entered the waiting room and addressed Lily. "Excuse me. I'm Dr. Williamson. Can I talk to you alone?"

Ian reached out his hand. "I'm Ian McPherson, and this is my son, Jason. He's my grandfather. Lily, why don't you take Jason and find him a snack or a drink? I'll talk to the doctor."

The doctor looked confused. "It's lucky your sister got him here so quickly."

"Yes it is," Ian said, staring at Lily.

Lily took Jason's hand and walked over to the snack machine.

The doctor continued, "He's still unconscious, but it appears he's had a mild heart attack. He must have fallen down during it and banged his head hard enough to cause a concussion."

Ian sighed. "Can you treat him?"

"He should wake up in few hours, we'll watch and see."

"And his heart?"

The doctor looked down at her pager before answering.

"If all the other tests are negative, we can treat the heart with medication, but he'll have to do some lifestyle changes too. Otherwise, he appears in good health for a man his age."

"How long before we can see him?" Ian asked.

"He's resting right now and under observation. Let's wait a little while to be sure he's stable. I'll send a nurse for you when he's ready for company."

"Thank you, doctor."

Lily and Jason wandered over and handed Ian a cup of coffee.

The doctor beamed. "I think he has the best medicine waiting for him right here."

She turned to go. "You all get some rest now, he's going to be fine."

"Do you want me to take Jason home, put him to bed, and look after Gretel?" Lily asked. Ian could barely get the words out, and there was no way he could convey the gratitude he felt. "Yes, Lily, that would be so helpful."

She looked concerned. "Call me."

Ian nodded. He watched her take Jason's hand and walk out the door. It was going to be a long night.

✦✦✦✦

"Are you Ian McPherson?"

He shook himself awake. He must have dozed in the lobby. "That's me."

"I'm Piper, your grandfather's night nurse." She pointed down a corridor. "Room 220B. You can see your grandfather now, but he's still unconscious."

Ian checked his watch; it was 3:30 in the morning. Shouldn't Gramps have been awake by now? He hurried down the hall and located the room. John was wired to machines beeping on and off, and an IV was hooked into his arm. He looked like he was sleeping peacefully. Ian fell into the leather chair beside the bed, pulled up the footrest, and curled up for some sleep. Certainly John would be awake in a few hours.

Chapter Thirty-Four

They'd just finished Jason's favorite breakfast, Frosted Corn Puffs and milk. The sugar rush was already making her dizzy. She had brought him to her house to sleep so he wouldn't see the stained carpet where John had fallen. Lily waited while Jason got dressed in her room.

"I'm ready," he said, joining her in the parlor. "Is Dad still at the hospital too?"

Lily nodded, pulling out her car keys. "Yep, let's go."

"Wait," Jason said. "I want to pick some flowers to bring Grandpa."

Why didn't she think of that? The upper field near John's house was full of wildflowers, and they made a cheerful bouquet. Just as they turned to go back to her car, a cab pulled up and a dark haired woman, deeply tanned and wearing bright colored clothes, jumped out with a suitcase.

"Jason," she yelled, arms wide open.

"Grandma!" Jason ran into her arms.

This had to be Ian's mother. He'd never said much about her before except that she was an artist and lived outside of the States.

The woman reached out her hand. "I'm Celeste. Do you know how my father's doing?"

"Lily, I live next door." She shook the woman's hand. "We were just heading over to the hospital to find out." Lily directed Celeste to the passenger's seat of her Honda. "As of late last night, John was stable but still unconscious."

Celeste looked out the window. "After Ian's last call, I figured I better get on the next plane. Lucky I caught the early shuttle or I would have missed you."

The day was clear and sunny. Everyone out there was going about their business like nothing happened, but for Lily, time had stopped for a while. An antiseptic smell permeated the air as they entered the hospital lobby and made their way to John's room.

"Just act like we belong here," Celeste said. "It may not be visitors' time."

They tiptoed into the patient room. A blue curtain was pulled around John's bed, and Ian was sitting on the empty bed next to it. He looked like he'd slept in his clothes and hadn't had a shower.

"Mom." He rose from the bed and gave her a hug. "Glad you came. When the old guy finally wakes up, he'll be happy to see you."

A doctor pulled the blue curtain open and walked over to them. "Good morning. We have been monitoring Mr. McPherson, and things look pretty good right now. His heart is stable, but we're going to run a few tests and see if we can figure out why he hasn't woken up yet."

"Is this normal?" Celeste asked.

The doctor looked concerned. "Could be the combination of the heart attack, the fall, and his age. If he doesn't wake up by tomorrow, I'll get the neurologist back in for a consult."

Celeste walked over and stood by her father. "Hi, Pops."

Jason followed. "Can we talk to him?" he asked the doctor.

"Sure thing, but not too loud. His head is probably still hurting from the fall." When the doctor left the room, Lily took Ian's hand. He looked down at her, worry sketched across his face. "I'm here for whatever you need, so just ask."

"Thanks," he said.

"I think I'll go back to John's and clean up a bit before you all come back."

"You don't need to do that," he said.

"Yes, I do," she whispered. "There's still some blood on the carpet and things knocked over."

His eyes widened in his pale face. "Thanks."

Lily waved goodbye after they promised to call if John woke up. Once she got home, Lily called Jude and told her what had happened.

"I'm so sorry," Jude said. "I'll meet you at your house, and we'll tackle the cleanup at John's together."

That was a relief. Lily was not looking forward to going back into the room she'd found him lying in last night.

Jude's old Mustang pulled up in front of Lily's house, and she ran out and jumped into the passenger seat. When they pulled up to John's farmhouse, Lily felt the blood drain from her face. Instinctively, she grabbed the door handle for support.

"Lily, you're not gonna faint on me now, are you?"

She shook her head no.

Gray clouds began to roll in, casting a dismal gray over the Sound. The lights were still on inside, and it seemed impossible that John would not be there, sitting in his chair, tinkering with something or watching TV. Jude pulled the car over to park under a large Madrona tree and turned to Lily.

"Are you up to this? I can turn this car around and take

you home if you want."

"Thanks, Jude, I can do it. It's just so sad."

"I know, honey, I'm sure he'll pull through just fine. Those farmers are strong as an ox."

Lily got out of the car and leaned against the hood, staring out toward the water. Tall, aged pines stood guard over the gentle slopes of rolling green hills. In the distance, the hills ended abruptly and sandstone cliffs cascaded down toward the water's edge. The overwhelming scent of jasmine made Lily feel light-headed. Without warning, her surroundings started to blur and spin. She seized Jude's arm for balance. Her heart felt like it would beat right out of her chest. "I just can't bear the thought of losing him...oh, Jude."

Jude hugged her tightly while she wept on her shoulder, then rummaged inside her purse and produced some Kleenex. "I think we both need these. How about we just go inside and get this done so the family can come home and get some sleep?"

◆◆◆◆

The house still held John's presence, she could almost hear his warm chuckle, but the leather recliner showed only the well-worn indent in the aging cushion. Lily started cleaning up while Jude scrubbed the carpet. How could this be happening? Was it only a week ago that John had come over to her house to sample breakfast menus? They had laughed and, as so often happened, she had cried on his ever-ready shoulders. He was the wisest and most compassionate man she'd ever known. No wonder her grandmother had loved him so dearly.

Lily's cell rang and she lunged for it, hoping to hear John was awake.

"I'm sorry to hear that, Ian. We're almost done, come on

home." Lily ended the call and stared at Jude. "He's still un-conscious. The doctor told them all to go home and get some sleep for the night."

Jude washed her hands in the kitchen sink. "Well, at least they'll come home to a clean house. Guess I better get back to the café. Should I give you a lift home?"

"That's okay, I'll wait here and see if they need anything." Lily took a seat on the couch in the den. She didn't have to wait long before the three McPhersons pulled up and entered the house. She hurried for the door. She heard Ian's voice, but when she spotted him, her legs would move no further. Ian... the raw pain in his eyes was more than she could bear. Jason was right beside him, steady, growing taller every day, so like his father.

And then Ian caught her gaze. In that moment, as their eyes locked, Lily knew with stunning certainty the truth— this was not a guilt-driven or rebound affair. The truth was, to the very depth of her soul, she loved Ian...and Jason. Goose-bumps rose with a prickle to cover her arms and legs—*a sure sign of confirmation*, Kyla had said.

With an unexpected effortlessness, Lily walked over and stood beside Ian. A look of recognition passed between them. Jason took Lily's hand, and Celeste moved in for a group hug.

"By the way, Celeste," Lily said, "I put your suitcase in the back bedroom."

Celeste sat down on the couch and raised her feet onto the coffee table. "Thanks. I'm sure I'll be wanting to go to sleep soon."

Ian turned to Lily. "Thank you."

Lily looked at her two boys, both pale, both hoping the same thing she was: Grandpa John would wake up and be home soon.

Jason curled in beside his grandmother on the couch and

put his head on her shoulder.

"You both look like you could use a glass of wine," Celeste said, waving them to go. "Ian, why don't you let me put Jason to bed and you go take Lily home?"

Ian stopped pacing and looked at Lily.

"Are you up to coming over, Ian?" she asked.

"C'mon," he said, "I'll walk you home."

They walked up the steps to her house and into the parlor. "Wine?" she asked.

He tossed off his jacket and sank down with a sigh. "Something warm would be good."

Lily retreated to the kitchen and started a pot of tea, happy to have something to keep her hands busy and to feel useful. She entered the living room with steaming mugs in hand and placed them on the coffee table.

"Have a seat," he said.

Lily curled up beside him and laid her head on his shoulder. Neither spoke for a while, and the companionable silence echoed tenderly into the night.

"Ian...would you like to get back home so you can get some sleep?"

He turned to her, his deep blue eyes raw with emotion. "What if Gramps...? I just couldn't bear..."

Lily hesitated for a moment, then stood up and reached out her hands to him. "Come on." She guided him to her bedroom. The bright light of the moon filtering through the window reflected silver white. They both needed each other tonight.

Ian held her gently by the shoulders. "Lily, you mean so much to me."

She took a step back. He stroked her cheek with his fingertips. "Don't be afraid," he whispered into her hair as he kissed her forehead, her eyelids, the tip of her nose. "I don't want to take anything from you, I just want you to be happy."

She fell into his arms. "Ian, my Ian," she whispered.

He lifted up her chin and his lips pressed against hers. "I love you, Lily, of that I am sure. I can and will wait if you want."

She looked up into his languid eyes. He was everything she wanted; she did not want to wait. She wrapped her arms around his neck, kissing him, pulling him to her. A startling heat shot down her body, making her legs quiver. Her knotted heartstrings broke open, and the love she had so carefully held at bay poured out. "Ian, my love."

He moved to the edge of the bed and awkwardly tried to unbutton his shirt. She watched his artist's hands, each beautiful, long finger, struggle with the buttons, then reached over to help. She stood before him, longing to give comfort and with the intense desire to touch. She stroked his cheek and let her trembling hand explore the smooth lines of his shoulders.

He grabbed her wrists, his tear-filled eyes staring into hers. His coarse black hair tumbled over his face. He smelled of forest and mist, of sweat and lust. Her fingers slid to his mouth, across his full lips.

Ian wrapped his long arms around her waist and buried his face in her breasts. Heat and longing rushed through her as the room melted away and only this moment, this man existed. Trembling, he drew her down onto the bed beside him. Hands in her hair, he pulled her mouth to his, their lips crushing against each other. Hearts pounding, their grip tightened, both frantically trying to merge into the other, to reclaim life and block out the grasping hand of grief.

Ian's kisses trailed down her neck, his warm breath setting every nerve on fire. She moaned with pleasure, melting into his arms. She was lost, swept away into the blissful sensations rippling through her body.

She ran her hands across his incredible body. Her bold eyes met his, and it was the last signal he needed. Hardly breathing, she watched as he unsnapped his jeans and slid them down his strong legs and onto the floor. She could feel the hardness of his body, the warmth of his raspy breath as his hands wandered along the curves of her back and then lingered between her thighs.

"Lily, you're so beautiful," he whispered, pushing aside her hair. His deft hands removed her pants and drew her naked body to his.

Their bodies entwined, Lily melted into the blissful union. Complete ecstasy; this was the man of her heart, the love of her life.

✦✦✦✦

Robins sang, cherio, cherio. Lily opened her eyes to the early bird calls that often woke her at 4:30 in the morning. She turned toward the window and was startled by Ian's profile. The creamy olive skin of his cheek lay on the pillow next to hers. His jet-black hair lingered down his neck and touched his bare shoulder. A day-old beard roughened his cheek.

Not wanting to let go of his image, the robin's cry alerted Lily to the sun's light and the necessity of Ian going back home.

She caressed his shoulder and shook him gently. "Ian, it's time to wake up."

He opened his eyes, pools of black staring back at her. He reached out and pulled her close for a kiss. "Good morning," he whispered.

"Ian, the sun's coming up. Probably best if you get back home before your mom and Jason wake up."

He sat straight up in the bed. "Right, I forgot. Someone

distracted me last night." As he pulled his jeans and t-shirt on, she watched his face fill with yesterday's worries. "Sorry to have to leave like this."

Lily rose on her toes and let her lips linger on his. "It's fine, go."

She followed him to the front door. "Call me as soon as you hear anything."

He started down the steps and turned back to her. "You'll be the first to hear."

From the porch, she watched him cross the field, dawn's light setting his body aglow. Ten years of marriage and she had never known love before now.

Chapter Thirty-Five

The phone ringing in the distance brought her back from her dreams. Lily shot up in bed. Nine o'clock, how had she slept so long after Ian left? She seized the phone. "Hello."

"He's awake, Lily. Gramps is awake."

She released a long breath. "Oh, Ian, I'm so happy to hear that."

"He woke up twenty minutes ago, and his first words were, 'I'm hungry.'"

Lily laughed. "Sounds like John. What did the doctor say?"

She could hear Ian catch his breath. "They're perplexed why he was unconscious so long, but she said he appears normal in all areas. They're going to keep him for observation for twenty-four hours and then he can come home."

She could hear Jason in the background cheering yippee. Lily held the phone away, knowing her voice would crack through her tears of relief. She took a tissue and dabbed her eyes. "Is there anything I can do?"

"My mom's got everything covered on this end for now. The doctor suggested we wait to visit until the afternoon and let him rest. I'll let you know when."

"I'm here if you need anything."

"I know, Lily, and I for you."

She showered, dressed, and headed for the kitchen. She needed to do something, and baking usually helped. She pulled out the recipe card. Flour, sugar, butter, and chocolate chips were her companions. This was the final recipe she would use for Grandma Maggie's Cowgirl Cookies with coconut and almonds. John would love these when he got home.

On second thought, they would probably put him on a special diet after the heart attack. She would freeze a few of this batch and then experiment with a low fat version to have ready in hand. Lily put the cookies into the oven; she wanted to be sure she had plenty of John's favorites.

While they baked, she wandered out to the porch with a pencil and paper. The sunny morning hinted at a warm day ahead. She rocked on the porch swing, legs curled under her just like when she was a child. The breeze off the Sound brought memories of the past and the present, merging for just a moment—the happiness of a young girl and a grown woman, swinging, smiling and waiting for the cookies to be done in the oven.

Most of the event plans were in progress, but she needed to get right back to work if everything would be ready on time. Her thoughts wandered back to last night, and her body trembled at the memory. She scribbled in the corners of the page, "Lily and Ian" and drew a heart. She felt like a young schoolgirl with a crush. For just a minute, she allowed the daydream to float pleasantly through her mind. Ian and Jason and her, together in a house, playing ball in the yard, sitting down to a family dinner, and even... She imagined herself pregnant, glowing, ecstatic.

Dreams were a scary thing sometimes. Wanting something so badly, yet fearing it just as much. All she'd ever wanted was here, right where it had always been, on Madrona Island. Bunnies played in the yard, running through the rock roses and fragrant alyssums. She looked out over the Sound; the beauty astounded her. Blues and greens blended in the current, reflecting the golden sunlight and snowcapped mountains that towered majestically toward heaven. A lone bald eagle swept over the tree tops, taking his usual perch to observe the landscape.

The buzzer went off on the antique range, and Lily rushed inside to be sure the cookies did not over-bake. The smell was heavenly…roasted almonds with coconut dreamily enhanced by melting chocolate. Potholder in hand, she pulled out the cookie sheet and placed it on a rack to cool. Impatient, she slipped one cookie off with a spatula, broke it open, blew on it and tossed it from hand to hand to cool it quickly, before taking a large bite. She savored the texture and flavors…even with whole-wheat flour and much less fat and sugar, the cookie was delicious.

He was alive. John was fine, coming home. Truly he was like a grandfather and father and best friend all rolled into one. She could not have borne to lose him.

The grand opening loomed in just over a week, and there was still much to do. Lily raced around the kitchen, packaging up the cookies and checking her list. She wished the new labels were ready, but Ian promised he'd have the final sketch to her tomorrow if he could. Once the logo was complete, she could begin the mail order business in earnest and get the new brochure printed. She read over her to-do list: finish painting outside trim and Lavender Guestroom, sew seat covers for parlor couch, pick up the new duvet for the Honeymoon Suite, and order all the final groceries and champagne. And, she thought, find the darned brownie recipe. She needed more help and for more days like this without rain. It was June, not January.

Jude, she needed to call Jude.

"He's fine, yes, I know, amazing. Home tomorrow." She hung up the phone and headed back outside. The white paint and brushes were waiting for her to finish up the porch trim outside. The repetitive gliding of the brush across the window trim soothed her nerves. The place was looking beautiful, restored and ready for business.

✦✦✦✦

Lily paced the front porch, waiting to see Ian's Volvo turn into the drive across the field. John's tests were all clear, and the family had gone to pick him up from the hospital. She couldn't wait to see him and give him a big hug. The dark blue Volvo made the curve and slowed. Down the steps running, she raced across the field to greet them.

Ian waved when he saw her approach. "Got the old man with us," he said, winking at his grandfather.

John emerged looking a bit tired, but good. "Who's calling me old? I can still fish you under the wharf."

Celeste took his arm and guided him toward the house. "I'm sure you can, Dad, but the doctor said you need to rest for a while."

John waved her over. "Lily, come give me a hug."

He did not have to ask twice. "I am so glad to see you home," she said.

"I'm not going anywhere," John said.

Ian opened the door and guided everyone inside. "On to the couch, Gramps. We'll be waiting on you for a while."

John settled onto the couch. "Sounds good to me. When's lunch?"

Lily stepped forward. "I talked to Jude, and she said to let you know she'll be bringing by a few days' worth of heart-healthy meals this afternoon."

John frowned. "No fish and chips?"

"That's really nice," Celeste said. She sat down on the couch and put her arm around John. "Ok, everyone, he's home, he's well, and I'm staying awhile to help out."

"Yippee," Jason said.

She looked up at Ian. "And that means you can go back home for Jason's last week of school, and you, Lily, can get back to work." She turned to her father. "And you can watch."

John sighed and leaned back into the sofa. "Anything's better than lying around in the hospital."

"I don't want to go back to school. I want to stay here with Gramps." Jason glared at his dad, and when he got no response, he threw himself down in a chair.

Ian walked over and rumpled his son's hair. "Ok, I'll give the school a call, see if I can pick up your work and bring it here."

Jason jumped back up and hugged Ian. "You're the best, Dad!"

Ian's eyes met Lily's. "And this way I can help Lily out too with all her last-minute plans."

"Good idea," John said. "Now, let's get to the important stuff: Where's lunch?"

Chapter Thirty-Six

*L*ily collapsed into the kitchen chair and put the list on the table, wondering if she'd ever finish in time. She laid a new paintbrush on the table and closed her eyes.

She heard footsteps at the back door. "Knock, knock. It's Ian and dog."

"Come in, it's open. I'm here in the kitchen," she yelled out. She tried to straighten up her hair but gave up quickly. She was glad he was staying on the island.

Ian entered, followed by Gretel. He had a stern look on his face and something behind his back. "Sitting down on the job, I see."

Lily put her hands on her hips. "I'll have you know I've been working since six a.m. baking cookies, answering phones, fixing another leaky faucet and—"

"Whoa, just kidding. You look a little down in the dumps is all. I'm trying to cheer you up." He leaned over, kissed the top of her head, and handed her a bouquet of delicate blue forget-me-nots.

"They're so pretty, I love these little flowers."

He began to rub her shoulders and neck. His hands felt

like sunshine on ice, melting away every drop of tension until she felt like a pool of still water.

She leaned her head against Ian's chest and moaned, "Please, never stop."

Ian laughed. "We could take a quick run to the bedroom for a full body massage." His hands moved down her back while he trailed kisses down the side of her neck.

"There's just too much to do. I need to paint trim in the suite and…"

He covered her mouth with his to muffle her protests and whispered, "We'll have to remedy this dilemma. I know an excellent painter who works cheap…for cookies and kisses."

"Ian, you're already doing so much."

Ian lifted her chin. "Look at me, Lily," he said gently. "Let me help you. It would make *me* happy."

She stared at this man offering from his heart. How vulnerable it felt to let a man help her, but this was not Brad. There were no hidden agendas. Sunlight filled the room. "The sun has come out," Lily said. "Looks like it will be a good day to paint after all."

"I'll go get my brushes. We can finish the Rose Room in a flash." He tousled her hair. "And I have a surprise for you."

She frowned at him. "What kind?"

"A surprise kind," he said with a grin. "It's just outside. Close your eyes and I'll be right back."

What in the world, she wondered. She heard him enter and place something on the chair beside her.

"You can open your eyes now," he said.

Propped on the chair in front of her was a framed canvas painted in Ian's style. Her eyes widened as she took in the subject. It was her face, cheeks aglow, eyes closed, and her hair floating on a pillow of billowy clouds. Her body was covered by a blanket of wings–a blue heron in flight hovering above her sleeping form. Below her airy bed of clouds, turquoise water bubbled and steamed, sending mist into the air. She looked up at him.

"I sketched it while you slept that morning at the hot springs."

"It's beautiful, Ian."

She stood and reached out to him. They fell into each other's arms. "I love you, Lily."

It felt so right. "I love you too, Ian."

Gretel barked startling them. "What is it, girl?" Ian said. "Do you want some love too?"

The dog bounded between them, covering them with kisses. "Okay, okay," Lily said, petting Gretel's sleek back. "It's time to get back to work."

"At your service, ma'am. What colors did you plan in the suite again?"

"Rose pink, accented with white trim and forest green accessories."

Ian smirked. "No browns? Blues? Plaids?"

Lily scooted him out the door. "Get out of here and get your brushes before we lose our natural light."

Ian smiled, ran his fingertips over her cheek, and brushed his lips across hers. For a moment the room spun and her knees buckled. "After we finish, we could curl up in the bed and be the first guests in the new Lavender Room!"

Lily threw her brush at him. "Back to work! Fun later."

✦✦✦✦

Tomorrow was the grand reopening of the bed and breakfast, and the one thing still missing was Grandma Maggie's Heavenly Brownies. Lily's heart sank; it just wouldn't be a tribute to her grandmother without the brownies. Why didn't she leave me the recipe, she left me everything else?

Jude pulled up the driveway and started unloading boxes of mini-quiches. "Hey, Lily, come give me a hand with this stuff."

Lily walked out on the porch and stared in amusement. "Do you think you brought enough, Jude?"

Jude's face dropped, "You don't think it's enough?"

Lily tried to hold a serious face but burst out laughing. She threw her arms around Jude and hugged tight. "What would I do without you, my dear friend?"

"We can always freeze all the leftovers." Jude hugged Lily. "Girlfriend, we're almost there."

"I can't believe we pulled this off and the place is truly mine now."

"You did this, Lily, some of us helped." Jude looked over to Ian's house. "Some of us helped more than others though!"

"He is a good man…I can't believe I'm saying that either!"

"Well, I guess you might just have to smile more often now, Miss Bed and Breakfast owner."

The two women began carrying the boxes into the kitchen and unloading the contents into the refrigerator. Lily began rearranging the trays and bowls. "Pretty crowded in here, but I think I can make a bit more room."

"So, is there anything else I can help with, Lily, anything?"

"Jude, the one thing I need help with is finding the darn brownie recipe." Lily pulled out some tall glasses and filled them with fresh ice-cold raspberry lemonade.

"You got me there, Lily, that's a hard one. Have you looked through every cupboard and drawer?"

"I've literally torn the place apart. She didn't even leave me a clue. I've found recipes for every dish from scones to cheesecake, but no brownie recipe," Lily sighed.

"Do you want me to help you look for it again?" Jude offered.

"That's okay, Jude. You go ahead back into town. You still have your lunch rush to deal with. Thanks again for everything!"

"No problem, any time," Jude said with a wink.

Lily sat in the porch swing and watched Jude drive away. She rocked softly, remembering all the times she'd played on the porch with her grandmother. A cool breeze, sweet with jasmine, blew in from the Sound. In the distance a ferry horn blasted. And she could almost hear Grandma Maggie calling, "Time for supper, my little pony, whoa now." She had loved running around the yard, her long pale hair loose in the wind. Lily closed her eyes and remembered the sweet smell of fresh chocolate chip cookies and spiced apple cider that her grandmother would serve her while she played dolls in the afternoon. They'd had their games and secrets between them. When Lily couldn't fall asleep at night, Grandma would tell her the never-ending stories about a little girl named Kayla who ran away to the forest because she was so sad at home. Lily would listen intently. There was always a kind old woman, or a guardian angel or friendly fairy, who would lead Kayla back home and tell her wonderful things about herself.

A smile spread across her face. She no longer wanted to run away, she had found home. She remembered her favorite game—find the hiding place. And when she'd found the hiding place, her grandmother always left a treasure to uncover as well. Lily abruptly stopped rocking. Her mind snapped back to the secret place they had left messages for each other. My pony...THE PONY, the white ceramic horse they always hid secret messages in. Of course, sitting in plain sight in the china cabinet, the beautifully sculpted, silky smooth porcelain horse that had been her mother's as a little girl. That was it! Hopes building, she tore into the house and threw open the glass door of the mahogany china cabinet. On the bottom shelf, where it had been kept since her grandmother was a little girl, stood the shiny white horse with the hole in the bottom of its platform.

Lily carefully lifted out the horse. Of course, where else would her grandmother leave her the most important message of all? She turned the horse upside down and reached in carefully, her fingers a bit larger than when she was eight years old. Deep inside she could feel a stiff piece of paper, just out of her reach. She tried again, this time using her little and ring fingers, and was just able to grasp it. Slowly, she slid the paper down through the small hole. Sure enough, rolled up into a tiny scroll and inserted in the hiding place was a message just for her.

Her heart skipped a beat. Memories flooded. She could smell Grandma Maggie's familiar gardenia scent, hear her sparkling laugh. "You finally found it, dear."

Time and place blended together…she was a child anticipating the treasure, she was a granddaughter cherishing a last message, she was a woman hoping for the last secret to be revealed. She unrolled the scroll. Her grandmother's curvy scrawl covered the page.

My dear Lily,

I know in my heart you will find this message meant only for you. Never have you left my heart, not a day has gone by that I did not dream of you and wonder what kind of incredible woman you had grown up to be. Know, my granddaughter, that I am still with you and pray that you will find the love I have on Madrona Island and recapture the pure joy we found here together when you were a child. Everything I hold dear is yours, from the beautiful inn to the magical people who will fill it once you have touched it with your grace and love.

My last legacy to leave you is your favorite, and many others as well, the Grandma Maggie's Heavenly Brownie recipe. May it bring you blessings in all forms.
   For eternity,
   Your Grandma Maggie

Lily stared at the recipe, trying to read it between her tears. The ingredients registered on her palate. She lowered herself into the velvet rocker and held the recipe to her heart.

Grandma Maggie's Heavenly Brownies. "YES!" Lily yelled. "Thank you, Grandma."

Her eyes scanned the recipe, making a mental note of each ingredient and checking off if the needed item was already stocked in her kitchen. Then she smiled smugly; tomorrow there would be a big treat for everyone who attended: The richest, chewiest, fudgiest brownies in the world would be at the Madrona Island Bed and Breakfast Grand Reopening Celebration.

Lily hurried to the computer to type in the recipe and save it in a section only she knew the password for. The possibilities of selling these brownies online were unlimited; she'd be the Mrs. Fields of the Internet. Grandma Maggie's Heavenly Brownies, what a great brand name. She would need newly designed labels and, of course, a new variety of gourmet flavors. Hmm, how about Lavender Chardonnay, or spicy cayenne bites? She would use Valrhona chocolate, she would swear that brand had magical properties. A brownie test baking was in order, and she was sure she would have plenty of tasters volunteering.

The parlor clock struck 7:00. The sun was just beginning to set. Tomorrow was the grand opening; she would have to stay up pretty late to get a few batches baked, but it would be worth it. For now, she would stick with the standard recipe that everyone adored and bake as many as her stock of ingredients and her waning energy would allow.

She pulled out the dry ingredients and then a dozen eggs and mounds of butter. Probably enough for two large batches, she assessed. The chocolate melted over a low flame in the double boiler while she beat the eggs and measured the flour. A flash of fur flew by as Gretel came blundering into the kitchen, nails tapping on the wooden floor. She landed head on into Lily's arms.

"Hey, girl, how'd you get in here?"

Gretel licked away at Lily's buttery hands.

"Oh, I see, you must have smelled the brownie prepping all the way across the field."

Ian leaned against the kitchen entry, holding back a guilty smile. He looked like a little boy caught stealing cookies. "I confess, we saw your kitchen light still on and knew something good had to be going on in here."

"*We* saw?" she chided.

He moved toward her and brushed a wisp of flour from her nose. "Well, I saw, Gretel smelled, and we decided to explore."

Lily kissed his lips, holding her flour-stained body at a distance. He pulled her close, running his hands up her back. The kitchen timer went off, and Lily broke the kiss and rushed to the stove to check the chocolate. "Ah, not burned. Thank you to the kitchen gods."

Ian leaned over to inspect the glistening chocolate mixture. "So, what's up? I thought you were going to bed early, not diving into a container of Valrhona."

Lily flashed the neatly typed recipe before his eyes. "I found it," she said, waving in the air. "The brownie recipe!"

Ian eyed the recipe that quickly disappeared behind Lily's back.

Her eyes narrowed. "It's a secret family recipe. Even from

you...for now."

A grin lit her face. "This could be a very valuable commodity soon."

Ian took a seat at the table, rolled up his sleeves, and asked, "So, how can I help? Beat eggs, line pans?"

Hair spilling into his face, tiredness around his eyes, and he was still there for her. It meant a lot.

"We might make it to bed by midnight at this rate," he said, staring at her with invitation in his eyes.

The same butterflies went through her as the first time he kissed her.

"Perhaps."

Chapter Thirty-Seven

A fluorescent hummingbird made kamikaze dives from feeder to flower, gathering nectar. The green of the cedar trees provided a sharp contrast against the deep rusty oranges of the flickering bird. Nestled in the corner office overlooking the lawn, Lily watched, mesmerized by the tiny creature as its wings turned a rainbow of colors in the morning sunlight.

The crape myrtle trees were in bloom; their vibrant petals floated on the breeze and dropped to the ground, creating the effect of rosy snow on the lawn. Everything looked like a fairytale on this early summer day: Puffy white clouds on the horizon, birdsong echoing in the garden, and the sweet smell of alyssum in the air. A perfect day for a party.

Betty was in her yard snipping flowers for the table bouquets. Lily marveled at how much energy the eighty-year-old woman had—up at dawn, full of energy, positive attitude, what a great neighbor and friend. Mary was in the kitchen, and soon Lily would need to leave her perch and join her there.

Daisies bloomed abundantly along the east fence in shades of purple and white. Whenever she walked out the back door lately, the sweet scent overwhelmed her senses. Tired of paperwork, she left her desk and headed outside to the tool shed. She pulled out a pair of garden clippers. Daisy bunches would make great bouquets for the parlor and dining room today. She could hardly believe how well everything had come together. Her mother, first showing up unexpectedly a few weeks ago in jeans and a work shirt, and now back again, had almost been worth the whole experience. Finally, she had a mother who not only helped her with her complicated divorce, but painted trim and pulled weeds. The check was a very welcome gift too.

There were so many things to do to get ready, and here she was out in her sweats snipping more of the gloriousdaisies blooming in her yard. A smile crossed her face; there was nowhere else she would rather be. July fourth weekend was the perfect time to launch her new inn, and she would give one heck of a party to thank everyone too. She could hardly believe how well everything had gone. She thought of her new adopted family, Ian, Jason, and Gretel, and of course, the angel with the white hair, Grandpa John. She had two soul sisters, Jude and Kyla. With their unflinching support, Lily now felt like she belonged.

She gathered the sweet blossom stalks and brought them into the kitchen to put in water. While Lily had baked and planned, Mary had spent the last two days cleaning and waxing until the inn gleamed. Lily and Mary put the flowers in vases, then pulled out the finely ironed tablecloths, lace doilies, and placemats and brought them into the parlor. The counters were piled high with trays of breads, brownies, and cookies securely covered with pink plastic wrap. Cases of cabernet and merlot were stacked in the pantry, and in the refrigerator, bottles of chardonnay and the local strawberry wine were chilling.

Lily surveyed the trays one more time. Stuffed mushrooms with feta and pine nuts, Roquefort cheese balls rolled in crushed pecans, platters of roasted turkey, and smoked salmon. The outside refrigerator was overflowing too. The smell of freshly ground French roast coffee dominated the room. The last three days had been nonstop cooking, baking, and last-minute cleaning. The fact that the phone had been ringing off the hook for reservations and RSVPs had been gratifying. The magazine article had really helped to get exposure.

She walked upstairs and checked out the rooms one more time before placing a thick velvet rope across the doorways of the guest rooms so they were available for viewing but not entering. In the Rose Suite, all of her mother's things had been moved out of sight and into the closet. Lily heard a car pulling into the driveway and glanced out the hall window to see who was driving up. She looked at her watch, 8:00 a.m. Ian was true to his word when he promised yesterday to have the brochures to her first thing in the morning. She couldn't wait to see the glossy, full-color work of art that Ian had designed. *That man is so creative.* From graphic artist to painter, he had amazed her. The watercolor rendition of the B&B for the logo was gorgeous. Ian had wrapped the entire inn with climbing roses and in delicate calligraphy written Madrona Island Bed and Breakfast–Lily Parkins, Innkeeper.

It was Independence Day. And in two more weeks her independence day would come too. After today, she would be truly an independent business owner too. All her hopes were coming true. Only a year ago, she didn't even know *how* to dream.

Jude's car flew into the driveway behind Ian's. She had insisted on arriving early too. "We come bearing gifts," Jude and Katherine said, carrying containers of food.

Ian followed, holding a box of brochures and waving one in the air. "Just in time."

They crowded around Ian, admiring the slick new brochure.

"This makes me want to vacation here myself," Jude said. "Karen will be here soon to help supervise the food, and her husband has promised to take photos today for you to put on the website."

"Everyone has been so great, thank you guys." Lily hugged them both.

Jude led the way up the stairs to the kitchen. "Now, let's get this party started."

The dining room table would act as the indoor buffet table. Coffee, ice-cold strawberry lemonade, and some appetizers on silver platters would line the kitchen counters, garnished with herbs and edible flowers. Ian and Katherine were setting up the round tables on the grass. Under the shade of the cedar and dogwood trees was another long buffet table covered in an antique linen floral tablecloth. People kept arriving to help, and pretty soon the place was being transformed into a fairytale setting.

Betty and Shirley were placing huge bouquets of roses, foxgloves, and daisies on every table. Lily set out the coffee urn and the beautiful silver tea set. Mary, dressed in a gauzy floral skirt and hot-pink top, carried out several boxes of heavenly scented baked goods and a large sheet cake. The smooth, white icing on the cake was lined with red, white, and blue roses. In the center of the cake was a golden sugar star. The cake, which was baked by Betty and decorated by Shirley, read "To our island star. Good luck, Lily."

Lily hugged her neighbors. "You both have been wonderful. Betty, you're like a magic elf, fixing everything, and, Shirley, you're a mother lion protecting her cub."

"And with a mane to prove it," Betty said.

Shirley glared at her. "At least I'm not an elf."

"Come on, group hug. I love you two."

Ian walked over and saw the three women a bit teary. "Are you okay?" he asked.

"Yes, yes," Lily replied. "Just happy."

Jude walked out. "Lots of work to do, Lily." Jude clapped her hands. "Get a move on, ladies and gentlemen, it's almost show time."

It was 11 a.m., and Lily assessed their progress. Her mother was directing the delivery men where to store the champagne. The food was ready, the parking marked. Not much was needed here on this glorious, sunny day. The pond sparkled with droplets of sunlit gold, and an occasional white puffy cloud floated in a brilliant blue sky. Across the Sound, the jagged outline of the Olympic Mountains jutted out across the turquoise sky. And to the south, the imposing peak of Mount Rainier presented itself. "Gorgeous," she whispered to herself.

Jude took Lily by the hand. "Off to the shower with you. I'm going to go pick up Kyla."

She hurried inside and bumped straight into Ian. Instead of letting her through, he swept her into a corner for a kiss. She was lost in that blissful place that lovers go, floating in the colors and sensations.

"How are you doing, Miss Innkeeper?"

Lily sighed, still breathless from the kiss. "A bit frazzled, but happy."

He held her close, pressing his face into her hair. "I knew you could do it. Not for a moment did I doubt this would turn out so well."

Lily raised her eyes to him. "Thank you, Ian."

A loud car horn blasted outside. "Go," Ian said. "I'll take care of it."

A bit panicked, she hurried off to the shower. She looked

back to see Ian grinning as he watched her stumbling up the stairs. She blew him a quick kiss.

✦✦✦✦

Celtic music floated in the open windows of her bedroom. She took a last look in the mirror and walked outside to greet her arriving guests. Lily glided across the lawn, her rosy linen dress picking up the breeze. Katherine was already greeting guests as she walked over to join them. Ian, dressed in a pale blue shirt and jeans, waved to her as she passed by. He'd set up a face painting station for the kids, and Jason was running around it blowing bubbles. Gretel jumped at the floating objects, punctuating the air with barks.

People smiled, said hello, made their way to the food and wine. Many people she recognized, several were new. The overnight guests with reservations for the weekend would be settling into their rooms after the party ended.

"Why, you must be Lily," a silver-haired lady said. "I knew your grandmother. She would be so pleased how wonderful everything looks."

"Thank you," Lily said as people complimented the remodel, the food, her fortitude in reopening in the inn.

Thank you, Grandma Maggie, she whispered to herself.

Chapter Thirty-Eight

Jude knocked on Kyla's door and wondered why she was not waiting outside as planned. A voice yelled, "Come in." Jude walked in and found her friend standing over the table trying to tie a ribbon around a potted bouquet. Kyla's hands were shaking, and crushed, fragrant leaves spilled to the wooden floor. "Darn, I'm already late and now this. I'm sorry, Jude, everyone must be wondering where the heck I am."

"Are you all right?" Jude asked.

"Fine, fine," Kyla said, brushing loose dirt back into the pot. "I'll just go wash my hands."

Something was wrong, Jude was sure of it. She followed her friend to the bathroom and watched her briskly comb through her mane of fiery red hair, tightening tortoise shell and amber combs in place. The July sun poured through the window, but Kyla was shaking and rubbing her arms as if she were freezing. She removed a small clump of hair from the comb and tossed it in the wicker wastebasket.

"I guess I have to go, for Lily," she said.

"Don't you want to go?" Jude asked.

Kyla just stared at her with a faraway look. "I guess running is no longer an option," was all she said. Then she hiked her green satin skirt up, laced up the leather thongs of her knee-high sandals, and adjusted the embroidered belt over her peasant blouse. She looked like a gypsy princess with gathered sleeves falling gently over her porcelain-like shoulders. But her pupils, wide as a spooked horse's and surrounded by emerald eyes the color of an Irish hill, betrayed her. Jude kept silent. Kyla would tell her when she was ready.

Kyla dropped onto the velvet sofa. "Remember when we posed for *Coast Flight Magazine*, when they featured the inn's grand opening?"

"Sure," Jude said. "The picture of the three of us smiling, toasting Madrona Island B&B looked great."

"What had I been thinking that day?" Kyla said, looking at Jude her eyes pools of sadness.

"What do you mean, Kyla? Tell me."

"The story was picked up by the travel section of the *Seattle Times*. I was recognized and he tracked me down."

Jude felt concern building in her chest. "Who tracked you down?"

Kyla rambled on, "He must hate me for leaving like that without a word. How can I face him again?"

"What do you mean?" Jude asked, hoping Kyla would make some sense.

Kyla walked over to her answering machine and pushed play. "Kyla, my love, per chance do you remember me? It's Lucas. How lovely you look in the *Coast Flight Magazine*, flowering herbs in your hair, not at all the NY model splashed across *Vogue* that I remember."

There was a sharp edge to the voice, each word pronounced with precision and aim. Kyla was frozen in place. Jude tried to compute all the information being spilled out in this message.

"Imagine my astonishment finding enchanting little you on this remote island. Ah yes, I am here too. I wouldn't miss this grand opening for anything. Until then…"

Breathing deeply, Kyla reached for a glass of water and took a sip. "Enough," she said, rising to her feet. "Let's go, Jude. I will not give in to fear." Rushing now, she jumped into Jude's car. "Please don't ask me about this now. I'll tell you everything after the party."

Jude drove, her mind reeling. Who was this woman she called her friend? All the missing pieces started to fill in, Kyla's secrecy and fatigue.

There were cars lining the lane and filling the parking lot when they got there. "Good for you, Lily!" Jude said aloud. Kyla emerged from her car, a vision of green satin and red curls, holding a large woven basket of rosemary and other flowering herbs. Jude watched her eyes scan the crowd and lock into another pair watching her from his lone perch on a nearby bench.

He was at their side before Jude could catch her breath. "May I help you carry anything, Kyla? It is you, right? I just had to see for myself." His eyes went from her hair to her eyes, from her clothes to her shoes. "From sophisticate to country gypsy, I didn't think that was your style."

Both women tried to walk past him, but he blocked Kyla's way and Jude would not leave her there alone.

"I can see the allure of this lifestyle," he said, staring out at the water. "You could have given me the choice to follow." He moved closer, his lightning-gray eyes searching her own. "Or was that part of the plan…to leave me behind?"

Kyla's voice came out in a whisper. "Lucas." She averted her eyes and clutched her chest.

Jude stepped over to rescue her friend. "Kyla, let's go greet Lily."

"It's okay, Jude. I owe him some explanation." Kyla turned to Lucas. "I have no good excuse, my fears took over and I just had to run."

The anger in his face seemed to drain out and uncover the grief lurking below. Lucas ran his fingertips over Kyla's arm and shoulder. "What were you really running from Kyla... from me?"

Tears spilled down her sun-touched cheeks. "No, Lucas, I was just..." Kyla covered her eyes.

Jude had had enough. She took Kyla's arm and guided her toward the house, leaving Lucas behind and praying he wouldn't follow them.

✦✦✦

Lily tightened her grip on Ian's warm hand. They stood motionless, watching the scene unfold between Kyla and a man Lily had not seen before. She could feel Ian's body stiffen, and his eyes never left the couple. Jude was with them, so she was not too worried. Ian did not share his thoughts with her, but Lily was pretty sure he knew more than he was saying right now.

"What the heck? Who is that man and why is Kyla crying?" Lily said, loosening her grip on Ian's hand. "Should I go after her or let her have her space? She's such a private person."

Ian kept his eyes on Kyla. "I'll go," he said. "Trust me, Lily, she needs support. It appears the whole story will probably come out now."

Lily cocked her head. "What story, Ian?"

His eyes softened and he kissed her cheek. "Let me go now, we can talk later."

She watched him head toward the back door, and an uneasy feeling moved through her stomach. She considered following him. Did she still not trust this man she loved? Brad's face crossed her mind, and she banished it to where it belonged, gone. She noticed the golden boy who had caused all the trouble with Kyla was watching Ian too. His face looked like he had seen a ghost.

The man walked over to Lily and introduced himself. "You have one fantastic place here, and I'm sure you will be very successful." He put out his hand to shake hers. "Lucas Bradford."

She shook his hand. One thing for sure, he was not hard to look at. "Nice to meet you," she said.

"I'll be leaving now, but I'm sure I will be back. Good luck with your new endeavor."

She watched him walk away. Who the heck was he and where was Kyla to ask? Perhaps she would check in the house.

Lily peeked into the kitchen. "Everything going okay in here?"

Mary smiled. "Couldn't be better, especially with Jason, my little helper, here."

Jason was so busy decorating trays with sprigs of fresh herbs that he didn't even notice Lily was there. She crept up behind him and covered his eyes. "Guess who?"

He pulled her hands down, turned, and gave her an enthusiastic hug. "I love helping with the food and tasting it too. Mary said I have a good plate."

Lily laughed. "You mean palate, good tasting ability. You have your dad's creative eye too. I see. Maybe one day you'll be a master chef."

Jason clapped his hands joyfully. "Yes, yes, I want to be a baker too."

"Speaking of your dad, have you seen him lately?"

Jason thought for a moment. "Oh yeah, I saw him a few minutes ago go up the stairs with Kyla."

She ruffled his hair. "Thanks, Jason, I'll just go find him. Keep up the good work." She winked at Mary and headed up the steps.

A cloud of fear crept over her heart. Images of the two of them in one of the bedrooms raced through her mind. Old wounds from her life with Brad propelled her up the stairs while trepidation nipped cruelly at her heels. When she reached the closed door to the Lavender Room, she could hear muffled voices inside. At least it wasn't the Rose Room, where she and Ian had declared their love.

Quietly, she cracked open the door and saw them sitting on the edge of the bed. Ian had his arms around Kyla, and her head was resting on his chest. Kyla's head jerked up, startled, eyes wide and puffy and tears staining her cheeks. Ian was comforting her. But why here, now, why him? Was he breaking up with her? Kyla was supposed to be Lily's friend and Ian... Her thoughts came to a halt as her body began to tremble.

Kyla and Ian darted over toward her. All Lily could do was put up her hands in a stop motion. Ian looked at Kyla, as if for permission. Silence, then Kyla wiped her cheeks with a handkerchief and nodded to him.

"Lily, please come in," she said. "It's time I told you more about me. I am so sorry I waited this long to confide in you."

Heart thumping violently inside her chest, Lily took a seat in the rocker by the bed. The scent of lavender filled the air, and though it was one of her favorites, the smell turned her stomach sour now. Ian moved behind her and placed his hands on her shoulders. She reflexively flinched at his touch. "Why don't you start by telling me what's going on here?"

Kyla sat on the edge of the bed facing Lily. Staring down at her clasped hands she took a deep breath and began. "Lily, Ian and I knew each other before I moved to the island. It was in New York."

Lily pushed herself from the chair. "I've changed my mind. I really don't need to know—"

Ian stopped her, pressing down gently on her shoulders. "Lily, it's not what you think, not even close. Please listen, just for a minute." He tipped her chin up so she could meet his eyes. "You know me, Lily. Trust me for just a few moments... please."

Kyla began again. "Five years ago, I was a top New York fashion model. It was a glamorous life, money flowed, and it was one long fantasy. Ian and I met at his premier art showing at the Findley Rose Gallery in Manhattan. My fiancé, Lucas, bought some of Ian's work and invited him to the loft to join us for drinks."

Lily started to breathe again. "Go on."

"The three of us spent several days together hitting NY's finest clubs, restaurants, and theaters. We sailed on the bay and enjoyed the good life that Lucas and his family fortune could amply provide. One afternoon, when Lucas was conducting one of his endless business calls, Ian told me all about Madrona Island. At the time, it sounded like the far end of the Earth."

Kyla looked up at Ian, "You have been such a good friend to me." She turned back to Lily. "Lily, you are a good friend. I would never intentionally hurt either one of you."

Ian took Lily's hand. "I'm sorry I couldn't tell you."

"Until now," Kyla said, "it was important to me that Ian keep my secret, even from you, Lily."

"So, what was so important that you couldn't tell me?" Lily asked. She watched Kyla's face grow pale. The room grew very still, except for faint sounds coming from the party outside. Lily looked from Ian's face to Kyla's and saw nothing but pain in both.

"Lily, I have advanced lupus."

"I'm so sorry to hear that, Kyla, but I still don't understand why you couldn't tell Jude and me. We would have been there for you, helped you out."

"Lily, it wasn't just the disease, it was every other lie I wove to hide the fact that I was even on Madrona Island. My lies all began to unravel when I became friends with you both. I knew you wondered about Ian and me, but I hoped after you realized there was nothing between us except friendship, your fears would just fade away."

Ian turned Lily toward him. "My love, I did not like keeping any secrets from you, but I had made a sacred promise to Kyla. I was in a tough position trying to be honorable."

Lily was still confused and looked questioningly at Kyla. "Tell me more."

"Less than a month after I first met Ian, I could no longer cover up my symptoms. I was horrified, worried about my career and losing my jet-set fiancé, not to mention my life. Without telling anyone, I saw a specialist and began steroid and then chemotherapy treatments."

Lily stared at her friend. All the pieces started falling together. Why Kyla never wanted to go out and kept to herself so much. How alone she must have felt. The times she was whispering to Ian. "Why did you come here?"

"I decided it would be easier to just vanish to the wonderful little island Ian had spoken of. I was a fool. I know this now. And I couldn't be sorrier for dragging Ian into my complicated little drama and causing you a moment of pain or doubt."

"It must have been very hard on you. What about your family, couldn't you go to them?"

"My family lives in New York, and if they knew I was ill, they would never have let me leave, particularly alone, and I was determined to disappear. I fell back on my family legacy of herbalists and healers, and started a new life here."

Ian broke in. "You've been hiding so much for so long. Maybe it's time to let all of that worry go and reveal yourself to those who love you."

"You're probably right," Kyla said. "I knew my career would be over, and I didn't want to find out if Lucas would stick by me without all my worldly trappings. I loved him so much."

Ian took Lily's hand and picked up the thread of the story. "It was about three years ago that I got a call at my studio from Kyla. I thought she and Lucas wanted to purchase some of my art. But as we talked, all she wanted was to know more about Madrona Island."

"Intuitively, I felt that Ian was a trustworthy soul and I could safely ask him to respect my privacy and keep my secret. So Ian became my very kind co-conspirator. He helped me find a location for the *Tea & Comfort* shop, introduced me to some local people, and occasionally checked up on me. That's all. Unfortunately for me, my heart still remains stubbornly in love with Lucas."

Lily considered the heartbreaking confession. Her own self-doubt and fear seemed paltry next to Kyla's difficulties. She took Kyla's hand. "I only wish you had told me this before so I could have been there for you as a friend."

"I wanted to tell you and Jude, and almost did so many times. That night of our slumber party, the whole story almost spilled out. But one slip and the chance that it might get out threatened my hard-earned peace and privacy and this life I have come to love on Madrona Island."

One last shadow of doubt flickered in Lily's mind. "So, just why are you two up here in the Lavender Room today?"

Color drained from Kyla's face once again and her voice

came out in a thin whisper. "Lucas is here. Today. He has found me."

Lily gasped. "The man who introduced himself? How did he find you?"

"The picture of all of us in *Coast Flight Magazine* to help promote the B&B reopening landed in his hands."

"Oh, Kyla, I'm so sorry."

"Don't be, Lily. It's time I let go of this haunting secret and face it head on. I'm older and wiser now, and it will be good for my health to lay this burden down."

"I think I can speak for Ian and Jude. We are all here to help you. Just ask."

Kyla returned Lily's gentle gaze and managed a faint smile. "Nothing beats the old Irish healing methods," she said wryly, "and the love of good friends! The doctors are quite amazed how well I'm doing, so don't worry about me."

Lily stood and started for the door. "I had better get back to my guests. You take as long as you want up here. Lucas has left, so just come down when you are ready. ."

"Thanks, Lily. Ian, you go with her. I want a moment alone to re-center myself before I go down again. Thank you both."

Lily slipped her hand into Ian's, twining her fingers gratefully in his as they walked down the stairs. The emotional rollercoaster ride was over...at least for the moment.

Jason came out of the kitchen to greet them. "I see you found my dad," he said.

Lily looked up at Ian. "Finding your dad, Jason, has been one of the best things I've ever done in my life."

Jason looked puzzled. "I don't get it. I thought he was just upstairs?"

Ian and Lily chuckled. "Come on, big boy," Ian said as he whisked Jason off his feet and placed him on his shoulders.

"Let's go outside to join the party and have some fun."

Hand in hand, they walked outside to celebrate the special day.

◆◆◆◆

The musicians had changed to an upbeat jazz band, and some of the guests were dancing on the grass. "The party is a success," she whispered to herself. "As good as I could have hoped it would be." She looked up to the sky and silently thanked the sun gods for this glorious day. Keyboard music wafted on the breeze, setting just the right mood.

"We're going to get something to drink, can I bring you something?" Ian asked.

"I would love some lemonade," Lily said. "And Ian... thanks."

Lily checked on Mary and Karen, who were watching over the food tables, and replenishing the dishes that were the most popular. She'd seen Karen's husband somewhere, baby in a stroller, kids in tow. It was time for her to take a break, if only for a moment.

Her mother waved and motioned her over. Katherine kissed Lily's cheek. "Look who's here...Roma."

Lily hugged her friend. "I can't believe you flew all the way up here from LA for this."

"Wouldn't miss it," Roma said. "This feast you've prepared could rival any top chef. Great job, Lily."

"Thank you, it means it lot. And I thank *you* for all your help, Mom."

Katherine leaned in and whispered, "Everything all right with you and Ian?"

"You don't miss much do you, Mom?" Lily looked over at Ian and Jason walking toward her with a tall drink. "Much more than all right."

Jason hurried over, balancing the icy lemonade. "Here you go," he said. "There's a strawberry in yours and mine too!"

"Here's yours, buddy," Ian said, handing Jason his drink. "Can I get you a glass, Katherine?"

"No thanks, I've had my fill. But I do think I will head over and get another one of those brownies now."

Lily stood and sipped her drink. A light breeze carried the scent of lilacs as the bright sun warmed her face and shoulders. Everywhere people were smiling and having fun. Jude was dancing on the lawn with her new chef. Ryan's shyness seemed to melt away under the radiance of Jude's smile as he twirled her under his arm. A young couple walking arm-in-arm approached her. "Excuse me, are you the innkeeper?"

"Yes, I am. Can I help you two?"

The lithe woman gazed up at the striking young man on her arm. "We would like to talk to you about planning our wedding here. It's one of the prettiest, most romantic places we have ever seen."

"Well, thank you," Lily said. Her eyes moved lovingly over the grounds, the remodeled inn, and the sweeping view of the Sound. "It's a very magical place, and we would love to help you plan your special celebration here. Why don't you get something cool to drink, have a seat? I'll bring you a brochure shortly."

"You boys will have to excuse me for a minute while I take care of business."

"That's fine," Ian said. "Jason wants to get his face painted."

Lily waved after them. "Have fun."

On her way to the office, Lily spotted Shirley and Betty across the lawn under a flowered umbrella and headed their way. They appeared to be enthralled by a stack of brownies set before them.

"Well, don't you two ladies look as lovely as ever? And you must tell me where you got that gorgeous hat, Shirley."

Shirley glared at Betty. "See? This girl has some fashion sense, unlike someone I know."

"To each his own," said Betty, popping another bite of brownie into her mouth.

Shirley continued, "Thank goodness someone can recognize good taste on this island. I ordered this hat special from the Nordstrom catalog." She flicked the edges of the large-brimmed sunhat with her fingers and struck a dramatic pose, as if for a camera.

Betty muttered under her breath, "I wouldn't be caught dead in that thing."

"Now, now, ladies, I love you both just as you are. I couldn't have done all this without both of your help."

Shirley looked both flustered and moved by Lily's quip. Betty looked Lily right in the eye. "You're one tough lady, Lily, and you did one heck of a job on this party, not to mention the inn."

Not to be outdone, Shirley squeezed Lily's hand. "You are one heck of a woman, too. I don't have to read tea leaves to foresee success and romance in your future."

Lily's grin filled her face. "You two really know how to make me feel good." She wiped her tears away. "Enough of this sentimentality. Can I get you something more to eat? Ice tea? More brownies?"

Betty stood up. "We can get our own goodies, you just run along now and chat up all those other guests. After this day, the 'No Vacancy' sign will stay up on a permanent basis!"

Lily brought the couple the brochure and continued mingling from table to table, taking compliments and answering questions. When the late afternoon sun started to drop behind the Olympic Mountains, guests began to leave, but not without promising to come back soon.

Lily wandered over to the old wooden bench and took a seat facing the glistening waters of the Puget Sound. Gretel bounded over and plopped at her feet. It had been a long day, and definitely one worth waiting for.

"May we join you?" Ian asked.

"I wouldn't have it any other way."

Jason scooted in next to her and laid his head on her shoulder. Ian nuzzled in on her other side. Lily encircled them both in her arms.

Epilogue

The bride stirred, allowing the luxurious satin sheets to caress her skin. Morning sun peered through the sheer window curtains, creating patterns on the bed's ruffled canopy. She yawned and turned her head to her new husband beside her. His lips were slightly open, breath moving through them, soft and even. She let her lips brush his in this perfect moment. Lucky, blessed...was there a word to describe how she felt? Blissful, contented...were there enough words? She wanted to go to the window and yell to everyone on the island...thank you.

Careful not to wake him, she tiptoed to the window and watched the sun spreading its crimson and apricot rays across the water. A lone heron crossed the sky, probably in search of breakfast. In a short while, a tray would be delivered to their door, courtesy of Mary. Coffee, black and rich, almond and chocolate croissants, and a dish of blackberries and cream would cover the silver tray.

She pulled the chenille spread off the rocking chair and wrapped it tightly around her shoulders as she sat down by the window. Her gaze landed on a vine maple in the yard, its vibrant fall foliage tinged with orange and reds. A few scattered leaves already lined the mossy ground.

Her husband tossed under the blanket then opened his eyes and yawned. "Good morning, my love."

She dropped her wrap and hurried back to the bed. His arms wide, she cuddled beside him. "Are we truly awake?" she asked.

His warm laugh filled the room. "It may be a dream, but I think I smell coffee coming from under the door."

"I'll go. You prop up the pillows and I'll bring back the tray."

The two lounged in bed, sipping the warm liquid, letting the flaky pastries crumble onto the down quilt. They fed each other blackberries covered in cream, following most bites with a kiss.

Both in their robes now, they settled on the loveseat by the fire. On the side table lay the Guestbook for the Honeymoon Suite.

The bride picked up the laminated pen and opened the book to an empty page.

October 4
   We couldn't have been happier to spend our first night of marriage in this enchanted place. Every happy memory for the rest of our life begins here.

She signed her name and so did the groom…

Lily and Ian McPherson.

The story continues in the Madrona Island Trilogy

Book Two–*Tea & Comfort*

This second volume features the puzzling yet sensuous, Kyla Nolan. The story unravels the mystery behind her hasty departure from her glamorous New York life as a top model and her transformation to shop proprietor, herbalist, and local tea leaf reader on Madrona Island. Follow her battle with a reoccurring illness and the return of Lucas, the wealthy winery owner and former fiancé whom she left behind. Can a love that was so based on outside trappings survive illness and loss? With a touch of the paranormal, and her island friends, Kyla comes to terms with her fears and her heart's longings.

Coming Soon 2016 Book Three–*Island Thyme Café*

The final book features the vivacious and loving, Jude Simon, owner of the popular Island Thyme Café. After Kyla's wedding festivities are over, Jude finds her own relationship with Ryan in jeopardy. This forces her to face the tragedy surrounding her husband's abandonment many years ago. Left a single mother of an infant daughter, Jude went on to make a success of her café, but still hides her broken heart behind her radiant smile. At almost 40 years old, she finds herself falling hard for her new chef, Ryan. Her feelings are returned, and just when she thinks she has found love at last, Ryan's own dark secret returns in the form of a seductive ex-lover. With the help of Kyla and Lily, Jude decides to fight for what she wants most and find the happy ending she has always longed for.

Grandma Maggie's Baking Company
RECIPES

Grandma Maggie's Heavenly Brownies

2 squares 100% Cacao
½ cup butter
¾ cup dark brown sugar
2 eggs
1 tsp. vanilla
¼ cup flour
¼ cup special dark cocoa powder
¼ tsp. salt
1 Tbs. mayonnaise
½ cup milk chocolate chips

Melt chocolate and butter together. Add sugar, vanilla and mayonnaise. Add eggs, one at a time, beating well after each addition. Carefully stir in flour, cocoa powder and salt. Add chocolate chips. Pour into well-greased 8 x 8 inch glass dish and bake at 325 degrees for 40-45 minutes. Do not over bake.

Inn Style Cookies
Created by Michaelene McElroy

½ cup unsalted butter–room temperature
¼ cup white sugar
½ cup brown sugar
1 egg
1 tsp. vanilla
¾ cup flour, plus 1 Tbs. - separated
½ tsp. baking soda
½ tsp. cinnamon
¼ tsp. salt (omit if salted butter is used)
1½ cups oatmeal (not instant)
1 cup toasted coconut

½ cup toffee bits
½ cup raisins
½ cup bittersweet chocolate pieces
½ cup chopped pecans

Preheat oven to 350 degrees. In a pan, over low heat, toast coconut until golden (approximately 10 minutes). Let cool. In a bowl, toss together toasted coconut, toffee bits, raisins, bittersweet chocolate pieces, and chopped pecans with 1 tablespoon flour. Set aside. Sift together flour, salt, cinnamon, and baking soda.

Beat butter until softened. Add white sugar and beat until blended, then add brown sugar and beat until light and fluffy (approximately 2 minutes). Add egg and vanilla, and beat until incorporated. Add dry ingredients and beat on low speed until blended. Add oatmeal and coconut mixture and blend well.

Lily likes big cookies. Place a ¼ cup of mixture (a ¼ cup ice cream scoop is perfect for this job) for each cookie, on a well greased cookie sheet. Bake at 350 degrees for 15-17 minutes. Check at 15 minutes. Makes approximately 18 mouthwatering cookies.

Mt. Rainier Cookies
Created by Michaelene McElroy
Filling:

1 cup peanut butter (strictly peanuts, no fillers)
2 Tbs. caramel sauce (store bought is fine as long as it's high quality)
1 cup powdered sugar, sifted

Mix peanut butter with caramel sauce, add powdered sugar, and mix until smooth. Shape into one inch balls. Freeze.

Cookie Dough:

   12 oz. bittersweet chocolate
   2 Tbs. butter
   2 Tbs. caramel sauce
   1 cup sweetened condensed milk
   1 tsp. vanilla
   2 cups flour
   ¼ tsp. salt

Melt bittersweet chocolate and butter in microwave at 50% power until chocolate is melted. Stir until smooth. In a mixing bowl, add caramel sauce and sweetened condensed milk to chocolate mixture and beat on low speed until incorporated. Sift flour and salt and add to mixture. Mix on low speed. Dough will be firm.

Assembly:

Break off pieces of the cookie dough and wrap around the frozen peanut butter filling. Make sure the filling is well sealed within the dough.

Baking:

Bake at 350 degrees for 10-12 minutes. Time varies based on size and accuracy of oven temperature. Let cool. Once cool, roll in powdered sugar.

Lavender Orange French Toast

Egg Mixture:
    1 loaf egg bread (Challah works great)
    10 eggs
    ½ cup of half and half
    1 Tbs. sugar
    ½ tsp. cinnamon
    2 Tbs. orange zest
    1/8 tsp. culinary lavender
    1 tsp. vanilla

Whisk 10 eggs in a bowl and beat in half and half, sugar, cinnamon, orange zest, culinary lavender, and vanilla. Prepare filling.

Filling:
    1 Tbs. fresh orange juice
    2 8-oz packages of cream cheese
    ½ tsp culinary lavender
    4 heaping Tbs. orange marmalade

Take 1 slice of bread. Spread generously with cream cheese mix and put another slice on top. Then soak in egg mixture. Grill on medium heat in skillet with generous amounts of butter. Grill both sides. Smother in syrup.

Syrup Mixture:
    1 cup real maple syrup
    2 tsp. orange zest
    1 tsp. fresh orange juice
    ½ tsp. culinary lavender

Heat syrup before serving then add other ingredients, stir and serve.

Fennel Sausage Frittata

Created by Andrea Hurst & Carol Reaf

2 Tbs. butter
½ lb. Chicken Sausage
8 oz. can artichoke hearts
¼ cup olive oil
2 cups onion, chopped
3 cloves minced garlic
2 cups portabella mushrooms
2 cups chopped fresh fennel
¼ tsp. salt
6 large eggs
1 tsp. basil
½ tsp. pepper
2 tsp. oregano
1 cup parmesan cheese grated
½ cup provolone grated

On a high flame, sauté chopped sausage and half of the vegetables except for the mushrooms in ¼ cup oil and 1 Tbs. butter in frying pan until translucent. Repeat with the rest of vegetables, oil, and butter. Place in flat low casserole dish (9x9). Preheat oven: 350 degrees. Sauté mushrooms on medium high in 1 Tbs. butter until brown. Add to casserole.

Drain canned artichokes, quarter and add to casserole dish. In blender, mix together 6 eggs, cheeses, salt, pepper and other seasonings and pour over casserole. Squeeze garlic through press over ingredients. Bake approximately 25-30 minutes until knife in center comes out dry. Cut and serve hot or cold. Four to Six servings.

Acknowledgements

Cover Design: Lidia Vilamajo
Copy Editors/Proof Readers: Audrey Mackaman & Marie DeHaan
Interior Layout: Brian C. Short
Developmental Editor: Cate Perry
Marketing: 2MarketBooks
Original Cover photo courtesy of Auberge on the Vineyard B&B (Cloverdale, CA)
www.sonomabedbreakfastinnwinecountry.com

Just like Lily had wonderful people helping her on her journey, I've had many supporters who have helped me on my journey with this book.

I'd like to thank Barbara Scharf, whose friendship and love for reading guestbooks inspired me to tell this story. To my expert editor, Lisa Siegel, I couldn't have done this without you. For her undying support and reading multiple versions, Jean Galiana's input has been invaluable. Cate Perry, writer, friend and extraordinary manuscript critiquer, I appreciate all you have done and continue to do. Audrey Mackaman has been an irreplaceable colleague both technically and with her exquisite cover design.

Gratitude goes to my fellow writers at Just Write for their encouragement and for showing up to write. Rowena Williamson and Mare Chapman, I thank you for your unwavering support, ideas, and friendship. And to William Bell at Local Grown Coffee, for giving us a place to write. Thank you Cherise Hensley and Cindy Hurn for proofreading.

To the expert readers and editors along the way, Dick Magnuson, Marie de Haan, Hanna Rhys Barnes, Lexi Hughes-Wooton, Julia Ringo, and Kelsi Lindus, your feedback helped shape this story. Acknowledgement goes to my original critique group, Rex Browning and Jan Carpenter, Judy Petersen, Shannon Thompson, and Tesia Lund who read the very first draft and encouraged me to continue.

Special thanks to amazing author, Anjali Banerjee for not only endorsing the book but helping me more than she knows.

I am grateful to my family for instilling in me the love of books at a very early age. To my children, Justin and Geneva, thanks for believing in me.

Lastly I would like to acknowledge the Farmhouse Bed and Breakfast in Clinton, WA, where I got the idea for this book, and the Inn at Barnum Point (Camano Island, WA), and the Flower Farm Inn (Loomis, CA), where I spent many hours writing and gained ideas for my setting. To Auberge on the Vineyard (Cloverdale, CA), who graciously offered the cover photo, I can't wait to visit. www.sonomabedbreakfastinnwinecountry.com

Recipes –
Mt. Rainier and Inn Style Cookies created by Michaelene McElroy
Grandma Maggie's Brownies created by Carol Reaf and Andrea Hurst, Sausage Frittata created by Carol Reaf and Andrea Hurst

Readers Group Discussion Questions for *The Guestbook*
www.andreahurst-author.com

1. Why do you think Lily stayed in an unhappy marriage for so long? Do you agree with her decision to give up everything she knew—including a life of financial security—in order to brave the waters of the unknown?

2. Do you feel Lily was right in leaving Brad for good? What do you think Brad would have needed to truly change his ways—or was it possible at all? Under what circumstances do you feel a cheating spouse deserves a second chance?

3. Discuss the role of food in *The Guestbook*. How did it play into Lily's childhood memories? How did it bring people together? How was it used as a source of comfort? As a sign of turbulence?

4. Friendship is a major theme in *The Guestbook*. Discuss the various friendships Lily develops on Madrona Island. How do these new friends help care for Lily and assist her in building her business and her self-worth? Do you have friends that have made a difference in these ways in your life?

5. Lily develops a "surrogate family" on Madrona Island. Who does her new family consist of? Has anyone ever adopted you as a "surrogate" mother, sister, or daughter? Do you have people in your life who are "surrogate" family members to you?

6. In Lily's family, three generations of women have

made choices based largely around the men in their lives. How has each woman's decision impacted her and those around her?

7. There are several generational parallels throughout *The Guestbook*, including Lily and her mother both being abandoned for other women; Lily and her grandmother's passion with food and care-taking; and Lily and Ian finding the same second chance at love their grandparents had enjoyed years before. Why might a younger generation parallel their parentage? Has your life paralleled your parents' or grandparents' lives in any way?

8. While Lily's grandmother wasn't physically present for most of *The Guestbook*, her presence was often felt. How did Lily's grandmother guide her using the guestbook as a medium? Have you ever felt someone from the other side guiding you in your life?

9. Because of Brad's infidelity, Lily has had difficulty trusting Ian not to hurt her in the same way. By the end of the book, do you feel Lily can truly trust Ian?

10. How has Lily grown by the end of *The Guestbook*? What other characters have shown growth in this book? How so?

11. Was Kyla right in keeping her illness from her friends? Why or why not?

12. Jude feels an immediate attraction to her new employee, Chef Ryan. How would you handle romantic

feelings for someone you had to work with on a daily basis?

13. At the beginning of this story, when Lily "takes the wheel" of her Honda to leave Brad, she is essentially taking the wheel of her life. Symbols emerge throughout *The Guestbook*, from nature imagery to the soulwarming cooking of food. What symbols emerged for you and how did they deepen the meaning of the story?

14. In *The Guestbook*, John and Grandma Maggie–as well as Lily and Ian–get a second chance at love. Do you believe each person has one soul mate, or is it possible to find another love? Share the stories of people you know.

15. Is it possible to have it all–your job, your talent, your passion, your love, *and* your dreams? Or is sacrifice inevitable? To what extent should a person sacrifice him/herself in the name of love, if at all?

16. How does setting play an important role in this story? Is Madrona Island a place you would like to visit?

Please visit Madrona Island at
www.andreahurst-author.com

When not visiting local farmers markets or indulging her love for chocolate, ANDREA HURST is an author and literary agent. Her passion for books drives her to find and write stories that take readers on a journey to another place and leave them with an unforgettable impression. She is a developmental editor for publishers and authors, an instructor in creative writing at the Northwest Institute of Literary Arts, and a webinar presenter for Writers Digest. She lives with her dachshund in the Pacific Northwest, on an island much like the fictional Madrona, with all of its natural beauty and small town charm.

Her published books include *The Guestbook*, *Tea & Comfort*, *Always with You*, The *Lazy Dog's Guide to Enlightenment* and *Everybody's Natural Food Cookbook*, and she co-authored *A Book of Miracles*. To learn more about Andrea and her books, visit www.AndreaHurst-Author. com or www.andreahurst.com.

Woe Is I

The Grammarphobe's Guide to Better English in Plain English

Patricia T. O'Conner

RIVERHEAD BOOKS
NEW YORK

For Stewart

RIVERHEAD BOOKS
Published by The Berkley Publishing Group
A division of Penguin Group (USA) Inc.
375 Hudson Street
New York, New York 10014

Copyright © 1996, 2003 by Patricia T. O'Conner
Book design by Brian Mulligan/Lovedog Studio
Cover design © Archie Ferguson

First Riverhead hardcover edition: July 2003
First Riverhead trade paperback edition: July 2004
Riverhead trade paperback ISBN: 1-59448-006-0

The Library of Congress has catalogued the Riverhead hardcover edition as follows:

O'Conner, Patricia T.
Woe is I : the grammarphobe's guide to better English in plain English /
Patricia T. O'Conner.
p. cm.
Rev. ed. of: Woe is I. c1996.
Includes bibliographical references and index.
ISBN 1-57322-252-6
1. English language—Grammar—Handbooks, manuals, etc.
2. English language—Usage—Handbooks, manuals, etc.
I. Title: Woe is I.   II. O'Conner, Patricia T. Woe is I.   III. Title.
PE1112.O28   2003   2003041416
428.2—dc21

Printed in the United States of America

10   9   8   7   6   5   4

Patricia T. O'Conner, a former editor at *The New York Times Book Review*, has written for many magazines and newspapers, and is a popular radio and television commentator. She is the author of two other books on language and writing, *Words Fail Me: What Everyone Who Writes Should Know About Writing* and, with Stewart Kellerman, *You Send Me: Getting It Right When You Write Online*. She lives in Connecticut.

PRAISE FOR
Woe Is I

"Wow! Who would have thought that you could have such a delicious time with a grammar book? *Woe Is I* is great fun."

—Susan Isaacs

"When we all come to our senses and start recognizing truly important deeds, Patricia T. O'Conner will get a ticker-tape parade and a big, shiny medal. Maybe even a flattering statue in a New York City park. This former *New York Times Book Review* editor has done more to keep the streets safe from bad grammar than just about anyone else, and we all owe her. First published in 1996, *Woe Is I* has been expanded and fine-tuned, making a great resource even more useful and entertaining. . . . It's no small trick to make grammar fun, or to write one smallish book that will suit professional writers and struggling beginners alike, but O'Conner manages."

—*Seattle Post-Intelligencer*

"[O'Conner's] commonsense, well-informed approach makes the book useful, but what makes it engaging—even entertaining—is her indefatigable wit. . . . High school teachers, employers, and editors might do their charges a favor and put *Woe Is I* in easy reach."

—*San Francisco Chronicle*

"*Woe Is I* is the best primer on English usage to come along since Strunk and White's *The Elements of Style*."

—*The Atlanta Journal-Constitution*

"A gem."

—*The Arizona Republic*

continued . . .

"This clever little book is packed with useful information. The new edition even includes e-mail etiquette, a category of which most Americans are abysmally ignorant."

—*Chattanooga Times Free Press*

"The breezy, bend-but-don't-break approach to rules of grammar in *Woe Is I* can really help. The book is quite user-friendly."

—*The Post Standard* (Syracuse, NY)

"I wouldn't call a grammar book easy and enjoyable reading. That was until I read *Woe Is I*. O'Conner delves into this seemingly boring topic, and, true to her claim, makes grammar understandable."

—*Staten Island Advance*

"Delightful . . . witty, economical and fun to read, it explains the secrets of grammar in refreshingly jargon-free sentences illustrated by numerous examples. While the volume is certainly handy to someone struggling with grammar basics—there are few style guides so breezy—the Verbal Abuse section will appeal to language experts and purists."

—*Publishers Weekly*

"This grammar book has a twist: It's fun. O'Conner . . . gives readers a witty and humorous look at grammar and the oddities of the English language in a way that doesn't intimidate or bore. . . . A pleasure to read . . . Highly recommended."

—*Library Journal*

"A lighthearted guide written for the grammatically challenged giving straight advice on the most common mistakes made by writers. O'Conner considers pronouns, split infinitives, subject-verb agreement, and clichés, handing over understandable, adult explanations devoid of jargon and dashed with humor."

—*Reference & Research Book News*

Contents

Preface to the Second Edition

Second editions often make a bashful entrance, pink about the ears and somewhat apologetic. Their very existence, after all, suggests that the original now lacks a certain something. But language books are different. They're expected to grow and change along with languages and the people who use them. And that goes double for books about English, that miracle of flexibility and verbal renewal.

When *Woe Is I* first appeared, English was establishing itself as the global language. Seven years later, it's established. English has become the voice of international business, science, politics, technology, medicine, culture—and, not least, of the Internet. More and more, communicating means communicating in English.

This new edition takes a fresh look at what "better English" is, and isn't, in the twenty-first century. But don't expect any earthshaking changes in what's considered grammatically correct. We don't ditch the rules of grammar and start over every day, or even every generation. The things that make English seem so changeable have more to do with vocabulary and how it's used than with the underlying grammar. And never before have words and usage changed so rapidly, thanks in part to the Internet.

In the age of e-mail, we're continually being called on to alter our notions of what's acceptable and what's not. So *Woe Is I* now includes a chapter about e-mail and other online writing.

Despite the alterations, though, the philosophy of *Woe Is I* remains unchanged. English is a glorious invention, one that gives us endless possibilities for expressing ourselves. Grammar is there to help, to clear up ambiguities and prevent misunderstandings. Any "rule" of grammar that gets in the way or doesn't make sense or creates problems instead of solving them probably isn't a rule at all. (Check out Chapter 9.)

And, as the book's whimsical title hints, it's even possible to be *too* correct. While "Woe is I" may appear technically correct (and that's a matter of opinion), the expression "Woe is me" has been good English for generations. Only a pompous twit—or an author trying to make a point—would use "I" instead of "me" here. As you can see, English is nothing if not reasonable.

Many of the good citizens who were acknowledged in the original *Woe Is I* also made valuable suggestions for the second edition, especially my old friends Charles Doherty and

Tim Sacco. I'm indebted as well to all the readers whose kibitzing from the sidelines helped make the book better, particularly David A. Ball, Jason W. Brunk, Liz Copeland, Don Corken, Jr., Victor Carl Friesen, Mary Laura Gibbs, David Hawkins, Hunt B. Jones, Anita Kern, Zilia L. Laje, Ruth M. McVeigh, Ed Pearson, Jessica Raimi, Louie G. Robinson, James Smith Rudolph, and Scott Summerville. And salaams to Wendy Carlton and the staff at Riverhead Books for seeing the new edition into print.

Acknowledgments

Countless friends and colleagues helped make this book by contributing ideas, pointing out omissions, and sneering at my mistakes. I'm glad that I was able to provide you all with a socially acceptable outlet for your more aggressive impulses. Your patience and good humor were second only to mine, and I can't thank you enough.

I'm particularly grateful to those who read the manuscript: Laurie Asséo; David Feldman; Margalit Fox; Elizabeth Frenchman; Anita Gates; Neal, Margo, and Garth Johnston; Dimi Karras; Peter Keepnews; David Kelly; Eden Ross Lipson; Deborah Nye; Allan M. Siegal; Rachel Elkind Tourre; Gloria Gardiner Urban; Elizabeth Weis; and my mother, Beverly J. Newman.

For their support, encouragement, and advice, I thank Michael Anderson; Michael Barson; Alida Becker; Brenda

Berkman; Charles Doherty; Tom Ferrell; Ken Gordon; Pamela and Larry Kellerman; Harvey Kleinman; Charles Mc-Grath; Merrill Perlman; Tim Sacco; Michael Sniffen; Katlyn Stranger; Yves Tourre; Marilynn K. Yee; Arline Youngman; my sister, Kathy Richard; my encyclopedic father-in-law, Allen G. Kellerman; my agent, Dan Green; and Kate Murphy and Anna Jardine at Putnam.

Sam Freedman was generous with his time and advice, and passed along much valuable insight (especially about danglers) from his experiences as a reporter, an author, and a teacher. William Safire was kind enough to acquaint me with the invaluable Jeff McQuain, who expertly scoured the manuscript for errors. (Any boo-boos that remain are mine alone.) And this book couldn't have been written without the help of Jane Isay, whose idea it was in the first place.

Finally, heartfelt thanks to my husband, Stewart Kellerman, for his conjugal as well as conjugational expertise. He put his own book aside many, many times to help me with mine. He's my best friend, and the best editor I know.

Introduction

We all come from the factory wired for language. By the time we know what it is, we've got it. Toddlers don't think about language; they just talk. Grammar is a later addition, an ever-evolving set of rules for using words in ways that we can all agree on. But the laws of grammar come and go. English today isn't what it was a hundred years ago, and it's not what it will be a hundred years from now. We make up rules when we need them, and discard them when we don't. Then when *do* we need them? When our wires get crossed and we fail to understand one another.

If language were flawless, this wouldn't happen, of course. But the perfect language hasn't been invented. No, I take that back—it has been done. There are so-called rational languages (like the "universal" tongue Esperanto and the computer-generated Eliza) that are made up, designed to be logical, reasonable, easy to speak and spell, to make sense. And guess what? They're flat as a pancake. What's missing is the quirkiness, as well as the ambiguity, the bumpy irregularities that make natural languages so exasperating and shifty—and so wonderful. That's wonderful in the literal sense: full of wonders and surprises, poetry and unexpected charm. If English weren't so stretchy and unpredictable, we wouldn't have Lewis Carroll, Dr. Seuss, or the Marx Brothers. And just try telling a knock-knock joke in Latin!

But we pay a price for poetry. English is not easy, as languages go. It began 1,500 years ago, when Germanic tribes (mainly Angles and Saxons) invaded Britain, a Celtic-speaking land already colonized by Latin-speaking Romans. Into this Anglo-Saxon stew went big dollops of French, Italian, Spanish, German, Danish, Portuguese, Dutch, Greek, and more Latin. Within a few hundred years, English was an extraordinarily rich broth. Today, it's believed to have the largest lexicon (that is, the most words) of any modern language—and it's still evolving. Is there any wonder the rules are a little screwy?

And let's face it, English *is* screwy. Bright, educated, technologically savvy people who can run a computer spreadsheet with their toes are heard every day saying things like:

"Come to lunch with the boss and I."

"Somebody forgot their umbrella."

"Already housebroken, the Queen brought home a new corgi."

Every one of those sentences has an outrageous howler (if

you don't see them, check out chapters 1 and 7). Some kinds of flubs have become so common that they're starting to sound right to our ears. And in some cases, they are right. What used to be regarded as errors may now be acceptable or even preferred. What are we supposed to make of all this?

Woe Is I is a survival guide for intelligent people who probably never have diagrammed a sentence and never will. Most of us don't know a gerund from a gerbil and don't care, but we'd like to speak and write as though we did. Grammar is mysterious to each of us in a different way. Some very smart people mess up pronouns, and I've known brilliant souls who can't spell. Many people can't tell the difference between *it's* and *its*. Others go out of their way to avoid using quotation marks. Whatever your particular boo-boo, *Woe Is I* can help you fix it without hitting you over the head with a lot of technical jargon. No heavy lifting, no assembly required. There are sections on the worst pitfalls of everyday language, along with commonsense tips on how to avoid stumbling into them. Wherever possible, I've tried to stay away from grammatical terms, which most of us relish about as much as a vampire does garlic. You don't need them to use English well. If you come across a term that gives you trouble, there's a glossary in the back.

One last word before you plunge in. A dictionary is a wonderful tool, and everybody should have at least one. Yet the fact that a word can be found in the dictionary doesn't make it acceptable English. The job of a dictionary is to describe how words are used at a particular time. Formal or standard meanings are given, but so are colloquial, slang, dialect, sub-standard, regional, and other current meanings. A dictionary may tell you, for example, what's meant by words like "restau-ranteur" and "irregardless" (both, as you'll see, impostors)—but you wouldn't want to embarrass yourself by using them. Buy a standard dictionary (there are recommendations in the bibliography), and read the fine print.

The best of us sometimes get exasperated with the com-plexities of using English well. Believe me, it's worth the ef-fort. Life might be easier if we all spoke Latin. But the quirks, the surprises, the ever-changing nature of English—these are the differences between a living language and a dead one.

Chapter 1

Woe Is I

Therapy for Pronoun Anxiety

When a tiny word gives you a big headache, it's probably a pronoun.

Pronouns are usually small (*I, me, he, she, it*), but they're among the biggest troublemakers in the language. If you've ever been picked on by the pronoun police, don't despair. You're in good company. Hundreds of years after the first Ophelia cried "Woe is me," only a pedant would argue that Shakespeare should have written "Woe is I" or "Woe is unto me." (Never mind that the rules of English grammar weren't even formalized in Shakespeare's day.) The point is that no one is exempt from having his pronouns second-guessed.

Put simply, a pronoun is an understudy for a noun. *He* may stand in for "Ralph," *she* for "Alice," *they* for "the Kramdens," and *it* for "the stuffed piranha." Why do we need them? Take the following sentence: *Ralph smuggled his stuffed piranha*

1

into the Kramdens' apartment, sneaked *it* out of *his* jacket, and was slipping *it* into *his* wife's curio cabinet, when suddenly Alice walked into *their* living room, clutched *her* heart, and screamed, "*You* get *that* out of *my* house!"

If no one had invented pronouns, here's how that sentence would look: *Ralph smuggled Ralph's stuffed piranha into the Kramdens' apartment, sneaked the stuffed piranha out of Ralph's jacket, and was slipping the stuffed piranha into Ralph's wife's curio cabinet, when suddenly Alice walked into the Kramdens' living room, clutched Alice's heart, and screamed, "Ralph, get the stuffed piranha out of Alice's house!"*

See how much time pronouns save?

Simple substitutions (like *his* for *Ralph's*) are easy enough. Things get complicated when a pronoun, like any good understudy, takes on different guises, depending on the roles it plays in the sentence. Some pronouns are so well disguised that you may not be able to tell one from another. Enter *that* and *which*; *it's* and *its*; *who's* and *whose*; *who* and *whom*; *everybody* and *nobody*; and *their*, *they're*, and *theirs*.

Now let's round up the usual suspects, as well as a few other shady characters.

✴   ✴   ✴

The Which Trials: That or Which?

Bite on one of these: *Nobody likes a dog **that** bites* or *Nobody likes a dog **which** bites.*

If they both sound right, you've been spooked by *which*es (the first example is the correct one).

The old *that*-versus-*which* problem haunts everybody sooner or later. Here are two rules to help you figure out whether a clause (a group of words with its own subject and verb) should start with *that* or *which*.

- If you can drop the clause and not lose the point of the sentence, use *which*. If you can't, use *that.*
- A *which* clause goes inside commas. A *that* clause doesn't.

Now let's put the rules to work. Look at these two sentences:

*Buster's bulldog, **which** had one white ear, won best in show.*
*The dog **that** won best in show was Buster's bulldog.*

The point of each sentence is that Buster's dog won. What happens when we remove the *that* or *which* clause?

In the first example, the *which* clause (**which** *had one white ear*) is disposable—without it, we still have the gist of the sentence: *Buster's bulldog won best in show.*

But in the second example, the *that* clause (**that** *won best* *in show*) is essential. The sentence misses the point without it: *The dog was Buster's bulldog.*

Some people consider *which* more refined or elegant than *that.* Not so! In fact, *that* is more likely to be grammatically correct than *which.* That's because most of us don't put un-essential information in the middle of our sentences, especially when speaking.

Here's a little memory aid:

C o m m a   S e n s e
Commas, *which* cut out the fat,
Go with *which,* never with *that.*

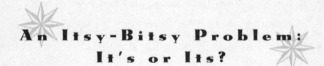

An Itsy-Bitsy Problem: It's or Its?

The smaller the word, the handier it is. And *it* is about as useful as they come. *It* can stand in for anything—a stuffed piranha, existentialism, the Monroe Doctrine, or buttered toast. It's a very versatile pronoun! But did you notice what just happened? We added an *s* and got *it's*—or should that be *its*? Hmmm. When do you use *it's,* and when do you use *its*?

This is an itsy-bitsy problem that gives lots of intelligent people fits. They go wrong when they assume that a word with an apostrophe must be a possessive, like *Bertie's aunt.* But an apostrophe can also stand for something that's been omitted (as in contractions, which are run-together words like *can't* and *shouldn't*). In this case, *it's* is short for *it is*. Plain *its* is the possessive form. So here's the one and only rule you need:

- If you can substitute *it is*, use *it's*.

  NOTE: *It's* can also be short for *it has*. There's more on *its* versus *it's* in the chapter on possessives, page 39.

Who's (or Whose) on First?

This problem is a first cousin of the one above (which you should look at, if you haven't already). As with *it's* and *its*, remember that *who's* is shorthand for *who is*, and unadorned *whose* is the possessive form.

- If you can substitute *who is*, use *who's*.

  NOTE: *Who's* can also be short for *who has*. There's more on *whose* versus *who's* in the chapter on possessives, page 40.

You're on Your Own

"Your our kind of people," reads the hotel marquee. Eek! Let's hope impressionable children aren't looking. The sign should

Who's That?

Choose one: *The girl* **that** *married dear old dad* or *The girl* **who** *married dear old dad.*

If both sound right, it's because both are right.

A person can be either a *that* or a *who*. A thing, on the other hand, is always a *that*.

But what about Benjy and Morris? Dogs and cats aren't people, but they aren't quite things, either. Is an animal a *that* or a *who*?

If the animal is anonymous, it's a *that*: *There's the dog* **that** *won the Frisbee competition.*

If the animal has a name, he or she can be either a *who* or a *that*: *Morris is a cat* **who** *knows what he likes.*

read: "You're our kind of people." *You're* is short for *you are*; *your* is the possessive form.

- If you can substitute *you are*, use *you're*.

Whom Sweet Whom

Poor *whom*! Over the years, wordsmiths from Noah Webster to Jacques Barzun have suggested that maybe we should ditch it altogether and let *who* do the job of both. Not a bad idea. It's pretty hard to imagine an outraged populace protesting, "*Whom* do you think you're messing with! Get your hands off our pronouns!" There's no doubt that in everyday speech, *whom* has lost the battle.

So has the bell tolled for *whom*?

Not quite. Here we are, well into a new millennium, and against all odds, creaky old *whom* is still with us. With a few minor adjustments, we can get away with dropping it when we speak (I'll show you how on page 9), though even that may raise an eyebrow or two. But since written English is more formal than conversational English, anyone who wants to write correctly will have to get a grip on *whom*.

If you want to be absolutely correct, the most important thing to know is that *who* does something (it's a subject, like *he*), and *whom* has something done to it (it's an object, like *him*). You might even try mentally substituting *he* or *him* where *who* or *whom* should go: if *him* fits, you want *whom* (both end in *m*); if *he* fits, you want *who* (both end in a vowel). *Who* does something to (*at, by, for, from, in, toward, upon, with,* etc.) *whom*. The words in parentheses, by the way, are prepositions, words that "position"—that is, locate— other words. A preposition often comes just before *whom*, but not always. A better way to decide between *who* and *whom* is to ask yourself *who* is doing what to *whom*.

This may take a little detective work. Miss Marple herself might have been stumped by the convolutions of some *who* or *whom* clauses (a clause, you'll recall, is a group of words with its own subject and verb). For instance, other words may get in between the subject and the verb. Or the object may end up in front of both the subject and the verb. Here are two pointers to help clear up the mystery, and examples of how they're used.

- Simplify, simplify, simplify: strip the clause down to its basic subject, verb, and object.
- Move the words around mentally to make it easier to identify the subject and the object.

Nathan invited only guys [who or whom] he thought played for high stakes. If you strip the clause of its false clues—the words separating the subject and verb—you end up with *who . . . played for high stakes. Who* did something (played for high stakes), so it's the subject.

Nathan wouldn't tell Miss Adelaide [who or whom] he invited to his crap game. First strip the sentence down to the basic clause, *[who or whom] he invited.* If it's still unclear, rearrange the words in your mind: *he invited whom.* You can now see that *whom* is the object—*he* did something to (invited) *whom*—even though *whom* comes ahead of both the verb and the subject.

NOTE: A preposition isn't necessarily followed by *whom.* It can be followed by a clause that starts with *who.* Consider this sentence: *After the crap game, Nathan was confused about [who or whom] owed him money.* Don't be misled by the preposition *about;* it's one of the

A Cure for the Whom-Sick

Now for the good news. In almost all cases, you can use *who* instead of *whom* in conversation or in informal writing, like personal letters and casual memos.

Sure, it's not a hundred percent correct, and I don't recommend using it on the most formal occasions, but *who* is certainly less stuffy, especially at the beginning of a sentence or a clause: **Who**'s *the letter from? Did I tell you* **who** *I saw at the movies?* **Who** *are you waiting to see? No matter* **who** *you invite, someone will be left out.*

A note of caution: *Who* can sound grating if used for *whom* right after a preposition. You can get around this by putting *who* in front. *From* **whom**? becomes **Who** *from?* So when a colleague tells you he's going on a Caribbean cruise and you ask, "Who with?" he's more likely to question your discretion than your grammar.

false clues mentioned above. Instead, simplify, simplify, simplify, and look for the clause—in this case it's *who owed him money*. Since *who* did something (owed him money), it's the subject.

Object Lessons

THE *ME* GENERATION

These days, anyone who says "It is I" sounds like a stuffed shirt. It wasn't always so. In bygone days, you might have had your knuckles rapped for saying "It's me" instead of "It is I." Your crime? A pronoun following the verb *to be,* the English teacher insisted, should act like a subject (*I, he, she, they*) and not an object (*me, him, her, them*). But language is a living thing, always evolving, and *It is I* is just about extinct. In all but the most formal writing, some of the fussiest grammarians accept *It's me.* Most of us find the old usage awkward, though I must admit that I still use "This is she" when someone asks for me on the phone. Old habits die harder than old rules.

Next time you identify the perp in a police lineup, feel free to point dramatically and say, "That's him, Officer!"

JUST BETWEEN *ME* AND *I*

Why is it that no one ever makes a mistake like this? *You'll be hearing from I*.

It's instinctive to use the correct form (*from **me***) when only a solitary pronoun follows a preposition. (Prepositions— *after, as, at, before, between, by, for, from, in, like, on, toward, upon, with*, and a slew of others—position other words in the sentence.) But when the pronoun isn't alone, instinct goes down the drain, and grammar with it. So we run into abominations like *The odds were **against you and** I*, although no one would dream of saying "against I."

I wouldn't be at all surprised to learn that the seeds of the *I*-versus-*me* problem are planted in early childhood. We're admonished to say, "I want a cookie," not "Me want a cookie." We begin to feel subconsciously that *I* is somehow more genteel than *me*, even in cases where *me* is the right choice—for instance, after a preposition. Trying too hard to be right, we end up being wrong. Hypercorrectness rears its ugly head!

My guess is that most people who make this mistake do so out of habit, without thinking, and not because they don't know the difference between *I* and *me*. If you find yourself automatically putting *you and I* after a preposition, try this: In your mind, eliminate the other guy, leaving the tricky pronoun (*I* or *me*) all by itself. Between you and me, it works.

NOTE: I can hear a chorus of voices shouting, Wait a minute! Doesn't Shakespeare use *I* after a preposition in *The Merchant of Venice*? Antonio tells Bassanio, "All debts are clear'd between you and I, if I might but see you at my death." That's true. But then, we're not Shakespeare.

More Than Meets the I

Some of the smartest people I know hesitate at the word *than* when it comes before a pronoun. What goes next, *I* or *me*? *he* or *him*? *she* or *her*? *they* or *them*?

The answer: All of the above! This is easier than it sounds. Take *I* and *me* as examples, since they're the pronouns we use most (egotists that we are). Either one may be correct after *than*, depending on the meaning of the sentence.

- *Trixie loves spaghetti **more than** I* means ***more than** I do*.
- *Trixie loves spaghetti **more than** me* means ***more than** she loves me*.

NOTE: If ending a sentence with *than I* or *than she* or *than they* seems awkward or fussy (particularly in speaking), you might simply add the missing thought: *Harry smokes more **than they do**.*

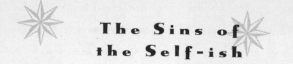

The Sins of the Self-ish

In the contest between *I* and *me*, the booby prize often goes to *myself*.

That's why we see sentences like *Jack and myself were married yesterday*. (It's *Jack and I*.) Or like this more common *self*-promotion: *The project made money for Reynaldo and myself*. The speaker isn't sure whether it's *Reynaldo and me* or *Reynaldo and I*, so she goes with *Reynaldo and myself*. Tsk, tsk. (It's *for Reynaldo and me*.)

Myself and the rest of the *self*-ish crew (*yourself, himself, herself, itself, ourselves, yourselves, themselves*) shouldn't take the place of the ordinary pronouns *I* and *me*, *she* and *her*, and so on. They are used for only two purposes:

- To emphasize. *I made the cake myself. Love itself is a riddle. The detective himself was the murderer.* (The emphasis could be left out, and the sentence would still make sense.)

- To refer to the subject. *She hates herself. And you call yourself a plumber! They consider themselves lucky to be alive. The problem practically solved itself.*

They and Company:
They're, Their, Theirs
(and There and There's)

These words remind me of the stateroom scene in the Marx Brothers movie *A Night at the Opera*. There seem to be half a dozen too many, all stepping on one another's feet.

Taken one at a time, though, they're pretty harmless.

- *They're* is shorthand for *they are*: **They're** *tightwads, and they always have been.*
- *Their* and *theirs* are the possessive forms for *they*: **Their** *money is* **theirs** *alone.*
- *There* (meaning "in or at that place," as opposed to "here") isn't even a pronoun, unlike the rest of the crowd in the stateroom. Neither is *there's,* which is shorthand for *there is.* But *there* and *there's* frequently get mixed up with the sound-alikes *they're, their,* and *theirs.*

Sometimes a limerick says it best:

The Dinner Guests

They seem to have taken on airs.
They're ever so rude with *their* stares.
They get *there* quite late,
There's a hand in your plate,
And *they're* eating what's not even *theirs.*

How Many Is Everybody?

This may seem like a silly question, but what's wrong with saying, *Are everybody happy?* After all, when you use the word *everybody,* you're thinking of a crowd, right? Then why do we say, *Is everybody happy?*

In other words, just how many people do we mean when we say *everybody* or *everyone?*

The answer is one. Odd as it may seem, these pronouns are singular. We often use them when talking about whole gangs of people, but we treat them grammatically as individual gang members. The result is that each takes a singular verb: *Everybody **loves** a lover, but not everybody **is** one.*

There's No Their There

A lot of people start seeing double when they use *anybody, anyone, everybody, everyone, nobody, no one, somebody, someone, each, either,* and *neither.*

Actually, each of these pronouns is singular—yes, even *everybody* and *everyone* (if you have doubts, see the item above). Then why do so many people use the plurals *they, them, their,* and *theirs* as stand-ins? *Somebody forgot **their** coat. If anyone calls, tell **them** I'm out.* I cringe when I hear things like that.

Stick to singular stand-ins (*he, she, it, his, her, hers,* or *its*) for singular pronouns like *everybody* and company: *Somebody forgot her coat. If anyone calls, tell him I'm out.* You may be tempted to use *their* and *them* because you don't know whether the somebody is a he or a she. Well, your nonsexist intentions are good, but your grammar isn't.

Frankly, this is one of the few times when English lets us down. The only unisex singular pronoun we have is *it,* which doesn't always fill the bill. Since time immemorial, English speakers have used the masculine *he* and *him* and *his* to refer to a person in general. Understandably, some people can't help thinking of those as . . . well . . . male.

If you can't bring yourself to use the all-purpose masculine and you hate the clunky *him or her* alternatives, don't resort to *they* and company. Bad English isn't the answer. My advice is to reword the sentence: *Somebody forgot a coat. If anyone calls, say I'm out.*

When you do use the stand-ins, though, get them right. Here are some examples. If they sound odd, that's because you're used to making mistakes. Join the club.

*Has **anybody** lost **her** purse?* Not: ***their** purse.*

*If **anyone** makes trouble, throw **him** out.* Not: *throw **them** out.*

*Everybody has **his** priorities.* Not: ***their** priorities.*

*Everyone seems happy with **his or her** partner.* Not: ***their** partner.*

*Nobody works overtime because **she** likes it.* Not: ***they** like it.*

No one appreciates **her** husband. Not: **their** husband.

Somebody must have **his** head screwed on backward. Not: **their** head.

Someone has locked **himself** out. Not: **themselves** or (even worse!) **themself**.

Each has **its** drawbacks. Not: **their** drawbacks.

Either has earned **his** stripes. Not: **their** stripes.

Neither was wearing **his** earring. Not: **their** earring.

NOTE: *Either* and *neither* can sometimes be plural when paired with *or* or *nor*. For more, see page 52.

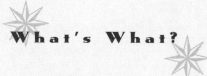

What's What?

Which sentence is correct?

Lou sees **what appears** *to be ghosts* or *Lou sees* **what appear** *to be ghosts.*

Leaving aside the issue of Lou's sanity, should we choose *what appears* or *what appear*? And what difference does it make? Well, what we're really asking is whether the pronoun *what,* when used as a subject, takes a singular verb (*appears*) or a plural one (*appear*). The answer is that *what* can be either singular or plural; it can mean "the thing that" or "things that." In this case, Lou is seeing "things that" appear to be ghosts. So this is the correct sentence: *Lou sees* **what appear** *to be ghosts.*

NOTE: When *what* is the subject of two verbs in the same sentence, make the verbs match in number—both singular or both plural, not one of each. ***What scares** Lou the most **is** Bud's sudden disappearance.* (Both verbs are singular.) *But **what seem** to be supernatural events **are** really sleight-of-hand.* (Both verbs are plural.)

By the way, it takes a certain effort to get your *what*s straight. Few people do it automatically, so take your time and watch out for trapdoors. For more on *what* with verbs, see page 54.

Chapter 2

Plurals Before Swine

Blunders with Numbers

With grammar, it's always something. If it's not one thing, it's two—or four, or eight—and that's where plurals come in. Without plural words, we'd have to talk about one thing at a time! You couldn't eat a bag of *peanuts* at the ball game, you'd have to eat *peanut* after *peanut* after *peanut*. But language is very accommodating. A *bagful* here and a *bagful* there and—voilà—you've got *bagfuls*. See? There's nothing we can't have more of, even *infinities*, because anything that can be singular can also be plural.

✳   ✳   ✳

What Noah Knew

The ark was filled symmetrically:
For every boy, a girl.
Its claim to singularity
Resided in the plural.

In English, it's fairly easy to go forth and multiply. To make a singular noun (a word for a thing, person, place, or idea) into a plural one, we usually add *s* or *es* or *ies,* depending on its ending. In general, plurals are a piece (or pieces) of cake.

Of course, there are dozens of irregular plurals, but most of them are second nature to us by the time we're five or six. *Children* (not "childs") shouldn't play with *knives* (not "knifes"), and ganders are male *geese* (not "gooses"). A little later in life we pick up some of the more exotic plurals—*criteria, phenomena, tableaux,* and the like—that are the offspring of other languages.

For most of us, plurals get sticky mainly when they involve proper names, nouns with several parts, or words that can be either singular or plural. How do we refer to more than one *Sanchez* or *spoonful* or *brother-in-law*? Is a word like *couple* or *politics* singular or plural—or can it be both?

To get right to the points, let's start with names.

✳   ✳   ✳

Keeping Up
with the Joneses:
How Names Multiply

It baffles me why people mangle names almost beyond recognition when they make them plural. *In my daughter's
preschool class, there are two **Larries** [ouch!], three **Jennifer's**
[oof!], and two **Sanchez'** [yipes!].* It's *Larrys, Jennifers,* and
Sanchezes.

Getting it right isn't that difficult. Whether you're dealing
with a first name or a last, form the plural by adding *s,* or (if
the name ends in *s, sh, ch, x,* or *z*) by adding *es.* A final *y*
doesn't change to *ies* at the end of a name. And please, no
apostrophes!

*Charles and his friend Charles are just a couple of **Charleses**.*

*When Eliza dated three guys named Henry, she couldn't keep
her **Henrys** straight. What's more, two of them were **Higginses**.*

*There are eight **Joneses**, two of them **Marys**, in Reggie's little
black book.*

*The **Ricardos** and the **Mertzes** had dinner with the **Simp-
sons** and the **Flanderses** at the home of the **Cleavers**.*

Compound Fractures:
Words That Come Apart

Some nouns aren't simple; they're more like small construction projects. When a *spoon* is *full,* it's a *spoonful*—but are two of them *spoonsful* or *spoonfuls*? If your better half has two brothers, are they your *brothers-in-law* or your *brother-in-laws*? In other words, how do you make a plural of a noun with several parts? The answer, as it turns out, comes in parts:

- If a compound word is solid and has no hyphen (-), put the normal plural ending at the *end* of the word:

  Churchmen love soapboxes.

  Kipling appeals to schoolchildren and fishwives.

  Doormen are good at getting taxicabs.

  You hardly ever come across Biedermeier bookcases in alleyways.

  Babies dump spoonfuls of jam on footstools.

- If the word is split into parts, with or without hyphens, put the plural ending on the root or most important part (underlined in the examples):

  Mothers-in-law like to attend courts-martial.

  Are they ladies-in-waiting or just hangers-on?

  Those counselors-at-law ate all the crêpes suzette.

  Garter belts aren't required on men-of-war.

- Watch out for *general* when it's part of a compound word. In a military title, *general* is usually the important part, so it gets the *s*. In a civilian title, *general* isn't the root, so it doesn't get the *s*:

Two **attorneys** *general went dancing with two* **major generals**.

Those **consuls** *general are retired* **brigadier generals**.

The ics Files

Figuring out the mathematics of a noun can be tricky. Take the word *mathematics*. Is it singular or plural? And what about all those other words ending in *ics—economics, ethics, optics, politics,* and so on? Fortunately, it doesn't take a Ph.D. in mathematics to solve this puzzle.

If you're using an *ics* word in a general way (as a branch of study, say), it's singular. If you're using an *ics* word in a particular way (as someone's set of beliefs, for example), it's plural.

"**Politics** *stinks,*" *said Mulder.*

"*Mulder's* **politics** *stink,*" *said Scully.*

Statistics *isn't a popular course at the academy.*

Alien-abduction **statistics** *are scarce.*

Ifs, Ands, or Buts

In English, there are exceptions to every rule. When *man* or *woman* is part of a compound, often both parts become plural. For example, *manservant* becomes *menservants; woman doctor* becomes *women doctors; gentleman farmer* becomes *gentlemen farmers.* Two other exceptions to the rules for making compound words plural make no sense at all: *hotfoot* becomes *hotfoots* (believe it or not), and *still life* becomes *still lifes.* Go figure.

On occasion you may need to form a plural of a word like *yes, no,* or *maybe.* Well, since you're referring to them as nouns, just follow the normal rules for making nouns into plurals:

WORDS TO THE WHYS

Ups and downs and ins and outs,
Forevers and nevers and whys.
Befores and afters, dos and don'ts,
Farewells and hellos and good-byes.
Life is a string of perhapses,
A medley of whens and so whats.
We rise on our yeses and maybes,
Then fall on our nos and our buts.

Two-Faced Words:
Sometimes Singular,
Sometimes Plural

A noun can be double trouble if it stands for a collection of things. Sometimes it's singular and sometimes it's plural. How do you know which is which? Amazingly, common sense (yes, it does have a place in English usage!) should tell you. Ask yourself this question: Am I thinking of the baseball team, or the players? Let's take a swing at these problem words a few at a time.

COUNSELING FOR COUPLES

What is a *couple*, anyway? Is it a pair (singular), or two of a kind (plural)? Is it two peas (plural) in a pod, or a pod (singular) with two peas?

Couple is probably the most common of the two-faced words. It can be either singular or plural, depending on whether it's supposed to mean two individuals or a package deal. Ask yourself whether you have the two peas in mind, or the pod. Here's a hint: Look at the word (*a* or *the*) in front. *The couple* is usually singular. *A couple,* especially when followed by *of,* is usually plural. Each of these examples illustrates both uses (the verbs are underlined, one plural and one singular):

A **couple** of tenants <u>own</u> geckos. The **couple** in 5G <u>owns</u> a family of mongooses.

*Only a **couple** of appointments <u>are</u> available. That **couple** <u>is</u> always late.*

There's more about *couple* in the chapter on verbs; see page 53.

GROUP THERAPY

Many words that mean a group of things—*total, majority,* and *number,* for example—can be singular or plural. Sometimes they mean the group acting as a whole, sometimes the members of the group.

As with the other two-faced words, ask yourself whether you are thinking of the whole or the parts. A little hint: *The* before the word (*the total, the majority*) is usually a tip-off that it's singular, while *a* (*a total, a number*), especially when *of* comes after, usually indicates a plural. Each of these examples illustrates both (the verbs are underlined, one singular and one plural):

*The **majority** <u>is</u> in charge. Still, a **majority** of voters <u>are</u> unhappy.*

*The **total** <u>was</u> in the millions. A **total** of six <u>were</u> missing.*

*The **number** of hats Bette owns is astounding. A **number** of them <u>are</u> pretty ridiculous.*

There's more about *total, majority,* and *number* in the chapter on verbs, page 53.

✦   ✦   ✦

ALL OR NOTHING

All is a versatile word. It's all things to all people; in fact, it's all-encompassing. So all-inclusive is this little word that it can be either singular or plural. Another two-faced word!

Luckily, it's all too simple to decide whether *all* is singular or plural. Here's a foolproof way (the verbs in the examples are underlined):

• If *all* means "all of it" or "everything" or "the only thing," it's singular: "*All I eat is lettuce,*" said Kate. "*But all I lose is brain cells. All is not well with my waist.*"
• If *all* indicates "all of them," it's plural. "*All the men I date are confused,*" said Kate. "*All prefer slender women with big appetites.*"

NOTE: The same logic holds for *any*. If it means "any of it," it's singular; if it means "any of them," it's plural. There's more about *any* and *all* in the chapter on verbs, page 53.

NONE SENSE

None is the most difficult of the two-faced words, those that can be either singular or plural. One reason it's so confusing is that generations of us were taught (incorrectly) as schoolchildren that *none* is always singular because it means "not one." Legions of people think of rather stiff sentences—*None of Dempsey's teeth was chipped,* or *None of Tunney's fingers was broken*—as grammatically correct.

But *none* has always been closer in meaning to "not any," and most authorities agree it's usually plural: ***None** of Tyson's teeth* <u>were</u> *chipped.* ***None** of Holyfield's fingers* <u>were</u> *broken. None* is singular only when it means "none of it" (that is to say, "no amount"): ***None** of the referee's blood* <u>was</u> *shed.*

Here's an easy way to decide whether *none* is singular or plural (the verbs are underlined):

- If it suggests "none of them," it's plural: ***None** of the fans* <u>are</u> *fighting.* ***None*** <u>are</u> *excited enough.*
- If it means "none of it," it's singular: ***None** of the bout* <u>was</u> *seen in Pittsburgh.* ***None*** <u>was</u> *worth broadcasting.*

NOTE: When you really do mean "not one," it's better to say "not one," and use a singular verb: ***Not one** of Holyfield's fingers was broken.*

Y's and Wherefores: Words That End in Y

Some plurals are just a bowl of cherries. Words ending in *y* either add *s* or change the *y* to *ies*. Here's the scoop.

- If a word ends in *y* preceded by a consonant (a hard sound, like *b, d, l, r, t,* etc.), drop the *y* and add *ies*: ***Ladies*** *don't throw* ***panties*** *off the decks of* ***ferries.***

- If a word ends in *y* preceded by a vowel (a soft, open-mouthed sound, like *a, e, o, u*), add *s*: **Boys born in alleys** *can grow up to be* **attorneys**.

For making plurals out of names that end in *y,* see page 21.

One Potato, Two Potato: Words That End in O

O for a simple solution to this one! Unfortunately, there's no hard-and-fast rule that tells you how to form the plural of every word that ends in *o.*

- Most form their plurals by adding *s*: **Romeos** *who wear* **tattoos** *and invite* **bimbos** *to their* **studios** *to see their* **portfolios** *are likely to be* **gigolos**.
- A small number of words that end in *o* form their plurals by adding *es*. Some of the most common are in this example: *The* **heroes** *saved the* **cargoes** *of* **tomatoes** *and* **potatoes** *from the* **mosquitoes** *and* **tornadoes** *by hiding them in* **grottoes**.

If you're unsure about the plural of an *o* word, look it up in the dictionary. And if two plurals are given, the one that's listed first is the preferred spelling.

Plurals on the Q.T.:
Abbreviations, Letters, and Numbers

No two authorities seem to agree on how we should form the plurals of abbreviations (*GI, rpm, RBI*), letters (*x, y, z*), and numbers (*9, 10*). Should we add *s*, or *'s*? Where one style maven sees *UFO's*, another sees *UFOs*. One is nostalgic for the *1950's*, the other for the *1950s*. This is more a matter of taste and readability than of grammar, and frankly, we have better things to worry about. For the sake of consistency and common sense, here's what I recommend. To form the plurals of all numbers, letters, and abbreviations (with or without periods and capitals), simply add *'s*.

CPA's, those folks who can add columns of 9's in their heads, have been advising MD's since the 1980's to dot their i's, cross their t's, and never accept IOU's. Things could be worse: there could be two IRS's.

Still not convinced? Just try making a plural of the lowercase letter *a* (or *i* or *u* or *s*, among others) without an apostrophe.

Between and From:
The Numbers Game

OK, it's not something that's been keeping you awake nights. But it comes up all the time. The question: When a noun follows *between* or *from,* is it singular or plural? *The elevator stalled* **between** *the ninth and tenth [***floor*** or* ***floors***], stranding the boss* **from** *the first to the third [***week*** or* ***weeks***] in August.* See what I mean? A small problem, perhaps, but a common one.

The answer: *Between* is followed by a plural noun, and *from* is followed by a singular one: *The elevator stalled* **between** *the ninth and tenth* **floors,** *stranding the boss* **from** *the first to the third* **week** *in August.*

Another pair of examples:

Veronica said she lost her charm bracelet somewhere **between** *Thirty-third and Thirty-seventh* **streets**. *Archie searched every inch of pavement* **from** *Thirty-third to Thirty-seventh* **Street** *before realizing that she had been in a cab at the time.*

The Soul of Kindness: All Kinds, Sorts, and Types

You've probably heard sentences like this one: *I hate* **these** **kind** *of mistakes!* If it sounds wrong to you, you're right. It's **these** **kinds** *of mistakes* (or **that** **kind** *of mistake*).

The singulars—*kind* of, *sort* of, *type* of, and *style* of—are preceded by *this* or *that,* and are followed by singular nouns: *Dagwood wears* **this kind of hat**.

The plurals—*kinds* of, *sorts* of, *types* of, and *styles* of—are preceded by *these* or *those,* and are usually followed by plural nouns: *Mr. Dithers hates* **those kinds of hats**.

Here are some more examples to help you sort things out:

"I enjoy **this sort of cigar**," said Dagwood.

"**These sorts of cigars** disgust me," said Mr. Dithers.

"**That type of car** is my ideal," said Dagwood.

"Only gangsters drive **those types of cars**," said Mr. Dithers.

Never use a or an after the expressions kind of, sort of, type of, or variety of: The beagle is some **kind of a** hound. (Arf!)

> **NOTE:** Some singular nouns can stand for just one thing (Is the **meat** done?) or a whole class of things (The butcher sells many varieties of **meat**). Other singular nouns always stand for a set of things (The **china** matches the **furniture**). When a singular noun stands for a group of things, it's all right (though not necessary) to use it with those kinds, these sorts, and so on. **Those kinds of china** break easily. This can be a subtle distinction. If you find it hard to make, you're safer sticking to the all-singular or all-plural rule (this kind of china).

Some Things Never Change

You're already familiar with nouns from the animal kingdom that can stand for one critter or many: fish, deer, moose, vermin, elk, sheep, swine. Well, some words ending in s are also the same in singular and plural: series, species, and headquar-

ters, which can mean a base or bases: *Gizmo's* **headquarters** *was designed by Rube Goldberg. The rival companies'* **headquarters** *were on opposite sides of town.*

✴ Looks Can Be Deceiving ✴

Loads of nouns look plural because they end in s, but they're actually singular: *checkers* (also *billiards, dominoes,* and other names of games); *measles* (also *mumps, rickets, shingles,* and many other diseases); *molasses; news;* and *whereabouts. Basil says* **checkers** *takes Sybil's mind off her* **shingles,** *which is driving her nuts.*

If that's not confusing enough, how about this? Some nouns that end in s and are regarded as pairs—*scissors, trousers, tongs, pliers, tweezers,* and *breeches,* for instance—are singular but treated as plural. *The* **scissors** *were found, as were the* **tweezers,** *in the drawer where the* **pliers** *are kept.*

NOTE: Some words are often used as singular (*data, media*), though for years the traditional meaning has been plural. The ground has shifted here, so for the scoop on such words, see page 184. And if you want a little thrill—all right, I said a *little* thrill—look up *kudos* (singular or plural?) on page 112.

✻   ✻   ✻

Plurals
with Foreign Accents

A Californian I know, Dr. Schwartz, is a cactus fancier. Is his garden filled with *cactuses* . . . or *cacti?*

As most dictionaries will tell you, either form is right. *Cacti* may sound more exotic, but it's not more correct; in fact, many American dictionaries favor *cactuses.*

As for other nouns of foreign origin, how do you know whether to choose an Anglicized plural (like *memorandums*) or a foreign one (*memoranda*)? There's no single answer, unfortunately. A century ago, the foreign ending would have been preferred, but over the years we've given Anglicized plural endings to more and more foreign-derived words. When you have a choice, take the plural that's listed first in the dictionary.

Here's a partial list of current preferences.

Anglicized: *antennas* (except those on insects), *appendixes, beaus, cactuses, châteaus, curriculums, dictums, formulas, gymnasiums, indexes, memorandums, millenniums, referendums, stadiums, syllabuses, symposiums, ultimatums, virtuosos.*

Multiple Mollusks
In the oceans, wriggling by,
Are *octopuses,* not *octopi.*

Foreign: *analyses, antennae* (on insects), *addenda, algae, axes* (for *axis*), *bacteria, bases* (for *basis*), *crises, criteria, fungi, hypotheses, kibbutzim, larvae, oases, parentheses, phenomena, radii* (but *radiuses* is on the rise), *stimuli, strata, tableaux* (*tableaus* is gaining fast), *theses, vertebrae.*

Plurals can be singularly interesting. Take the octopus—a remarkable creature, grammatically as well as biologically. *Octopus* is from the Greek and means "eight-footed." The original plural was *octopodes,* Anglicized over the years to *octopuses.* Along the way, someone substituted the Latin ending *pi* for the Greek *podes* and came up with the polyglot *octopi.* Though it's technically incorrect, *octopi* is now so common that dictionaries list it as a second choice after *octopuses,* the preferred plural. *Octopi* is for suckers.

Chapter 3

Yours Truly

The Possessives and the Possessed

For an acquisitive society, we're awfully careless about possessives. Have you ever driven through a vacation community and noticed the offhanded signs identifying the properties? *The Miller's, The Davis', The Jone's, Bobs Place.* Businesses are no better, imagining possessives where there aren't any. A now defunct theater near Times Square in New York called itself *The Ero's.* We've all seen places like *Harrys Muffler Shop* or *Glorias' House of Beauty* or *His' and Hers' Formal Wear.*

The word *its* is an Excedrin headache, a possessive that does not take the apostrophe (') we've come to expect. There are scores of other possessive puzzles: Are you a friend *of Jake,* or a friend *of Jake's?* Are you going to your *aunt and uncle's* house, or to your *aunt's and uncle's* house? Do you mind *me smoking,* or do you mind *my smoking?*

As long as there are haves and have-nots, there will be questions about possessives. This chapter should answer the most troublesome ones.

Possession Is Not Demonic: The Simple Facts

The tool kit couldn't be simpler. All you need to make almost any word possessive is an apostrophe and the letter *s*. You add both of them together (*'s*) or just the apostrophe alone, depending on the circumstances:

- If the word is singular, always add *'s*, regardless of its ending. (This is true even if the ending is *s*, *z*, or *x*—whether sounded or silent.) *The waiter spilled red wine on* **Eula's** *dress, which came from* **Paris's** *finest shop. The* **dress's** *skirt, which resembled a tutu from one of* **Degas's** *paintings, was ruined.* **Flem's** *attitude was philosophical because he had been reading* **Camus's** *essays. "It wasn't* **Jacques's** *fault," he said, defending the waiter. "Besides, it's not this* **Bordeaux's** *best vintage."*
- If the word is plural and doesn't already end in *s*, add *'s*: *The* **children's** *menu was a rip-off, and the* **men's** *room was painted fuchsia.*
- If the word is plural and ends in *s*, add just the apostrophe: *The* **Snopeses'** *car was stolen by the valet parking*

attendant. The **cops'** attitude was surly. The **victims'** evening was now demolished.

And by the way, when you need a comma or a period after a possessive word that ends with an apostrophe, the comma or period goes after the apostrophe and not inside it: *The idea was the **girls'**, or maybe the **boys'**, but at any rate the responsibility was their **parents'**.*

NOTE: Be sure you've formed the plural correctly before you add the apostrophe to the end. There's more about plural names in the chapter on plurals, page 21. In a nutshell, if a name ends in *s* (like *Snopes*) the plural adds *es* (the *Snopeses*) and the plural possessive adds *es'* (the *Snopeses'* car). For a name that doesn't end in an *s* sound (*Babbitt*), the plural adds *s* (the *Babbitts*) and the plural possessive adds *s'* (the *Babbitts'* car).

Its (or It's?): Public Enemy Number 1

What a difference an apostrophe makes. Every possessive has one, right? Well, not necessarily so. *It* (like *he* and *she*) is a pronoun—a stand-in for a noun—and pronouns don't have apostrophes when they're possessives: *His coat is too loud because of **its** color, but **hers** is too mousy.*

Now, as for *it's* (the one with the punctuation), the apostrophe stands for something that has been removed. *It's* is short for *it is*, and the apostrophe replaces the missing *i* in *is*. *The parakeet is screeching because it's time to feed him.*

Here's how to keep *its* and *it's* straight:

● If the word you want could be replaced by *it is*, you want *it's*. If not, use *its*. (There's more on *its* and *it's* in the chapter on pronouns, page 4.)

NOTE: Sometimes *it's* can be short for *it has*, as in: *It's been hours since he ate.*

✳ Who's Whose? ✳

The battle between *whose* and *who's* comes up less frequently than the one between *its* and *it's* (see above), but the problems are identical. If you can solve one, you've got the other one whipped.

Don't be misled by the apostrophe. Not every possessive has one. *Who* (like *it* and *he*) is a pronoun—a stand-in for a noun—and pronouns don't have apostrophes when they're possessives: *"Whose frog is this?" said Miss Grundy.*

Now, as for *who's*, the apostrophe stands for something that has been removed. *Who's* is short for *who is*, and the apostrophe replaces the missing *i* in *is*. *"And who's responsible for putting it in my desk?"*

Here's how to keep *whose* and *who's* straight:

● If you can substitute *who is,* use *who's.* If not, use *whose.*

NOTE: Sometimes *who's* can be short for *who has,* as in: **Who's had lunch?**

✸ Their Is But to Do or Die ✸

His newest book, Monster Truck, *is written especially for the child with machinery on **their** mind.* Hmm . . . *their?* Let's hope this children's book is better written than the ad.

Their, the possessive form of *they,* is often used mistakenly for *his* or *her,* as in: **No one in their right mind pays retail.** Ouch! *No one* is singular, and the possessive that goes with it should be singular, too: **No one in her right mind pays retail.**

I suspect many people are reluctant to use *his* or *her* when they aren't referring to anyone in particular. But until our language has a sex-neutral possessive to use instead, we are stuck with *his,* or *her,* or the clumsy compound *his or her.* To substitute *their* may be politically correct, but it's grammatically impaired.

For problems with *their* and its sound-alikes, see the chapter on pronouns, page 14.

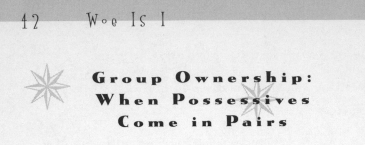

Group Ownership: When Possessives Come in Pairs

If something has two owners, who really owns it? If two people share an experience, whose experience is it? Who, in other words, gets the apostrophe when Sam and Janet spend an evening out—is it *Sam and Janet's evening,* or *Sam's and Janet's evening?*

- If two people (*Sam and Janet*) possess something (an *evening*) in common, consider them a single unit and put a single *'s* at the end: *Sam and Janet's evening was ruined when their date ended at the police station.*

- If two people possess something (or some things) individually, rather than jointly, each name gets an *'s*: *Sam's and Janet's furniture—his Danish modern, her French rococo—would never work in the same apartment.* Or *Sam's and Janet's couches came from the same store.*

- If the names of the two owners are replaced by pronouns (stand-ins for nouns, like *your, my, our,* etc.), don't use them side by side, as in *"Your and my furniture can't live together,"* said Janet. It sounds better with the noun in between: *"Your furniture and mine can't live together."*

Nobody's Fool

Body language is no problem in the possessive. Words like *anybody, everybody, somebody,* and *nobody* become possessive when you add *'s: anybody's, everybody's, somebody's, nobody's.*

When *else* is added, the *'s* goes after *else*: *"Stella is mine, and **nobody else's**," said Stanley.* This seems pretty obvious to us now, but there was a time when it was considered correct to leave the apostrophe with the pronoun: *Is that your suit of armor, Sir Lancelot, or **somebody's else**?*

For Goodness' Sake!

Some word formations are just too much for us to get our tongues around. That's the only good reason I can think of for this next exception to the usual rules on possessives.

We may do something for *pity's* sake, for *heaven's* sake, for the *nation's* sake, for our *children's* sake. But some of the "sake" phrases—for *goodness'* sake, for *conscience'* sake, for *appearance'* sake, for *righteousness'* sake—don't take the final *s* that normally follows the apostrophe. Call it tradition. I suppose our English-speaking forebears decided there was enough hissing in those words already, without adding another sibilant syllable (say those last two words five times in rapid succession).

It's often customary to drop the final *s* when forming the possessives of ancient classical names that already end in *s*: *Whose biceps were bigger, **Hercules'** or **Achilles'**?*

Are You Too Possessive?

One way to make a noun possessive is to add *'s*; another way is to put *of* in front of it.

What about using both? Are two possessives better than one? Should we say *a friend **of Jake**?* Or *a friend **of Jake's**?* I'll end the suspense quickly. Both are correct.

But when a pronoun is involved, make it a possessive: *a friend of **his**,* not *a friend of **him**: Jake is a guest of my **daughter** [or **daughter's**], which makes him a guest of **mine**.*

Doing Time

Time is money, they say, and both are valuable, which may be why they're sometimes expressed in a possessive way. It's long been the custom in English that we may, if we wish, describe periods of time and amounts of money by using possessives: *After an **hour's** wait in court, Butch was given **two years'** pro-*

*bation for stealing **fifty dollars'** worth of change from the collection plate.*

Of course, you can say the same thing without using any possessives: *After waiting an hour in court, Butch was given two years of probation for stealing fifty dollars in change from the collection plate.*

Do You Mind Me . . . Uh . . . My Smoking?

For many of us, this one is the Gordian knot of possessive puzzles. Actually, it's not hard to untie, once you know the secret. First, let's see how you do on your own. Which of these is correct?

1. *He resents **my going**.*
2. *He resents **me going**.*

If you picked number 2, you goofed, but don't beat up on yourself. You're a member of a large and distinguished club. To see why so many of us slip up, let's look at two similar examples:

1. *He resents **my departure**.*
2. *He resents **me departure**.*

I'll bet you didn't have any trouble with that one. Obviously, number 1 is correct. *Departure* is a noun (a thing), and when it is modified or described by a pronoun (a word that stands in for a noun), the pronoun has to be a possessive: *my, his, her, your,* and so on.

Now look again at the first set of examples:

1. *He resents* ***my*** *going.*
2. *He resents* ***me*** *going.*

If you still feel like picking number 2, it's because *ing* words are chameleons. They come from verbs—*go,* in the case of *going*—and usually act like verbs. But every once in a while they step out of character and take on the role of nouns. For all intents and purposes they may as well be nouns; in this example, *going* may as well be the noun *departure.*

The $64,000 question: How do we figure out whether an *ing* word is acting like a verb or like a noun? Here's a hint: If you can substitute a noun for the *ing* word—*departure* in place of *going,* for example, or *habit* for *smoking*—then treat it like a noun. That means making the word in front a possessive (*my,* not *me*): *He can't stand* ***my*** *smoking.*

Loose Ends

The preceding explanation unties the Gordian knot, and you can stop there if you want. But there are a couple of loose ends you may want to finish off.

Sometimes it's too clumsy to use a possessive with an *ing* word—for instance, when you'd have to make a whole string of words possessive, not just one. Here's an example: *Basil objects to* **men and women kissing** *in public*. Using the possessive (*men's and women's kissing*) would create a monster. It's good to follow a rule, except when it leads you off a cliff. Since there's no way to mistake the meaning, leave it alone. But if there's just a pronoun in front, stick to the rule and make it a possessive: *Basil objects to* **our kissing** *in public*. (Not: *Basil objects to* **us kissing** *in public*.)

Another complication is the kind of sentence that can go either way:

Basil dislikes that **woman's wearing** *shorts*.

Basil dislikes that **woman wearing** *shorts*.

Both are correct, but they mean different things. In the first example, Basil dislikes shorts on the woman. In the second, he dislikes the woman herself. The lesson? Lighten up, Basil!

Chapter 4

They Beg to Disagree

Putting Verbs in Their Place

The verb is the business end of a sentence, the sentence's reason for being. That's where the action is. Without a verb, even if it's only suggested, there's nothing going on, just a lot of nouns standing around with their hands in their pockets. A verb is easy to spot. Just look for the moving target, the center of activity, the part that tells you what's going on. No wonder the verb is often the most interesting word in a sentence.

It's also the most complicated. Because a verb expresses action, it has a dimension that other words lack—time. It has to tell you whether something happened in the past, the present, the future, or some combination of times: *sneeze, sneezed, will sneeze, would have sneezed,* and so on. The verb has another dimension, too. It varies according to the subject (who or what is performing the action): *I sneeze, he sneezes, they sneeze,* and so on.

There are plenty of reasons a verb can go astray. The most common is that it doesn't match the subject: one is singular and the other plural (*Harry and I **was sneezing**,* for example). The next most common reason is that the verb's timing—its tense—is off (*Yesterday she **sneezes***).

Then there are those pesky little verbs that are as annoying as ants at a picnic, and just about as hard to tell apart: *sit* and *set, rise* and *raise, lie* and *lay.*

This makes verbs sound daunting, but they're actually not that bad. Taken one at a time (which is how you encounter them, after all), problems with verbs can be made to disappear.

Making Verbs Agreeable

Some rules of grammar may shift every eon or so, but you can bet the bank that this one will never change: Subject and verb must agree. If the subject is singular, so is the verb (*Ollie stumbles*). If the subject is plural, so is the verb (*Stan and Ollie stumble*).

If your verb (the action word) doesn't match its subject (who or what is doing the action), you probably have the wrong subject in mind. That's not unusual, since the real subject isn't always easy to see. If you find it a breeze to write a simple sentence, but start hyperventilating when a few bells and whistles are added, you're not alone. Here's what I mean:

*Every part of Ollie **needs** a massage.*

No problem. The subject (*part*) is singular, so the verb (*needs*) is singular. Now let's add a few of Ollie's aching parts:

*Every part of Ollie—his legs, his neck, his shoulders, his feet—[**needs** or **need**] a massage.*

Since the closest word is *feet*, a plural, you might be tempted to pick *need*. But in fact, the verb stays the same, *needs*, despite the added details. That's because the subject itself (*part*) hasn't changed. The key to making subject and verb agree is to correctly identify the subject, and for that you have to simplify the sentence in your mind and eliminate the extraneous stuff. Here are a couple of tips on simplifying a sentence:

- Extra information inserted between subject and verb doesn't alter the verb.

  *Spring's glory **was** lost on Ollie.*

  *Spring's glory, with its birds and its flowers and its trees, **was** lost on Ollie.*

  The subject, *glory*, is still singular, no matter how much information you add to it.

- Phrases such as *along with*, *as well as*, *in addition to*, and *together with*, inserted between subject and verb, don't alter the verb.

  *Spring **was** a tonic for Stan.*

*Spring, along with a few occasional flirtations, **was** a tonic for Stan.*

The subject is still *spring,* and is singular.

● Descriptions (adjectives) added to the subject don't alter the verb.

*A substance **was** stuck to Stan's shoe.*

*A green, slimy, and foul-smelling substance **was** stuck to Stan's shoe.*

The subject is *substance,* and it stays singular no matter how many disgusting adjectives you pile on.

SPLIT DECISIONS

Often the subject of a sentence—whoever or whatever is doing the action—is a two-headed creature with *or* or *nor* in the middle: ***Milk or cream** is fine, thank you.*

When both halves of the subject—the parts on either side of *or* or *nor*—are singular, so is the verb: *Neither alcohol nor tobacco **is** allowed.* When both halves are plural, so is the verb: *Ties or cravats **are** required.*

But how about when one half is singular and the other plural? Do you choose a singular or a plural verb? *Neither the eggs nor the milk [**was** or **were**] fresh.*

The answer is simple. If the subject nearer the verb is singular, the verb is singular: *Neither the eggs nor the **milk was** fresh.* If the subject nearer the verb is plural, the verb is plural: *Neither the milk nor the **eggs were** fresh.*

The same rule applies when subjects are paired with *not only* and *but also: Not only the chairs but also the **table was** sold.* Or: *Not only the table but also the **chairs were** sold.*

THE SUBJECT WITH MULTIPLE PERSONALITIES

Say you've identified the subject of a sentence, and it's a word that could be interpreted as either singular or plural, like *couple, total, majority, number, any, all,* or *none.* Is the verb singular or plural?

Here's how to decide.

Words that stand for a group of things—*couple, total, majority,* and *number*—sometimes mean the group as a whole (singular), and sometimes mean the individual members of the group (plural). The presence of *the* before the word (*the couple, the total, the majority*) is often a clue that it's singular, so use a singular verb: ***The couple lives** in apartment 9A.* When *a* comes before the word, and especially when *of* comes after (*a couple of, a number of*), it's probably plural, so use a plural verb: ***A couple of** deadbeats **live** in apartment 9A.*

The words *all, any,* and *none* can also be either singular or plural. If you're using them to suggest *all of it, any of it,* or *none of it,* use a singular verb: ***All** the money [all of it] **is** spent.* If you're suggesting *all of them, any of them,* or *none of them,* use a plural verb: ***All** the customers [all of them] **are** gone.*

There's more about these two-edged words in the chapter on plurals, pages 25–28.

WHAT AND WHATNOT

Here's another multiple personality—a word that can be either singular or plural. Take a look at these examples:

What is going on here? *What are* your intentions, Mister?

As you can see, *what* can be either singular or plural when it's the subject of a verb. If *what* stands for one thing, use a singular verb (*is,* in this case). If it stands for several things, use a plural verb (*are,* for example).

But how do you choose? Consider this sentence: *Phyllis is wearing* **what** [**look** *or* **looks**] *like false eyelashes.* Just ask yourself whether *what* refers to "a thing that" or "things that." In this case, she is wearing *things* that *look* like false eyelashes. Use the plural verb: *Phyllis is wearing* **what look** *like false eyelashes.*

NOTE: When *what* affects two verbs in the same sentence, the verbs should be alike—both singular or both plural, not one of each: **What gives** *away Phyllis's age* **is** *her bad knees.* In other words, the thing about Phyllis that gives away her age is the fact that she has bad knees. On the other hand, if you want to emphasize that both of Phyllis's knees have gone bad, you should choose plurals for both verbs: **What give** *away Phyllis's age* **are** *her two bad knees.* As you may suspect, there can be room for disagreement about whether *what* should be singular or plural. What's important to remember is that if *what* affects two verbs, they should match—both singular or both plural.

There's more about *what* in the chapter on pronouns; see page 17.

THERE, THERE, NOW!

When a statement starts with *there*, the verb can be either singular or plural. We can say *there is* or *there are*:

*"**There is** a fly in my soup!" said Mr. LaFong. "And **there are** lumps in the gravy!"*

The choice can be tricky, because *there* is only a phantom subject. In the first example, the real subject is *fly*; in the second, it's *lumps*. If the subject is hard for you to see, just delete *there* in your mind and turn the statement around: *"A fly **is** in my soup! And lumps **are** in the gravy!"*

For more on *there* at the head of a sentence, see pages 184 and 192.

Wishful Thinking: I Wish I Was . . . or . . . I Wish I Were?

"Difficult do you call it, Sir?" the lexicographer Samuel Johnson once said after hearing a violinist perform. "I wish it were impossible."

Were? Why not *I wish it **was** impossible*? Well, in English we have a special way of speaking wishfully. We say, *I wish I* *were in love again,* not *I wish I was in love again.* There's a peculiar, wishful kind of grammar for talking about things that are desirable, as opposed to things as they really are. When we're in a wishful mood (a grammarian would call it the subjunctive mood), *was* becomes *were:*

I wish I were in Paris. (I'm not in Paris.)

They wish he weren't so obnoxious. (He is so obnoxious.)

She wishes New York were cleaner. (New York isn't cleaner.)

He wishes Julia were home more often. (Julia isn't home more often.)

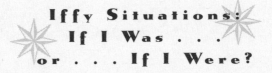

Iffy Situations: If I Was . . . or . . . If I Were?

What a difference an *if* makes. An ordinary, straightforward statement like *I was taller* becomes quite another proposition when we insert one little word: *If I were taller.*

Why is this? It's because there's a special, "what if" sort of grammar that kicks in when we talk about something that's untrue. When we're in this iffy mood (the subjunctive mood, if you want to be technical), *was* becomes *were.* This happens when a sentence or a clause (a group of words with its own subject and verb) starts with *if,* and what's being talked about is contrary to fact:

If I were king, no one would pay retail. (I'm not king.)

*If she **were** older, she'd know better.* (She's not older.)

*We could go shopping if it **were** Saturday.* (Today is not Saturday.)

NOTE: Not all *if* statements fall into this category, only those that are undeniably contrary to fact. In cases where the statement may actually be true, *was* remains *was*.

*If I **was** rude, I apologize.* (I may have been rude.)

*If she **was** there, I guess I missed her.* (She may have been there.)

*If it **was** Thursday, I must have gone to bed early.* (It may have been Thursday.)

As If You Didn't Know

The same rules that apply to *if* statements apply to those starting with *as if* or *as though*:

*He acts as if he **were** infallible.*

(He's not infallible.)

*She behaves as though money **were** the problem.*

(Money is not the problem.)

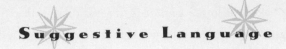

Suggestive Language

Sometimes, English slips through a time warp and into another dimension. In cases where we'd normally use the verbs *was* or *were*, we use *be* instead. You might have wondered why we say, *I **was** quiet*, but *They requested that I **be** quiet*. What's going on here? The answer is that in English we have a special way of suggesting or demanding something (another example of the subjunctive mood). This is what you need to remember:

Use *be* instead of *was* or *were* after someone *suggests, demands, asks, requests, requires,* or *insists* that something be done:

*I demanded that I **be** excused.*

*The judge ordered that he **be** executed.*

*Olivia insists they **be** admitted free.*

*The law requires that you **be** fingerprinted.*

If *be* sounds unnatural to your ear, just imagine an unspoken *should* in front of it:

I demanded that I (should) be excused.

The judge ordered that he (should) be executed.

Olivia insisted they (should) be admitted free.

The law requires that you (should) be fingerprinted.

By the way, the form of the verb used here—*be* instead of *was* or *were*—is similar to the one used for a command: *Be good! Be quiet! Be there or **be** square!*

NOTE: Although *was, were,* and *be* give us the most trouble when we're suggesting or demanding something, other verbs must also be in the command form when they're forced to give "command" performances: *Mom demands that Ricky eat. We insist that she walk. He urged that Barbra negotiate. I suggested he go.* Again, if this feels unnatural, imagine an unspoken *should* in front of the verb: *I suggested he (should) go.*

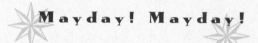

Mayday! Mayday!

If there were a club for people who confuse *may* and *might,* I would be its president. Also its vice-president, treasurer, and recording secretary. I'm always using the search function on my computer to find *may* in my work, because it is often wrong and should be *might.*

May is a source of our word *maybe,* and that's a good clue to how it's used. We attach it to another verb (*happen,* for example) to indicate the possibility of something's happening. If we say something *may* happen, we mean it's possible or even probable.

Might is a slightly weaker form of *may.* Something that *might* happen is a longer shot than something that *may* happen. *I may get a raise* is more promising than *I might get a raise.*

Although your dictionary will tell you that *might* can be the past tense of *may,* either one can be used in the present tense (*She **may** break a leg; She **might** break a leg*) or in the past (*She **may** have broken a leg; She **might** have broken a leg*). The form you choose depends on the degree of possibility and can radically change your meaning. *A bulletproof vest **may** have saved him* implies that he was saved. *A bulletproof vest **might** have saved him* implies that he wasn't.

There's an exception to this rule of possibility, which is why I'm grateful for search keys. If a sentence has other verbs in the past tense, use only *might*: *She thought* [past] *she **might** have broken a leg. Eloise was* [past] *afraid they **might** lose everything. Frank said* [past] *he **might** leave early.*

Just One of Those Things

Here's one of the things that [*drives* or *drive*] us crazy. Should the verb be singular or plural? *Drives*? Or *drive*? In other words, what kind of verb goes with a phrase like *one of the, one of those,* or *one of these*? The answer in a nutshell:

- If *that* or *who* comes before the verb, it's plural: *He's one of the authors who **say** it best.*
- If not, it's singular: *One of the authors **says** it best.*

In the first example, *one* is not the subject of the verb *say.* The actual subject is *who,* which is plural because it refers to *authors.* In the second example, the subject really is *one.* If you don't trust me, just turn the sentences around in your mind and you'll end up with the correct verbs: *Of the authors who say it best, he is one. Of the authors, one says it best.*

Never-Never Land

Poor verbs! We tend to spread them a little thin sometimes. Any sentence with *never have and never will* is probably doomed. There's almost no way to finish it correctly, because so few verbs go with both *have* and *will.*

Here's the kind of sentence I mean: *They **never have and never will** forget Paris.* What we intend to say is, *They never have forgotten and never will forget Paris.* But what we've actually said is, *They never have [forget] and never will forget Paris.* That odd, crackling noise you hear is the sound of a sentence short-circuiting! This problem comes up when we use *have* and *will* with the same verb. Another major culprit is *always have and always will.*

Only when a verb appears the same way twice (like *forget* in *I never could forget and never would forget Paris*) can you omit the first one and avoid repeating yourself: *I never could and never would forget Paris.*

NOTE: If you don't want to repeat yourself when using different forms of the same verb, you can cheat by rearranging the sentence: *They never have forgotten Paris and never will.* That way, the part you omit—*forget Paris*—is at the end of the sentence, where it won't be missed very much. This isn't perfect grammar, mind you, but it's reasonable. And nobody will blow a fuse.

Ize in Our Heads: Are These Verbs Legit?

For centuries, we've been creating instant verbs in English simply by adding *ize* to nouns (*demon* ⇒ *demonize*, for instance) or to adjectives (*brutal* ⇒ *brutalize*). The ancient Greeks were the ones who gave us the idea. The *ize* ending (often *ise* in British spellings) has given us loads of useful words (*agonize, burglarize, fantasize, mesmerize, pasteurize, pulverize*). It's just as legitimate to add *ize* to the end of a word as it is to add *un* or *pre* to the beginning.

Yet there can be too much of a good thing, and that's what has happened with *ize*. Verbs should be lively little devils, and just adding *ize* to a word doesn't give it life. Fortunately, many recent horrors (*credibilize, permanentize, respectabilize, uniformize*) didn't catch on. But some lifeless specimens have slipped into the language, among them *colorize, prioritize,* and *finalize,* and they're probably going to be around for a while.

Infinitively Speaking

Many of us misuse the infinitive (a verb that usually has *to* in front of it) after certain words. *Anxious*, for example. Are you *anxious to go*, or are you *anxious about going*? If you picked *anxious to go*, you should be anxious about your grammar. Here's a list of words that shouldn't be followed by infinitives:

anxious: *I was* **anxious about going**. Not: *I was anxious to go*. With the infinitive, use *eager* instead: *I was* **eager to go**. For more about *anxious* and *eager*, see page 91.

convince: *They* **convinced** *us* **that** *we should go*. Not: *They convinced us to go*. With the infinitive, use *persuade*: *They* **persuaded** *us* **to** *go*. For more about *convince* and *persuade*, see page 96.

prevent: *We* **prevented** *him* **from** *going*. Not: *We prevented him to go*. If you keep the infinitive, use *did not permit* instead: *We* **did not permit** *him* **to** *go*. Another way to say this is: *We* **prevented** *his going*.

prohibit: *She was* **prohibited from** *going*. Not: *She was prohibited to go*. With the infinitive, use *forbid*: *She was* **forbidden to** *go*. For more about *forbid* and *prohibit*, see pages 111 and 113.

I have two pieces of advice about verbs ending in *ize*:

- Don't coin any new ones.
- Don't use any recent ones you don't like. If we ignore them, maybe they'll go away.

Ants at the Picnic: Pesky Look-alikes

Who hasn't confused *lie* and *lay*? *Sit, set,* and *sat*? *Rise* and *raise*? It's nothing to be ashamed of. You could commit them all to memory, of course. Or you could *lay* your cares aside, *sit* tight, *rise* to the occasion, and look up the answer.

Here's the *lay* of the land (or, as they say in Britain, the *lie* of the land):

lie (to recline): *She **lies** quietly. Last night, she **lay** quietly. For years, she **has lain** quietly.*

lie (to fib): *He **lies**. Yesterday he **lied**. Frequently he **has lied**.*

lay (to place): *She **lays** it there. Yesterday she **laid** it there. Many times she **has laid** it there.* (When *lay* means "to place," it's always followed by an object, the thing being placed.)

sit (to be seated): *I **sit**. I **sat** last week. I **have sat** many times.*

set (to place): *He **sets** it there. He **set** it there yesterday. He **has set** it there frequently.* (*Set* meaning "to place" is always followed by an object, the thing being placed.)

rise (to go up or get up): *You **rise**. You **rose** at seven. You **have risen** even earlier.*

raise (to bring something up): *I **raise** it. I **raised** it last year. I **have raised** it several times.* (The verb *raise* is always followed by an object, the thing being brought up.)

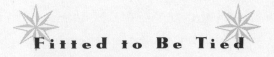

Fitted to Be Tied

Several verbs ending in *t* or *d* have all but dropped the *ed* ending in the past tense. Once we would have said, *Mr. Pecksniff **quitted** the firm, **betted** on the horses, and **wetted** his whistle, then **wedded** his sweetheart in a suit that **fitted** him perfectly.* The British still use those endings, but Americans are now more likely to use the shorter *quit, bet, wet, wed,* and *fit. Mr. Pecksniff **quit** the firm, **bet** on the horses, and **wet** his whistle, then **wed** his sweetheart in a suit that **fit** him perfectly.*

We still use *wedded,* but only as an adjective (a word that describes people or things): ***Wedded** life is a thrill a minute.*

We also use *fitted* as an adjective (*a fitted sheet, a fitted suit*). And we use *fitted* when we speak of someone whose clothes are, shall we say, under construction: *Alice was **fitted** for a new dress.* But later we would say, *When it was finished, the dress **fit** like a glove.*

✦ Happy Endings: Burned or Burnt?

He *spilled* the milk, or he *spilt* it? He *burned* the toast, or he *burnt* it? Actually, they're all correct, although in these cases the *ed* spellings are preferred.

A number of verbs can form the past tense with either *ed* or *t.* For some of them, the preferred ending is *ed,* and for others it's *t.* In these examples, the favored spellings are given first, and the less common ones follow in parentheses: *bereaved (bereft), dreamed (dreamt), dwelt (dwelled), knelt (kneeled), leaned (leant), leaped (leapt), learned (learnt), smelled (smelt), spelled (spelt), spoiled (spoilt).*

> **NOTE:** Some verbs no longer have alternative *ed* endings: *bent* (the obsolete form survives in the phrase *on bended knee*), *crept, dealt, felt, kept, left, lost, meant, slept, swept,* and *wept.*

✦ Wake-up Calls

Wake . . . woke . . . have *woken*? Or is it have *waked*? Some days it's a challenge just to get up in the morning. If you lie awake nights worrying about this one, don't bother. Either form is correct, though many dictionaries now prefer *have woken*, long favored by the British but once considered obsolete in American English.

For the record, the accepted forms of the verb *wake* are *wake, woke* (or *waked*), and *have woken* (or *have waked*). Here they are in action: *I usually* **wake** *at seven. Yesterday, I* **woke** (or **waked**) *at nine. In the past, I* **have woken** (or **have waked**) *as early as five.* By the way, it's fine to add *up* to any of the *wake* forms: *Wake* **up** *and smell the coffee!*

If you're like me, and you think both *have woken* and *have waked* sound weird, try *have wakened* or *have awakened*. Those are past tenses of related verbs, *waken* and *awaken*.

There are lots of ways to greet the morning—maybe more than we need. You can *wake*, or you can *waken*, or you can *awake*, or you can *awaken*. So rise and shine, already!

What's the Use?

One way to say *he formerly did* is *he used to*: *Andre* **used to** *have a good lob.*

What about when the sentence becomes a question or a negative statement? Let's see if we can choose the right form:

*Did Andre [***use*** or ***used***] to have a good lob?*

*Andre didn't [***use*** or ***used***] to have a good lob.*

The answer in both cases is *use*. Why? Because *did use* is another way of saying *used,* just as *did walk* is another way of saying *walked.* You wouldn't say "did walked," would you? Then why would you say "did used"?

> **NOTE:** The British, as you might have noticed, have a different way of dealing with *used to.* Instead of using *did* in a question or a negative statement, they prefer these forms: *Used Andre to have a good lob? Andre usedn't to have a good lob.* Forget you ever saw them.

Getting the Hang of Hung

No! It's not true that *hung* is never right. I would like to impress this on the magazine writer who described somebody's walls as "hanged with handsome black-and-white photographs."

Both past tenses have been around for hundreds of years, but since the sixteenth century it's been customary to reserve *hanged* for referring to executions, and to use *hung* for other meanings.

So, except at the gallows, *hung* is the correct past tense of *hang: He* **hung** *around. They* **have hung** *around.* This is true whether you've *hung* pictures, *hung* loose, *hung* out, *hung* laundry, or *hung* up.

Anyone who still uses *hanged* in such cases should be suspended.

That's That

There are two kinds of editors. One kind sticks in *that* wherever it will fit. The other kind takes it out.

They're both wrong.

Many verbs (*think, say, hope, believe, find, feel,* and *wish* are examples) sometimes sound smoother—to my ears, at least—when they're followed by *that: Carmela believed [**that**] Tony was unfaithful.* You may agree that the sentence sounds better with *that,* or you may not. It's purely a matter of taste. The sentence is correct either way.

Some writers and editors believe that if *that* can logically follow a verb, it should be there. Others believe that if *that* can logically be omitted, it should be taken out. If you like it, use it. If you don't, don't. Here are some cases where adding *that* can rescue a drowning sentence.

- When a time element comes after the verb: *Junior said on Friday he would pay up.* This could mean either: *Junior said **that** on Friday he would pay up,* or *Junior said on Friday **that** he would pay up.* So why not add a *that* and make yourself clear?
- When the point of the sentence comes late: *Johnny found the old violin hidden in a trunk in his attic wasn't a real Stradivarius.* Better: *Johnny found **that** the old violin hidden in a trunk in his attic wasn't a real Stradivarius.* Otherwise, we have to read to the end of the

sentence to learn that Johnny's finding the violin isn't the point.

● When there are two more verbs after the main one: *Silvio thinks the idea stinks and Paulie does too.* What exactly is Silvio thinking? The sentence could mean *Silvio thinks **that** the idea stinks and **that** Paulie does too.* Or it could mean *Silvio thinks **that** the idea stinks, and Paulie does too.* Adding *that* (and a well-placed comma) can make clear who's thinking what.

S p l i t s v i l l e

Many people seem to believe that there's something sacred about a verb, and that it's wrong to split up one that comes in parts (*had gone* or *would go,* for example). You've probably heard at one time or another that you're cheating if you slip a word (say, *finally*) in between (as in *had finally gone* or *would finally go*). Well, it just isn't so.

The best place to put a word like *finally*—that is, an adverb, a word that characterizes a verb—is directly before the action being described: in this case, *go* or *gone*. It's perfectly natural to split the parts of a verb like *have gone* by putting an adverb between them: *The goombahs **have finally gone**.* If you prefer to put the adverb before or after all the parts of the verb (as in, *The goombahs **finally have gone**,* or *The goombahs **have gone finally***), that's all right, too. But don't go out of your way to avoid the "splits." And keep in mind that adverbs usually do the most good right in front of the action words they describe.

This fear of splitting verb phrases, by the way, has its origins in another old taboo—the dreaded "split infinitive" (*to finally go,* for instance). The chapter on dead rules has more on that one, and on how the myth got started. See pages 182 and 185.

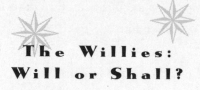

The Willies: Will or Shall?

In George Washington's day, schoolchildren on both sides of the Atlantic were admonished to use *shall* instead of *will* in some cases. (Don't ask!) Americans have since left *shall* behind and now use *will* almost exclusively. Although *shall* survives in parts of England, even the British are using it less and less these days.

Shall can still be found in a few nooks and crannies of American English, such as legalese (*This lease **shall** commence on January 1*) and lofty language (*We **shall** overcome*). It's also used with *I* and *we* in some kinds of questions— when we're asking what another person wishes: **Shall** *we dance, or* **shall** *I fill your glass?*

Shall is one of the "living dead" discussed in the chapter on outdated rules, page 189.

The Incredible Shrinking Words: Contractions

The contraction—two words combined into one, as in *don't* or *I'm*—seldom gets a fair shake from English teachers. It may be tolerated, but it's looked down upon as colloquial or, according to one expert, "dialect" (what a slur!). Yet despite its esteem problem, the humble contraction is used every day by virtually everyone, and has been for centuries. Quaint antiquities like *shan't* (shall not), *'tis* (it is), *'twas* (it was), *'twill* (it will), *'twould* (it would), and even *'twon't* (it will not) are evidence of the contraction's long history.

Today's contractions usually include a verb, along with a subject or the word "not."

Isn't it time we admitted that the contraction has earned its place in the sun? It has all the qualities we admire in language: it's handy, succinct, and economical, and everybody knows what it means. Contractions are obviously here to stay, so why not give them a little respect? Here's the long and the short of it: the contractions that are respectable, followed by a few that aren't.

Fit to Print

aren't	are not	mustn't	must not
can't	cannot	oughtn't	ought not
couldn't	could not	she'd	she would;
didn't	did not		she had
doesn't	does not	she'll	she will
don't	do not	she's	she is;
hadn't	had not		she has
hasn't	has not	shouldn't	should not
haven't	have not	that's	that is;
he'd	he would;		that has
	he had	there's	there is;
he'll	he will		there has
he's	he is;	they'd	they would;
	he has		they had
I'd	I would;	they'll	they will
	I had	they're	they are
I'll	I will	they've	they have
I'm	I am	wasn't	was not
I've	I have	we'd	we would;
isn't	is not		we had
it'll	it will	we'll	we will
it's	it is; it has	we're	we are
let's	let us	we've	we have
mightn't	might not	weren't	were not

what'll	what will	who's	who is;
what're	what are		who has
what's	what is;	who've	who have
	what has	won't	will not
what've	what have	wouldn't	would not
where's	where is	you'd	you would;
who'd	who would;		you had
	who had	you'll	you will
who'll	who will	you're	you are
who're	who are	you've	you have

OUT OF BOUNDS

ain't. It's not OK and it never will be OK. Get used to it. If you're tempted to use it to show that you have the common touch, make clear that you know better: *Now, **ain't** that a shame!*

could've, should've, would've, might've, must've. There's a good reason to stay away from writing these. Seen in print, they encourage mispronunciation, which explains why they're often heard as *could of, should of, would of, might of,* and *must of* (or, even worse, *coulda, shoulda, woulda, mighta,* and *musta*). It's fine to pronounce these as though the *h* in *have* were silent. But let's not forget that *have* is there. Write it out.

gonna, gotta, wanna. These are merely substandard English. Unless you're talking to your sister on the phone, make it *going to, got to, want to,* and so on.

how'd, how'll, how're, how's, when'll, when're, when's, where'd, where'll, where're, why'd, why're, why's. Resist the urge to write any contractions with *how, when, where,* or *why,* except that old standby *where's.* We all say things like, *"How'm I supposed to pay for this?"* But don't put them in writing.

it'd, that'd, there'd, this'd, what'd. Notice how these *'d* endings seem to add a syllable that lands with a *thud?* And they look ridiculously clumsy in writing. Let's use the *'d* contractions (for *had* or *would*) only with *I, you, he, she, we, they,* and *who.*

that'll, that're, that've, there'll, there're, there've, this'll. Ugh! These clumsies may be fine in conversation, but written English isn't ready for them yet. Do I use *that'll* when I talk? Sure. But not when I write.

Where There's a Will, There's a Would

Do you waffle when faced with the choice of *will* or *would?* Take your pick: *Harry said he [will or would] make waffles for breakfast.*

All Tensed Up

If we used only one verb per sentence, we'd never have trouble choosing the tense—past, present, future, or whatever: *They waltzed. He tangos. She will polka.* And so on. Many sentences, though, have several things going on in them—actions happening at different times, each with its own verb. You can't just string these verbs together like beads in a necklace. It takes planning.

With most sentences, we don't give this much thought, and we don't have to. When all the actions happen at about the same time, we can just put them in the same tense and rattle them off in order: *On Sundays, Elaine* **rises** *at seven,* **makes** *tea,* **showers**, *and* **goes** *back to bed. Last Sunday, Elaine* **rose** *at seven,* **made** *tea,* **showered**, *and* **went** *back to bed.*

When we have different things happening at distinctly different times, sentences get more complicated: *Elaine* **says** *she* **made** *tea last Sunday, but she* **will make** *coffee next week.*

Common sense tells us how to do most of these adjustments in timing. But some verb sequences are harder to sort out than others. Pages 77–80 deal with some of the most troublesome ones.

Follow the lead of the first verb (*said*). Since it's in the past tense, use *would*: *Harry said he **would** make waffles for breakfast*. When the first verb is in the present tense (*says*), use *will*: *Harry says he **will** make waffles for breakfast*.

Now here's an example with three verbs (the same principle applies): *Harry thought that if he [**eats** or **ate**] one waffle, he [**will** or **would**] want another.*

Since the first verb (*thought*) is in the past, use the past tense, *ate*, and *would*: *Harry thought that if he **ate** one waffle, he **would** want another*. When the first verb is in the present (*thinks*), use the present tense, *eats*, and *will*: *Harry thinks that if he **eats** one waffle, he **will** want another*.

In the Land of If

Think of *if* as a tiny set of scales. When a sentence has *if* in it, the verbs have to be in balance. When the *if* side of the scale is in the present tense, the other side calls for *will*. When the *if* side of the scale is in the past tense, the other side gets a *would*.

*If he **shops** [present] alone, he **will spend** too much.*

*If he **shopped** [past] alone, he **would spend** too much.*

Balancing the scales becomes more complicated as the tenses get more complicated. When you use a compound tense with *has* or *have* on the *if* side of the scale, you need a *will have* on the other side. Similarly, when you use a compound tense with *had* on the *if* side of the scale, you need a *would have* on the other.

*If he **has shopped** alone, he **will have spent** too much.*

*If he **had shopped** alone, he **would have spent** too much.*

The *if* part doesn't have to come first, but the scales must stay in balance: *He **will spend** too much if he **shops** alone. He **would spend** too much if he **shopped** alone.*

After Thoughts

Some people tense up when one action comes after another in a sentence. Let's test your tension level. Which verbs would be better in these examples?

*I will start dinner after the guests [**arrive** or **have arrived**].*

*I started dinner after the guests [**arrived** or **had arrived**].*

If you chose the simpler ones, you were right: *I will start dinner after the guests **arrive**. I started dinner after the guests **arrived**.* Why make things harder than they have to be?

No matter what the tense of the main part of a sentence, and no matter how complicated, the verb that follows *after* should be in either the simple present (*arrive*) or the simple past (*arrived*).

When the main action in a sentence takes place in the present or in a future tense, the verb that follows *after* is in the simple present:

I start dinner after the guests **arrive**. *I will have started dinner after the guests* **arrive**.

When the main action takes place in a past tense, the verb that follows *after* is in the simple past:

I would have started dinner after the guests **arrived**.

The rule is the same if the sentence is turned around so the *after* part comes first: *After the guests* **arrive**, *I will have started dinner.*

Sometimes the simple solution is the best. Keep that in mind, and may all your verbs live happily ever after.

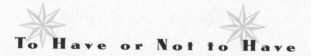

To Have or Not to Have

Have is a useful word, but we can have too much of it.

Which is correct? *I would have liked* **to go**, or *I would have liked* **to have gone**.

The first example is correct. One *have* is enough, though it can go with whichever half of the sentence you want to emphasize: *I would* **have** *liked to go*, or *I would like to* **have** *gone*.

Here's a case in which even one *have* is a *have* too many.

Incorrect: *Two years ago, Whiskers was the first cat to have flown on the Concorde.*

Correct: *Two years ago, Whiskers was the first cat to fly on the Concorde.*

You need to use *have* only if you're talking about two different times in the past: *Until last year, Whiskers was the only cat **to have flown** on the Concorde.* If you find the concept hard to grasp, think of it this way. One of the times was last year and the other was the period before that.

I could go on about the subtleties of *have,* but I suspect that by now you've had it.

Chapter 5

Verbal Abuse

Words on the Endangered List

The give-and-take of language is something like warfare. A word bravely soldiers on for years, until one day it falls face-down in the trenches, its original meaning a casualty of misuse. *Unique* is a good example: a crisp and accurate word meaning "one of a kind," now frequently degraded to merely "unusual."

Then there are what I call mixed doubles: pairs of words and phrases that are routinely confused, like *affect* and *effect*. Finally, there are the words that are mispronounced, misspelled, or so stretched out of shape that they aren't even words anymore—like that impostor *irregardless*.

Keep in mind, though, that today's clumsy grotesquerie may be tomorrow's bon mot. Dictionaries are forever changing their minds about what's acceptable, and they're supposed to. Their job is to reflect the language people use at a particular time—the good, the bad, the indifferent. So spellings, pronunciations, and meanings that once were considered substandard or even illiterate (words like *irregardless,* spellings like *alright,* pronunciations like NOO-kyoo-lur) may find acceptance in dictionaries as more people use them. But what's common isn't necessarily correct.

If correctness is what you're after, your computer spell-checker may only add to the confusion. Mine tells me, for instance, that *restauranteur* and *judgement* and *straightlaced* are preferred spellings, but I know better. And it doesn't care whether I use *affect* or *effect.* There's more about spell-checkers in the chapter on e-mail, page 214.

What's a reasonable person to do? Let's take a closer look at some of the more commonly mauled words and phrases. Where authorities disagree, I've tried to weigh the best evidence and make decisions that reflect what thoughtful, literate people consider good English.

Here, then, are the walking wounded. Bloodied but unbowed, they shouldn't be given up for dead. Give them back their proper meaning, spelling, usage, and pronunciation, and they'll live to fight another day.

What's the Meaning of This?

decimate. Who says grammar books don't have sex and violence? To *decimate* means literally "to slaughter every tenth one," although most people don't intend it literally. It can be used loosely to mean "to destroy in part" (*Gomez says the mushroom crop in the cellar has been **decimated** by rats*), but don't use it to mean "to destroy entirely." And definitely don't attach a figure to the damage: *The earthquake **decimated** seventy-five percent of Morticia's antiques.* Ouch!

diagnose. The disease is *diagnosed,* not the patient. *Miss Mapp's rash was **diagnosed** as shingles.* Not: *Miss Mapp was **diagnosed** with shingles.*

dilemma. This is no ordinary problem; the *di* (from the Greek for "twice") is a clue that there's a *two*ness here. A *dilemma* is a situation involving at least two choices—all of them bad. (This idea is captured neatly in the old phrase about being caught on the *horns of a dilemma.*) *Richie faced a **dilemma**: he could wear the green checked suit with the gravy stain, or the blue one with the hole.*

eclectic. This word is mistakenly used to mean discriminating or sophisticated; in fact, it means "drawn from many sources." *Sherman has an **eclectic** assortment of mud-wrestling memorabilia.*

effete. Don't use this if you mean weak, effeminate, soft, or affected. *Effete* means barren, used up, or worn out. *Frazier considers abstract expressionism an **effete** art form.*

enervating. Energizing it's not. On the contrary: if something's *enervating,* it drains you of energy. *Frazier's date found his conversation **enervating**.*

enormity. Don't confuse this with *enormousness,* because *enormity* isn't a measure of size alone. It refers to something immensely wicked, monstrous, or outrageous. *Sleepy little Liechtenstein was shocked by the **enormity** of the crime.*

fortuitous. No, this word doesn't mean fortunate. Formally speaking, *fortuitous* means accidental. (*It was entirely **fortuitous** that Ralph bought a filly instead of a colt.*) Still, those notions of good fortune and chance have blended so much that dictionaries now accept a hybrid definition— something *fortuitous* is a happy accident. (*Pie-O-My was a **fortuitous** choice.*) The upshot? To avoid misunderstanding, use another word to describe an *un*lucky accident.

fulsome. You may think this means abundant; it also means overdone or disgustingly excessive. *Eddie's insincere and **fulsome** speeches got on Mrs. Cleaver's nerves.* Avoid it if you might be misunderstood.

hero. There was a time when this word was reserved for people who were . . . well . . . heroic. People who performed great acts of bravery or valor, often facing danger, even death. But lately, *hero* has started losing its luster. We hear it applied indiscriminately to professional athletes, lottery winners, and kids who clean up at spelling bees. There's no other word quite like *hero,* so let's not bestow it too freely. It would be a pity to lose it. *Achilles was a **hero**.*

hopefully. These days, it's hopeless to resist the evolution of *hopefully*. Purists used to insist (and some still do) that there's only one way to use it correctly—as an adverb meaning "in a hopeful manner." (*"I'm thinking of going to Spain," Eddie told Mrs. Cleaver. "Soon?" she asked **hopefully**.*) If the holdouts had their way, nobody would use *hopefully* to replace a phrase like "it is hoped" or "let us hope," as in: *"**Hopefully** the cuisine in Spain will be as delectable as your own,"* Eddie said. But here in the real world, language changes, and upright citizens have been using *hopefully* in that looser way for ages. It's time to admit that *hopefully* has joined that class of introductory words (like *fortunately, frankly, happily, honestly, sadly, seriously,* and others) that we use not to describe a verb, which is what adverbs usually do, but to describe our attitude toward the statement that follows. The technical term for them is sentence adverbs. When I say, "Sadly, Eddie stayed for dinner," I probably don't mean that Eddie was sad about staying. I mean, "I'm sad to say that Eddie stayed for dinner." And "Frankly, he's boring" doesn't mean the poor guy is boring in a frank way. It means, "I'm being frank when I say he's boring." Frankly, I see no reason to treat *hopefully* otherwise. But be aware that some sticklers still take a narrow view of *hopefully*. Will they ever join the crowd? One can only hope.

irony. I hope some TV news reporters are tuning in. A wonderful word for a wonderful idea, *irony* refers to a sly form of expression in which you say one thing and mean another. (*"You're wearing the green checked suit again, Richie! How fashionable of you,"* said Mrs. Cunningham, her voice full of **irony**.) A situation is *ironic* when the result is the opposite—or pretty much so—of what was intended. It isn't merely coincidental or surprising, as when the newscaster thoughtlessly reports, "Ironically, the jewelry store was burglarized on the same date last year." If the burglars take great pains to steal what turns out to contain a homing device that leads the police to them, that's *ironic*. (And forget the correct but clunky *ironical*.)

literally. This means actually or to the letter. (*Martha sprayed a dried bouquet with metallic paint, **literally** gilding the lily.*) *Literally* is often confused with *figuratively*, which means metaphorically or imaginatively. No one says *figuratively*, of course, because it doesn't have enough oomph. I am reminded of a news story, early in my editing career in Iowa, about a Pioneer Days celebration, complete with covered wagons and costumed "settlers." Our reporter proposed to say that spectators "were literally turned inside out and shot backwards in time." Gee, we should have sent a photographer along. (For the proper use of *backward*, see **toward**, page 117.)

long-lived. How do you pronounce the *i*—like the one in "life," or the one in "to live"? Both ways are acceptable, but the first is preferred. In fact, *-lived* (as in *short-lived, clean-lived, nine-lived,* and so on) comes from the word *life* and started out as *-lifed*. That's why those in the know make these *i*'s rhyme: *"Here's to life!" cried the **long-lived** Carmine*.

noisome. If you think this means noisy, you're not even close. *Noisome* and *noisy* are as different as your nose and your ear. *Noisome* means evil-smelling or offensive. It's related to *annoy*, so think of it as a clipped form of *annoysome. The **noisome** fumes of the stink bomb forced officials to evacuate the school.*

nonplussed. It means baffled or confused, not calm and collected. *Tony was **nonplussed** at finding his golf clubs in the driveway.* (Hint: *Non* means "no," and *plus* means "more." A guy who's *nonplussed* is so perplexed he can do no more.)

presently. Misuse strikes again. If Kramer tells his landlord he's *presently* sending his rent, does that mean . . . uh . . . the check is in the mail, or the check really *is* in the mail? The answer is, don't hold your breath. *Presently* doesn't mean now or at present. It means soon, before long, any minute (hour, day) now, forthwith, shortly, keep your shirt on, faster than you can say Jack Robinson, or when I'm darn good and ready.

restive. Here's one that's worse than it sounds. *Restive* doesn't mean impatient or fidgety (that's *restless*). It means unruly or stubborn. *Even on a good day, Pugsley is a **restive** child.*

scarify. Sounds terrifying, doesn't it? Well, it's not. *Scarify* doesn't mean scare. Primarily, it means cut or scratch marks into the surface of something. A memory hint: If you *scarify* something, you leave *scars*. *Ricky promised that his Rollerblades wouldn't **scarify** the floor.*

unique. If it's *unique,* it's the one and only. It's unparalleled, without equal, incomparable, nonpareil, unrivaled, one of a kind. There's nothing like it—anywhere. There are no degrees of uniqueness, because the unique is absolute. Nothing can be more, less, sort of, rather, quite, very, slightly, or particularly *unique*. The word stands alone, like *dead, unanimous,* and *pregnant. The Great Wall of China is* **unique**.

via. This means "by way of," not "by means of." *Itzhak drove to Tanglewood* **via** *Boston.* Not: *Itzhak drove to Tanglewood* **via** *car*.

Mixed Doubles

abjure/adjure. The first means swear off. The second means command. *"***Abjure** *cigars or move out of the house!" Ethel* **adjured** *Fred.*

abridge/bridge. To *abridge* something is to shorten it (think of the word *abbreviate*). An *abridged* book, for instance, is a condensed version. To *bridge* something means what you'd expect—to connect or to span a gap. *The producers hope to* **abridge** *Philip's nine-hour opera about an engineer who tries to* **bridge** *the Grand Canyon.*

accept/except. To *accept* something is to take it or agree to it. *Except* can also be a verb—it means exclude or leave out—but its usual meaning is "other than." *"I never* **accept** *presents from men," said Lorelei, "***except** *when we've been properly introduced."*

adverse/averse. The longer word is the stronger word. *Adverse* implies hostility or opposition, and usually characterizes a thing or an action. *Averse* implies reluctance or unwillingness, and usually characterizes a person. *Georgie was not averse to inoculation, until he had an adverse reaction to the vaccine.*

affect/effect. If you're referring to a thing (a noun), ninety-nine times out of a hundred you mean *effect*. (*The termites had a startling effect on the piano.*) If you mean an action (a verb), the odds are just as good if you go for *affect*. (*The problem affected Lucia's recital.*)

> **NOTE:** Then there's that one time out of a hundred. Here are the less common meanings for each of these words:
>
> • *Affect,* when used as a noun (pronounced with the accent on the first syllable), is a psychological term for "feeling." *Termites display a lack of affect.*
> • *Effect,* when used as a verb, means achieve or bring about. *An exterminator effected the removal of the termites.*

aggravate/irritate. Don't use them interchangeably. Use *irritate* to mean inflame, *aggravate* to mean worsen. *Poison ivy irritates the skin. Scratching aggravates the itch.*

Aggravate is widely used to mean vex or annoy, but sticklers find this irritating.

ago/since. Use one or the other, not both. *Fluffy died three days* **ago**. Or: *It's been three days* **since** *Fluffy died.* Not: *It's been three days* **ago since** *Fluffy died.*

allude/refer. To *allude* is to mention indirectly or to hint at—to speak of something in a covert or roundabout way. (*Cyril suspected that the discussion of bad taste* **alluded** *to his loud pants.*) To *refer* is to mention directly. (*"They're plaid!" said Gussie,* **referring** *to Cyril's trousers.*)

allusion/illusion/delusion. An *allusion* is an indirect mention. (*Gussie's comment about burlesque was a snide* **allusion** *to Cyril's hand-painted tie.*) An *illusion* is a false impression. (*It created the* **illusion** *of a naked woman.*) A *delusion* is a deception. (*Cyril clung to the* **delusion** *that his tie was witty.*) *Delusion* is much stronger than *illusion,* and implies that Cyril has been misled or deceived—in this case, by himself.

alternate/alternative. The first means one after the other; the second means one instead of the other. *Walking requires* **alternate** *use of the left foot and the right. The* **alternative** *is to take a taxi.*

among/between. When only two are involved, the answer is easy: *between.* (*Miss Bennet sensed a barrier* **between** *her and Mr. Darcy.*) With three or more, you have a choice. Use *between* if you're thinking of the individuals and their relations with one another. (*There were several embarrassing exchanges* **between** *Lydia, Kitty, and Jane.*) Use *among* if you're thinking of the group. (*Darcy's arrival created a stir* **among** *the guests.*)

amused/bemused. If you're having a good time, you're *amused*. If you're befuddled or puzzled or plunged deep in thought, you're *bemused*. *"I fail to see why you're **amused**," said the **bemused** Mr. Peepers, whose missing spectacles were perched on his head.*

anxious/eager. In ordinary speech, these are used interchangeably. But in writing, use *eager* unless there is actually an element of *anxiety* involved. And note that *eager* is followed by *to*, but *anxious* is followed by *about* or *for*. *Nancy is **eager** to have a pony, but Aunt Fritzi is **anxious** about the expense.* For more on these, see page 63.

appraise/apprise. *Appraise* means evaluate or size up; *apprise* means inform. *Sotheby's **apprised** Mr. Big of the fact that his "Rembrandt" was **appraised** as worthless.*

as if/as though. These mean the same thing and can be used interchangeably. Once upon a time, *if* was one of the meanings of *though*. It's not anymore, except in the phrase *as though*. *Cliff and Norm looked **as though** they could use a drink.*

assume/presume. They're not identical. *Assume* is closer to suppose, or "take for granted"; the much stronger *presume* is closer to believe, dare, or "take too much for granted." *I can only **assume** you are joking when you **presume** to call yourself a plumber!*

> **NOTE:** *Presume* in the sense of believe gives us the adjective *presumptive*. And *presume* in the sense of "take too much for granted" gives us the adjective *pre-*

sumptuous. As her favorite nephew, Bertie was Aunt Agatha's **presumptive** *heir. Still, it was* **presumptuous** *of him to measure her windows for new curtains.*

assure/ensure/insure. All three have their roots in a Latin word for "safe" or "secure." In American English, to *assure* is to instill confidence or certainty. As for *ensure* and *insure,* both can mean to make certain of something, but only *insure* is used in the commercial sense (to issue or take out insurance). *"I* **assure** *you," said the grieving widow, "I* **ensured** *he was* **insured** *to the hilt."*

avert/avoid. *Avert* means prevent, ward off, or turn away. *Avoid* means shun or stay clear of. *Mr. Smithers* **avoided** *the open manhole,* **averting** *a nasty fall.*

bad/badly. When it's an activity being described, use *badly,* the adverb (a word that describes a verb; many adverbs, you'll notice, end in *ly*). When it's a condition or a passive state being described, use *bad,* the adjective (a word that describes a noun). *Josh ran the race* **badly***; afterward, he looked* **bad** *and he smelled* **bad***.* If the difference still eludes you, try mentally substituting a pair of words less likely to be confused: *Josh ran the race* **honestly***; afterward, he looked* **honest** *and he smelled* **honest***.*

The same logic applies for *well* and *good.* When it's an activity being described, use *well,* the adverb. (As you can see, not all adverbs end in *ly*.) When it's a condition or a passive state being described, use *good,* the adjective.

*Donna sang **well**; at the recital she looked **good** and she sounded **good**.*

> **NOTE:** There's a complication with *well*. It's a two-faced word that can be an adjective as well as an adverb. As an adjective, it means healthy (*Josh feels **well***).

beside/besides. *Beside* means "by the side of." *Besides* means "in addition" or "moreover." *Pip was seated **beside** Miss Havisham in an uncomfortable chair. He had a fly in his soup **besides**.*

bi/semi. In theory, *bi* attached to the front of a word means two and *semi* means half. (*Although Moose is **bilingual**, he's **semiliterate**.*) In practice, *bi* sometimes means *semi*, and *semi* sometimes means *bi*. You're better off avoiding them when you want to indicate time periods; instead, use "every two years" or "twice a week" or whatever. I don't recommend using the following terms, but in case you run across them, here's what they mean. (You can see why they're confusing.)

biennial: every two years

biannual: twice a year *or* every two years (Here again, dictionaries tend to disagree, so they aren't much help.)

semiannual: every half-year

bimonthly: every two months *or* twice a month

semimonthly: every half-month

biweekly: every two weeks *or* twice a week

semiweekly: every half-week

both/as well as. Use one or the other, but not both. *Carrie had **both** a facial and a massage.* Or: *Carrie had a facial **as well as** a massage.*

bring/take. Which way is the merchandise moving? Is it coming or going? If it's coming here, someone's *bringing* it. If it's going there, someone's *taking* it. (**"Bring** *me my slippers," said Samantha, "and **take** away these stiletto heels!"*) That much is pretty straightforward, but there are gray areas where the *bringing* and the *taking* aren't so clear. Say you're a dinner guest and you decide to tote a bottle of wine along with you. Do you *bring* it or do you *take* it? The answer depends on your perspective—on which end of the journey you're talking about, the origin or the destination. "What shall I bring, white or red?" you ask the host. "Bring red," he replies. (Both you and he are speaking of the wine from the point of view of its destination—the host.) Ten minutes later, you're asking the wine merchant, "What should I take, a Burgundy or a Bordeaux?" "Take this one," she says. (Both you and she are speaking of the wine from the point of view of its origin.) Clear? If not, pour yourself a glass, take it easy, and say what sounds most natural. You'll probably be right.

callous/callus. One's an adjective (it characterizes something), and one's a noun. *Hard-hearted Hannah is **callous**, but the thing on her toe is a **callus**.*

can/may. The difference is between being able and being allowed or permitted. *Can* means able to; *may* means permitted to. *"I **can** fly when lift plus thrust is greater*

*than load plus drag," said Sister Bertrille. "May I demon-
strate?"*

> **NOTE:** *May* is used in another sense: to indicate possibility. See the section on *may* and *might,* page 105.

chord/cord. A *chord* is a combination of musical notes; it has an *h,* for "harmony," which is what *chords* can produce. (*"That **chord** is a diminished seventh," said Ludwig.*) A *cord* is a string or cable, like the ones found in the human anatomy: spinal cord, umbilical cord, and vocal cords. (*Wolfgang never had to worry about tripping over an electrical **cord.***) A mislaid rope may be called a *lost cord,* but the familiar musical phrase is *lost chord.*

compare with/compare to. Don't lose sleep over this one. The difference is subtle. *Compare with,* the more common phrase, means "to examine for similarities and differences." The less common *compare to* is used to show a resemblance: ***Compared with** Oscar, Felix is a crybaby. He once **compared** his trials **to** those of Job.*

complement/compliment. To *complement* is to complete, to round out, or to bring to perfection; a *complement* is something that completes or makes whole. (A little memory aid: Both *complement* and *complete* contain two *e*'s.) To *compliment* is to praise or admire; a *compliment* is an expression of praise or admiration. *Marcel loved to **compliment** Albertine. "That chemise **complements** your eyes, my little sparrow," he murmured.*

continually/continuously. Yes, there is a slight difference, although most people (and even many dictionaries) treat them the same. *Continually* means repeatedly, with breaks in between. *Continuously* means without interruption, in an unbroken stream. *Heidi has to wind the cuckoo clock **continually** to keep it running **continuously**.* (If it's important to emphasize the distinction, it's probably better to use *periodically* or *intermittently* instead of *continually* to describe something that starts and stops.) The same distinction, by the way, applies to *continual* and *continuous*, the adjective forms.

convince/persuade. You *convince* her *of* something. You *persuade* her *to do* something. *Convince* is usually followed by *of* or *that,* and *persuade* is followed by *to. Father* **convinced** *Bud* **that** *work would do him good, and* **persuaded** *him* **to** *get a job.* For more about *convince* and *persuade,* see page 63.

credibility/credulity. If you've got *credibility,* you're believable; you can be trusted. *Credulity* is a different quality—it means you'll believe whatever you're told; you're too trusting. The descriptive terms (adjectives) are *credible* (believable) and *credulous* (gullible). The opposites of these, respectively, are *incredible* (unbelievable) and *incredulous* (skeptical). *Councilman Windbag has lost his* **credibility**, *even among suckers known for their* **credulity**.

NOTE: Out in left field, meanwhile, is an entirely different player: *creditable,* which means deserving of credit, or praiseworthy.

deserts/desserts. People who get what they *deserve* are getting their *deserts*—the accent for both is on the second syllable. (*John Wilkes Booth got his just deserts.*) People who get goodies smothered in whipped cream and chocolate sauce at the end of a meal are getting *desserts*—which they may or may not deserve: *"For dessert I'll have one of those layered puff-pastry things with cream filling and icing on top," said Napoleon.* (As for the arid wasteland, use one *s* and stress the first syllable: *In the desert, August is the cruelest month.*)

differ from/differ with. In general, things *differ from* one another, but people who disagree *differ with* one another. (*Seymour insisted that his left foot differed from his right in size. His chiropodist, however, differed with him.*) In either sense, *differ* may be used alone: *Seymour says his feet differ. His chiropodist differs.*

different from/different than. What's the difference? The simple answer is that *different from* is almost always right, and *different than* is almost always wrong. You can stop there if you like.

> **NOTE:** You may use either one just before a clause (a group of words with its own subject and verb). Both of these are accepted: *Respectability is different from what it was fifty years ago. Respectability is different than it was fifty years ago.*

discomfit/discomfort. Here's a horse that's gotten out of the barn. Back when men were men and words had some muscle, *discomfit* meant defeat, rout, or overthrow. A *discomfited* enemy may well have been a dead enemy. (*Robin Hood and his merry men* **discomfited** *the Sheriff of Nottingham.*) But *discomfit* has lost its punch. Perhaps because of confusion with *discomfort* and *dismay,* it is widely used to indicate uneasiness or vague dissatisfaction. Dictionaries now accept this usage, a development I find *discomforting*.

discreet/discrete. If you're gossiping, you probably want *discreet,* a word that means careful or prudent. The other spelling, *discrete,* means separate, distinct, or unconnected. *Arthur was* **discreet** *about his bigamy. He managed to maintain two* **discrete** *households.*

disinterested/uninterested. They're not the same. *Disinterested* means impartial or neutral; *uninterested* means bored or lacking interest. *A good umpire should be* **disinterested**, *said Casey, but certainly not* **uninterested**.

each other/one another. The rule: Use *each other* for two, *one another* for three or more. (*Nick and Nora found* **each other** *adorable. Nick and his cousins all heartily despised* **one another**.) You'll never go wrong by following the rule, but keep in mind that many respected writers ignore it, using *one another* when referring to a pair. (*Husband and wife should respect* **one another**.) So if the more relaxed usage sounds better to your ear and you're not concerned about being strictly correct, allow yourself some latitude. (Speaking of *other* and *another,* here's a whole other issue. Some people jumble *whole other* with *another* and end up with *a whole nother*. Ugh! Not that you or I would ever do such a thing, of course.)

e.g./i.e. Go ahead. Be pretentious in your writing and toss in an occasional *e.g.* or *i.e.* But don't mix them up. Clumsy inaccuracy can spoil that air of authority you're shooting for. *E.g.* is short for a Latin term, *exempli gratia,* that means "for example." (*Kirk and Spock had much in common,* **e.g.,** *their interest in astronomy and their concern for the ship and its crew.*) The more specific term *i.e.,* short for the Latin *id est,* means "that is." (*But they had one obvious difference,* **i.e.,** *their ears.*) Both *e.g.* and *i.e.* must have commas before and after (unless, of course, they're preceded by a dash or a parenthesis).

emigrate/immigrate. You *emigrate from* one country and *immigrate to* another. (*Grandma* **emigrated from** *Hungary in 1923, the same year that Grandpa* **immigrated to** *America.*) Whether you're called an *emigrant* or an *immigrant* depends on whether you're going or coming, and on the point of view of the speaker. A trick for remembering:

> Emigrant as in *Exit.*
> Immigrant as in *In.*

eminent/imminent/immanent. If you mean famous or superior, the word you want is *eminent*. If you mean impending or about to happen, the word is *imminent*. If you mean inherent, present, or dwelling within, the word is the rarely heard *immanent*. *The **eminent** Arch-bishop Latour, knowing his death was **imminent**, felt God was **immanent**.*

NOTE: The legal term is *eminent domain*.

farther/further. Use *farther* when referring to physical distance; use *further* to refer to abstract ideas or to indicate a greater extent or degree. *Lumpy insisted that he could walk no **farther**, and he refused to discuss it any **further**.*

faze/phase. To *faze* is to disconcert or embarrass; it comes from a Middle English word, *fesen*, which meant "drive away" or "put to flight." A *phase*, from the Greek word for "appear," is a stage or period of development; the word is used as a verb in the expressions *phase in* and *phase out*, to appear and disappear by stages. *Jean-Paul's infidelity is just a **phase**, says Simone, so she never lets it **faze** her.*

fewer/less. Use *fewer* to mean a smaller number of individual things; use *less* to mean a smaller quantity of something. *Mr. Flanders is a practical man. The **less** money he makes, the **fewer** dollars he spends.*

flounder/founder. To *flounder* is to stumble awkwardly or thrash about like a fish out of water. (*Harry **flounders** from one crisis to another.*) To *founder* is to collapse, fail completely, or sink like a ship. (*His business **foundered** when the market collapsed.*)

flout/flaunt. *Flout* means defy or ignore. *Flaunt* means show off. *When Bruce ran that stop sign, he was **flouting** the law and **flaunting** his new Harley.*

gantlet/gauntlet. You run the *gantlet,* but you throw down the *gauntlet.* Why? It seems that in days of yore, a knight in a fighting mood would defiantly fling his *gauntlet* (a heavy, armored glove) to the ground as a challenge. To pick up the *gauntlet* was to accept the challenge. Meanwhile, a form of military punishment (a *gantlet,* from the Swedish word for the ordeal) required the hapless offender to run between parallel lines of his colleagues, who hit him with switches or clubs as he passed. *Wearing her mink to the ASPCA meeting, Tiffany ran a **gantlet** of hostile stares. "So what?" she said, throwing down the **gauntlet**.* It's a distinction worth preserving, even if some dictionaries no longer think so.

good/well. These are cousins to **bad/badly** (page 92).

historic/historical. If something has a place in history, it's *historic.* If something has to do with the subject of history, it's *historical. There's not much **historical** evidence that the Hartletops' house is **historic**.*

hyper/hypo. Added to the front of a word, *hyper* means over or more; *hypo* means under or less. *I become **hyperactive** and get a rash if I don't use a **hypoallergenic** soap.*

if/whether. When you're talking about a choice between alternatives, use *whether: Richie didn't know **whether** he should wear the blue suit or the green one.* The giveaway is the presence of *or* between the alternatives. But if there's a *whether or not* choice (*Richie wondered **whether or not** he should wear his green checked suit*), you can usually drop the *or not* and use either *whether* or *if: Richie wondered **if***

[or **whether**] *he should wear his green checked suit.* Occasionally you'll need to keep *or not* for emphasis: *Richie wanted to wear the green one,* **whether** *it had a gravy stain* **or not**.

imply/infer. These words are poles apart. To *imply* is to suggest, or to throw out a suggestion; to *infer* is to conclude, or to take in a suggestion. *"You* **imply** *that I'm an idiot," said Stanley. "You* **infer** *correctly," said Blanche.*

in behalf of/on behalf of. The difference may be tiny, but it's worth knowing. *In behalf of* means "for the benefit of" or "in the interest of." *On behalf of* means "in place of" or "as the agent of." *Bertie presented the check* **on behalf of** *the Drones Club, to be used* **in behalf of** *the feebleminded.*

in to/into. Yes, there is a difference! Don't combine *in* and *to* to form *into* just because they happen to land next to each other. *Into* is for entering something (like a room or a profession), for changing the form of something (an ugly duckling, for instance), or for making contact (with a friend or a wall, perhaps). *Get* **into** *the coach before it turns* **into** *a pumpkin, and don't bang* **into** *the door!* Otherwise, use *in to*. *Bring the guests* **in to** *me, then we'll all go* **in to** *dinner.* (You wouldn't go *into* dinner, unless of course you jumped *into* the soup tureen.) And be careful with *tune* and *turn*: *I think I'll* **tune in to** *my favorite TV show and* **turn into** *a couch potato.*

Still having a hard time with *into* and *in to*? Here's a trick to help keep them straight. If you can drop the *in* without losing the meaning, the term you want is *in to.* *Bring the guests [in] to me, then we'll all go [in] to dinner.* (Yes, there's also a difference between *on to* and *onto,* page 105.)

ingenious/ingenuous. Something that's *ingenious* (pronounced in-JEEN-yus) is clever or brilliant; the tip-off is that it has the pronunciation of *genius* built right in. *Ingenuous* (in-JEN-you-us) means frank, candid, unworldly, or innocently open; it's related to *ingénue,* a word for an inexperienced girl. (Calling somebody *disingenuous*— insincere—is a roundabout way of saying he lies.)

lay/lie. To *lay* is to place something; there's always a "something" that's being placed. To *lie* is to recline. *If you're not feeling well, lay your tools aside and lie down.* (These two get really confusing in the past tense. There's more about *lay* and *lie,* and how to use them in the past, on page 64.)

lend/loan. Only the strictest grammarians now insist that *loan* is the noun and *lend* is the verb, a distinction that is still adhered to in Britain (**Lend** *me a pound, there's a good chap*). American usage allows that either *loan* or *lend* may be used as a verb (**Loan** *me a few bucks till payday*). To my ears, though, *lend* and *lent* do sound a bit more polished than *loan* and *loaned.*

liable/likely. They're not interchangeable, but they come mighty close sometimes. Use *likely* if you mean probable or expected. Use *liable* if you mean bound by law or obligation (as in *liable for damages*), or exposed to risk or misfortune. *If Madeline goes skating, she's **liable** to fall, and not **likely** to try it again.*

like/as. Which of these is correct? *Homer tripped, [as or like] anyone would.* The answer is *as*, because it is followed by a clause, a group of words with both a subject (*anyone*) and a verb (*would*). If no verb follows, choose *like*: *Homer walks **like** a duck.*

Those are the rules, but the ground is shifting. In casual usage, *like* is gaining steadily on *as* (*She tells it **like** it is*), and on its cousins *as if* and *as though,* which are used to introduce clauses that are hypothetical or contrary to fact (*She eats chocolate **like** it's going out of style*).

The informal use of *like* to introduce a clause may be fine in conversation or casual writing, but for those occasions when you want to be grammatically correct, here's how to remember the *"as* comes before a clause" rule: Just think of the notorious old cigarette ad—*"Winston tastes good **like** a cigarette should"*—and do the opposite. On those more relaxed occasions, do as you like.

like/such as. Which is correct? *Rachel prefers cool colors, [**like** or **such as**] blue, violet, and aqua.* It's a matter of taste—either is acceptable. To my ear, *like* sounds better; *such as* has a more formal air. Of course, there are times when a bit of stiffness is appropriate: *"I've got my reasons for always using **like**," said Rufus T. Firefly. "**Such as**?" said Mrs. Teasdale.*

loath/loathe. The one without an *e* is an adjective describing somebody who's unwilling or reluctant, and it's usually followed by *to*: *Dmitri is* **loath** *to eat in Indian restaurants.* The one with an *e* is a verb: *He* **loathes** *chicken vindaloo.*

may/might. These are tricky. In the present tense, *might* is used rather than *may* to describe an iffier situation. Something that *might* happen is more of a long shot than something that *may* happen. For more, see page 59.

nauseated/nauseous. It's the difference between sick and sickening. You are made sick (*nauseated*) by something sickening (*nauseous*). Never say, "I'm nauseous." Even if it is true, it's not something you should admit. "*I'm* **nauseated** *by that* **nauseous** *cigar!" said Ethel.*

on to/onto. If you mean on top of or aware of, use *onto*. (*The responsibility shifted* **onto** *Milo's shoulders. "I'm really* **onto** *your shenanigans," he said.*) Otherwise, use *on to*: *Hang on to your hat.* Sometimes it helps to imagine a word like "ahead" or "along" between them: *Milo drove* **on to** *Chicago. He was moving* **on to** *better things.* (Confused about *in to* and *into*? See page 102.)

oral/verbal. They're not the same, though the meanings do overlap. *Oral* means by mouth or by spoken word. *Verbal* means by written or spoken word. That's why *verbal* is so easily misunderstood. What's a *verbal* contract? Written or spoken? It can be either. When it's important to make the distinction, use *oral* when you mean spoken, *written* when you mean written. In the words of Sam Goldwyn: "A verbal contract isn't worth the paper it's written on."

ought/ought to. Which is proper? You'll always be correct if you use *ought to.* Omit *to,* if you wish, in a negative statement: *Children **ought** not take candy from strangers. Pigs **ought** never be allowed in the kitchen.*

overwhelming/overweening. The more familiar *overwhelming* means just what you think it does—too much! *Overweening,* a useful word that we don't see very often, means conceited or pretentious. *The arrogance of that **overweening** little jerk is simply **overwhelming**.*

palate/palette/pallet. Maybe you don't have any trouble telling these apart, but I have to look them up every time. The *palate* is the roof of the mouth, and the word also refers to the sense of taste (the letters spell "a plate"). A *palette,* the board a painter mixes colors on, is also a range of colors. A *pallet* is a rustic bed, usually a makeshift mattress of straw or some other humble material. *Vincent painted his supper, then ate it. Having satisfied his **palate,** he cleaned his **palette** and retired to his **pallet**.*

pore over/pour over. You *pore over* an engrossing book, but it's gross to *pour over* one. *While Charlotte **pored over** a steamy novel, the bathtub **poured over**.*

presume/presumptive/presumptuous. See the discussion of **assume/presume,** page 91.

principal/principle. Still can't keep these straight? A *principal* is a leading figure (the head of a school, for example), and plays a leading, or *principal,* role. A *principle,* on the other hand, is a rule or standard. Here's a memory aid: If you're good in school, the *principal* is your *p-a-l.*

prophecy/prophesy. The *prophecy* (noun) is what's foretold. To *prophesy* (verb) is to foretell. As for pronunciation, *prophecy* ends in a "see," *prophesy* in a "sigh." *Madame Olga charged $50 per* **prophecy**, *claiming she could* **prophesy** *fluctuations in the commodities market.*

rack/wrack. Are you *racked* with guilt, or *wracked*? Is tax time nerve-*racking*, or nerve-*wracking*? Are you on the brink of *rack* and ruin, or *wrack* and ruin? Most of the time, you are *racked* (tortured, strained, stretched, punished). Just think of the *rack*, the medieval instrument of torture. If you're *wracked*, on the other hand, you're destroyed—you're *wreckage* on the beach of life (the words *wrack* and *wreck* are related). In sum: *You are* **racked** *with guilt, you've had a nerve-***racking** *time, and you're facing* **wrack** *and ruin.* You need a less stressful life!

raise/rise. To *raise* is to bring something up; there's always a "something" that's being lifted. To *rise* is to get up. *When they* **raise** *the flag, we all* **rise**. (There's more about *raise* and *rise*, and how they're used in the past tense, on page 65.)

ravage/ravish. When the ocean liner *Queen Elizabeth* caught fire and burned in Hong Kong harbor, a newspaper in Minnesota heralded the news with this headline: "Queen Elizabeth Ravished." What the headline writer intended was *ravaged*, meaning damaged or destroyed. There's an element of lust in *ravish*, which means to carry off (either by force or by emotion) or to rape. These days we're more likely to use *ravish* in the emotional than in the violent sense. *Though it was **ravaged** by the cleaners, the dress still looked **ravishing***.

regretfully/regrettably. A person who's full of regret is *regretful,* and sighs *regretfully.* A thing that's a cause of regret is *regrettable,* and *regrettably* that's the situation. *Hazel **regretfully** swept up the Ming vase, which **regrettably** had smashed to smithereens.*

reluctant/reticent. These aren't even distant cousins. A *reluctant* person is unwilling, but a *reticent* one is silent. *The **reluctant** bride was **reticent** when asked to say "I do."* By the way, *reticent* comes from the same Latin verb (meaning "to keep silent") as *tacit* (unspoken) and *taciturn* (uncommunicative).

set/sit. To *set* is to place something; there's always a "something" that's being placed. To *sit* is to be seated. *Set the groceries on the counter and sit at the table.* (There's more about *set* and *sit,* and how they're used in the past tense, on page 64.)

spade/spayed. People who confuse these must drive veterinarians crazy. A *spade* is a small, skinny shovel. An altered female dog or cat is *spayed.* To *spade* a garden is to dig it up; to *spay* a cat is to keep her from having kittens. *Ashley took up a **spade** and **spaded** the flower bed, while Melanie took Boots to be **spayed***.

stationary/stationery. If the *stationery* (paper) is *stationary* (fixed or still), you can write on it, and it won't move. (Hint: Both *stationery* and *paper* contain *er.*) *"If you* *haven't become* **stationary**, *Barney, please get up and bring me my* **stationery**," *said Thelma Lou.*

than/then. Does it make your hair stand on end when someone writes: *"He's taller* **then** *his brother"*? No? Go stand in the corner. *Than* and *then* are similar only in the way they sound. If you're comparing or contrasting things, use *than*, as in *more* **than** or *less* **than**. If one thing follows or results from another, use *then* (as in, *Look,* **then** *leap*). *The next morning, Paolo was sicker* **than** *a dog. He took some aspirin,* **then** *went back to bed.* "*If gin disagrees with you,* **then** *avoid it," said Francesca.* For advice on *than* when it comes before a pronoun (*I, me, he, she,* etc.), see page 12.

though/although. These are interchangeable, except in two cases, when only *though* will do:

- in the phrases *as though* or *even though*;
- when it's used to mean "however." *Madame Olga predicted it would rain in Brazil; it didn't,* **though**.

tortuous/torturous. The first means winding, crooked, full of turns. The second, as you may suspect from its root word, *torture*, means painful. *On the* **tortuous** *drive through the mountains, Jake developed a* **torturous** *headache.*

try and/try to. The proper phrase is *try to*, as in: "*Try to eat your soup without slurping," said Nancy.* But *try and* is gaining acceptance in spoken and informal use, and seems appropriate when there's an added note of defiance or stiffening of resolve: "*Try and make me," said Sluggo.*

until/till. Either of these is correct, but not "til." And using *up* or *since* with *until* is unnecessary. *Until* [not *Up until*] *recently, Sluggo's tie was spotless.*

will/would. These are often confused when paired with other verbs. Use *will* after a verb in the present tense (*He says he will*) and *would* after a verb in the past (*He said he would*). For more, see page 75.

Use It (Right) or Lose It

both. The pair (of people, things, ideas, etc.) following *both* should have the same accessories:

If one has a preposition (*as, by, for, to,* and so on), so must the other: *Phineas has proposed both **to Mary** and **to Laura***. Or: *Phineas has proposed to both **Mary** and **Laura***.

If one has a verb (an action word), so must the other: *His attentions both **pleased them** and **flattered them***. Or: *His attentions were both **pleasing** and **flattering***.

comprise. It means include or contain. *Vladimir's butterfly collection **comprises** several rare specimens.* Avoid *comprised of.* You wouldn't say "included of," would you? The *of* is correct, however, in *composed of* and *consists of.*

couple. It takes *of: Elaine considers them a **couple of** idiots.* Not: *Elaine considers them a **couple** idiots.* Similarly, *plenty of, type of, variety of, breed of, kind of: What **breed of** dog is he?*

NOTE: Sometimes *couple* is singular and sometimes it's plural. See pages 25 and 53.

depend. It takes *on.* *"Well,"* said Buster, *"that **depends on** what* [not ***depends what***] *you mean by housebroken."*

due to. When you want to be on your very best grammatical behavior, use *due to* only if you mean "caused by" or "resulting from": *The damage was **due to** moths.* In recent years, dictionaries have come to accept a looser usage, meaning "because of" or "on account of": *Richie threw the suit away **due to** the hole.* But be warned that some find this grating, especially at the front of a sentence: ***Due to** the hole, Richie threw the suit away.*

equally as. Forget the *as*: *Ken and Midge are **equally** obnoxious.* Or: *Ken is **as** obnoxious **as** Midge.*

forbid. Use *forbid* with *to*, never with *from*: *I **forbid** you to spit.* (Not: *I **forbid** you **from** spitting.*) As an alternative, you can use *forbid* with an *ing* word alone: *I **forbid** spitting.* For more about *forbid,* see page 63.

graduated. There are three rights and a wrong:
Right: *Moose **graduated from** college.*
Right: *Moose **was graduated from** college.*
Right: *The college **graduated** Moose.*
Wrong: *Moose **graduated** college.*

hardly. Don't use *hardly* with a negative verb, as in: *She **can't hardly** see without her glasses. Hardly* is already a negative word, and you don't need two of them. Either of these is correct: *She **can hardly** see without her glasses.* Or: *She can't see without her glasses.*

hardly/scarcely/no sooner. Watch your *when*s and *than*s with these. Use *when* with *hardly* and *scarcely*: *We had **hardly** begun to cook **when** the smoke alarm went off.* Or: *We had **scarcely** begun to cook **when** the smoke alarm went off.* Use *than* with *no sooner*: ***No sooner** had we begun to cook **than** the smoke alarm went off.*

hence. Like its cousin *whence* (see below), *hence* has a built-in "from"—it means "from here" or "from now." So using "from" with *hence* is redundant. *"My birthday is three days **hence**," said Corky, "and I could really use a dehumidifier."* Another meaning of *hence* is "thus": *It's damp, **hence** the mildew.*

HIV. This is the AIDS virus; the letters stand for "human immunodeficiency virus." Since *virus* is already part of the name, it's redundant to repeat it. *He's doing research on HIV* (not "on the HIV virus").

inside of. Drop the *of*: *Penelope keeps her hankie **inside** her glove.*

kudos. This is a singular noun meaning praise or glory (*Bart won **kudos** for his skateboarding skill*), not a plural form of some imaginary "kudo." Show me one kudo and I'll eat it.

likely (with a verb). When you use *likely* to describe an action, don't use it all by itself; precede it with *very, quite,* or *most*: *Nathan will **quite likely** lose his shirt at the track* (not "will likely lose"). If you prefer, use *is **likely** to* instead:

Nathan is likely to lose a bundle, and Miss Adelaide is likely to kill him.

myriad. It originally meant "ten thousand," but *myriad* now means "numerous" or "a great number of." (*Lulu has myriad freckles.*) Avoid the redundant "myriads" or "a myriad of."

oblivious. It's better with *of,* not *to. Olivia was oblivious of her liver.*

only. Aside from conversational or casual language, don't use *only* in place of *but* or *except: I would go to Paris, but* [not *only*] *I'm broke.* For more on *only,* see page 122.

prohibit. Use *prohibit* with *from,* never with *to: The rules prohibit you from spitting.* (Not: *The rules prohibit you to spit.*) As an alternative, you can follow *prohibit* with an *ing* word alone: *The rules prohibit spitting.* For more about *prohibit,* see page 63.

whence. Not *from whence.* The "from" is built in. *Whence* means "from where." (*Go back whence you came, brigand!*) The same is true of *hence* and *thence:* use them alone, since "from" is implied. Their cousins *whither, hither,* and *thither* have "to" built in. If you must use a grizzled old word, treat it with respect. (See **hence** above.)

whether or not. You can usually ditch *or not: Phoebe knows whether Holden is telling the truth.* (See **if/whether,** page 101.)

while. The classic meaning is "during the time that": *Doc whistles while he works.* But *while* has also gained acceptance as a substitute for *although* or *whereas* at the beginning of a sentence or clause: *While Grumpy can whistle, he prefers not to.*

NOTE: If you use *while* in place of *although*, be sure there's no chance it could be misunderstood to mean "during the time that." You could leave the impression that unlikely things were happening at the same time, as in: *While Dopey sleeps late, he enjoys vigorous exercise.* Only if Dopey is a sleepwalker! For how to use *a while* and *awhile*, see page 120.

You're Getting Warmer: Spelling and Saying It Right

accommodate. It has two *c*'s and two *m*'s. *"I believe I can accommodate you, even without a reservation,"* said Mr. Fawlty.

advertise/advertisement/advertising. Here in the United States, each of these has an *s* (the preference in Britain is to use a *z*). *When Jack got his job at the advertising agency, he didn't advertise the fact that he'd never written an advertisement.*

all-round. *Shep is a good all-round dog. All-round* is better than *all-around,* in the sense of complete or rounded. This is a case where it's better to round off the word.

arctic. Not "artic" (don't forget the middle *c*). The lower-case *arctic* means very cold. The capitalized *Arctic* means the region. And it's *Antarctica,* not "Antartica" (a common misspelling). *The **Arctic** expedition reached the North Pole. Next year's goal, **Antarctica**, is in the opposite direction.* I was once astonished to see a big sign from Coors advertising a frosty beverage called Artic Ice. Never trust anything you read on the side of a bus.

artifact. Not "artefact." That's with an *i,* not an *e*: *"An 1840 saxophone is a rare **artifact**," said Lisa.*

desiccated. One *s,* two *c*'s. *"A raisin is simply a **desiccated** grape," said Uncle Fester.*

ecstasy. Two *s*'s (not "ecstacy"; and there's no *x*). *Miranda was in **ecstasy**.*

embarrass. Two *r*'s and two *s*'s. *Spock was not **embarrassed** by his pointy ears.*

fulfill. One *l* in the middle, two at the end. *Did Paulie **fulfill** his obligation?*

guerrilla. Two *r*'s and two *l*'s. *Che raised a **guerrilla** army.* (It's the ape that's a *gorilla*.)

harass. One *r* and two *s*'s. As for pronunciation, you may accent either syllable, although the preference on this side of the Atlantic is to stress the second. *"Wally, stop **harassing** your brother," said Ward.*

hyperbole. It is not pronounced like the name of a sporting event, the Hyper Bowl; it's high-PER-buh-lee. It means exaggeration or overstatement. *Buster's claim that his dog could read was **hyperbole**.*

NOTE: If you've seen **hyper/hypo** (page 101), you may wonder whether there's such a word as *hypobole*. As a matter of fact, there is (it means something like "suggestion"), but I've never heard anybody use it.

indispensable. It ends in *able*, not *ible*. "*Nick, you're in-dispensable,*" *said Nora.*

irresistible. It ends in *ible*, not *able*. I wish there were an easy way to tell the *ibles* from the *ables*, but there isn't. You're at the mercy of your dictionary. "*Nora, you're irre-sistible,*" *said Nick.*

judgment. No *e* after the *g*. (The same goes for *acknowl-edgment*, but not *knowledgeable*.) "*I never make snap judg-ments,*" *said Solomon.*

lightning. Flash! There's no *e* in *lightning*, the kind that leaves us thunderstruck: *A bolt of **lightning** split the sky.* The word with an *e* (*lightening*) comes from *lighten*: *I'll bet she's **lightening** her hair.*

marvelous. One *l*. (The British spell it with two, but pay no attention.) "*Gertrude, that's a **marvelous** haircut!*" *said Alice.*

memento. It's not spelled—or pronounced—"momento." Think of the word remem*brance*. *The embroidered pillow was a **memento** of Niagara Falls.*

minuscule. It's not spelled—or, again, pronounced—"miniscule." Think of *minus* as the root, not *mini*. *Barbie's accessories are **minuscule**.*

nuclear. Pronounce it NOO-klee-ur (not NOO-kyoo-lur). "*My business is **nuclear** energy,*" *said Homer.*

rarefied. It's spelled with one *i*, not "rarified." (If in doubt, think of *rare*.) *McCoy feared that the **rarefied** air in the* Enterprise *was enervating the crew.* (If you don't know what *enervating* means, see page 83.)

restaurateur. Notice that there's no *n* (and don't believe dictionaries or spell-checkers that tell you there is). The root is a word meaning "restore." The *restaurateur* (the person who restores you) runs the *restaurant* (where you go to get restored). *When Apu became a **restaurateur**, he called his **restaurant** Curry in a Hurry.*

skillful. Two *l*'s in the middle, one at the end. *Tex was **skillful** with a lasso.*

sprightly. The word meaning energetic has a *gh*; it's not "spritely": *Ed and Trixie were feeling **sprightly**.* Someone who's like a sprite, a little imaginary creature resembling a pixie or an elf, is *spritelike*. *Ed looked **spritelike** in his leprechaun costume.*

straitjacket/straitlaced. There's no *gh* in either—not "straightjacket" or "straightlaced." ***Straitlaced** people who go over the edge may find themselves in **straitjackets**.* The word *strait* is from the Latin *strictus,* which means "constricted" or "tight." *Straight,* from an Anglo-Saxon word for "stretch," means uncurved. The word you run across in geography, by the way, is *strait,* referring to a tight waterway: the *Strait* of Gibraltar, the Bering *Strait*.

toward. No final *s* ("towards"), although that's how they say it in Britain. Similarly, in American English, standard practice is not to add a final *s* to *forward, backward, up-ward, onward, downward,* and so on. *George and Kramer were last seen heading **toward** the buffet.*

weird. It's spelled *ei*, not *ie*. *"You're looking particularly **weird** this evening, Morticia, my love,"* said Gomez.

"Seedy" Endings

Words that end with a "seed" sound are notoriously hard to spell. It helps to keep in mind that all but four end with *cede*. Three end with *ceed*, and only one ends with *sede*.

- **cede:** accede, antecede, cede, concede, intercede, precede, recede, secede (and others)
- **ceed:** exceed, proceed, succeed
- **sede:** supersede

✳ **One Word or Two?** ✳

all ready/already. They're not the same. *All ready* means prepared; *already* means previously. *Carrie and Samantha are* **all ready** *to boogie; in fact, they've* **already** *started.*

all together/altogether. They differ. *All together* means collectively—all at once or all in one place: *Bertie's aunts were* **all together** *in the living room. Altogether means in sum or entirely:* **Altogether** *there were four of them. Bertie was* **altogether** *defeated.*

any more/anymore. Use *any more* if you mean any additional; use *anymore* if you mean nowadays or any longer. *Shep won't be chasing* **any more** *cars. He doesn't get around much* **anymore***.*

any one/anyone. If you can substitute *anybody*, then the single word *anyone* is correct; if not, use two words, *any one.* **Anyone** *can fool Lumpy.* **Any one** *of his friends is smarter than he is.* (See also **every one/everyone** below.)

any place/anyplace. One word is acceptable if you mean *anywhere* (though *anywhere* is usually better). If in doubt, use two. *I can afford to live* **anyplace***, but I can't live in* **any place** *that doesn't accept pets.*

any time/anytime. Use two words if you mean "any amount of time," one if you mean "whenever." *The boss will see you* **anytime** *she has* **any time***.*

any way / anyway. It's one word if you mean "in any case." Otherwise, use two words, *any way.* Never "anyways." *I don't know of **any way** to visit the dungeons without bumping into Snape. You wouldn't want to see them, **anyway**.*

awhile / a while. These are often confused when they're written. *Awhile* means "for a time"; "for" is part of the meaning and shouldn't be added. *A while* means "a period of time." *Heloise rested **awhile**; she put her feet up and dozed for **a while**.* (For how to use *while,* see page 113.)

every day / everyday. We mix them up daily (or *every day*). The single word, *everyday,* is an adjective. It describes a thing, so it can usually be found right in front of a noun: *"I just love my **everyday** diamonds," said Magda.* The time expression *every day* is two words: *"That's why you wear them **every day**," said Eva.*

every one / everyone. If you can substitute *everybody,* then the single word *everyone* is correct; if not, use two words, *every one.* ***Everyone** fears Dagmar's children. **Every one** of them is a little terror.*

Detour—Dangerous Construction Ahead

all . . . not / not all. Many sentences that are built around *all . . . not* face backward. Use *not all* instead: *Not* *all* Swedes are blond. To say, *All Swedes are not blond,* is to say that not a single Swede has golden hair.

as bad or worse than. Stay away from this kind of sentence: *Opie's math is **as bad or worse than** his English.* Do you see what's wrong with it? Well, there are two kinds of comparisons going on, *as bad as* and *worse than.* When you telescope them into *as bad or worse than,* you lose an *as.* Putting it back in (*Opie's math is **as bad as or worse than** his English*) is correct but cumbersome. A better idea is to put the rear end of the comparison (*or worse*) at the end of the sentence: *Opie's math is **as bad as** his English, **or worse.*** (Another way to end the sentence is *if not worse.*)

as good or better than. This is a variation on the previous theme. It's better to split up the comparison: *Harry's broom is **as good as** Malfoy's, **or better.*** (Another way to end it is *if not better.*)

as much or more than. Here's another variation on *as bad or worse than* (see above). Don't use this phrase all at once; split it up: *Otis loves bourbon **as much as** rye, **or more.*** (Another ending is *if not more.*)

See **one of the . . . if not the** below, for a way out of another common trap.

either . . . or. Think of the elements joined by *either* and *or* as the two sides of a coin. Make sure the sides are even. If what follows *either* has a subject and a verb (is a clause, in other words), what follows *or* should, too: ***Either Kenny did or he didn't.*** If what follows *either* starts with a preposition (a word that "positions," or locates, other words in the sentence), then what follows *or* should, too: *Kenny is **either** at school **or** in trouble.* If what follows *either* is an adjective (a word that characterizes something), then so is what follows *or*: *Truant officers are **either** spiteful **or** misguided.* In short, the two sides of the coin, the *either* and *or* parts, must match grammatically—subject with subject, verb with verb, preposition with preposition, adjective with adjective, and so on. If the sides aren't equal, you can often fix the problem by moving *either* a few words over. So this blunder, ***Either** Mrs. McCormick is angry **or** amused,* becomes *Mrs. McCormick is **either** angry **or** amused.*

> **NOTE:** Several other pairs should be treated as flip sides of the same coin: *neither . . . nor; not only . . . but also; both . . . and.* As with *either . . . or,* they may take some arranging; all require that the two sides match.

one of the . . . if not the. Here's another corner you can avoid backing yourself into: *Jordan was **one of the** best, **if not the** best, player on the team.* Oops! Can you hear what's wrong? The sentence should read correctly even if the second half of the comparison (*if not the best*) is removed; but without it you've got: *Jordan was one of the best player on the team.* One of the best *player*? Better to put the second half of the comparison at the end of the sentence: *Jordan was **one of the** best players on the team, **if not the** best.*

only. This slippery word—meaning "alone," "solely," or

"and no other"—can be found almost anywhere in a sentence, even where it doesn't belong. To put *only* in its place, make sure it goes right before the word or phrase you want to single out as the lone wolf. Take this sentence as an example: *The butler says he saw the murder.* By inserting *only* in various places, you can give the sentence many different meanings. Keep your eye on the underlined words—those are the wolves being singled out of the pack:

- *Only the butler says he saw the murder.* (The butler, and no one else, says he saw the murder.)
- *The butler only says he saw the murder.* (The butler says, but can't prove, he saw the murder.)
- *The butler says only he saw the murder.* (The butler says he, and no one else, saw it.)
- *The butler says he only saw the murder.* (He saw—but didn't hear—the murder.)
- *The butler says he saw only the murder.* (He saw just the murder, and nothing else.)

Remember: *Only* the lonely! It's easy to slip *only* into a sentence carelessly, so get into the habit of using it right in front of the word you want to single out.

NOTE: The whole point of putting *only* in its place is to make yourself understood. In the examples above, the various locations of *only* make a big difference. But in informal writing and conversation, if no one's likely to mistake your meaning, it's fine to put *only* where it seems most natural—usually in front of the verb: *I'm **only** going to say this once; This food can **only** be called swill.* The more grammatically correct versions—*I'm going to say this **only** once; This food can be called **only** swill*—only sound unnatural.

reason . . . is because. Here's a redundancy for you, a wording that seems to repeat itself: *The **reason** Rex stayed home **is because** robbers tied him up.* Can you hear the echo effect? *Because* means "for the reason that," so the example says, in effect: *The **reason** Rex stayed home is **for the reason that** robbers tied him up.* Use one or the other, not both: *The **reason** Rex stayed home is that robbers tied him up.* Or: *Rex stayed home **because** robbers tied him up.*

Overwriters Anonymous

at this time. A bit overstuffed, no? (*Dr. Melfi has no openings **at this time**.*) Why not just *now*? (*Dr. Melfi has no openings now.*)

if and when. Wordy people are very fond of this phrase (*I'll punch out his lights, **if and when** I see him*). Use either *if* or *when*; you seldom need both.

in order to. Unless there's some need for special emphasis, drop *in order* and simply use *to*: "*I work **to** live, and I live **to** boogie*," said Tallulah.

unless or until. (*"I'm not talking, unless or until I see my lawyer!" said Mr. Bluster.*) One or the other will usually do, unless or until you're getting paid by the word.

Sensibility and Sense

gender. Let's hope *gender* never replaces *sex*. An old and durable word, *sex* (from the Latin *sexus*) has long meant either of the two divisions—male and female—that characterize living things. (*Annie Oakley was a credit to her sex.*) By extension it has also come to refer to the sexual act. *Gender,* a grammatical term for "kind," describes the ways some languages categorize nouns and pronouns by sex (masculine, feminine, or neuter). Perhaps it was inevitable that as we began speaking more openly about sex and sex roles, some people would feel a need for a more neutral word to refer to the Great Divide, one with no taint of the act itself. *Gender* seemed to fit the bill. (*Little Emily plays with dolls of both genders.*) Well, this horse, too, is out of the barn. But to my ear, *gender* sounds prudish as an alternative to *sex.* Until a better word comes along, I'll stick with the three-letter original. If *sex* was good enough for Jane Austen ("Miss de Bourgh is far superior to the handsomest of her sex"), it's good enough for me.

-man/-woman/-person. Speaking of sex, here's something else to think about. For a thousand years, give or take, the word *man* has done double duty, as a term for both the male of the species and the species as a whole. In the last half-century or so, sensibilities have changed, and this state of affairs now strikes many people as lop-sided. *Man* and its variations no longer seem appropriate as catch-alls, especially when we refer to women: *When Cynthia was* **chairman**, *she provided most of the* **manpower**. See what I mean? If you know a person's sex, why not call her a *chairwoman* or him a *chairman*? If you don't know, there's always an alternative, like *head* instead of *chairman*, *press officer* instead of *spokesman*, *firefighter* instead of *fire-man*, *representative* instead of *congressman*, and so on. Of course, there are always the *person* words (*chairperson*, *spokesperson*, *councilperson*, *businessperson*, *ombudsperson*). Personally, I find them clunky and self-conscious. Then there's *chair*, a solution inspired, perhaps, by the prece-dent of *table* as a parliamentary term. I'm in the minority on this one, but I think of a chair as an article of furniture. Feel free to disagree.

Department of Hot Air

dialogue. Can we *dialogue*? No, thanks. I'd rather talk, chat, gossip, speak, converse, exchange ideas, or shoot the breeze. Some people prefer to *dialogue*, or to *have a dia-*

logue. Don't talk to them. (For a related cliché, see **meaningful dialogue**, page 174.)

impact. The kind of person who uses language as a sledgehammer is likely to use *impact* as a verb meaning affect. (*"The third-quarter loss will **impact** our earnings projections for the year," said Daddy Warbucks.*) If you don't want to give the rest of the world a headache, use *impact* only as a noun. (*"Will this have any **impact** on my allowance?" asked Annie.*)

interface. People who like to *dialogue* also like to *interface.* By this they mean interact, or work together. Don't work with them.

monies. This is how a bureaucrat says *money.* *"But where will these **monies** come from?" asked Councilman Windbag.*

paradigm. It masquerades as a two-dollar word, but it's really worth only about twenty cents. A *paradigm* (the *g* is silent: PAIR-a-dime) is simply a pattern or example. It's not a standard of perfection (that's a *paragon*). Still, homely old *paradigm,* along with its cousin *paradigmatic* (here the *g* is sounded), has become the darling of those who like to dress up ordinary ideas in technicalities. *"Our ad campaign has a **paradigmatic** resonance," said Mr. Palaver.*

parameter. There's nothing like a scientific word to lend an air of authority to a weak sentence. (*"Let us review the **parameters** of the issue," said Senator Blowhard.*) That's how a word like *parameter* (a mathematical term for a type of arbitrary constant or independent variable) worms its way into the Official Overwriters' Vocabulary. Don't let it get into yours. Weak writers use *parameter* to mean a boundary, a characteristic, a component, an element, a feature, an ingredient, a part, a perimeter, a quality, or a requirement. When a word is used for too many things, it ends up meaning nothing. Unless you know an independent variable from an arbitrary constant, stay away from *parameter*.

say. You've *said* it before, and you'll *say* it again, because if there's a word that *says* it all, surely it's the verb *say*. ("*I love you," he **said**.*) So why do some writers avoid it? The problem with *say* is that it's just too simple and clear and straightforward for many people. Why *say* something, when you can declare, assert, expostulate, whine, exclaim, groan, peal, breathe, cry, explain, or asseverate it? I'm all for variety and freshness of expression, but let's not go overboard. As Freud said, sometimes a cigar is just a cigar.

transpire. This is how a stuffed shirt says *happen* or *occur* or *take place*: "*Let us review exactly what **transpired** at the First Continental Congress," said Professor Jawbone.*

unprecedented. *Judge Hearsay's action was **unprecedented***. Oh yeah? Very few things are unprecedented. Don't use this word to mean unusual, uncommon, odd, unexpected, rare, exceptional, curious, irregular, offbeat, or surprising. No matter how extraordinary something sounds to you, there's probably a precedent for it. *Mr. Scrooge's generosity was **unprecedented**—for him.*

You Call That a Word?

ahold. A horror! Either it's two words (*"Gal, you've really got a hold on me," said Roy*), or it's simply *hold* (*"For heaven's sake, Roy, get hold of yourself," said Dale*).

ain't. It's still misbehavin'. Not: *"I ain't hanging up my six-guns just yet," said Shane.*

alot. Ouch! It's two words: *a lot. He hasn't done his friends a lot of good.*

alright. No, *alright* is not *all right*—it's all wrong! *"All right, I'll let you whitewash the fence!" said Tom.*

anywheres. Never. It's *anywhere. "The aliens could be almost anywhere," said Ripley.*

being that. This clunker is sometimes used as an alternative to *since* or *because*: *Being that he was hungry, he ate a piece of Mildred's fruitcake.* It may squeak by in conversation (not with me, please!) but should be avoided in writing. *Being as* and *being as how* are just as bad. They aren't felonies, but neither is snoring at the ballet. (The same goes for *seeing that, seeing as,* and *seeing as how.*)

complected. No; the word traditionally favored is *complexioned. After years of riding the range with no sunscreen, Yosemite Sam was dark-complexioned.*

dove (for **dived**). *Dived* is still the preferred past tense for what Esther Williams did off a diving board, but *dove* is surfacing more and more. In writing, stick to *dived;* in conversation, especially if it's casual, you can get by with *dove* (though I'd rather see it sink). *With the swamp before him and an angry rhino at his heels, Indiana **dived** into the murky waters.*

irregardless. This isn't a word—it's a crime in progress! The word you want is *regardless.* (*Dick and Nicole do as they like, **regardless** of the consequences.*) Irrespective of what you hear and read, there is no such word as *irregardless.*

orientate. The extra syllable is ugly and unnecessary, though not a hanging offense. *Orient* is sufficient. *Santiago tried to **orient** himself without a compass.*

preventative. The extra syllable isn't wrong, but it's unnecessary. Use *preventive. Always wear sunscreen as a **preventive** measure.*

seeing that. See **being that** above.

Plug Ugly

Words are easy to stretch. Just add *ly* to a word like *neat* and you end up with *neatly*: *It's a **neat** trick to pack a suitcase **neatly**.* What could be neater?

But not all words like having *ly* tacked on to them, especially if they already end in *ly,* like *ugly, friendly, surly,* and *jolly.* Sure, the dictionary says we can use lame adverbs like *uglily, friendlily, surlily,* and *jollily,* but nobody says we have to.

If a word doesn't want to be stretched out of shape, don't force it.

Et Cetera

a/an. Sometimes it's the little things that give us away. For instance, we all know the rule about using *an* in front of words that begin with vowels (*a, e, i, o, u*), and *a* in front of those starting with consonants (letters with a "hard" sound, like *b, c, d, f, g, h,* and so on). But what happens when *h* sounds like a vowel or *u* sounds like a consonant? A pair of handy rules:

- Use *a* (not *an*) in front of words that start with these sounds: a "sounded" *h* (the *ha-ha* variety, as in *history, horror, hotel*); a "long" *u* (the *yew* variety, as in *university, utopia, eulogy, European*).
- Use *an* in front of words that start with these sounds: a "silent" *h* (*hour, honor, herbal*); a "short" *u* (*uncle, umbrella, undertaker*).

and/or. This ugly wrinkle (*Tubby, would you like apple pie and/or ice cream?*) can be smoothed out: *Tubby, would you like apple pie, ice cream, or both?*

at. Avoid using it unnecessarily with *where,* as in *Where is Silvio at? The at* is understood, so all you need is *Where is Silvio?* Understood?

but. It's common practice to use *but* to mean *nothing but* or *only*—just be careful not to get tangled in negatives, since *but* in these cases already has a negative sense built in. *Tom is but a boy.* Not: *Tom isn't but a boy.*

*Aunt Polly **weighs but** 105 pounds.* Not: *Aunt Polly **doesn't weigh but** 105 pounds.*

> **NOTE:** Avoid using *help but,* as in: *Huck **can't help but** look silly in those pants.* Drop the *but* and use the *ing* form: *Huck **can't help** looking silly in those pants.*

etc. Since this abbreviation (it stands for *et cetera*) means "and others," it's redundant to say or write "and etc." It's even worse to use "etc., etc." (*A conscientious groupie knows all the members of a band: drummer, lead guitar, rhythm, bass, **etc**.*) And by the way, if you're one of those people who pronounce it ek-SET-ra, shame on you. There's no *k* sound.

of. Don't use it if you don't need it. *Paulie says his new TV fell off **of** a truck. The missing warranty is not that big **of** a problem.* Whack the *of*: *Paulie says his new TV fell off a truck. The missing warranty is not that big a problem.* (For exceptions, see page 191.)

Chapter 6

Comma Sutra

The Joy of Punctuation

An editor I know at *The New York Times* once received a gift from a writer friend. It was the tip of a lead pencil, broken off and wrapped up and presented along with a card that said, "A gross of commas, to be used liberally throughout the year as needed." Now, that writer understood the gift of punctuation!

When you talk, your voice, with its pauses, stresses, rises, and falls, shows how you intend your words to fit together. When you write, punctuation marks are the road signs (stop, go, yield, slow, detour) that guide the reader, and you wouldn't be understood without them.

If you don't believe me, try making sense out of this pile of words:

Who do you think I saw the other day the Dalai Lama said my aunt Minnie.

There are at least two possibilities:

- *"Who do you think I saw the other day?" the Dalai Lama said. "My aunt Minnie."*
- *"Who do you think I saw the other day? The Dalai Lama!" said my aunt Minnie.*

(I know, I know. I've taken liberties with *who* and *whom*. You can, too, in conversation and informal writing. See the chapter on pronouns, page 9.)

Punctuation isn't some subtle, arcane concept that's hard to manage and that probably won't make much of a difference one way or another. It's not subtle, it's not difficult, and it can make all the difference in the world.

The Living End: The Period (.)

The period is the red light at the end of a sentence. When you reach the period, it's all over. Whatever thought you were trying to convey has been delivered. A straightforward sentence that states rather than asks or exclaims something starts with a capital letter and ends with a period.

But what if there's a dot there already, as when a sentence ends with an ellipsis (. . .) or an abbreviation that has periods (A.M., for example)? And what if a sentence has a smaller sentence within it? Here's what you do:

- If a sentence ends with an abbreviation that has a final period, don't add another period: *As a new immigrant, Apu's nephew felt welcome in the U.S.* (More and more abbreviations, like MD, are losing their dots these days, so check your dictionary for updates.)

- If a sentence ends in an ellipsis (three dots that indicate an omission), put a period first to show that the sentence is over: *"You'd like to borrow fifty dollars?" said Apu. He recalled the old saying, Neither a borrower nor a lender be. . . .*

But if you want to emphasize a deliberate trailing off, you may omit the period. End the sentence with a space, then the three dots: *"Well . . ."*

- If a sentence concludes with the title of a work that ends in a question mark or an exclamation point, don't add a final period: *Liz gained twenty pounds for* Who's Afraid of Virginia Woolf? *We couldn't get seats to* Oklahoma!

- If a sentence has a smaller sentence within it (surrounded by dashes or parentheses), don't use a period to end the "inside" sentence: *When Apu made him an offer—"I could use some help around the store"—he accepted.*

NOTE: This last point doesn't apply to question marks or exclamation points: *Apu criticized his nephew's manners ("Speak up! How are the customers supposed to hear you?") and his grooming ("Do you call that a beard?").*

Uncommonly Useful:
The Comma (,)

There's nothing much to punctuating a sentence, really, beyond a little comma sense. Get the commas right, and the rest will fall into place.

Yeah, yeah, I hear you saying. What's a comma or two—or three? How can something so small, so innocuous, be important? Well, that attitude can get you tossed into grammatical purgatory. You don't believe it? Take a look:

Cora claimed Frank planned the murder.

Without commas, the finger of guilt points to Frank. But add a pair of commas, and Cora becomes the suspect:

Cora, claimed Frank, planned the murder.

Here's another pair of examples with completely different meanings:

Augie quit saying he was looking for another job.

Augie quit, saying he was looking for another job.

In the first sentence, Augie quit talking; in the second, he quit his job.

The lesson: Don't take commas for granted. They're like yellow traffic lights. If you ignore one, you could be in for a bumpy ride.

Most problems with commas have to do with dividing a sentence into parts—larger parts like clauses (each with its own subject and verb), or smaller ones like items in a series. Commas are also used to interrupt a sentence and insert another thought. Here's how to get out of some of the most common comma complications.

Long and Short Division

- Use a comma to separate clauses (big chunks of a sentence) joined by *and* or *but*. *Tina hadn't left the city in months, and by Friday she was climbing the walls.* If there's no *and* or *but* in between, use a semicolon instead: *Tina hadn't left the city in months; by Friday she was climbing the walls.*
- Use commas to separate a series of things or actions. *She packed a toothbrush, a hair dryer, her swimsuit, and her teddy bear. She finished packing, paid some bills, ate a few Oreos, and watered the plants.*

NOTE: The final comma in those two series, the one just before *and*, can be left out. It's a matter of taste. But since its absence can sometimes change your meaning, and since there's no harm in leaving it in, my advice is to stick with using the final comma.

As I Was Saying

- Use commas before and after the names of people you're talking to: *"Good-bye, Mom. Dad, be good,"* she said, and hung up the phone. You can skip the comma before the name if all that precedes it is *and* (*"And Mom, don't worry"*) or *but* (*"But Dad, you promised"*).

• Use commas before or after a quotation: *"Let's see,"* said Tina. Or: *Tina said, "Let's see."* But don't use a comma after a quotation that ends with an exclamation point or a question mark: *"Have I forgotten anything?" she wondered. "Sunscreen!" she exclaimed.*

LET ME INTERRUPT

• Use a comma after an introductory phrase if a pause is intended: *As usual, she checked to make sure the stove was turned off. Of course, it always was. You see, Tina was a bit compulsive.*
• Use commas around an aside—information that could just as well go in parentheses: *Her upstairs neighbor, the one without the tattoos, promised to collect her mail.*
• Use commas around a *which* clause: *The airport bus, which was usually on time, never came.* You need only the first comma if the clause comes at the end: *So she took a taxi, which cost her an arm and a leg.*

But don't use commas around *that* clauses: *The bus that she had planned to take never came, so she grabbed the first taxi that she saw.*

For more on *which* and *that,* see page 3.

✳   ✳   ✳

Semi-Avoidance: The Unloved Semicolon (;)

The semicolon is one of the most useful but least used punctuation marks. For whatever reason, many of us avoid it. Maybe it intimidates us; it shouldn't. (See, wasn't that easy?) If a comma is a yellow light and a period is a red light, the semicolon is a flashing red—one of those lights you drive through after a brief pause. It's for times when you want something stronger than a comma but not quite so final as a period. Here's when to use it.

- Use a semicolon to separate clauses when there's no *and* in between: *Andy's toupee flew off his head; it sailed into the distance.*
- Use semicolons to separate items in a series when there's already a comma in one or more of the items: *Fred's favorite things were his robe, a yellow chenille number from Barneys; his slippers; his overstuffed chair, which had once been his father's; murder mysteries, especially those by Sue Grafton; and single-malt Scotch.*

Let Me Introduce You:
The Colon (:)

Think of the colon as a traffic cop, or punctuation's master of ceremonies. Use it to present something: a statement, a series, a quotation, or instructions. But remember that a colon stops the flow of traffic. Use one only if you want to step on the brake. Keep these guidelines in mind.

- Use a colon instead of a comma, if you wish, to introduce a quotation. *I said to him: "Harry, please pick up a bottle of wine on your way over. But don't be obsessive about it."* Many people prefer to introduce a longer quotation with a colon instead of a comma.

- Use a colon to introduce a list, if what comes before the colon could be a small sentence in itself (it has both a subject and a verb). *Harry brought three wines: a Bordeaux, a Beaujolais, and a Burgundy.*

- Don't use a colon to separate a verb from the rest of the sentence, as this example does. *In Harry's shopping bag were: a Bordeaux, a Beaujolais, and a Burgundy.* If you don't need a colon, why use one? *In Harry's shopping bag were a Bordeaux, a Beaujolais, and a Burgundy.*

NOTE: If what comes after the colon is a complete sentence, you may start it with a capital or a lowercase letter. I use a capital when I want to be more emphatic: *My advice was this: Bring only one next time.* (This is a matter of taste, and opinions differ. Whatever your choice, be consistent.)

Huh?
The Question Mark (?)

The question mark is the raised eyebrow at the end of a sentence. It's used with a question, of course, but also to show skepticism or surprise. (*"Lost? My luggage got lost on a direct flight?"*) Here are some of the most common questions about questions.

● What do you do when a sentence has a series of questions? This gets an either/or answer.

You can put the question mark at the very end: *Would Tina have to buy a new hair dryer, toothbrush, swimsuit?*

Or, for emphasis, you can put a question mark after each item (you don't need capital letters for each item, since it's still one sentence): *Would Tina have to buy a new hair dryer? toothbrush? swimsuit?*

● How do you introduce a question within a longer sentence? The simplest way is to use a comma and start the question with a capital letter. *The question was, How long should she wait for her luggage?*

The same is true if the question is a quotation: Introduce it with a comma. *Tina cried, "What next?"*

But if the introduction is a complete sentence, especially if it's a long one, a colon works better. *The question she asked herself was this: How long should she wait for her baggage?*

● What comes after a question mark? If the sentence continues after the question, don't use a comma after the question mark. *What will I do without my hair dryer? she asked herself.* *"What more can go wrong?" she said to the ticket agent.*

The Silent Scream: The Exclamation Point (!)

The exclamation point is like the horn on your car—use it only when you have to. A chorus of exclamation points says two things about your writing: First, you're not confident that what you're saying is important, so you need bells and whistles to get attention. Second, you don't know a really startling idea when you see one.

When you do use an exclamation point, remember this:

● Use it alone (don't add a comma afterward): *"Holy cow!" said Phil.*

And keep your voice down.

A Brief Interlude: Parentheses ()

Once in a while you may need an aside, a gentle interruption to tuck information into a sentence or between sentences. One way to enclose this interruption is with parentheses (the end rhymes with *cheese*), and you just now saw a pair.

The thing to know about parentheses is that they can enclose a whole sentence standing alone, or something within a sentence. The tricky part is determining where the other punctuation marks go: inside or outside the closing parenthesis. Punctuation never precedes an opening parenthesis (not in the same sentence, anyway).

- When the aside is a separate sentence, put punctuation inside the parentheses, and start with a capital letter: *Jimmy thinks he has won the lottery. (He is mistaken, however.)*
- When the aside is within a sentence, put punctuation outside the parentheses, and start with a small letter. *Jimmy thinks he has won the lottery (fat chance).*

An exception occurs when the remark inside parentheses is an exclamation (*wow!*) or a question (*huh?*). The exclamation point or question mark goes inside the parentheses, but any accompanying punctuation marks go outside: *Jimmy has already made plans for the money (poor guy!), but his wife is skeptical. He may have misread the numbers on his lottery tick-ets (how dumb can you get?).*

Too Much of a Good Thing: The Dash (—)

We could do with fewer dashes. In fact, the dash is prob-ably even more overused these days than the exclamation point—and I admit to being an offender myself (there I go again).

The dash is like a detour; it interrupts the sentence and in-serts another thought. A single dash can be used in place of a colon to emphatically present some piece of information: *It was what Tina dreaded most—fallen arches.* Or dashes can be used in pairs instead of parentheses to enclose an aside or an explanation: *Her new shoes had loads of style—they were Ferragamos—but not much arch support.*

Dashes thrive in weak writing, because when thoughts are confused, it's easier to stick in a lot of dashes than to organize a smoother sentence. Whenever you are tempted to use dashes, remember this:

● Use no more than two per sentence. And if you do use two, they should act like parentheses to isolate a re-mark from the rest of the sentence: *After the flight, Tina looked—and she'd be the first to admit it—like an un-made bed.*

- If the gentler and less intrusive parentheses would work as well, use them instead. *Tina's luggage (complete with her return ticket) appeared to be lost.*

By the way, don't confuse the dash with the hyphen (see below). The dash is longer. If you want a dash but your computer keyboard doesn't have one, use two hyphens (--).

Betwixt and Between: The Hyphen (-)

A hyphen is not just a stubby version of the dash. The two of them do very different things. While the dash separates ideas or big chunks in a sentence, the hyphen separates (or connects, depending on how you look at it) individual words or parts of words: *My mother-in-law works for a quasi-official corporation that does two-thirds of its business with the government.*

When a word breaks off at the end of a line in your newspaper and continues on the next line, a hyphen is what links the syllables together. But the hyphen most of us have problems with is the one that goes (or doesn't go) between words, as in terms for some family members (*mother-in-law*), or in two-word descriptions (*quasi-official*), or in fractions (*two-thirds*). Here are some guidelines for when you need a hyphen and when you don't.

THE PART-TIME HYPHEN

One of the hardest things to figure out with hyphens is how to use them in two-word descriptions. When two words are combined to describe a noun, sometimes you use a hyphen between them and sometimes you don't.

The first question to ask yourself is whether the description comes before or after the noun.

- If it's after the noun, don't use a hyphen: *Father is strong willed*. *My cousin is red haired*. *This chicken is well done*. Ducks are *water resistant*.
- If it's before the noun, use a hyphen when either of the two words in the description wouldn't make very much sense by itself. *He's a strong-willed father. I have a red-haired cousin. This is well-done chicken. Those are water-resistant ducks.*

EXCEPTIONAL SITUATIONS

Here are some exceptions to the "before or after" rule for hyphens in two-word descriptions:

- If *self* or *quasi* is one of the words, always use a hyphen: *Robert is self-effacing; still, he's a self-confident person. He's our quasi-official leader; the position is only quasi-legal.*
- If both words could be used separately and still make sense, don't use a hyphen even if they come before a

noun: *Hodge was a **naughty old** cat. Alicia is a **sweet young** thing.*

● If *very* is one of the two words, forget the hyphen: *That Hepplewhite is a **very expensive** chair.* If *very* is added to a description that would ordinarily take a hyphen (**much-admired** *architect,* for example), drop the hyphen: *Sam's a **very much admired** architect.*

● If one of the two words ends in *ly,* you almost never need a hyphen: *That's a **radically different** haircut. It gives you an **entirely new** look.*

● If one of the words is *most, least,* or *less,* leave out the hyphen: *The **least likely** choice, and the **less costly** one, is the **most preposterous** hat I've ever seen.*

Is Your Hyphen Showing?

Here are some cases where you must use hyphens:

● With *ex* (meaning "former"). *Hal is the **ex-president** of the company.*

● When adding a beginning or an ending to a word that starts with a capital (*anti-British, Trollope-like*). Two exceptions are *Christlike* and *Antichrist.*

● When adding *like* would create a double or triple *l* (*shell-like*).

● When adding a beginning or ending would create a double vowel (*ultra-average, anti-isolationist*). But *pre* and *re* are often exceptions to this (*preempt, reexamine*), so when you have a duplicate vowel, look up the word in the dictionary. (The vowels are *a, e, i, o, u*.)

• With fractions. ***Three-quarters*** *of the brownies and* ***two-thirds*** *of the cookies are gone.* For how to go halves, see below.

Half Measures

I wish there were a rule for *half,* but it's all over the map. Some formations involving *half* are one word (*halfhearted, halfway*), some are two words (*half note, half sister*), and some are hyphenated (*half-hour, half-moon*). Check the dictionary.

HEADS OR TAILS

Many of us can't add a beginning or an ending to a word without sticking in a hyphen for good measure. If we put *mini* in front of *van,* it inexplicably becomes *mini-van* instead of *minivan;* if we put *like* after *life,* it unaccountably becomes *life-like,* not *lifelike.* Many hyphens show up where they're not wanted. Here are some common endings and beginnings that don't usually need them:

Endings

ache: I'll trade my **toothache** for your **headache**.

less and *most*: The **ageless** soprano can still hit the **uppermost** notes.

like: What a **lifelike** Gainsborough.

wide: Sewer rats are a **citywide** menace.

Beginnings

anti: Samson was **antifeminist**.

bi: They're conducting a **bicoastal** romance.

co: This celebrity autobiography has no **coauthor**.

extra: His **extracurricular** schedule is full.

inter: Luke has **intergalactic** ambitions.

micro, mini, and *multi*: Excuse me for a moment while I **micromanage** a **minicrisis** among these **multitalented** children.

mid: Our raft sank **midstream**.

non: Hubert is a **nonperson**.

over and *under*: Be **overcautious** if your date is legally **underage**.

post: He lives in a **postwar** building.

pre and *pro*: The **prenuptial** atmosphere was definitely **promarriage**. (See NOTE on page 150.)

re: They have **reexamined** their situation. (See NOTE on page 150.)

semi: I wish I'd invented the **semiconductor**.

sub and *super*: Our **subbasement** got **supersaturated** in the flood.

Hyphens in the Family

Some family members get hyphens and some don't. Here's how to keep them straight.

USE A HYPHEN

- With *ex.* Meet my **ex-husband**.
- With *in-law.* Fred's my **brother-in-law**.
- With *great.* There goes my **great-aunt**.

DON'T USE A HYPHEN

- With *step.* His **stepson** Charlie is a doctor.
- With *half.* Bob's **half brother** is a thug.
- With *grand.* She can't be a **grandmother**!

trans: Leslie is a **transsexual**.
ultra: That Nancy is **ultrachic**.
un: Argyle socks with sneakers are **uncool**.

NOTE: There are exceptions, cases when you'll want to use a hyphen in words starting with *pre*, *pro*, and *re*. If a word starting with *pre* or *pro* is just too hard to read without a hyphen, add one (*pre-iron*, *pro-am*). And if a word starting with *re* could be confused with one that's spelled the same but means something else, add a hyphen. For instance, use *re-cover* (for "cover again") to avoid confusion with the word *recover*. Other examples include *re-creation, re-petition, re-press, re-sent, re-serve, re-sign, re-sort, re-treat.* (When the boss asks to renew your employment contract, it makes a big difference whether your reply memo says, "I'm going to re-sign" or "I'm going to resign.")

A Multitalented Mark: The Apostrophe (')

That little airborne mark that dangles over some words (including last names like O'Conner) is called an apostrophe. This is the punctuation mark that has many sign painters mystified. Store awnings and windows, sides of trucks, even neon signs, are peppered with wayward apostrophes that either don't belong at all or are in the wrong position. Beware, especially, of the unusual apostrophe in a plural word.

Here's how to use an apostrophe with . . .

• **Possessives.** To indicate ownership, add *'s* to a singular noun or to a plural noun that does not end in *s*: *Buster's bulldog has wrecked the **children's** room.* Add the apostrophe alone to a plural noun that ends in *s*:

This was the boys' idea. (Chapter 3 is all about possessives, in case you need to know more.)

● **Some unusual plurals.** Add *'s* to make plurals of numbers and letters, including abbreviations: *Libby, the daughter of two CPA's, was born in the 1940's, and earned all B's at Swarthmore.* When a number is written out, it gets no apostrophe: *She spent **millions** of dollars in **tens** and **twenties**.* For more on the sticky question of using apostrophes to make plurals, see page 30.

● **Missing letters.** An apostrophe can show where letters have been dropped in a shortened word or phrase. For example, *shouldn't* is short for *should not;* the apostrophe shows where the *o* in *not* was dropped. Some other clipped words are quite irregular, like *won't* and the illegitimate *ain't.* Shortened words and phrases are called contractions; there's a list of them on pages 73–74 (they're also in the dictionary). When in doubt, look it up.

● **A comma or period.** When you need a comma or period (or any other punctuation, for that matter) after a possessive word that ends with an apostrophe, the punctuation goes after the apostrophe: *The idea was the boys', but the responsibility was their **parents**'.*

✳   ✳   ✳

Enough Said:
Quotation Marks (" ")

Think of quotation marks as bookends that support a quotation in between.

The opening quotation marks always go right before the first word of the quotation: *"Can we talk?"* The trick is at the other end, where the closing quotation marks go. You'll have to decide whether the punctuation that follows the quoted material (period, comma, question mark, or whatever) goes inside or outside the closing quotation marks. Here's what's in and what's out.

The Ins

- **Period.** *"I think I'm going to be sick."*
- **Comma.** *"I shouldn't have eaten those strawberries,"* Gustav said.

The Outs

- **Colon.** *There are two reasons she hates the nickname* "Honey": *It's sticky and it's sweet.*
- **Semicolon.** *Frank's favorite song was* "My Way"; *he recorded it several times.*

Sometimes In,
Sometimes Out

- **Question mark.** In most cases, a question mark should be inside the quotation marks: *"Who goes there?" said the sentry. "What is the password?"* But the question mark must be outside if it's not part of the actual quotation: *Who starred in "Dynasty"?*

● **Exclamation point.** In most cases, an exclamation point goes inside the quotation marks: *"Captain!" said Sulu. "We're losing speed!"* But the exclamation point goes outside if it's not part of the quotation: *My God, the screen just went blank after reading "Situation Normal"!*

● **Parentheses.** If the entire quotation is in parentheses, then the closing parenthesis should go outside the quotation marks: *Uhura had the last word ("I told you so").* If only part of the quotation is in parentheses, then the closing parenthesis goes inside the quotation marks: *She added, "Maybe next time you'll listen to me (if there is a next time)."*

● **Apostrophe.** How do we get ourselves into messes like this one? To create the possessive of something that's normally in quotation marks—for example, the title of a poem, "The Raven"—you would have to put the apostrophe outside: *"The Raven"'s first stanza is the best.* Pretty awful-looking, isn't it? It's so awful that many publications even cheat to avoid it, and write *"The Raven's"*—definitely incorrect, although much prettier. My advice is to avoid this problem entirely. Instead of writing *"The Raven"'s author was Poe,* rearrange it: *Poe was the author of "The Raven."*

✳   ✳   ✳

NOTE: When one quotation appears within another, enclose the interior one in single quotation marks: *"Was it Linus who said, 'Get lost'?" asked Lucy.*

The Slant on Titles

You may have wondered why some titles, like *Vogue* and *Huckleberry Finn,* most often appear in the slanting letters called italics, while others, like "Bedroom at Arles" and "My Funny Valentine," usually appear in ordinary type enclosed in quotation marks.

Customs vary on how titles should be written. In most newspaper writing, for example, all titles are in plain type, though not all go inside quotation marks.

My advice is to follow conventional practice. Put the names of larger works, like books, movies, and plays (and magazines and newspapers), in italics. Put the names of smaller works, like poems, stories, and paintings, in ordinary type with quotation marks.

Use Italics

Books: *Gone With the Wind*
Magazines: *Newsweek*
Newspapers: *The Miami Herald*
Movies: *Million Dollar Legs*

The Less Said:
When Not to Quote

Sign painters seem to love quotation marks. They don't care how a word is spelled, as long as it's enclosed in quotes. I don't know much about the sign-painting business—maybe they get paid extra for punctuation. Here are a few signs of the times I've spotted:

Nail salon: *Our Instruments Are "Sterilized"*
Pizzeria: *"Free" Delivery*
Locksmith: *"Fast" and "Friendly" Service*

There's no reason for quotation marks in any of those signs. The intent may be to emphasize the quoted words, but a bright color or a different typeface would do a better job.

In fact, quotation marks used like that can mislead the reader. They're sometimes used in a skeptical or sarcastic way, to indicate that what's quoted isn't meant seriously: *Uncle Oscar's regular Friday-night "volunteer work" turned out to be a poker game.*

The moral is: Don't quote it if you don't have to. And the next time your pipes spring a leak and a truck marked *"Licensed" Plumber* pulls up to your door, don't say I didn't warn you.

Plays, musicals, operas, ballets: *Macbeth, Guys and Dolls, The Magic Flute, Swan Lake*

Use Quotation Marks

Articles: "The Cellulite Cure: Fact or Fiction?"

Essays: "Civil Disobedience," by Henry David Thoreau

Poems: "The Raven," by Edgar Allan Poe

Short stories: "The Secret Life of Walter Mitty," by James Thurber

Paintings, sculptures: "Nude Descending a Staircase," "Venus de Milo"

TV series: "Jeopardy!"

Song titles: "Begin the Beguine"

NOTE: Where titles are concerned, classical music has its own variations on the theme. Here, too, usage varies widely. I recommend writing the formal names of symphonies, concertos, sonatas, and similar compositions in ordinary type without quotation marks: Mahler's Symphony No. 2 in C Minor, Mozart's Serenade in D. But if you use a nickname, put it in quotation marks: Beethoven's "Emperor" Concerto, Schubert's "Trout" Quintet.

Chapter 7

The Compleat Dangler

A Fish out of Water

Life would be pretty dull if everyone's English were perfect. Without slips of the tongue, we wouldn't have spoonerisms, the tongue-tanglers named after the befuddled Reverend William A. Spooner. He was the Victorian clergyman who spoke of "Kinquering Congs" and greeted someone with, "I remember your name perfectly, but I just can't think of your face."

And we wouldn't have malapropisms, either. Mrs. Malaprop was a character in an eighteenth-century play whose bungled attempts at erudite speech led her to declare one gentleman "the very pineapple of politeness!" and to say of another, "Illiterate him . . . from your memory."

We're lucky that English, with its stretchy grammar and its giant grab-bag of a vocabulary, gives us so much room for verbal play, if not anarchy. As Groucho Marx said, "Love flies out the door when money comes innuendo," and it's hard to imagine him saying it in Esperanto.

Naturally, if you have room to play, you have room to make mistakes. And English sentences are often constructed without regard for building codes. I've grown almost fond of one common error, the dangler. It's a word or phrase (a group of words) that's in the wrong place at the wrong time, so it ends up describing the wrong thing. Here comes one now: *Strolling along the trail, Mount Rushmore came into view.* The opening phrase, *strolling along the trail,* is a dangler. Why? Because it's attached to the wrong thing, *Mount Rushmore.* The way the sentence stands, the mountain was out taking a stroll!

Danglers show up in newspapers and bestsellers, on the network news and highway billboards, and they can be endlessly entertaining—as long as they're perpetrated by someone else. When you're doing the talking or writing, the scrambled sentence isn't so amusing. See if you can tell what's wrong with these examples.

- *Born at the age of forty-three, the baby was a great comfort to Mrs. Wooster.* As the sentence is arranged, the baby—not his mother—was forty-three. (The opening phrase, *born at the age of forty-three,* is attached to *the baby,* so that's what it describes.) Here's one way to rearrange things: *The baby, born when Mrs. Wooster was forty-three, was a great comfort to her.*

- *Tail wagging merrily, Bertie took the dog for a walk.* See how *tail wagging merrily* is attached to *Bertie*? Put the tail on the dog: *Tail wagging merrily, the dog went for a walk with Bertie.*

- *As a den mother, Mrs. Glossop's station wagon was always full of Cub Scouts.* Whoa! The phrase *as a den mother* is attached to *Mrs. Glossop's station wagon.* Attach it to the lady herself: *As a den mother, Mrs. Glossop always had her station wagon full of Cub Scouts.*

Danglers are like mushrooms in the woods—they're hard to see at first, but once you get the hang of it they're easy to find. Although the wild dangler may lurk almost anywhere in a sentence, the seasoned hunter will look in the most obvious place, right at the beginning of the sentence. If the first phrase is hitched to the wrong wagon—or no wagon at all—it's a dangler. Some kinds of opening phrases are more likely than others to be out of place. I'll show you what to look for.

THE USUAL SUSPECT

Always suspect an *ing* word of dangling if it's near the front of a sentence; consider it guilty until proved innocent. To find the culprit, ask yourself whodunit. Who's doing the *walking, talking, singing,* or whatever? You may be surprised by the answer. In these examples, look at the phrase containing the *ing* word and look at whodunit.

- *After overeating,* the hammock looked pretty good to Archie. Who ate too much in this sentence? The hammock! If a person did the overeating, the opening *ing* phrase should be attached to him: *After overeating,* **Archie** *thought the hammock looked pretty good.*
- *On returning home,* Maxine's phone rang. Who came home? Maxine's phone! To show that the owner of the phone was doing the returning, put her right after the opening phrase: *On returning home,* **Maxine** *heard the phone ring.*
- *Walking briskly,* the belt of her raincoat was lost. Who's the pedestrian? The belt! What's attached to the opening phrase is what's doing the walking. If you want to say *she* was walking briskly, put her right after the opening phrase: *Walking briskly,* **she** *lost the belt of her raincoat.*

PIN THE TAIL ON THE DONKEY

Have you ever seen children at parties pinning the tail on the wrong part of the donkey? Well, sometimes adjectives (words that characterize nouns) get pinned to the wrong part of a sentence and become danglers. Here's a sentence with its "tail" in the wrong place:

Incorrect: **Dumpy and overweight,** *the vet says our dog needs more exercise.*

The description *dumpy and overweight* should be pinned on the dog, not the vet:

Correct: **Dumpy and overweight**, *our dog needs more exercise, the vet says.* A more graceful solution would be to rewrite the sentence completely: *The vet says our dog needs more exercise because she's* **dumpy and overweight**.

Adjectives (such as *dumpy* and *overweight*) like to be pinned on the nearest noun.

HITCH YOUR WAGON

A dangling adverb at the front of a sentence is a lot like a horse that's hitched to the wrong wagon. Adverbs (words that characterize verbs) can be easy to spot because they often end in *ly*. When you see one, make sure it's "hitched" to the right verb. In this example, what went wrong at the hitching post?

Incorrect: **Miraculously** *we watched as the surgeon operated with a plastic spoon.*

As the sentence stands, the opening word, *miraculously*, refers to the watching, not the operating. That's because the closest verb is *watched*. To fix things, put the *ly* word closer to the right action:

Correct: **Miraculously**, *the surgeon operated with a plastic spoon as we watched.*

Here's another solution: *We watched as the surgeon* **miraculously** *operated with a plastic spoon.*

Adverbs (such as *miraculously*) like to be hitched to the nearest verb. For another warning about troublesome adverbs, see page 130.

ROADS TO NOWHERE

You can easily be led astray when a sentence has a road sign at the very beginning. The kind of sign I mean is a preposition, a word that shows position or direction (*at, by, on, with,* and so on). If the sign is in the wrong place, you end up on the road to nowhere. Try to avoid this kind of dangler:

Incorrect: ***At the age of ten,*** *my father bought me a puppy.*

As the sentence is written, Dad was only a boy! That's because the opening phrase, *at the age of ten,* is attached to *my father*—an obvious mismatch. If the sign is to point in the right direction, the sentence has to be rearranged:

Correct: ***At the age of ten****, I got a puppy from my father.*
Or: *My father bought me a puppy* ***when I was ten.***

TO'S A CROWD

Some of the hardest danglers to see begin with *to.* Beware of the sentence that starts with an infinitive (a verb form usually preceded by *to,* for instance *to run, to see, to build*). The opening phrase has to be attached to whoever or whatever is performing the action. Here's an opening phrase that leaves the sentence scrambled:

Incorrect: ***To crack an egg properly****, the yolk is left intact.*

As the sentence is written, the yolk is the one cracking the egg. The opening phrase, *to crack an egg properly,* is attached to *the yolk,* not to whoever is doing the cracking. Let's put a cook in the kitchen.

Exceptions That Make the Rule

Some expressions are so common that they're allowed to dangle at the beginning of a sentence, even though they're not connected to anything in particular. We treat them as casually as throat-clearing. For example, we may say: **Generally speaking**, *pigeons mate for life*. The pigeons aren't the ones doing the speaking, naturally, and no one would make such a connection. Other stock phrases that can dangle to their hearts' content include *strictly speaking, barring unforeseen circumstances, considering the alternative, assuming the worst, judging by appearances, after all, by and large, on the whole, admittedly, put simply, given the conditions, in the long run, in the final analysis, to tell the truth, contrary to popular belief,* and *to be perfectly frank.* Introductory phrases like these have become so familiar that they have earned the right to be exceptions to the rule. Are they necessary? That's another issue. For more about throat-clearing, see page 197.

Correct: *To crack an egg properly, you must leave the yolk intact.*

Here's an even simpler way to say it: *To crack an egg properly, leave the yolk intact.* (The subject is understood to be *you*. This is called an imperative sentence, since someone's being told to do something.)

Owners' manuals, you'll notice, are chock-full of dangling infinitives. Does this sound familiar? *To activate widget A, doohickey B is inserted into slot C.* If the one trying to activate the silly thing is *you*, make *you* the subject: *To activate widget A, you insert doohickey B into slot C.* Or you can delete the *you*, since it's understood to be the subject: *To activate widget A, insert doohickey B into slot C.*

A LIKELY STORY

Looking for a dangler? Then look for a sentence that starts with *like* or *unlike*. More than likely, you'll find a boo-boo. Here's a likely candidate.

Incorrect: *Like Alice, Fran's nose job cost plenty.*

The phrase *like Alice* is a dangler because it's attached to the wrong thing: *Fran's nose job.* Presumably Fran, and not her nose job, is *like* Alice. Make sure the things being compared really are comparable. There are two ways to fix a sentence like this.

Correct: *Like Alice, Fran paid plenty for her nose job.* Or: *Like Alice's, Fran's nose job cost plenty.*

Chapter 8

Death Sentence

Do Clichés Deserve to Die?

Tallulah Bankhead once described herself as "pure as the driven slush." And bankruptcy has been called "a fate worse than debt." We smile at expressions like these out of relief, because we're braced for the numbing cliché that fails to arrive.

Nothing is wrong with using a figure of speech, an expression that employs words in imaginative (or "figurative") ways to throw in a little vividness or surprise. But it's an irony of human communication that the more beautiful or lively or effective the figure of speech, the more likely it will be loved, remembered, repeated, worn out, and finally worked to death. That's why some people will tell you that the Bible and Shakespeare are full of clichés!

So crowded is our stock of figurative language that every

profession—legal, corporate, fashion, artistic, literary, and so on—seems to have a collection all its own. A tired book critic, for example, will say a novel is "a richly woven tapestry," "a tour de force," or "a cautionary tale," one whose characters are either "coming of age" or experiencing "rites of passage." For corporate "high rollers," what matters is the "bottom line," or whether a company is "in play," or a stock has "gone south."

Then are all clichés and familiar turns of phrase to be summarily executed? No. Let your ear be your guide. If a phrase sounds expressive and lively and nothing else will do, fine. If it sounds flat, be merciless. One more point. It's far better to trot out a dependable cliché, and to use it as is, than to deck it out with lame variations (*the tip of the proverbial iceberg*) or to get it wrong ("unchartered seas" instead of *uncharted* ones; "high dungeon" instead of *dudgeon;* "heart-rendering" instead of *heart-rending*). And two unrelated figures of speech shouldn't be used one after the other, whether they're clichés or not (*He got off his high horse and went back to the drawing board*). That's called mixing your metaphors, and there's more about it at the end of this chapter.

There's no way to eliminate all clichés. It would take a roomful of Shakespeares to replace them with fresh figures of speech, and before long those would become clichés, too. Vivid language is recycled precisely because it's vivid. But think of clichés as condiments, the familiar ketchup, mustard, and relish of language. Use when appropriate, and don't use too much. When you're dressing up a hamburger, you don't use béarnaise sauce. You use ketchup, and that's as it should be. But you don't put it on everything. Some dishes, after all, call for something special. Here are some of today's more overworked condiments.

Acid test. Overuse and you flunk.

Agree to disagree. People never really *agree to disagree.* They just get tired of arguing.

Back to the drawing board. Back to *Roget's Thesaurus.*

The ball is in your court. Only if you're Andre Agassi.

Beat a dead horse. Anyone who uses this expression more than once a month should be required to send a donation to the ASPCA.

Bite the bullet. Save your teeth.

Bitter end. This is right up there with *making ends meet.*

Blanket of snow. Nature is a *fertile field* (there's another one) for clichés. Besides *blankets of snow,* beware *sheets of rain, calms before the storm, devastating earthquakes, raging torrents, bolts from the blue, steaming jungles, uncharted seas* (which are likely to become *watery graves*), *wide-open spaces, places in the sun,* and anything *silhouetted against the sky.* (See also *golf-ball-sized hail* below.)

Blessing in disguise. Not disguised well enough.

Boggles the mind. It's all right to be boggled once in a while, but don't make a habit of it.

Bone of contention. This expression is getting osteoporosis.

Bored to tears. There has to be a more exciting way to complain of boredom.

Bottom line. Unless—and even if—you're talking about finance, there's probably a better way to say it.

Broad daylight. The sun has begun to set on this one, and on *light of day.*

Brute force. This phrase is no longer forceful.

A bug going around. Another way of saying you don't know what you've got.

By hook or by crook. This one hangs out in the same crowd with *hook, line, and sinker* and *lock, stock, and barrel.*

Can of worms. Don't open this one too often. And don't unnecessarily disturb its cousins, *nest of vipers* and *hornet's nest.*

Can't see the forest for the trees. If you find yourself using this expression over and over again, you have a myopic imagination.

Champing at the bit. If you must use it, get it straight. Restless horses *champ* at their bits; they don't "chomp."

Come to a head. Sometimes seen as *bring to a head,* this phrase has its humble beginnings in dermatology. Need I say more?

Cool as a cucumber. Using this too much is uncool.

Cutting edge. Dull.

Days are numbered. A phrase that's not just overused, but depressing.

Dead as a doornail. Why a doornail, anyway? (Also see *passed away* below).

Diamond in the rough. And watch those *pearls before swine,* too. When accessorizing your language, remember that a little jewelry goes a long way.

Discreet silence. Silence makes good clichés (*chilly silence, eloquent silence*). And in the silence, of course, you can *hear a pin drop.*

Draw a blank. This is what you do when you run out of clichés.

Each and every. The resort of a weak writer, like *one and the same* and *any and all.*

Easier said than done. What isn't? As for *no sooner said than done,* it's a promise that's seldom kept.

Errand of mercy. The truly merciful don't resort to clichés.

Far be it from me. When you say this, you're about to butt in where you don't belong. If you do want to be a buttinsky, though, use it correctly (not "far be it for me").

Fell through the cracks. An unconvincing way of saying something is not your fault. And don't make it worse by saying "fell between the cracks."

Few and far between. This is what fresh expressions are becoming.

Food for thought. I'd say this expression is *from hunger,* but that's another cliché.

Fools rush in. And when they get there, they use clichés.

Foregone conclusion. A pedestrian way of saying that something was no surprise.

Foreseeable future. The future is not foreseeable. Anyone who knows otherwise should be in the commodities market.

General consensus. Disagreeable.

Generation gap. An even worse cliché, *Generation X,* is already geriatric.

Get nowhere fast. It's a cliché, all right, but it's better than *spinning your wheels.*

Get the show on the road. This expression closed in New Haven.

Glass ceiling. This phrase, like *level playing field,* is getting overworked. Hasn't it become a little transparent?

Golf-ball-sized hail. Why golf balls? How about plums or Ping-Pong balls for a change?

Grind to a halt. OK, you can use this maybe once a year.

Head over heels. I've never understood this one. Wouldn't *heels over head* make more sense?

Heated argument. Is there any other kind?

His own worst enemy. Not unless he stabs himself in the back.

Impenetrable fog. Maybe we should bring back *thick as pea soup.*

In the nick of time. "Just in time" isn't good enough?

Innocent bystander. Why is a *bystander* always *innocent*? Has anybody given him a lie-detector test?

It goes without saying. Then don't say it.

Last but not least. If it's not least, then don't put it last.

Leaps and bounds. Gazelles and antelopes, and maybe even lizards, move by *leaps and bounds;* few other things do.

Legendary. This and *fabled* are much overused. What legend? What fable? Unless you're Aesop or the Brothers Grimm, give these words a vacation.

Make a killing. The best thing to be said about this cliché is that it's better than being *taken to the cleaners.* Don't use either of them to excess.

Mass exodus. As opposed to an exodus of one? In most cases, *exodus* alone is enough.

Meaningful dialogue. This was a dumb expression to begin with. Drop *meaningful.* In fact, *dialogue* is pretty dumb, too. Don't people have talks anymore?

Moment of truth. Ever notice that it's always bad news?

More than meets the eye. If you've got a good eye, there's not that much more.

Nip it in the bud. This nipping of buds has to stop.

Pandora's box. Put a lid on it.

Passed away. You've probably noticed that death is a favorite playground of clichés. This is too bad. In situations where people most need sincerity, what do they get? Denial. There's no shame in saying somebody died, but the vocabulary of mortality avoids it. Think again before using expressions like *passed away* or *passed on* (sometimes reduced to just *passed*), *untimely end, cut down in his prime, called to his Maker, called away, great beyond, this mortal coil, bought the farm, hopped the twig* (a variation on *fell off his perch*), *kicked the bucket, gone to a better place, handed in his dinner pail, checked out, grim reaper, in the midst of life, irreparable loss, broke the mold, vale of tears, time heals all, words can't express, tower of strength,* or *he looks like he's sleeping.*

Play hardball. This expression seems to have edged out *no more Mr. Nice Guy.* But it's not as intimidating as it once was, so why not give it a rest?

Play it by ear. This is a nice old image. Let's not wear it out, except at the piano.

Political hopefuls. I vote no.

Powers that be. This is much overused by powers that wannabe.

Pre-existing condition. We're probably stuck with this, but it's a redundancy (that means it repeats itself, like *end result, final outcome, new initiative,* and *close proximity*).

Pushing the envelope. Isn't it amazing how fast a new phrase gets old? Like *A-OK,* this one is no longer state-of-the-art.

Raise the bar. May it go belly-up.

Reliable source. Are your other sources lying scoundrels?

Roller coaster. This phrase (usually preceded by some descriptive term like *emotional* or *fiscal*) comes up a lot in news stories about natural disasters, crippling illness, the federal budget, or the Olympic Games. Let's hope the ride will soon be over.

Sadder but wiser. Some people are *sadder but wiser* after hearing *a word to the wise.* These are nice old expressions that could be with us for a long time if they're treated gently, but *only time will tell.*

Sea of faces. These are often *bright and shining faces.* Commencement speakers, why not give these expressions a sabbatical?

Seat of the pants. And very shiny pants they are. Let's not wear them out.

Seriously consider. This isn't just hackneyed, it's insincere. If someone tells you he'll *seriously consider* your suggestion, he's already kissed it off. That goes double if he has promised to give it *active* or *due consideration.*

Shattered with grief. Why does this phrase make us think of insincere widows?

Sickening thud. This was a lively image in the first five thousand mystery novels where it appeared. The *sickening thud* usually came after *a shot rang out.*

Slippery slope. Don't fall for it.

Tarnished image. The *tarnished image* (distantly related to the old *blot on the escutcheon*) could use some polishing. Give it a leave of absence.

Team player. When your boss says you should be more of a *team player,* that means she wants you to take on more of her work.

Thick as thieves. Thieves are not that thick, anyway. Otherwise, plea bargaining would never work.

Tip of the iceberg. A tip of the hat to anyone who can come up with something better.

To the manner born. If you're going to use a cliché, respect it. This Shakespearean phrase (it comes from *Hamlet*) means "accustomed to" or "familiar with" a manner of living. It is not "to the manor born" and has nothing to do with manor houses.

Tongue in cheek. The only expression more trite than *tongue in cheek* is *tongue firmly in cheek.* I'd like to retire them both.

Trust implicitly. Never believe anybody who says you can trust him implicitly.

Tumultuous applause. This went out with the Monkees.

24/7. Time out!

Up in the air. Let's come up with a more down-to-earth way of saying this.

Viable alternative. Well, it beats the alternative that doesn't work.

War-torn. This cliché stays alive because, regrettably, there are always enough wars to go around. Anything that's *war-torn,* by the way, is bound to be *embattled* or *besieged.*

What makes him tick. This image is winding down. Don't overdo it.

World-class. No class.

Metaphors
Be with You

Is it any wonder we love figures of speech? Just think how dull language would be without them. The metaphor, the most common figure of speech, lets us use one image—any image we want!—to conjure up another. Imagination is the only limit. This gives us about a zillion ways (give or take a few) of saying the same thing.

The phrase *volley of abuse*, for example, uses the image of a fusillade of bullets to describe an outpouring of anger. This metaphor leaves behind a single vivid picture.

But if that image has to compete with another (as in, *The volley of abuse was the straw that broke the camel's back*), we have what's called a mixed metaphor. No clear picture emerges, just two dueling ideas (bullets versus straws). If you've heard it's unwise to mix metaphors, this is why: The competing images drown each other out, as in, *the silver lining at the end of the tunnel*, or *Don't count your chickens till the cows come home*.

Some people are so wild about metaphors that they can't resist using them in pairs. This may work, if the images don't clash: *Frieda viewed her marriage as a tight ship, but Lorenzo was plotting a mutiny.* Since the images of *tight ship* and *mutiny* have an idea in common (sailing), they blend into one picture. But usually when two figures of speech appear together, they aren't so compatible. In that case, the less said, the better.

Chapter 9

The Living Dead

Let Bygone Rules Be Gone

The house of grammar has many rooms, and some of them are haunted. Despite the best efforts of grammatical exorcists, the ghosts of dead rules and the spirits of imaginary taboos are still rattling and thumping about the old place.

Sometimes an ancient prohibition becomes outdated, or it may turn out that a musty convention was never really a rule at all. The trouble is that these phantoms are hard to displace, once they take hold in our minds. It's no longer considered a crime to split an infinitive or end a sentence with a preposition, for example, but the specters of bogus or worn-out rules have a way of coming back to haunt us. In the interest of laying a few to rest, I dedicate to each a tombstone, complete with burial service. May they rest in peace.

TOMBSTONE: Don't split an infinitive.

R.I.P. An infinitive is a verb in its simplest form, right out of the box. It can usually be recognized by the word *to* in front of it: *Blackbeard helped him to escape*. But the *to* isn't actually part of the infinitive and isn't always necessary: *Blackbeard helped him escape*. As a preposition, a word that positions other words, the *to* lets us know an infinitive is coming.

The truth is that the phrase "split infinitive" is misleading. Since *to* isn't really part of the infinitive, there's nothing to split. A sentence often sounds better when the *to* is close to the infinitive: *Dilbert decided **to mention** dating in the workplace*. But there's no harm in separating them by putting a descriptive word or two in between: *Dilbert decided **to discreetly mention** dating in the workplace*.

A sentence like that sounds natural because in English, the best place for an adverb (like *discreetly*) is right in front of the word it describes (*mention*). Where else could *discreetly* go? Putting it anywhere else—say, before or after *decided* or *dating*—would change the meaning. So go ahead and split, but don't overdo it. Not: *Dilbert decided **to discreetly and without referring to the boss's secretary mention** dating in the workplace*.

Sometimes, rearranging a sentence to avoid a "split" makes it ridiculous. Try this example: *Kiri's landlord wanted **to flatly forbid** singing*. Or this one: *He threatened **to more than double** her rent*. Or this: *The landlord is expected **to strongly oppose** weaker noise regulations*. See what I mean?

Writers of English have been merrily "splitting" infinitives since the 1300's. It was considered perfectly acceptable until the mid-nineteenth century, when Latin scholars—notably Henry Alford in his book *A Plea for the Queen's English*—misguidedly called it a crime. (Some linguists trace the taboo to the Victorians' slavish fondness for Latin, a language in which you *can't* divide an infinitive.) This "rule" was popular for half a century, until leading grammarians debunked it. But its ghost has proved more durable than Freddy Krueger.

TOMBSTONE: It's wrong to end a sentence with a preposition.

R.I.P. Here's another bugaboo that English teachers used to get worked up over.

We can blame an eighteenth-century English clergyman and Latin scholar named Robert Lowth for popularizing this one. He wrote the first grammar book to say that a preposition (a positioning word, like *at, by, for, into, off, on, out, over, to, under, up, with*) shouldn't go at the end of a sentence. This idea caught on, even though great literature from Chaucer to Shakespeare to Milton is bristling with sentences ending in prepositions. Nobody knows why the notion stuck—possibly because it's closer to Latin grammar, or perhaps because the word *preposition* means "position before," which seems to suggest that a preposition can't come last.

At any rate, this is a rule that modern grammarians have long tried to get us out from under.

🪦 **TOMBSTONE:** *Data* is a plural noun and always takes a plural verb.

R.I.P. It's time to admit that *data* has joined *agenda, erotica, insignia, opera,* and other technically plural Latin and Greek words that have become thoroughly Anglicized as singular nouns taking singular verbs. No plural form is necessary, and the old singular form, *datum,* can be left to the Romans. (*Media,* it seems, is going the same way, though it's not there yet. Ask me again in a few years.)

🪦 **TOMBSTONE:** Always put the subject of a sentence before the verb.

R.I.P. Says who? Tell it to Tennyson (*"Into the valley of Death / Rode the six hundred"*). He didn't mind putting his subject (*the six hundred*) after the verb (*rode*).

True, most of the time a sentence with its subject (the one doing the action) before the verb (the action being done) sounds more forceful and direct than one written the other way around. *Murray came later* has more oomph than *Later came Murray.* But every now and then it's appropriate to put the verb first (*Says who?* for instance), and literature is full of poetic examples of verbs preceding their subjects. (Just ask Poe: *"Quoth the Raven, 'Nevermore.'"*)

NOTE: If a sentence starts with *there,* its real subject probably follows the verb, as in: *There was a young*

man from Darjeeling. (The subject isn't *there;* it's *man.*)
Sentences starting with *there* get a bad rap in many
grammar guides. There's nothing wrong with them, either. See pages 55 and 192.

TOMBSTONE: It's wrong to start a sentence with *and*
or *but.*

R.I.P. But why is it wrong? There's no law against
occasionally using *and* or *but* to begin a sentence.

Over the years, some English teachers have enforced the
notion that *and* and *but* should be used only to join elements
within a sentence, not to join one sentence with another. Not
so. It's been common practice to begin sentences with them
since at least as far back as the tenth century. But don't
overdo it, or your writing will sound monotonous.

TOMBSTONE: Don't split the parts of a verb phrase
(like *has been*).

R.I.P. This has never been a rule. It's a by-product of
the famous superstition about splitting an infinitive (see the
first tombstone, page 182).

TOMBSTONE: *None* is always singular.

R.I.P. Not always. In fact, *none* is more likely to be
plural.

Many people seem to have been taught (mistakenly) that
none always means "not one" (as in, **None of the chickens is**

hatched). But most authorities have always believed that *none* is closer in meaning to "not any (of them)" than to "not one (of them)." So it's considered plural in most cases and takes a plural verb: **None** *of the chickens* **are** *hatched.*

None is singular only when it means "none of it"—that is to say, "no amount." (**None** *of the milk* **was** *spilled.*)

If you really do mean "not one," say "not one." (There's more about *none* in the chapter on plurals, page 27.)

TOMBSTONE: Don't use *whose* to refer to inanimate objects.

R.I.P. Here's a musty old custom whose time is up. There's nothing wrong with using the possessive *whose* for inanimate objects. *Never buy a* **car whose** *odometer doesn't work.*

A related misconception is that you shouldn't use *'s* with inanimate things (as in *This* **car's** *odometer is broken*). Apparently, the thinking goes, inanimate things aren't as possessive as living ones. Silly, right? Well this book's position is that yesterday's custom can be safely ignored.

TOMBSTONE: Use *It is I*, not *It is me*.

R.I.P. Here's another ordinance that's out-of-date. In all but the most formal circumstances, it's OK to use *It is me, That's him, It's her,* and similar constructions, instead of the technically correct but stuffier *It is I, That's he,* and *It's she.*

Similarly, it's fine to say *Me too.* The alternative, *I too,* is still grammatically correct, but unless you're addressing the Supreme Court or the Philological Society, you can drop the formality.

There's more about *I* and *me* on pages 10–12.

TOMBSTONE: Never use *who* when the rules call for *whom*.

R.I.P. We can't dump *whom* entirely, at least not just yet. But many modern grammarians believe that in conversation or informal writing, *who* is acceptable in place of *whom* at the beginning of a sentence or clause (a clause is a group of words with its own subject and verb): *Who's the package for? You'll never guess **who** I ran into the other day.*

Where *whom* should be used after a preposition (*to, from, behind, on,* etc.), you can substitute *who* in casual situations by reversing the order and putting *who* in front. *"From **whom**?"* becomes *"**Who** from?"*

There's a more detailed discussion of *who* versus *whom* on pages 6–10.

TOMBSTONE: Always use an active verb (*Bonnie **drove** the getaway car*) and avoid a passive one (*The getaway car **was driven** by Bonnie*).

R.I.P. It's true that a passive verb makes for a wimpier, more roundabout way of saying something. The more straightforward way is to put the one performing the action (*Bonnie*) ahead of the one being acted upon (*the getaway car*), with the verb in between: subject . . . verb . . . object.

But the direct way isn't always the best way. The passive might be more appropriate in cases like these:

- When there's a punch line. You might want to place the one performing the action at the end of the sentence for emphasis or surprise: *The gold medal in the five-hundred-meter one-man bobsled competition* **has been won** *by a six-year-old child!*
- When nobody cares whodunit. Sometimes the one performing the action isn't even mentioned: *Hermione* **has been arrested**. *Witherspoon* **is being treated** *for a gunshot wound.* We don't need to know who put the cuffs on Hermione, or who's stitching up Witherspoon.

TOMBSTONE: Never use a double negative.

R.I.P. My advice on double negatives: Never say never.

The double negative wasn't always a no-no. For centuries, it was fine to pile one negative on top of another in the same sentence. Chaucer and Shakespeare did this all the time to accentuate the negative. It wasn't until the eighteenth century that the double negative was declared a sin against the King's English, on the ground that one negative canceled the other. (Blame Robert Lowth, the same guy who decided we shouldn't put a preposition at the end of a sentence.)

As for now, stay away from the most flagrant examples (*I*

didn't do nothing; You never take me nowhere), but don't write off the double negative completely. It's handy when you want to avoid coming right out and saying something: *Your blind date is not unattractive. I wouldn't say I don't like your new haircut.* (There's more on double negatives in the glossary.)

TOMBSTONE: Use *I shall* instead of *I will.*

R.I.P. Once upon a time, refined folk always used *I shall* or *we shall* to refer to the simple future, not *I will* or *we will.* But *will* has edged out *shall* as the people's choice. *Shall* can still be used with *I* and *we* in an offer or a proposal: **Shall I freshen your drink, or shall we go?**

There's more about the demise of *shall* in the chapter on verbs (page 71).

TOMBSTONE: Use *more than* instead of *over.*

R.I.P. You may have been told by some pedant that *over* doesn't apply to numbers, only to quantities. Not so. It's fine to use *over* in place of *more than* or *in excess of: Dad's new car gets **over** ten miles to the gallon.*

TOMBSTONE: Don't use *since* to mean "because."

R.I.P. Now and then, an extremely conservative grammarian will suggest that *since* should be used only to indicate a time period (*since Thursday,* for example). Forget that, if you ever heard it. *Since* doesn't always mean "from the time that."

It can also mean "because" or "for the reason that." (**Since** *you asked me, I'll tell you.*) People have been using *since* in this way for five hundred years.

Just be sure the meaning can't be confused, as in, **Since** *we spoke, I've had second thoughts.* In that case, *since* could mean either "from the time that" or "because," so it's better to be more precise.

TOMBSTONE: Don't use *while* to mean "although."

R.I.P. Some grammarians believe that *while,* which comes from an Anglo-Saxon word meaning "time," should be used only to mean "during the time that."

But there's a long tradition, going back at least to the six-teenth century, of using *while* at the head of a sentence to mean "although" or "whereas": **While** *he may be short, he's wiry.*

Just be sure the meaning can't be confused, as in: **While** *he reads the* Times, *he watches the news on CNN.* In this case, *while* could mean either "during the time that" or "although." Pick one of those and avoid the confusion.

One more thing about *while.* Some people overuse it as a way to vary their sentences and avoid using *and.* Let's not wear out a useful word for no good reason. If *while* isn't meant, don't use it. Not: *Wally wears suspenders,* **while** *his favorite shoes are wingtips.*

✳   ✳   ✳

TOMBSTONE: Use *lighted*, not *lit*.

R.I.P. There's nothing wrong with using *lit* for the past tense of *light*: *Paul **lit** two cigarettes, then gave one to Bette.*

TOMBSTONE: Use *have got,* not *have gotten.*

R.I.P. People who take this prohibition seriously have gotten their grammar wrong.

At one time, everyone agreed that the verb *get* had two past participles: *got* and *gotten*. (The past participle is the form of a verb that's used with *have, had,* or *has.*) It's true that the British stopped using *have gotten* about three hundred years ago, while we in the Colonies kept using both *have got* and *have gotten*. But the result is not that Americans speak improper English. The result is that we have retained a nuance of meaning that the unfortunate Britons have lost.

When we say, *Fabio **has got** three Armani suits,* we mean he has them in his possession. It's another way of saying he *has* them.

When we say, *Fabio **has gotten** three Armani suits,* we mean he's acquired or obtained them.

It's a useful distinction, and one that the British would do well to reacquire.

TOMBSTONE: Drop the *of* in *all of* and *both of.*

R.I.P. Some members of the Redundancy Police think *of* is undesirable in the phrases *all of* and *both of*, except in front of a pronoun (*all of me, both of them,* etc.). They frown on sentences like *Both of the thieves spent all of the money,* and would prefer *Both the thieves spent all the money.*

Either way is correct. There's no law against keeping *of,* but by all means drop it if you want to. You can't please all of the people all the time. For more on dropping *of,* see page 132.

TOMBSTONE: Use *as . . . as* for positive comparisons, and *so . . . as* for negative ones. For example: *She's as old as Fran, but not so old as you.*

R.I.P. Not so fast! For centuries, it's been correct to use *as . . . as* in positive comparisons (*as fat as ever*) and to use either *as . . . as* or *so . . . as* in negative comparisons (*not as fat as before, not so fat as all that*). If you want to use *so . . . as* in a negative comparison, go right ahead. But *as . . . as* is correct in all cases.

If anyone tries to tell you otherwise, just remind him that in Old English, both *as* and *so* (*eall* and *swa*) appeared in the same word, *ealswa.* It was used in comparisons eight or more centuries ago pretty much the way we use *as* these days (*ealswa good ealswa gold*).

TOMBSTONE: Don't start a sentence with *there.*

R.I.P. There is no doubt that a statement starting with *there* begins on a weak note. It's weak because *there* is a phantom subject, standing in for the real one. *There is a party going on* is a different way of saying, *A party is going on.* The real subject in both cases is *party.*

Some English teachers frown on starting a sentence with *there,* possibly because they prefer keeping the real subject before the verb. Never mind. There's nothing wrong with it. In fact, literature is full of splendid examples: *"There is a tide in the affairs of men, which, taken at the flood, leads on to fortune."* There's more on pages 55 and 184.

Chapter 10

Saying Is Believing

How to Write What You Mean

A good writer is one you can read without breaking a sweat. If you want a workout, you don't lift a book—you lift weights. Yet we're brainwashed to believe that the more brilliant the writer, the tougher the going.

The truth is that the reader is always right. Chances are, if something you're reading doesn't make sense, it's not your fault—it's the writer's. And if something you write doesn't get your point across, it's probably not the reader's fault—it's yours. Too many readers are intimidated and humbled by what they can't understand, and in some cases that's precisely the effect the writer is after. But confusion is not complexity; it's just confusion. A venerable tradition, dating back to the ancient Greek orators, teaches that if you don't know

195

what you're talking about, just ratchet up the level of difficulty and no one will ever know.

Don't confuse simplicity, though, with simplemindedness. A good writer can express an extremely complicated idea clearly and make the job look effortless. But such simplicity is a difficult thing to achieve, because to be clear in your writing you have to be clear in your thinking. This is why the simplest and clearest writing has the greatest power to delight, surprise, inform, and move the reader. You can't have this kind of shared understanding if writer and reader are in an adversary relationship.

Now, let's assume you know what you want to say, and the idea in your head is as clear as a mountain stream. (I'm allowed a cliché once in a while.) How can you avoid muddying it up when you put it into words?

There are no rules for graceful writing, at least not in the sense that there are rules for grammar and punctuation. Some writing manuals will tell you to write short sentences, or to cut out adjectives and adverbs. I disagree. The object isn't to simulate an android. When a sentence sounds nice, reads well, and is easy to follow, its length is just right. But when a sentence is lousy, you can take steps to make it more presentable. These are general principles, and you won't want to follow all of them all of the time (though it's not a bad idea).

※   ※   ※

1. Say what you have to say.

Unless you're standing at a lectern addressing an audience, there's no need to clear your throat. Your listeners aren't finding their seats, putting down their forks, wrapping up a conversation, or whatever. Your audience—the reader—is ready. So get to it.

These are the kinds of throat-clearing phrases you can usually ditch:

At this juncture I thought you might be interested in knowing . . .

Perhaps it would be valuable as we arrive at this point in time to recall . . .

I can assure you that I'm sincere when I say . . .

In light of recent developments the possibility exists that . . .

(Of course, some messages could do with a bit of cushioning: *We at the bank feel that under the circumstances you would want us to bring to your attention as soon as possible the fact that . . . your account is overdrawn.*)

2. Stop when you've said it.

Sometimes, especially when you're on a roll and coming up with your best stuff, it's hard to let go of a sentence (this one, for example), so when you get to the logical end you just keep going, and even though you know the reader's eyes are glazing over, you stretch one sentence thinner and thinner—with a semicolon here, a *however* or *nevertheless* there—and you end up stringing together a whole paragraph's worth of ideas before you finally realize it's all over and you're getting writer's cramp and you have to break down and use a period.

When it's time to start another sentence, start another sentence.

How do you know when it's time? Well, try breathing along with your sentences. Allow yourself one nice inhalation and exhalation per sentence as you silently read along. If you start to turn blue before getting to the end, either you're reading too slowly (don't move your lips) or the sentence is too long.

3. Don't belabor the obvious.

Some writers can't make a point without poking you in the ribs with it. A voice isn't just pleasing; it's pleasing *to the ear*. You don't just give something away; you give it away *for free*. The reader will get the point without the unnecessary prepositional phrases (phrases that start with words like *by, for, in, of,* and *to*): pretty *in appearance*, tall *of stature*, few *in number*, blue *in color*, small *in size*, stocky *in build*, plan *in advance*, drive *by car*, assemble *in a group*. You get the picture.

Speaking of redundancies, think twice before using expressions like *advance reservations, final conclusion, foreign import, free gift, prerecorded, refer back,* or *safe haven.* Do I hear an echo?

4. Don't tie yourself in knots to avoid repeating a word.

It's better to repeat a word that fits than to stick in a clumsy substitute that doesn't. Just because you've called something a spider once doesn't mean that the next time you have to call it an arachnid or a predaceous eight-legged creepy-crawly.

Editors sometimes call this attempt at elegant variation the Slender Yellow Fruit Syndrome. It is best explained by example: *Freddie was offered an apple and a banana, and he chose the slender yellow fruit.*

5. Be direct.

Too many writers back into what they have to say. A straightforward statement like *He didn't intend to ruin your flower bed* comes out *His intention was not to ruin your flower bed.*

Don't mince words. If what you mean is, *Mom reorganized my closet brilliantly,* don't water it down by saying, *Mom's reorganization of my closet was brilliant.*

Here are a couple of other examples:

Their house was destroyed in 1993. Not: *The destruction of their house occurred in 1993.*

We concluded that Roger's an idiot. Not: *Our conclusion was that Roger's an idiot.*

If you have something to say, be direct about it. As in geometry, the shortest distance between two points is a straight line.

6. Don't make yourself the center of the universe.

Of course we want to know what happened to you. Of course we care what you think and feel and do and say. But you can tell us without making every other word *I* or *me* or *my*. E-mailers are often guilty of this. Next time you write an e-mail or a letter (remember letters?), look it over and see how many sentences start with *I*.

You can prune phrases like *I think that,* or *in my opinion,* or *let me emphasize that* out of your writing (and your talking, for that matter) without losing anything. Anecdotes can be told, advice given, opinions opined, all with a lot fewer first-person pronouns than you think.

This doesn't mean we don't love you.

7. *Put descriptions close to what they describe.*

A television journalist in the Farm Belt once said this about a suspected outbreak of hoof-and-mouth disease: *The pasture contained several cows seen by news reporters that were dead, diseased, or dying.*

Do you see what's wrong? The words *dead, diseased, or dying* are supposed to describe the cows, but they're so far from home that they seem to describe the reporters. What the journalist should have said was: *Reporters saw a pasture containing several cows that were dead, diseased, or dying.*

When a description strays too far, the sentence becomes awkward and hard to read. Here's an adjective (*bare*) that has strayed too far from the noun (*cupboard*) it describes: *Ms. Hubbard found her **cupboard**, although she'd gone shopping only a few hours before, **bare**.* Here's one way to rewrite it: *Although she'd gone shopping only a few hours before, Ms. Hubbard found her **cupboard bare**.*

And here's an adverb (*definitely*) that's strayed too far from its verb (*is suing*): She **definitely**, *if you can believe what all the papers are reporting and what everyone is saying*, **is suing**. Put them closer together: She **definitely is suing**, *if you can believe what all the papers are reporting and what everyone is saying*.

The reader shouldn't need a map to follow a sentence.

8. *Put the doer closer to what's being done.*

Nobody's saying that sentences can't be complex and interesting; they can, as long as they're easy to follow. But we shouldn't have to read a sentence twice to get it. Here's an example that takes us from Omaha to Sioux City by way of Pittsburgh:

The **twins**, *after stubbornly going to the same high school despite the advice of their parents and teachers,* **chose** *different colleges.*

Find a way to say it that puts the doer (the subject, *twins*) closer to what's being done (the verb, *chose*): *The* **twins chose** *different colleges, after stubbornly going to the same high school despite the advice of their parents and teachers.*

If you need a compass to navigate a sentence, take another whack at the writing.

9. *Watch out for pronounitis.*

A sentence with too many pronouns (*he, him, she, her, it, they, them,* and other words that substitute for nouns) can give your reader hives: *Fleur says Judy told* **her** *boyfriend about* **their** *stupid little adventure and* **she** *already regrets* **it**.

Whose boyfriend? Whose stupid little adventure? Who regrets what?

When you write things like this, of course you know the cast of characters. It won't be so clear to somebody else. Don't make the reader guess. Here's a possibility: *Judy told her boyfriend about her stupid little adventure with Fleur and already regrets telling him, according to Fleur.*

10. Make sure there's a time and place for everything.

Mr. Big's administrative assistant got a raise by hinting that she'd found a candid photo of him and Natasha in a compromising position in the file cabinet during Administrative Professionals Week.

What happened in the file cabinet? And when? Did the shenanigans take place during Administrative Professionals Week? Or is that when the administrative assistant put the squeeze on Mr. Big? This calls for some administrative assistance.

Mr. Big's administrative assistant got a raise by hinting during Administrative Professionals Week that she'd found in the file cabinet a candid photo of him and Natasha in a compromising position.

Where are we? What's going on? What time is it? These are questions the reader shouldn't have to ask.

11. Imagine what you're writing.

Picture in your mind any images you've created.

Are they unintentionally funny, like this one? *The bereaved family covered the mirrors as a reflection of its grief.* If you don't see what's wrong, reflect on it for a moment.

Are there too many images, as in this sentence? *The remaining bone of contention is a thorn in his side and an albatross around his neck.* Give the poor guy a break. One image at a time, please.

12. Put your ideas in order.

Don't make the reader rearrange your messy sentences to figure out what's going on. The parts should follow logically. This doesn't mean they should be rattled off in chronological order, but the sequence of ideas should make sense. Here's how Gracie Allen might have talked about a soufflé recipe, for instance:

It is possible to make this soufflé with four eggs instead of eight. But it will collapse and possibly even catch fire in the oven, leaving you with a flat, burned soufflé. Now, you wouldn't want that, would you? So if you have only four eggs, reduce all the other ingredients in the recipe by half.

Rearrange the ideas:

This soufflé recipe calls for eight eggs. If you want to use fewer, reduce the other ingredients accordingly. If the proportions aren't maintained, the soufflé could flatten or burn.

13. Get the big picture.

Forget the details for a minute. Now step back and take a look at what you've written. Have you said what you wanted to say? After all, leaving the wrong impression is much worse than making a couple of grammatical boo-boos. Get some perspective.

Assuming you've made your point, ask yourself whether you could make it more smoothly. Somebody once said that in good writing, the sentences hold hands. See if you can give yours a helping hand. It may be that by adding or subtracting a word here or there, you could be even clearer. Or you could switch two sentences around, or begin one of them differently.

14. Read with a felonious mind.

There's no easy way to raise your writing from competence to artistry. It helps, though, to read with a felonious mind. If you see a letter or memo or report that you admire, read it again. Why do you like it, and what makes it so effective? When you find a technique that works, steal it. Someday, others may be stealing from you.

Chapter 11

E-Mail Intuition

Does Anything Go?

And now, a word to the wired: E-mail is no excuse for lousy English.

Granted, virtual writing is usually more informal than writing in the "real" world. But informal doesn't mean incoherent—or it shouldn't. Unfortunately, much of the writing you see in cyberspace (and e-mail isn't the only culprit) barely qualifies as English. The words are chosen with little or no thought. The grammar is a mess. The punctuation is either absent or in your face. As for spelling, it's hit-or-miss— usually miss. No wonder the whole point of an e-mail is often lost in transmission.

Don't bother rounding up the usual suspects. Even people who are normally careful about their English may throw the rules out the window when they go online. Maybe they don't think of e-mail as writing. Maybe they don't realize that good English is just as important online as off.

In fact, misunderstandings are more likely in an e-mail than in a letter or a phone call or a face-to-face conversation. The speed, the brevity, the disengagement of online writing all conspire to muddle your message. And the short attention span of the wired reader only makes things worse.

What's more, the virtual world is full of strangers, people who know you only by your words. Sure, your best friend will overlook a few misspellings or lapses in grammar. But people you've never met will judge you solely by what they see on their computer screens. To them, you are what you write.

In short, online writing needs all the help it can get. Good English is clear English. It's efficient, precise, sensible, economical, sometimes even beautiful. And that's just as true in e-mail as it is in snail mail—or any other kind of writing.

E-mail that's hard to understand—ambiguous, poorly worded, misspelled, unpunctuated—takes only an instant to send but forever to decipher. So e-mail unto others as you would have them e-mail unto you.

That means you don't call time-out when you log on. Such niceties as grammar, spelling, and punctuation *do* matter online, plus a few more besides. Here are some things for the wired writer to consider before clicking Send.

✳   ✳   ✳

The Right Connection

How finicky are you about e-mail? Most people I know think of it as a new species, a cross between a phone call and a letter. Those who see it more like a letter are pickier about the fine points. The free-spirited types treat it more like a phone call and don't sweat the details.

Who's right? Both factions, some of the time. The issue isn't e-mail itself, but the person who's getting it. If you're e-mailing your English professor, for example, you'd better be letter perfect. But if you're messaging your flaky little brother, loosen up.

The point is, the audience should be your guide. That means customizing your e-mail—the vocabulary, the level of formality, the mood, the sophistication, the humor—to fit the reader.

So when you message the prof, keep it straight: *I don't understand the essay question on postmodernism.* When you e-mail little bro, go for it: *Say what?*

Subject Matter

You'd never know it by looking at the queue of unread messages in the typical in-box, but the subject line can make or break an e-mail.

The subject line determines how soon a message is read—if at all. Yet many e-mailers kiss it off and some don't even bother filling it in. What's the poor reader to make of a pointless subject line like *Hmmm* or *FYI* or *Stuff* or, worst of all, *<no subject>*?

If you'd like your e-mail read before it grows mold, here's some friendly advice on the subject.

- Be specific. Don't make readers guess what your message is about. Instead of saying *The project* or *A meeting*, give them a clue: *Opie's science project* or *Otis's AA meeting*.
- Don't cry wolf. If your message can wait, say so: *Query for Leonard—no rush*. On the other hand, if it's urgent, speak up: *Virginia: Need reply by noon*. But don't wear out the panic button if you want it to work when you really need it.
- Watch the spelling. A subject line is the last place you want a spelling (or grammar or punctuation) error to creep in. Why should the reader bother with your message when you obviously didn't?
- Hold the hype. Any hint of spam in the subject line, particularly if the reader isn't familiar with your e-mail address, can be the kiss of death. Nobody likes junk mail. If you're e-mailing Ben & Jerry's with an idea for a new ice cream flavor, for example, skip the hard sell (*This is your lucky day*) and say it straight (*Caramel Miranda*).

Imprint this on your noodle: The object of the subject is to inform the reader.

Screen Test

Imagine that Aunt Dahlia sends Bertie an e-mail about her plans to take a two-week tour of Tibet. After reading several screenfuls about a lamasery on the slopes of Mount Guopei, Bertie stores the message to finish later. Before he gets around to it, Aunt Dahlia is on his doorstep with her three favorite foxhounds and a fortnight's supply of kibble.

Yes, Bertie should have read the whole message. But Aunt Dahlia should have mentioned the dog-sitting job up front and saved the colorful travelogue for later.

As I've said before, wired readers have short attention spans. If you have something important to tell them, say it somewhere in the first screenful. What's less important can go later, but don't rattle on indefinitely. You're writing an e-mail, not the *Encyclopaedia Britannica*.

The computer makes it easy to go on and on and on. You empty all your ideas into the word processor. If you can't decide which ones are best, you keep them all. When you run out of ideas, you cut and paste someone else's. Isn't technology wonderful?

Well, not so wonderful when you're on the receiving end. Everyone knows that long messages are the ones that get read last. So be selective. It's easier to dump in everything, but resist the urge. (If you need help with the pruning, see Chapter 10.)

Getting to Know You

Call me old-fashioned, but I find it jarring to get an e-mail without a hello or a good-bye. Cyberia is chilly enough already. Why not warm things up with a greeting and a closing?

You don't have to be stiff or starchy about it. Most of the time, a simple *Hi, Alice* and *Bye, Trixie* will do. But keep it more formal when your message really matters—say, in an e-mail to the prospective boss of your dreams.

An e-mail without a salutation or a signature can seem abrupt and impersonal, even rude. It's like a phone call from someone who starts talking with no preliminaries, then hangs up without saying good-bye.

Politeness aside, there are other reasons for using a greeting and a closing. Perhaps you're writing to someone who shares an e-mail address with somebody else. Or maybe you share one yourself. Why leave any question about who's getting the message or who's sending it? Then again, you might be messaging people who don't recognize your address. Why make them puzzle it out?

Yes, you're in a hurry when you write e-mail. But it takes

only seconds to add a *Yo, Phoebe* and a *See ya, Holden.* And what a difference they make!

Copy Cats

In the old typewriter days, making copies was a hassle (remember carbon paper?). Nowadays copying is a snap. With a few clicks, you can send copies or forwards or attachments to everybody in your address book. The down side of all this wizardry is that the average in-basket is as stuffed as a Thanksgiving turkey.

Do you need to cc everybody in the book club that you'll be late Wednesday night? Should you send the boss an attachment every time you submit a report to a client? Must you forward that list of lightbulb jokes to everyone in your organic chemistry class? I think not.

If Uncle Fred really needs to see your e-mail to cousin Bamm-Bamm, by all means send him a copy. But if he doesn't need the whole thing, cut and paste just the part he has to see, and send it in a separate e-mail.

Do your bit to fight clutter. Don't copy or forward or attach something just because you can.

✳   ✳   ✳

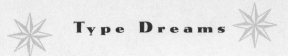

Type Dreams

The only thing more annoying than an unnecessary e-mail is an unreadable one—something you can't read without getting eyestrain. You know the kind: a message that's all UPPER-CASE or lowercase, especially one with no punctuation or paragraph breaks.

Hard-to-read messages do serve a purpose. By forcing us to squint at our computer screens, they keep things hopping at the optometrist's. And I'll bet all that peering with furrowed brow helps sell a lot of acetaminophen and wrinkle cream.

Headaches and wrinkles aside, punctuation and paragraph breaks and occasional capital letters are handy signals to the reader. They show where sentences begin and end, where the subject changes, and where people and places and dates come into the picture. Nobody likes to stare at an unbroken blob of indistinguishable type.

In addition to the vision thing, a lot of people think an e-mailer who uses all caps is SHOUTING. So turn down the volume.

Jargonistas

IMHO (in my humble opinion), those abbreviations that worm their way into online writing—like CUL (see you later) and BTW (by the way)—are juvenile and irritating. So are those little smileys and frownies made of punctuation marks that are supposed to show how the writer feels. Come on, kids. Aren't punctuation marks abused enough already? :-(

That stuff reminds me of grade school and secret handshakes. You may disagree, of course. A lot of reasonable people do. But I'd rather use words.

If you feel you must use a cutesy abbreviation or emoticon to save a few words or express an emotion, go ahead. Just make sure the reader understands your slanguage. An analog soul—and there are still a lot of us out there—might not get it.

Oh, I see. You're too busy to write complete sentences. So what are you doing with the time you save by using clever shortcuts? Volunteering at the homeless shelter? Delivering Meals on Wheels? Sure you are. I'm ROFL—rolling on floor laughing. :-)

Response Ability

Say Mr. Kane sends out a few hundred e-mails on a few hundred subjects to a few hundred people in the course of a month. Now let's say he gets back a few hundred replies along the lines of *That's possible* or *OK* or *Not just yet* or *I'll think it over.* Come again? Information please!

A cryptic reply won't do the job when you're answering a busy citizen like Mr. K., especially if a lot of time has passed or if the subject line is no help. The last thing he wants to do is slog through his outgoing mail to remind himself what he asked you.

Don't give the reader a hard time. Be clear about what you're replying to. Either sum up the original e-mail in a few words (*About your request for a potted palm in the lobby . . .*), or cut and paste the relevant parts. There's usually no need to quote the whole thing.

You can also do the summarizing in the subject line. If the one that pops up when you click Reply is too vague (*Re: A request*), rewrite it: *Your request for a potted palm.*

Spellbound

A spell-checker can be your best friend—and your worst enemy.

I use mine all the time, and I can't count the times it's saved my bacon. For example, I'm incapable of typing the word *substitution* correctly. My fingers simply can't do it. If it weren't for my speller, I'd have to use *replacement* or *stand-in* or *pinch hitter* instead.

I also tend to misspell *the*—it comes out *hte*. Or I write it twice: *the the*. Spell-check bails me out every time.

But the good old speller doesn't always come through. Turn your back on it, and it'll kick you in the but. There! That's what I mean. My software didn't catch that *but* because it can't tell the difference between sound-alike words: *but* and *butt*, *need* and *knead*, *sew* and *sow*, and so on.

Word processors may have dictionaries, but they don't have common sense—at least not yet. The lesson? Use your spell-checker, but don't follow it blindly. Don't automatically hit Replace every time the program tells you to. Yule bee sari!

As for your so-called grammar-checker, forget about it. Most of the "mistakes" it finds aren't mistakes at all, and much of the advice comes from the Twilight Zone. The other day, I wrote an e-mail with the phrase "an hour-long program" and ran my grammar checker just for the heck of it. I was told to change *an* to *a*. No, I did not hit Replace. (For the inside story on *a* and *an*, see page 131.)

Repeat Performance

If you haven't given your e-mail a second look, you're not ready to click Send.

I know what you're thinking: *It's only an e-mail. Getting it out is more important than getting it perfect.* Well, just because an e-mail travels instantly doesn't mean you have to send it instantly.

Sure you're busy. But your reader doesn't have all day, either. The time you save by not rereading an e-mail is time the other guy has to spend deciphering it. And what about all the time you'll spend clearing up what should have been clear the first time?

In other words, rereading isn't a time waster, it's a time saver. Think of it as preventive maintenance. With a little regular servicing, you can avoid lengthy visits to the repair shop to overhaul your e-mail clunkers.

A Civil Tongue

E-mail can turn the nicest person into a tactless lout. It's the nature of the medium. Unlike a phone call or an in-the-flesh conversation, an electronic message lacks the vocal nuances, the give-and-take, the body English that do so much to soften the sharp edges of a poorly chosen word.

Here on earth, a smile, a murmur, a nod, a chuckle can do the job of a missing courtesy like "May I?" or "Excuse me." But in cyberspace, words have to stand alone, unless you count such inadequate crutches as smileys and abbreviations.

Of course, words have to stand alone on paper too, but writing a "real" letter is a slower, more leisurely process, especially if you're using pen and ink. You're more careful, for one thing. If you flub the penmanship or word choice, you'll have to wad up the page and start over. And built-in delays like addressing the envelope, finding a stamp, and getting to the mailbox give you time to reconsider and avoid thoughtless blunders.

All in all, it's easier to inadvertently hurt someone's feelings in an e-mail than in a letter, a phone call, or a face-to-face talk. A casual comment or a brusque remark that would pass harmlessly at the water cooler, for instance, might touch off World War III in an e-mail.

Next time you log on and enter the ozone, don't check your manners at the portal. Here's what to do instead:

• Dust off a few Old World expressions like "please," "thank you," and "I'm sorry." There's no law against being nice online.

• Go for the extra word or two if that will make you clearer. Why be stingy, especially when you're dealing with a sensitive topic?

• Don't click Send when your blood is boiling. Try clicking Send Later and waiting for your temperature to drop to 98.6.

- Get real and ask yourself whether a phone call, a letter, or a "live" meeting would be better. One brief conversation might do the job of a dozen e-mails. And a letter might be more appropriate if you're thanking Great-Aunt Betsey for her generous graduation present.
- Be discreet about what you send and to whom, especially at work. E-mail isn't the place for sensitive personnel matters, criticism of third parties, office romance, hurtful gossip, or anything else that could find its way to the wrong mailbox.

So don't let e-mail bring out the beast in you. If you feel yourself growing fangs and sprouting hair from the backs of your hands, get a grip. You're a real person writing to real people. Yes, even in the virtual world.

Glossary

ADJECTIVE. A word describing or characterizing a noun. It can come before the noun (*pink* sweater) or after (*The sweater is* **pink**). Because an adjective adds something to a noun, it's called a modifier; we say it "modifies" the noun.

ADVERB. A word that describes or characterizes a verb (*He grunted* **lugubriously**). It can also characterize an adjective (*He is* **very** *lugubrious*) or another adverb (*He grunted* **very** *lugubriously*). An adverb is called a modifier, because it "modifies" another word.

APOSTROPHE. A mark of punctuation that's used to make nouns possessive (*Albert's coat*), to form some plurals (*the 1950's*), and to show where letters have been omitted, as in contractions (*wouldn't*).

ARTICLE. The three articles (*a, an, the*) are actually tiny adjectives that tell us whether a noun refers to a particular thing (*the chair*, *the ottoman*) or just one of those things (*a chair*, *an ottoman*). *The* is called the definite article; *a* and *an* are indefinite articles.

BRACKETS. Marks of punctuation used in quoted material or excerpts to enclose something that's not part of the original, like an explanatory aside. *"My weight [154 pounds] is a well-kept secret," said Leona.*

CLAUSE. A group of words with its own subject and verb. A simple sentence might consist of only one clause: *Ernest left for Paris.* More complex sentences have several clauses, as in this example: *I learned | that Ernest left for Paris | when Scott told me.* Independent clauses make sense alone (*I put on a sock . . .*), but dependent, or subordinate, clauses don't (*. . . that had no mate*).

CLICHÉ. A figure of speech that's lost its sparkle. When you find yourself using one, nip it in the bud—or maybe I should put that another way.

COLLECTIVE NOUN. A noun that stands for a group of people or things, like *total* or *number*. It can be considered singular (*The number is staggering*) or plural (*A number of them have gone their separate ways*).

COLON. A punctuation mark that can be used to introduce a statement, a series of things, a quotation, or instructions. It's a pause in the traffic, telling you to brake before going on.

COMMA. A punctuation mark that indicates a pause. If it were a traffic signal, it would be a yellow light. It can be used to separate clauses in a sentence, or items in a series.

CONDITIONAL CLAUSE. A clause that starts with *if, as if, as though,* or some other expression of supposition. The verb in a conditional clause has an attitude: that is, it takes on different forms, or "moods," depending on the speaker's attitude or intention toward what's being said. When the clause states a condition that's contrary to fact, the verb is in the subjunctive mood (*If I were you* . . .). When the clause states a condition that may be true, the verb is in the indicative mood (*If I was late* . . .). For more on the conditional, see VERB.

CONJUNCTION. A connecting word. The telltale part of this term is "junction," because that's where a conjunction is found—at the junction where words or phrases or clauses or sentences are joined. The most familiar conjunctions are *and, but,* and *or.* And it's fine to start a sentence with one. But not too often. Or you'll overdo it.

CONSONANT. Generally, a letter with a "hard" sound: *b, c, d, f, g, h, j, k, l, m, n, p, q, r, s, t, v, w, x, y, z.* Sometimes the consonants *w* and *y* act like vowels, which are letters with a "soft," openmouthed sound. And occasionally consonants (such as *g, h,* and others) are seen but not heard.

CONTRACTION. Two words combined into one, with an apostrophe showing where letters are omitted. There are three kinds of contractions: a verb plus *not* (*do + not = don't*); a pronoun plus a verb (*they + are = they're*); and a noun plus a verb (*Bob + is = Bob's*). Don't confuse the last example with the possessive (*Bob's dog*).

DANGLER. A word or phrase in the wrong place that ends up describing the wrong thing: *After napping, the card table was set up.* Who was napping? Unless it's the table, change the sentence: *After napping, Oscar set up the card table.*

DASH. A punctuation mark that interrupts a sentence to insert another thought. One can act like a colon: *It was every mother's nightmare—ringworm.* Or a pair of dashes can be used like parentheses: *The remedy was easy enough—a simple oral medication—but what would she tell the neighbors?*

DICTIONARY. A book that lists words in alphabetical order and gives their spellings and pronunciations, their meanings and origins—including words that aren't legit, like *alright.* The fact that a word can be found in the dictionary doesn't mean it's all right. Read the fine print.

DOUBLE NEGATIVE. A double negative is what you get when you combine a negative verb (like *have not* or *is not*) with a negative pronoun (like *nothing* or *nobody*), a negative adverb (like *hardly* or *never*), or a negative conjunction (like *neither* or *nor*). Not all double negatives are no-nos. Here are some flagrant examples of don'ts: *I have not seen nobody. It wasn't hardly worth it. He is not there, neither.* Some allowables: *It's not inconceivable. She's not unappealing.*

ELLIPSIS POINTS. Punctuation that indicates an omission, or ellipsis, in a quotation. The three dots can show the omission of a word—in this case a naughty one: *"Get off my lawn, and take your . . . dog with you!" he shouted.* Or they can show where a sentence trails off: *"Now let me think. . . ."* Notice that when the ellipsis points come at the end of the sentence, a period precedes them, so you end up with four dots instead of three. (If you want to emphasize the incompleteness of the trailing off, you may end with a space, then just three dots: "But . . .")

EXCLAMATION POINT. A punctuation mark that comes after something that's exclaimed: *"I passed!" said Pippa.* Go easy on the exclamation point and save it for the really startling stuff.

FIGURATIVE. Language is figurative when it uses words in imaginative or out-of-the-ordinary ways. In the process, the truth is often stretched to make a point. If you were being literal, you might say: *Jack's dog is big and stocky.* But to be more vivid, you could say: *Jack's dog is built like a refrigerator.*

FIGURE OF SPEECH. An imaginative (or "figurative") expression: *She knows how to push his buttons.* (See FIGURATIVE.) When a figure of speech gets stale, it becomes a cliché.

GERUND. A word that's made of a verb plus *ing* (*bowling*, for example) and that acts as a noun: ***Bowling*** *is his first love.* The same *ing* word is a participle if it acts as an adjective (*He's a **bowling** fool*) or part of a verb (*He was **bowling***).

GRAMMAR. A system of rules for arranging words into sentences. We adopt rules when we need them and discard them when we don't, so the rules are always changing.

HYPHEN. A mark of punctuation that looks like a stubby dash. It is used to join words together to make new ones (*self-conscious*), and to link syllables when a word, like *humongous* here, breaks off at the end of a line and continues on the next.

IMPERATIVE. A verb is imperative when the speaker is expressing a command or request: *Lose twenty pounds, Jack.* (See MOOD.)

INDICATIVE. A verb is indicative when the speaker is expressing a straightforward statement or question: *Jack lost twenty pounds.* (See MOOD.)

INFINITIVE. A verb in its simplest form (*sneeze*, for example). While the preposition *to* is usually a signal that the infinitive is being used (*to sneeze*), it's not part of the infinitive itself. Putting an adverb in the middle (*to loudly sneeze*) is fine—you're not really "splitting" anything.

INTERJECTION. A word (or words) expressing a sudden rush of feeling: *My word! Help! Wow! Oh, damn!*

INTERROGATIVE. An expression is interrogative if it asks a question: *Got that?*

INTRANSITIVE. See VERB.

JARGON. Language used by windbags and full of largely meaningless, pseudotechnical terms that are supposed to lend the speaker an aura of expertise. The advantage of jargon is that you can use it to discuss things you know little about, and without really saying anything. But even when you know what you're talking about, technical language can be confusing to someone who isn't another expert. *Jargon* comes from an old word for "chattering" or "twittering."

LITERAL. True or "to the letter"—the opposite of figurative. Don't use the adverb *literally* to modify a figure of speech, as in: *The boss literally had kittens.*

METAPHOR. The most common figure of speech. A metaphor takes the language normally used for one thing and applies it to something else: *His stomach began to growl. The moon was a silver coin upon the water.*

MOOD. Verbs have attitude. They take on different forms, called *moods,* or sometimes *modes,* that reflect the speaker's attitude toward what's being said. There are three moods in English. If what's being said is an ordinary statement or question about facts, the verb is in the indicative mood. (*He is on my foot.*) If what's being said is contrary to fact or expresses a wish, the verb is in the subjunctive mood. (*I wish he were not on my foot. If he were not on my foot, I could go.*) If what's being said is a command or a request, the verb is in the imperative mood. (*Get off my foot!*)

NOUN. A word that stands for a person, place, thing, or idea. A common noun starts with a small letter (*city* or *girl* or *religion,* for example); a proper noun starts with a capital letter (*Memphis* or *Molly* or *Methodist*).

OBJECT. A noun or pronoun that's acted on by a verb. It can be something you give, for instance, or somebody you give it to. An indirect object is the person or thing on the receiving end of the action, and a direct object is who or what ends up there: *Harry gave me* [indirect object] *the flu* [direct object]. Think of it like a game of catch—you throw a direct object to an indirect object.

Additionally, a noun or pronoun at the receiving end of a preposition (*to* and *from* in these examples) is an object: *Harry gave the flu to me. He is from Chicago.*

PARENTHESES. Marks of punctuation used to enclose an aside—either a whole sentence or words within a sentence.

PARTS OF SPEECH. The eight kinds of words: noun, pronoun, adjective, verb, adverb, preposition, conjunction, interjection. This sentence uses all of them: *But* [conjunction] *gosh* [interjection], *you* [pronoun] *are* [verb] *really* [adverb] *in* [preposition] *terrible* [adjective] *trouble* [noun]!

PERIOD. A punctuation mark that shows where a declarative sentence, one that states something, ends. The period is also used in some abbreviations (U.S. for "United States," Dr. for "Doctor," P.M. for "post meridiem"), but many abbreviations have dropped their dots.

PHRASE. A group of related words without subject and verb, like *glorious sunset* or *in the meantime* or *to spill the beans* or *gently swinging in the breeze*. A group of words with both a subject and its verb is a clause.

PLURAL. More than one; just one is singular. Plural nouns generally have endings different from singular ones (*berries* versus *berry,* for example).

POSSESSIVE. Showing ownership. With most nouns, you get the possessive form (or "case") by adding *'s* (***Alice's** cousin*) or the preposition *of* (*a cousin **of** Alice*). A "double possessive" uses both methods (*a cousin **of** Alice's*).

PREPOSITION. A word that "positions" or situates words in relation to one another. The roots of the term *preposition* mean "put before," which is appropriate, because a preposition usually comes before a noun or pronoun: *My cousin is from Philly.* (Contrary to what you might have heard, however, it can indeed go at the end of a sentence.) The prepositions we use most are *about, above, across, after, against, ahead* *of, along, among, around, as, at, away from, before, behind, below, beneath, beside, between, but* (in the sense of "except"), *by, down, except, for, from, in, in back of, in front of, inside, into, like, of, off, on, onto, out, out of, outside, over, past, since, through, throughout, to, toward, under, until, up, upon, with, within, without.* Some of these words can serve as other parts of speech as well (adverbs, conjunctions).

PRONOUN. A word that can be used in place of a noun. Pronouns fall into these categories:

- A **personal pronoun** can be a subject (*I, you, he, she, it, we, they*); an object (*me, you, him, her, it, us, them*); or a possessive (*my, mine, your, yours, his, her, hers, its, our, ours, their, theirs*). Some of these (*my, your, his, her, its, our, their*) are also called possessive adjectives, since they describe (or modify) nouns.

- A **reflexive pronoun** calls attention to itself (it ends with *self* or *selves*): *myself, yourself, himself, herself, itself, ourselves, yourselves, themselves.* Reflexive pronouns are used to emphasize (*She **herself** is Hungarian*) or to refer to the subject (*He blames **himself***).

- A **demonstrative pronoun** points out something: *this, that, these, those.* It can be used by itself (*Hold **this***) or with a noun, as an adjective (*Who is **this** guy?*).

- An **indefinite pronoun** refers to a vague or unknown person or thing: *all, another, any, anybody, anyone, anything, both, each, either, every, everybody, everyone, everything, few, many, much, neither, no one, nobody, none, one, other, several, some, somebody, someone, something,* *such* (***All** is lost*). Some of these, too, can serve as adjectives.

• An **interrogative pronoun** is used to ask a question: *what, which, who, whom, whose* (***Who's** on first?*).

• A **relative pronoun** introduces a dependent (or subordinate) clause: *that, what, whatever, which, whichever, who, whoever, whom, whomever, whose* (*He's the guy **who** stole my heart*).

PUNCTUATION. The signs and signals in writing that direct the traffic of language. They call for stops, starts, slowdowns, and detours. The marks of punctuation include the period, the comma, the colon, the semicolon, the question mark, the exclamation point, the apostrophe, the dash, the hyphen, parentheses, ellipsis points, and quotation marks.

QUESTION MARK. A punctuation mark that comes at the end of a question.

QUOTATION MARKS. Punctuation marks that surround spoken or quoted words.

SEMICOLON. A punctuation mark for a stop that's less final than a period. It's like a flashing red light—it lets you drive on after a brief pause. You'll often find it between clauses in a sentence and between items in a series.

SENTENCE. A word or group of words that expresses a complete thought; in writing, it begins with a capital letter and has a concluding mark like a period, a question mark, or an exclamation point. Most sentences have a subject and a verb, but not all. An imperative sentence, which demands an action, may have only a verb (*Run!*). An interrogative sentence, which asks a question, may also have only one word (*How?*). An exclamatory sentence, which expresses emotion, may have only a word or a phrase (*Good heavens!*). The declarative sentence, the most common kind, conveys information and is likely to have a subject, a verb, and an object—usually in that order: *He ate my fries.*

SIBILANT. A consonant sound that hisses, like *s, z, sh, zh, ch,* and *j.* Nouns that end in sibilants sometimes have special ways of forming plurals and possessives.

SINGULAR. Only one; more than one is plural. A noun or a verb is singular if it applies to a single person, place, or thing.

STUFFED SHIRT. A person likely to use jargon; similar to a windbag. (See JARGON.)

SUBJECT. That which initiates an action; in other words, who or what is doing whatever's being done. Subjects can be nouns (like *Harry*), pronouns (like *I*), or phrases (like *Harry and I*). *Good old **Harry and I** have fallen arches.* A subject with all its accessories (*Good old Harry and I*) is the complete subject. One stripped to its bare essentials (*Harry and I*) is the simple or basic subject.

SUBJUNCTIVE. A verb is in the subjunctive (see MOOD) when the intention is to express:

1. A wish (*I wish Jack **were** here*).

2. A conditional (*if*) statement that's contrary to fact (*If Jack **were** here . . .*).

3. A suggestion or demand (*We insist that Jack **be** here*).

SYLLABLE. Part of a word that is pronounced as a single unit. The word *syllable* has three syllables: SIL-la-bul. *Word* is a one-syllable word.

TENSE. What a verb uses to tell time. The basic tenses—present, past, future—and the variations on them tell us when an action takes place, took place, will take place, and so on. We're always telling time with verbs, since whenever we use one, there's a "when" built in. See VERB for examples of some common verb forms at work.

TRANSITIVE. See VERB.

VERB. An action word. In a sentence, it tells you what's going on: *She **sells** seashells*. Verbs are called transitive when they need an object to make sense (*Henry **raises** dahlias*) and intransitive when they make sense without one (*Flowers **die***). Also see MOOD and TENSE.

Here's what some common verb forms look like, for the first person singular (*I*) and the verb *eat*.

	PRESENT	PAST	FUTURE	CONDITIONAL
SIMPLE	I eat	I ate	I will eat	I would eat
PROGRESSIVE	I am eating	I was eating	I will be eating	I would be eating
PERFECT	I have eaten	I had eaten	I will have eaten	I would have eaten

VOWEL. A letter with a "soft," openmouthed sound: *a, e, i, o, u*. The other letters are consonants; two of them, *w* and *y*, sometimes act like vowels. (*Few boys own many cows*.)

Bibliography

Here are some books you may find helpful, including many that I turn to again and again. (A dictionary isn't optional, though. It's required.)

The Careful Writer: A Modern Guide to English Usage. Theodore M. Bernstein. New York: The Free Press, 1995.

A Dictionary of Contemporary American Usage. Bergen Evans and Cornelia Evans. New York: Random House, 1957.

A Dictionary of Modern American Usage. Bryan A. Garner. New York: Oxford University Press, 1998.

A Dictionary of Modern English Usage. H. W. Fowler. 2nd ed., revised by Ernest Gowers. New York: Oxford University Press, 1983.

The Elements of Style. William Strunk, Jr., and E. B. White. 3rd ed. New York: Macmillan, 1979.

Essentials of English Grammar. Otto Jespersen. Tuscaloosa: University of Alabama Press, 1964.

Harper's English Grammar. John B. Opdycke. Revised ed. New York: Warner Books, 1991.

The Language Instinct. Steven Pinker. New York: Harper Perennial, 2000.

Modern American Usage: A Guide. Wilson Follett. Edited and completed by Jacques Barzun et al. New York: Hill & Wang, 1966.

The New York Public Library Writer's Guide to Style and Usage. Edited by Andrea J. Sutcliffe. New York: HarperCollins, 1994.

Plain Words: Their ABC. Ernest Gowers. New York: Knopf, 1954.

Simple & Direct: A Rhetoric for Writers. Jacques Barzun. Revised ed. Chicago: University of Chicago Press, 1994.

Style: Toward Clarity and Grace. Joseph M. Williams. Chicago: University of Chicago Press, 1995.

Words Fail Me: What Everyone Who Writes Should Know About Writing. Patricia T. O'Conner. San Diego: Harvest, 1999.

Words into Type. Marjorie E. Skillin, Robert M. Gay, et al. 3rd ed. Englewood Cliffs, NJ: Prentice-Hall, 1974.

You Send Me: Getting It Right When You Write Online. Patricia T. O'Conner and Stewart Kellerman. New York: Harcourt, 2002.

DICTIONARIES

The American Heritage Dictionary of the English Language. 4th ed. Boston: Houghton Mifflin, 2000.

Webster's New World College Dictionary. 4th ed. New York: John Wiley & Sons, 1999.

Note: If you spend a lot of time on the computer, consider getting a CD-ROM dictionary. When you're busy, the answer is just a click away. *The New Oxford American Dictionary,* published by Oxford University Press, is a good choice.

Index

233